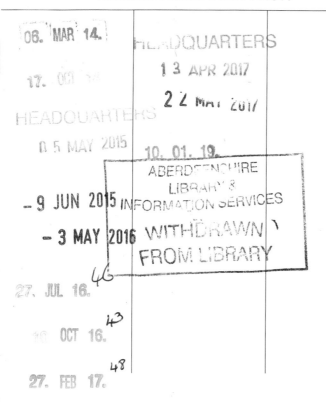

TRINIDAD STREET

The Isle of Dogs at the turn of the century is a close-knit community, and in Trinidad Street loves and lives tangle and interweave... When Tom Johnson is sacked and set upon, his daughter Ellen has to leave school and her dreams of an office job, but she can still dream of Harry Turner. Harry is bewitched by silver-tongued Siobhan O'Donaghue, who will use any weapon to repay the people of Trinidad Street for her disappointments – and Gerry Billingham, if he doesn't go a deal too far in pursuit of a retail empire, will be there to pick up the pieces...

To Pam and Marion, friends extraordinary

Trinidad Street

by

Patricia Burns

Magna Large Print Books
Long Preston, North Yorkshire,
BD23 4ND, England.

British Library Cataloguing in Publication Data.

Burns, Patricia
  Trinidad Street.

  A catalogue record of this book is
  available from the British Library

  ISBN   978-0-7505-2976-1

First published in Great Britain 1992 by Random Century Group

Cover illustration © Nigel Chamberlain by arrangement with
Alison Eldred

The right of Patricia Burns to be identified as the author of this work
has been asserted by her in accordance with the Copyright, Designs
and Patents Act, 1988

Published in Large Print 2008 by arrangement with
Patricia Burns, care of Dorian Literary Agency

LP

Magna Large Print is an imprint of Library Magna Books Ltd.

Printed and bound in Great Britain by
T.J. (International) Ltd., Cornwall, PL28 8RW

PART I

1898

1

Half-past four and a tribe of children erupted from the gates of Dock Street school. Boots clattering on the pavement, jackets and scarves and pinafores flying, they burst out into the street, girls from one entrance, boys from another, infants dragging behind big brothers and sisters. They mingled in the street outside and separated to go their various ways home through the packed terraces of Millwall. It was Friday afternoon, already dusk, and they were free of the three-storey prison for two whole days.

Ellen walked slowly, jostled by the shrieking throng, hardly noticing her young sister Daisy pulling at her arm.

'Come on, Ellen, come on! I want to get home.'

But Ellen refused to be hurried. Her own thoughts engrossed her.

'All right, all right,' she said vaguely, oblivious to the urgent tugging at her sleeve.

Daisy gave up in disgust and ran on with a gang of friends. Yelling their joy at being let out, they scampered off down the street hand in hand. Ellen let her go. At eight, Daisy was quite old enough to take herself home. She thrust her hands into her pockets and frowned at the toes of her patched boots, turning over the events of the day in her mind. She did not notice the pair of boys closing in on either side of her.

7

'Who's the teacher's pet, then?'

She started. Their faces leered at her, one sharp as a ferret, the other round and pasty. She knew just who they were. They were always in trouble for bullying. She tried to dodge round them but they danced about in front of her, grinning.

'Toffee nose, toffee nose. Don't want to play with us no more.'

One snatched at her tam-o'-shanter and ran off. With a yell, Ellen was after him.

'Give it us back!'

'Teacher's pet.' He threw it to his friend.

'Give it back!'

Grinning, the thin boy backed away, holding it in the air, the wool stripes bright against the blackened brick of the high schoolyard wall.

'Pig. Beast. Give it us!' Ellen tried to jump up and grab it, but the fat boy held her back while his mate whirled it round and round on his finger, faster and faster. The colours became a blur. Any minute now it would fly off and land in the dirt of the cobbled street. Her beautiful new hat, the only brand-new thing she had had for ages and ages. Tears of rage gathered behind Ellen's eyes. She kicked and struggled while the two boys laughed and taunted her.

'Come on then, swanky, come and get it!'

'Lovely big hat for a big head!'

She managed to kick the shins of the one who was holding her. He swore and twisted her arm behind her back. A yelp of pain escaped from Ellen, making them laugh all the more.

'Two on to one ain't fair.'

A taller boy strode up and calmly caught hold

8

of the tam-o'-shanter.

'Let go of her or I'll fetch you one.'

The tormenters glared defiance. The big boy thrust the hat into his pocket, grabbed each of them by the collar and with one swift jerk knocked their heads together. The crack echoed loud in the raw winter air.

Ellen was released. Panting, she rubbed her arms where hard fingers had bitten into them, her heart still beating wildly. She grinned at the two sulky faces. They glared back at Ellen and her champion, who gave them a final shake and released them.

'Now beat it,' he told them.

For a few moments they tried to hold out, attempting to save face, but finally they backed down and turned away.

'Blooming Trinidad Street lot,' the thin one muttered as they both slunk off.

Interested spectators disappeared. Already the street was nearly empty of children. Gravely the big boy handed the hat back.

'There you are, Ellen.'

Hero worship shining in her eyes, Ellen took it from his hands. Carefully she dusted the contamination of the bullies from it and pulled it back into shape, dwelling lovingly on the bright coloured stripes. Her mum had knitted this just for her, for Christmas. She arranged it over her plaits. Her head felt right now, with the hat's woolly warmth on top.

'Thanks, Harry. You saved my life.'

Harry Turner, blue eyes old in a youthful face, shrugged off the compliment.

''Snothing.'

'If this hat'd got spoilt my mum'd go mad.'

'Yeah, well – we got to stick together, ain't we? Trinidad Street lot.'

'Oh yes,' Ellen agreed fervently. A lifetime's loyalty bound them together. 'What you doing up here, anyway? Shouldn't you be at work?'

'I'm on my way now. We're taking a barge up-river overnight with one load and coming back down with another in the morning. I just called in here to give the kids a message.'

He started to walk up the street. Ellen tagged along.

'Lucky for me you did.'

She wanted to keep him here. Harry was sixteen, five years older than she was, practically grown up. Once they had been friends, in a distant sort of way, for he was the brother of her best friend Florrie. But now he had a man's job on the lighters and she was still a schoolkid. She felt undersized and gawky beside him. He had an air of strength and confidence about him rarely seen amongst the lads of her acquaintance who laboured long hours in unhealthy factories. His job on the river had built up his shoulder muscles and tanned his wide-boned face. All the girls in the street fancied him. She tried to think of something to say, something about his job. He forestalled her.

'What was all that about, anyway?'

A pink blush rose in Ellen's cheeks.

'Oh – because I got called in to see Mr Abbot.'

'You?' Harry looked amazed. 'I thought you was good at school.'

10

'It wasn't that, it was – it was about going to the Central.'

Harry whistled. 'You going, then? Going to the Central?'

She shrugged, trying to feign unconcern, but somehow it did not work. 'Dunno. Dunno what my mum and dad'll say.'

Harry paused, considering. 'They're all right, your mum and dad.'

'Yeah.' Ellen smiled. 'Yeah, they are. They're the best.'

'Do you want to go?'

Did she want to go? She longed to, yearned to, more than she had ever wanted anything in her short life.

'Oh yes,' she said, with such fervour that her whole face lit up.

Harry shook his head in disbelief. 'Funny girl. Couldn't wait to get out, myself. But each to his own.'

At the corner he stopped. 'I best be getting along.'

'Oh.' Disappointment dragged at her. She knew very well that he would not be walking home with her, that she was just a kid of eleven, beneath his notice, but still she did not want to part.

'Best of luck with your mum and dad.'

'What?'

'About the Central.'

'Oh – yeah. Yeah, thanks, Harry. Thanks for everything.'

He brushed it off with a hunch of the shoulders and set off in the opposite direction to Trinidad Street, cap on the back of his head, a slight swag-

11

ger to his walk. Her saviour. Ellen watched him until he was out of sight, swallowed up by the traffic from the factories. Then she turned for home.

Gradually her own preoccupations absorbed her again. Shaking off the fury and the triumph of the fight, she dawdled along Alpha Road, trying to decide what her mum and dad would say to the news.

Would they agree, would they be proud and say something like, 'You always were the bright one'? Or would they say that no one in their family had gone to Millwall Central and there was no reason to start now? Or that she was to stay on at Dock Street and leave at fourteen to start paying her way in the world like everyone else – like Harry? Harry had not even considered doing anything but start work the day he was old enough. His mum had been desperate for a bit more money to come in. She couldn't go on feeding a great boy who could be earning his own keep. A realization of her selfishness crept through the hope. There was no reason on earth why she, Ellen Johnson, should expect to be any different from anyone else, except – except – the small persistent belief that she was different. But how could she explain that to her mum and dad? They would not understand. Even worse, they might laugh.

She simply did not know how they would take it. Running over the alternatives in her head, trying to act it out, they all seemed possible. But most possible was a no of some sort.

Fear and excitement chased round her stomach, turning the emptiness of hunger into a hollow sickness.

'Oi! Watch it, girlie!'

Ellen jumped back on to the pavement just in time. A van came sweeping round the corner into the side road just as she was stepping off. The pie-bald horse's legs flashed by at a smart trot and the iron-bound wheels passed inches from her nose.

'You all right, dearie?' a passing woman asked.

Ellen nodded. 'Yeah.' Her knees felt a bit shaky. She simply hadn't seen the thing at all.

'Blooming van drivers – think they own the place. You look where you're going, dear. Run you down without a second thought, they will.'

'Yeah. Thanks,' Ellen said.

She crossed the road with exaggerated care.

The incident shook her out of her preoccupation for fully a block of houses. She even paused to look at the knife grinder with his painted handcart, joking with the housewives as they waited with their knives and scissors to be sharpened. She watched as he pumped the foot pedal and the band made the stone wheel go round. His blackened hands held the blade, steady and sure, and with a nerve-grating sound the edge came up sharp and bright. The women paid with ha'pence or sometimes with bundles of rags, though the knife grinder grumbled and said he wasn't a rag-and-bone man and didn't have time to go trading all this stuff. Ellen stayed until the last knife was sharpened, watching and listening, tracing with her eyes the swirls and lines of the patterns on the cart, green and red and yellow.

'You going to my road?' she asked. 'My mum's got a knife needs doing. She said so only the other day.'

The man took a pull from the bottle of beer he had tucked down the side of the cart and wiped his mouth on the back of his hand.

'And where might that be?'

'Trinidad Street.'

'Done it.'

'Oh.' She was disappointed. It was more fun watching your own knife being sharpened. Not as good as the rag-and-bone man – you could bargain with him – and certainly not as good as the barrel-organ man, but still fun. 'Oh well, my mum'll be pleased,' she said.

The man grunted in reply, bent his stooped shoulders to grasp the handles of his cart and went trundling on.

Overhead the air was smutty with smoke from the multitude of steam engines running round the quays and warehouses of the docks. Mixed with it was the grey dust of the cement works and a reek of chemicals and oil and burning fat from dozens of factories. Ellen coughed. Like many of the Islanders she had a permanent cough, but she hardly noticed the smells. They were part of the Island, always there, like the ships' sirens, the masts and the cranes, the trams and trains and the endless procession of horses and carts on the main roads to and from the docks. The docks dominated their lives. Behind the high walls of the warehouses to her right lay the Millwall dock. Looking down the length of Alpha Road, she could see tall masts and spars of sailing ships rearing over the chimneypots, together with the red and blue funnels of a liner. They were tied up in the West Indias. Her dad was up there, at the

14

West Indias. When he came in, she would ask him about going to Millwall Central.

She played games, defying fate. *If it's an odd number of windows to the corner, they will let me; if it's an even number, they won't.* Counting along the row, not letting herself cheat by looking ahead and working it out. *If I can hopscotch all the way up to the shop, they'll let me. If three McDougal's vans pass me before I get home, they'll let me.* Twice she won. McDougal's let her down.

She turned the corner by the Rum Puncheon into Trinidad Street. Home, her territory. She knew everyone in these houses. They might argue and squabble at times, but when it came to the push they would always stick up for each other against any outsiders. She was safe here. It wasn't posh like Mellish Street, where the ministers and schoolteachers lived, but neither was it rough like Manilla Street, where there were fights nearly every night. It was just right.

''Evening, Ellen!' An old man dragging a little trolley piled with scavenged pieces of wood raised a hand in greeting.

''Evening, Mr Bright! Good day?'

'Mustn't grumble, girl, mustn't grumble.'

Two rows of flat-fronted two-up and two-down houses faced each other in unbroken lines across the cobbled road, the tops of their windows slightly curved, their front doors letting straight out on to the pavement. One plane tree struggled to survive just about at the point where the Irish end gave way to the English. Ellen walked past a noisy group of boys playing football, their boots skidding and clumping on the cobbles. She looked at the places belonging to her particular friends. Here was the Turners', over there the O'Donaghues', by the tree her big brother and Harry's big sister, newly married, lodged with Harry's aunty Alma. Past Granny Brown's and Peg-leg Gibbons' and Loony Mike's. Last year, on the Queen's jubilee, they had all dragged tables and chairs into the street and had a party. Smiling to herself at the memory, she pushed open the door of number thirty-two.

'Wipe your feet!' Mum's voice boomed through from the kitchen.

Ellen carefully erased all traces of dirt from boots a size too big for her narrow feet. Inside, it was almost dark. She negotiated the black islands of the put-you-up and table and hung up the tam-o'-shanter with her coat under the stairs, touching it with grateful fingers. She hesitated. Tell her now, straight out? Or wait for later and tell both of them together? She could not decide. Light and voices came through the kitchen door. Still dithering, Ellen went in.

The black range was alight, giving out a comfortable fug. Daisy and Jack were already sitting drinking mugs of tea at one end of the scrubbed table while Mum, massive in the cramped room, was ironing at the other end.

'You took your time. Others've been back ten minutes.'

'Oh–'

'Always in a dream. Come here.'

Ellen nestled into the warm squashy body. Mum smelt of cooking and steam and Fairy soap.

'Been a good girl today?'

16

Ellen nodded against the pillow of her mother's bosom. Now was the moment, now. She opened her mouth but only a squeak came out.

'That's my chick.' Mum released her and exchanged the cooling flat-iron for the one on the range. She spat on it, was satisfied with the sizzle and thumped it down on the shirt laid out on the table. 'Pour y'self a cup of tea, lovey.'

Ashamed of her own cowardice, Ellen lifted the heavy brown teapot with its frilly cosy of multi-coloured wool, added a drop of precious milk and two spoons of sugar.

'Mum—'

'But *why* can't I go out and play football?' Jack interrupted.

'You know very well why. You tore all up the back of your jacket yesterday. I got better things to do than mend your clothes every day.'

Jack, nine years old but looking younger, kicked at the table leg. His thin face with its almost colourless eyes took on a mutinous look.

'Ain't fair.'

Daisy and Ellen exchanged a covert grin, waiting for the explosion. Mum thumped the iron down on the range. Arms akimbo, she glared down at him.

'Fair? What's fair? Me wearing my eyes out mending for you? And you can take that look off of your face, my lad. Any more trouble from you and your dad'll have something to say when he comes in. When you've finished that tea you can go and fetch some more coal in for me.'

Scowling, Jack obeyed. He picked up the bucket and disappeared out into the yard. The

17

back door slammed behind him in protest.

'I'm a good girl,' Daisy said self-righteously. 'I got a merit mark today, I did.'

'Did you, lovey? What for?'

Ellen sipped the scalding tea as Daisy chattered on. The warmth of the room seeped into her, making the chilblains on her fingers itch. On the range a pot bubbled, sending a delicious smell of stew into the room. It was mostly vegetables and barley by now, with just a trace of Wednesday's neck of lamb, but it made her stomach lurch and growl. Home, familiar and secure, enfolded her. Resting her chin on her hands, she went over the morning's momentous events again. Miss Evans calling her out in front of all the class, sending her to see Mr Abbot. The shame and the fear, wondering what she had done, wondering what crime she had committed. The walk down the brown-tiled corridor to his office was the longest she had ever taken. Then standing outside the door, plucking up courage to knock, wondering whether to make a run for it, where she could go all day until home time. She dreaded the smart of his withering tongue, so much worse than the sting of the cane. And then the amazement when she finally went in and saw he was smiling. Smiling! Mr Abbot!

'...Ellen?'

She came back to the present with a start. Mum was looking at her, iron in hand.

'Wake up, girl, do. Light the candle, I can hardly see.'

The room took on a homely glow, the feeble light heightening the cosiness, hiding the cheapness of the few possessions, the lack of colour, the damp patches.

Jack banged back in with the coal bucket, making the candle gutter in the draught.

'Anyway,' he declared, thumping it down beside the range, 'Ellen got sent to Mr Abbot today, so there.'

'You never?' Mum stopped folding up a shirt and stared at her. 'What you bin and gone and done?'

It was out. Ellen did not know whether to be relieved that the subject was in the open or angry that Jack had pushed her into it.

'Nothing bad, Mum, honest!' she said, gazing back earnestly at the accusing eyes.

'I should hope not. You may be a dreamer but at least you never get into any trouble at school. What did he want?'

'It was about this exam, Mum, this test. Mr Abbot said...' Ellen took a deep breath, spoke more slowly, considering each word as it came out. 'He said you can take this exam when you're eleven, and if you pass it, you can go to Millwall Central. And he said he was sure I could pass it, and then he would be *pleased* to rec-recommend me. But you got to agree to it first, you and Dad.'

'Millwall Central?'

The way the mother said it, she might have been saying Buckingham Palace. The dream receded, became hazy and distant, a castle in the clouds.

'Yes.'

'Cor, posh,' Jack commented.

Ellen waited, heart thudding, for the verdict. The silence seemed to stretch to hours, years. Her mother was frowning, iron cooling slowly in

19

her hand as she put her thoughts in order.

'Don't that mean staying on till you're sixteen?'

'Yes,' Ellen admitted.

Again she thought of Harry leaving the day he was fourteen, like everyone else, going straight out to work. To stay on at school another two years seemed gloriously, impossibly selfish. School work she could do, she was good at. She was no good at drawing or sewing; people never picked her for their teams – she dropped balls and was last in races – but reading, writing, sums and learning by heart came easily to her. To be allowed two further years of it was a priceless gift.

'Blimey.' Mum's voice was sharp. 'You must think we're made of money.'

A lurch of disappointment hit her in the stomach. They couldn't afford it.

So that was that. No money. And yet she could not give it up just like that. She opened her mouth to plead, good reasons for staying on crowding her mind: the honour, making them and Mr Abbot proud of her, and more importantly the better job she would be able to get at sixteen.

But before she could get so much as a word out there was a thumping at the front door, uneven, desperate, and the words died on her tongue.

'Martha – Martha!'

The street door handle rattled.

For a second all four froze. Then Mum moved across the room, surprisingly fast for such a large woman, negotiated the semi-darkness of the parlour with practised ease and opened the door. The three children sat motionless in the kitchen, listening.

'Martha, thank God...' The words were blurred with tears.

'All right, Milly, all right, come in now, that's it.'

They all knew the voice. It was Harry's mother. They could all guess why she was here. Jack's face took on a ghoulish interest.

'What's he done to her this time?' he hissed.

Ellen felt queasy.

Mum came back into the kitchen, manoeuvring with difficulty through the door. She was supporting a thin woman who sagged inside her encircling arm, her breath rasping in great sobs. Ellen could not help staring. Milly Turner's hair was half loose and straggling down. One eye was closed and swollen, blood poured from a cut on her lip and splattered the front of her soiled apron. She sank into the chair that Mum pulled out for her and doubled over, arms clutched round her stomach, groaning.

Over her head, Mum fixed the three pairs of wide eyes with a warning look and indicated the door with a thrust of the chin that said *Out* more plainly than words. Silently, they obeyed, Ellen swiftly, pulling Daisy and trying not to look at the abject woman, the dark welling blood. Jack followed reluctantly, dragging his gaze with difficulty from the fascinating sight.

The footballers were gathered in a bunch round the door, a dozen boys aged from eight to twelve or so, all bursting with interest, eager for the next stage of the entertainment.

'What's he done?' one demanded.

'Is she bad?'

'What's your mum said?'

21

'She's real bad, all blood.' Jack mimed Milly's posture, exaggerated her groans, working it up into a real performance. 'Oh God, oh help me, I'm dying.'

The boys shrieked with glee.

'She never!'

'Go on!'

'She did, she did. Bleeding all over the place, all down her front, all over the floor. Moaning and groaning. I think she's dying. I think he's killed her this time. Aaagh – aagh–'

Ellen could not bear it. She rushed at him, pushing him, beating him with her fists. Her brother laughed and dodged. The other boys danced around, imitating her in squeaky voices.

'Stop it, stop it, you're horrible!'

Jack leaned over and groaned one more time, then ran off up the darkened street.

'Come on, let's play football. What's the score?'

'Horrible boys,' Ellen muttered. 'I hate them.'

'Yeah, they're pigs,' Daisy agreed.

The pair of them stood in the doorway, shivering. They had come out in such a rush they had not collected their coats. Ellen was just wondering whether she could creep back in and get them, whether she even wanted to go in and perhaps hear something upsetting, when she saw the three youngest Turner children. Five doors down, they were huddled together in a defensive bunch. Without further thought, she hurried towards them.

'It's all right,' she said. 'My mum's looking after her. My mum'll see she's all right.'

In the middle of the little group, Florrie nodded dumbly. A year younger than Ellen and small for her age, with a narrow chest and dark-ringed eyes, she stood with one arm round six-year-old Ida and the other round little Johnny. Both younger ones were whimpering.

'You all right?' Ellen asked. 'He didn't hurt you?'

Florrie shook her head. There was something frozen about her. Instead of speaking, Ellen sat down on a step and tried to pull Johnny on to her lap to comfort him, but he squealed and clung to his sister, burying his face in her thigh. Florrie's hand caressed his tousled head, but she did not look at him. Her mouth was tightly clamped, her eyes hard and bright in the half-light. Her silence was disturbing. Ellen shivered. The cold was penetrating.

'Come and sit down,' she urged. 'Keep warm.' She patted the step beside her. All Trinidad Street steps were scrupulously clean, scrubbed each morning by women with calloused knees and rough red hands. Daisy complied immediately, plumping down beside her and nestling close.

'I'm cold,' she complained.

Ellen ignored her. She was looking at the strange doll-like creature that was her friend, except that no doll could look so dark and unyielding. The real Florrie did not seem to be there. She did not seem to be hearing or seeing anything. Ellen stared at her, biting her lip, wondering what to do. Then at last her words appeared to get through, as if they had had to go a long, long way. Florrie sat, slowly, stiffly. Johnny climbed on to her lap, Ida burrowed against her. Ellen put an arm round Florrie's bony shoulders and tried to be like her mum, comforting, making everything

23

right, but she did not know what to say. There was nothing she could say to a friend whose dad had just done that to her mum. It was not the first time it had happened and it would not be the last. Nothing Ellen could say would change it or make it better. She could only hug Florrie. The cold from the stone step seeped through pinafore, dress and drawers. Johnny was wet, and smelt.

Still Florrie sat rigid, staring across the street. Ellen spoke to the little ones, telling them not to worry, that their mum would be all right, all the while stealing sideways glances at her friend.

Then Florrie spoke.

'I hate my dad. I hate him. I'll kill him one day, so help me. I will, I'll kill him.'

The venom in her voice made Ellen catch her breath.

'Yes,' was all she could say.

The two little ones whimpered.

'Hate him–' There was a break in her words, then her shoulders were shaking, great dry sobs tearing at her chest. Ellen's throat tightened in sympathy and tears swelled behind her eyes. There must be some way she could protect Florrie, someone who would help. Then she swallowed hard. Of course – her hero.

'If only Harry'd been there. He'd've stuck up for you.'

Harry was like that, he looked after his little sisters and brother and he rescued Ellen's hat from the bullies.

Florrie said nothing. The sobs still shook her thin body.

'Wouldn't he?' Ellen insisted. She held on to

the conviction. There must be someone who could do something. Florrie could not be all alone bearing this terrible thing. 'Harry would look out for you,' she repeated.

'Last time' – Florrie spoke in gasps – 'Harry tried – to stop him – and my dad hit him – down the stairs–'

Ellen felt sick all over again. It was all too big for her. She felt powerless. The street that usually seemed so secure had a hostile feel to it. The windows were blank and unseeing, the doors hid unfriendly faces. There was no one to turn to.

The door opened behind them. Ellen nearly fell back into the empty space. A feeble light fell on their pinched faces.

'What you kids doing on my step?' a sharp voice demanded. 'Blooming kids, always up to no good. Time you was home. It's nearly dark.'

Ellen looked up at the small elderly figure. For a moment she was confused. She had not noticed whose doorstep they were sitting on. Some people minded, some didn't, but all grannies were formidable. She began to mutter an apology.

'Just you get off of my step. What–' The voice changed, became gruffly kind. 'Oh, it's you is it, Florrie Turner. P'raps you better come in. Sitting there in the cold with nothing on you. Catch your death. Why didn't you knock? Stupid girl.'

Florrie said nothing, so Ellen said thank you for all of them. She had got her bearings again now. It was Granny Hobbs. She was all right if you kept the right side of her, but woe betide you if you got on the wrong one. She could bear a grudge for years. She scrambled to her feet and

25

tried to pull the others up too.

'Florrie's a bit upset,' she said.

'I can see that, Ellen Johnson. I may be old, but I'm not blind. Not stupid, neither. I can guess why she's upset, too. Same old story, eh?'

Ellen nodded. Granny Hobbs grunted disapproval.

'Bring them little 'uns in, and hurry up about it. You're letting cold air into the house.'

Ellen tried to usher the Turners and Daisy through the door, but Florrie planted her slight body resolutely on the step and refused to move, while Ida and Johnny clung on to her like limpets.

Footsteps clumped down the street, breaking into a weary trot. Ellen looked up and realized why the Turners were waiting. Their aunty Alma was coming.

Even in the growing darkness, Alma Billingham struck an exotic note in the drab street. A purple coat trimmed with balding black velvet strained across her ample bust. On her floppy hat a garden of scarlet artificial poppies nodded and quivered as she moved. There was a strong reek of gin and cigarettes about her, and she was tired, a bone weariness from a long day's work that showed in her voice and her movements; but in spite of all this, relief flowed through Ellen. Here at last was someone to take charge, to lift this impossible responsibility.

'Been at it again, has he?' she asked, resigned.

Ellen nodded. 'My mum's looking after Mrs Turner.'

'Right, thanks ducky.' Alma looked down at the

26

three younger children. 'You lot come on in to my place. I'll find something for you to eat. Don't know what that big sister of yours is about. Why didn't she come down and get you in? Hope she's not ill again.'

'I see,' Granny Hobbs' voice piped up again, highly indignant. 'Going with her, are we? Going with her when you could have come in to a respectable house.'

Alma gave her a look of contempt. 'Oh, shut your mouth, you old bat.'

Ellen shrank away, trying to keep out of it. Granny Hobbs shut her door with a bang.

Alma shrugged and held out her hands to the children. Florrie got to her feet and picked up Johnny, Alma took Ida's hand and put an arm round Florrie.

'Come on, ducks, cheer up. It ain't the end of the world, you know.' She smiled at Ellen and Daisy. 'You're good girls, you are. Like your mum. You go and tell her to bring Milly over, will you? Say thank you for me and that I'll take care of her now.'

Ellen nodded. She could have hugged Alma, gin smell and all. Alma would make Florrie back into herself again.

'That's the ticket. You run along home.'

Thankfully, Ellen obeyed.

She opened the kitchen door cautiously and peeped round. There was a sharp smell of witch hazel in the room. Milly was silent, her eyes closed, wet rags on her bruises. Her mother looked up sharply from stoking the range.

'Mum.' Ellen kept her voice to a whisper. 'Mrs

27

Billingham has come home. She's taken the little ones in and she says will you bring Mrs Turner along 'cos she'll take care of her now.'

'Right.' Her mother put down the coal shovel and wiped her hands on her apron. She stooped over Milly Turner, her voice gentle. 'You hear that, Milly? Alma's back. Now you stand up – careful now – and I'll help you over. Your sister'll see you're all right.'

Ellen held the doors as her mother helped Milly hobble out of the house. Daisy came in and they both huddled close to the range, feeling the warmth thawing their chilled bodies. They heard their mother yelling at the door for Jack to come home, and soon they were all sitting round the kitchen table once more, drinking another cup of tea.

'Is she going to be all right?' Ellen asked.

Her mother sighed. 'I dunno, lovey. I hope so. Alma'll look after her. She's all right, Alma, whatever they might say. Heart's in the right place. You just thank your lucky stars your dad ain't like that.'

Daisy chattered, asking questions that their mother answered abstractedly or not at all. Jack tried to tell them about his game. Ellen could only think of Florrie, hard and frozen.

Her mother got up. 'We'll have our tea now,' she decided. 'You kids are cold and it's Friday night. There's no knowing what time your dad'll be in. I'll keep his for him.'

Daisy and Ellen stared in dumb amazement. Jack yelled 'Hooray!' and jumped up to get the knives and forks without even being asked. They bustled about, washing hands, fetching plates.

The stew was ladled out, potatoes and carrots and pearl barley with the odd scrap of meat swimming in gravy. Silently they shovelled it into grateful mouths, felt the tasty warmth of it filling empty stomachs. They mopped up the last drops and sat back. The world was a happier place.

'Just you girls learn a thing or two from this,' their mother told them. 'You make sure you choose the right boy when you get married. Get it wrong then and you're in for a life of misery. There's no backing out of it once you're married. Stuck with it, you are, whether you like it or not. And as for you, Jack, if I ever hear you've done something like that, I'll have the hide off you, grown man or not. You hear me?'

'Yes, Mum.'

Slowly the problems of the Turners faded in Ellen's head and the question of her own future came back into focus. As if reading her mind, her mother spoke.

'What was all that about Millwall Central?'

Ellen sighed. 'It's all right. I know I can't go.'

Her mother was silent, frowning into her tea-cup. 'Girls and boys from there get office jobs, don't they?'

Daisy came unexpectedly into the conversation. 'May Dobb's sister went there and she's got an office job at Maconochie's. May says it's a lovely job. She sits all day on a high stool writing things.'

'Sits!' Mum sounded impressed. 'I didn't never have a job sitting, not in all my life.'

'She wears a tailored coat and skirt to work,' Daisy added, warming to her theme. 'Not an apron. May says she wants to do that too. I don't.

I don't want to sit writing all day long. I hate writing.'

'Sounds better than bottling pickles or getting scalded by the jam,' Mum said. 'Meet a nicer class of young man, too.'

They all knew what she meant: nicer than Archie Turner.

Ellen was silent. She wanted to go to Millwall Central. Wanted it like she'd never wanted anything in her life before. But she knew it was impossible.

Her mother put the tea down and gathered Ellen to her.

'You're a good girl. I'd like to see you with a job in an office. Real nice, that'd be. Ladylike. You deserve a chance to better yourself, get away from what some have to suffer. We'll afford it somehow. I can always get a job if I have to. It's not as if you little 'uns are babies any more. But we'll have to see what your dad says. Wait till he's had his tea. Then we'll see.'

For several moments Ellen could not take it in. It was too good to be true.

'Oh, Mum – do you mean it? Do you really?'

''Course. Maybe I'm daft, but of course I mean it. Someone in our family with an office job! It's worth going out ship scrubbing for that.'

'Oh, Mum! Oh, thanks.' Ellen stood up and flung her arms round her mother's neck. She was nearly there.

2

Tom Johnson straightened up and kneaded the small of his back where it creaked in protest at the long day's work. Old, he was getting old. He couldn't take it like he used to. Half his life he had been here now, here at the West Indias, or over at the East Indias, and very occasionally – if times were bad – down at the Millwall. He had settled into his own specialization and was recognized as a skilful shipworker. Thousands upon thousands of tons he must have shifted in his time.

The raw products of the great British Empire and the untamed world beyond came rolling up the Thames in the holds of great timber sailing vessels and huge iron steamships, and an army of dockers unloaded them to be fed into the hungry factories of London. Wool from Australia, fruit from South Africa, coffee from Brazil, sherry from Spain, cotton from America, it all came ashore to be heaved into the warehouses by Tom and his like and disgorged again to feed and clothe and service the sprawling capital and the people of the lands and towns.

The romance of it all had fired his imagination once, but it was all too familiar now. Just another day to be got through, endless hours of lifting and carrying, with arms and legs and back aching more with each sack or bale or keg. He knew how to conserve his strength, how to lift so as to put

31

as little strain as possible on his body, how to pace himself through the day so that the foreman had nothing to hold on him. But the fact remained that he was forty-one and past his prime. Today he had been brought face to face with the fact that he could no longer keep up with the younger men. Here he was on the quay, trundling a truck, the two-wheeled carrying device used for taking goods into the warehouses or transit sheds. He, Tom Johnson, was down amongst the quay workers because he was not quick and strong enough to work on the ship any more. His pride had taken a bad blow, but it was the same pride that stopped him from showing it.

He glanced now at the foreman, king of the quay. They were old enemies, Tom and Alf Grant, well matched, but Alf always had the last say since it was he who had the power. He was the one who called the men on at the start of the day. He could get a man blacked so that no one would take him on.

Alf had his back to him, seeing to the gang on the forward hold, and Tom could relax for a moment.

'Grand sight, ain't she?' An old sailor stopped by his side, his white beard sticking out like wire wool all round his face. He was looking up at the ship they were unloading, pride in his seamed face.

'Yes – grand.' Tom rolled his fists into his stiff and aching back.

'You should see her under full sail, rolling through the roaring forties. Nothing to beat her bar the clippers. Wonderful old girl, the *Ariadne*. Wonderful.'

Tom cast an eye over the elegant lines of the windjammer – her four tall masts; her tangle of rigging; the long yellow bowsprit jutting along the quayside, and under it the garishly painted figurehead of a half-naked woman. Round her in the oily waters of the dock clustered a bunch of lighters and sailing barges receiving cargo to take up the river or round the coast to quays and small ports, waterside factories and warehouses. Beyond her a line of ships was moored, nearly all sailormen, passenger and cargo, discharging their loads on to the dockside before going round empty to the export pool to fill up with manufactured goods for the outward journey.

The old sailor was still talking. 'I remember when we was coming out of Rio with a cargo of coffee – '88 that would've been, or '89 – and we just...'

Tom was not listening. The ship did not hold his attention. She was right enough, but when all was said and done, just another set of holds to be unloaded. It was the men on the quayside he was watching, the sweating gangs toiling amongst the snaking ropes, the unstable heaps of cargo, the tall cranes with their dipping beaks and swinging chains, the slippery cobbles and the leaky barrels of inflammable oil or dangerous chemicals. *They* were the ones who laboured, who spent the strength of their youth for a tanner an hour. *They* were the ones who should have the power, not Alf Grant and the bosses. Down the line the money went, hand to hand with everyone taking his cut, till it came to the bottom, where the real work was done – with the dockers. Not much left for them.

But they were only casual labourers, after all, and there were plenty more at the gate. They didn't matter. It made him sick, the way they were treated. Tom was a lucky one, a 'Royal', taken on in preference to the masses for any job that was going. The foremen knew that he was strong and reliable, that he could be trusted and that he knew what he was doing. He could be sure of getting work if work there was, and his family never went cold or hungry. But his sympathy was with the casuals. His days were concentrated on fighting for a better deal for the men on the quay.

Tom's eyes sought his son, up on the deck. The vessel still had the old-fashioned hand winches, and Will was up there as winchman with one of the O'Donaghue boys. Stocky and straight-backed with well-muscled shoulders, he gave an illusion of height, though only in contrast with the under-sized race that grew up in the streets of the Island. He was grown bigger than Tom, with a mind and a life of his own. A fine man, his Will, but wild. He had hoped Will would get a steady job, free from the hand-to-mouth life of the docker, but regular work had not agreed with him. He'd got the sack from five different places before taking his chances here at the docks. Even now he was larking about with Pat O'Donaghue; Tom could hear his laugh ringing out. 'Don't worry yourself,' his wife Martha would say. 'Don't worry, he's a good boy. He'll settle, now he's a married man. That Maisie's a nice little thing. She'll be a decent wife and a good mother.' Tom hoped she was right.

'Young fools.' Brian O'Donaghue's voice sounded at his shoulder, just a faint hint of a

34

brogue softening the London accent. 'Get themselves thrown off.'

'No sense,' Tom said.

Both men watched their sons with a mixture of
irritation and pride.

'Ah well, you're only young once now, aren't
you?' Brian was tolerant. 'Let them have their
time. Never did me no harm. Though you were
always the serious one, now I call it to mind.'

'Yeah.' Things had been much worse when he
had started work. That was before the great strike.
At least now if you worked for an hour you were
paid a tanner. But there was a long way to go yet.
There was work to be done, battles to be won so
that life could be better for Will, and for his
unborn child.

'Johnson!' Alf Grant's voice sliced through the
rattle of machinery, through the rumble of engines, through countless human cries. 'Johnson!
Slacking again. Get back to work. I've no room for
idle men.'

'Slave-driving bastard,' Brian muttered, without rancour.

Tom stayed still for just long enough to save
face, holding Grant's eyes, then turned slowly to
pick up the next tub of molasses.

Up on the deck, Will Johnson and Pat O'Donaghue battled with the heavy winches, hauling the
cargo up out of the hold and down into the
lighters clustered round the ship. They worked
steadily for two hours or more, arms and backs
straining, until a problem with the crane held up
the rest of the gang. Will looked down at Alf
Grant, who was blowing his top over the delay.

35

'He's got his hands nice and full,' he said.

Pat nodded and grunted in reply. They let down the next load. Will straightened up.

'Oi,' he said, 'can you do this?'

He stepped over to the edge of the hatch, where a narrow lip of wood about eight inches high ran all round the gaping hole. He put his booted foot up on the rim, steadied himself with his arms outstretched, then brought the other foot up and walked all the way along like a circus performer.

'Easy!'

Not to be outdone, Pat O'Donaghue started doing the same along the opposite side. The younger men whistled and clapped. Flushed with danger and success, Will and Pat bowed.

'Johnson! O'Donaghue! Cut that out.'

Grant was on to them. Fists on hips, scarlet with anger, he yelled up at them from the quayside.

'What the hell d'you think you're doing, holding up the whole bloody ship?'

Will opened his mouth and shut it again. You didn't argue with Alf Grant. He'd have you thrown off as soon as look at you. But on the other hand he was damned if he was going to say sorry like a schoolboy. While he was still standing there making his mind up, his father joined in.

'They ain't holding up nothing, Mr Grant. It's the crane what's stopping us,' he pointed out.

Grant rounded on him. 'It ain't stopping them, Johnson, and well you know it. They should be working them winches. It's idleness what's stopping them.'

He bawled up at Will and Pat to get on with it, and set about Tom again.

'And as for you, Johnson, I had it up to here with you. You're for it now. You put your bloody nose in where it's not wanted once too often. I got no more room for troublemakers like you.'

Will glanced at his friend. 'Bloody hell, he's for it now, my old man.'

The pair of them went back to the winch. The break had given them enough energy to carry on to the end of the long day.

The crane was sorted out and the work resumed. Grant stationed himself near Tom's gang and barked every time one of them so much as paused for a breather. It was a grim afternoon, and at six o'clock it was practically dark. The cargo of glucose tubs was all neatly stacked in the huge warehouse. The men dumped their last burdens, flexed their aching muscles and knocked off. Will and Pat joined their fathers and Pat's brother Declan, ready to walk out together.

'Johnson!' Grant came striding along the quay, looking like the cat that had got the cream. 'You're wanted in the gov'nor's office.'

Tom, wooden-faced, met his eye.

'What for?' he asked.

'You'll find out.' The man was grinning at him, malicious satisfaction oozing from every pore.

Tom was not to be intimidated. 'All right, all right. There's a thing or two I want to see the gov'nor about and all.' He turned to Will and the O'Donaghues. 'Get one in for me. I'll see you at the Kingsbridge.'

'Right you are, mate,' Brian agreed.

Will watched his father walk off with Alf Grant and hesitated, wondering whether to wait for him.

37

'You coming, Will?' Pat O'Donaghue called to him.

He took one more look at the retreating back, and recognized by the set of his father's shoulders that this was going to be a long session. He didn't need him as much as Will needed a drink.

'Yeah, coming,' he called back.

He fell in beside the O'Donaghues as they joined the flood of men heading for the dock gates: small men, ill dressed in stained jackets and ragged trousers, all wearing flat caps and heavy much-mended boots, and slouching because it was the end of the day, wanting only to get out, to get paid, to get home or to the pub.

There was a queue at the main gate as they all funnelled under the impressive great archway with its bronze model of a three-masted sailing ship on top. Ahead of them the dock police stopped a man. There was an argument before he was led away to be searched. Will watched him with detached sympathy. He knew the man by sight; he lived over in Cubitt Town somewhere. He hoped the police were picking on him just because they didn't like the look of him. They often did that. You were searched and questioned and set free. They did it to try and stop you nicking stuff, but it didn't work. Everyone pocketed things, it was part of the game.

Out in the grey street at last, they walked along by the high prison-like wall of the dock until they came to the pub where the contractor paid out. They queued again, this time for their wages, had the customary squabble over hours, felt the warm weight of silver in their pockets. Six shillings for twelve hours' labour. Riches.

The O'Donaghues managed to get a table while Pat lined the drinks up.

'Here y'are, Will, one for you and one for your dad.'

'He won't be in for a while,' Will said. 'You know what he's like. Arguing the point with the gov'nor, most like.'

They all nodded. They knew Tom Johnson. But they had hardly finished agreeing on it before Will spotted him in the pay queue, and he did not look like a man who had just won a battle. Will sampled his beer, looking at his father over the top of the glass. He was standing hunched up, not speaking to anyone, which in itself was unusual. His dad was a great one for talking. Will wondered what was up.

At length Tom appeared, slumped down on the seat they had saved for him and took a long pull at his brown ale. Brian handed him a cigarette.

'It's a dog's life,' he said.

The others nodded in solemn agreement.

More pints arrived on their table. Pat, Will and Declan had a race to see who could down a pint the fastest. The pub was crowded. People were standing between the tables. It was Friday and there was only one more day till sainted Sunday off. Caps were tipped back, jackets unbuttoned, faces glowed red. Quite a few men had started in on the serious drinking, glasses of gin in front of them. A roar of laughter came from one corner and the joke was repeated from mouth to mouth. Brian was telling a long tale about his bantam cock.

'–So I shut the little bleeder up, but damn me if he didn't get out again. Must've pecked away at the catch. His own hens ain't enough for him, y'see. Half a dozen I got in that run, half a dozen little beauties! Bright eyes, lovely feathers. Won the Bantam hen prize last summer in the show with one of 'em, I did.'

'Oh, Jesus.' Declan pushed his chair back and heaved himself to his feet. 'I'm going to throw up.'

Of one accord, Pat and Brian grabbed his arms and started to shoulder a path towards the door, shouting at people to get out of the way. But they were too late. There were shouts of protest, curses. Those out of the way laughed and jeered. The landlord sent a barmaid over to clean up.

'If that boy of yours can't hold his drink, don't bother bringing him in here,' he grumbled.

Brian traded insults and manoeuvred his son into the fresh air.

'Finish the drinks for me, Tom,' he called back through the crowd. 'I'm taking the boy home. Must've been something he ate.'

The empty chairs were filled, Grant's character torn to shreds. Tom came out of his silent fit and became more like his normal self. Will almost forgot he had been worried. He looked at his father, who was leaning forward, jabbing at the sticky table top to emphasize a point he was making, a compact, sturdy man with a broken tooth and a frill of greying hair sticking out from under his cap.

Will listened to the older men's talk for a while. They respected his father, brought their problems and complaints to him, and trusted him to take up cudgels on their behalf. He watched as they listened to what his dad had to say, nodding sometimes in agreement. It gave him a feeling of family pride. His dad could get them all behind him. Will didn't know quite how he did it; but if there was another strike like the one back in '89, his dad would be there in the thick of it, organizing the action in their part of the Island.

His attention wandered. He didn't care about Alf Grant, or the governors. He knew he could earn a good day's wage whenever he wanted. He was young and strong and nearly always called on. A day's labouring left him tired, but nowhere near exhausted. A wash and a good meal inside him and he was ready for an evening out.

He started talking to a couple of mates about the Millwall Rovers' chances in the next game. He felt warm and relaxed. The beer slid easily down inside him, loosening his tongue, making him feel good. Friday night. His pay hung pleasantly heavy in his pocket, his mates were game for anything, and it was almost the best time of the week.

His dad was standing up. Will eyed the barmaid threading her way with difficulty through the crowd, collecting empties, exchanging banter. He'd fancied her for a while, with her wide smile and ripe body. He watched her as she raised her arms to lift the glasses over the heads of the close-packed men. When she did that, her full breasts moved. He envied the men she brushed against as she passed.

'Coming, Will?'

'Not yet.'

He would speak to the barmaid when she came

over here.

'Your Maisie'll be waiting for you.'

The words 'Let her wait' formed on his tongue, but something in his father's tone made him swallow them. He dragged his eyes away from the woman and looked at the remains of his drink, his filthy hands and grimy clothes. A wash, a good meal, an evening out and then Maisie. It was a prospect worth moving for.

'Yeah, yeah, I'm coming.'

He drained his glass and stood up. Perhaps he would take Maisie out with him. He followed his father out into the street.

The West Ferry Road was still busy. Buses filled with homeward-bound workers, brightly painted vans, huge heavy drays and carts of every size and description from hand barrows to flat waggons choked the roadway. On the pavement men and women heading home from factories and foundries and repair yards jostled with children scampering along on errands and street sellers shouting their wares.

'Oranges, who will buy my fresh oranges?'

'Chestnuts, chestnuts, all lovely and hot!'

Will ignored them with difficulty because he was hungry now that he was out in the air. Head down, shoulders hunched against the raw cold, he plodded along, matching his stride to his father's. He wondered what was for tea, hoped it was a bit of fried fish. It was some time before it struck him that his old man was very quiet.

'What's up?' he asked.

'Nothing.'

He remembered then, in a rush, Alf Grant

coming up to him at the end of the day, taking him off to the office.

'Come on, Dad, something's biting you. What did the gov'nor want?'

There was a silence for the length of half a block. Will wondered whether his father had not heard him, or if he was just not answering.

'He gave me the sack.' His tone was so matter-of-fact that it took a moment or two for the words to sink in. It was terrible. His dad was a preference man, called on first after the permanents for any job that was going. Their household was always fairly certain of something coming in each week, whereas the others, the casuals, never knew whether they would get work or not.

'*What?* They never give you the sack for sticking up for me and Pat?'

'That was just the excuse.'

'Bloody hell, Dad. I never thought – Christ, what can I say? I'm sorry.'

His father shrugged. 'It weren't you and Pat, lad. Like I said, that was just an excuse. It's been on the cards for a long time. They don't like me. I make things too uncomfortable for them.'

'It's bloody unfair,' Will said.

'The whole system's bloody unfair, son. Bosses in their big houses sitting on their arses making money out of the sweat of the workers is unfair. But don't you worry, it ain't the end of the world. I'll go casual. And I won't stop making things uncomfortable for them, neither. One of these days they'll have to have a proper reason for sacking a man. They won't be able to throw him out just because his face don't fit. They'll have to

43

prove he's no good at the job.'

Will agreed, fired with the idea of working with his father to right all these wrongs. When his father spoke like this, he saw great armies of working men rising up to make a new world, a fairer world, where the poor got their just deserts: decent homes, warm clothes, doctoring when they were sick; a fair day's wage for a fair day's work. When his father spoke, it was more than just a dream, it was a goal within reach. He saw himself at the head of the army, waving a banner, leading them to victory.

'That's right,' he said. 'They'll be licking our boots one day, begging us to work.'

Then he saw the girl, and all thought of improving the world went right out of his head.

She was standing on the street corner, shawl over her head, bundle in her hand, staring up at the street sign, bewilderment showing in every line of her body. Fresh off the boat, Will decided, his predatory interest stirring. Newly arrived and easy game. He quickened his stride, a spring in his step, and stopped in front of her.

'You lost, darling? Can I show you the way?'

Wary eyes looked up at him. Blue, he saw by the smeary light of the street lamp. Blue as a summer sky and fringed with great dark lashes. Cherry-sweet mouth. Round little face, pale with a weariness that tugged at his heart. He wanted to take her in his arms right there. He smiled down, showing his strong unblemished teeth.

She looked him up and down, rather as a mouse might size up a cat, and shifted from foot to foot, ready to make off. Clearly she did not trust him.

'You can tell me the way to where I'm going,' she said.

The soft brogue confirmed his first guess, but the carefully worded reply disappointed him in his second. She might be a bogtrotter but she was not completely green. Will tried a different approach.

'Just tell me the name, miss, and I'll tell you how to get there,' he invited, trying to look the very rock of dependability.

Still she hesitated. She was very young to be coming to London all on her own – not more than sixteen, at a guess.

'I know every road there is round here. Born and bred on the Island, I was,' Will told her, trying to sound reassuring.

She looked at him, biting her lip, her delicious nose wrinkled in the effort of making her mind up whether to confide in him. Will found he was holding his breath.

She came to a decision. 'I'm trying to find my way to Trinidad Street.'

Will could hardly believe his ears. 'Trinidad Street! Well, that's luck for you. I'm going that way m'self.'

She looked doubtful at that.

'Anything up?' Tom arrived at his side. Will was irritated. No chance now, not with his old man there.

'This young lady is looking for Trinidad Street. I said she should come along with us,' he explained.

'Ah.' Tom considered her.

Will knew just what the problem was. Strangers were always regarded with suspicion. You knew

45

where you were with people you grew up with, knew how they'd react, knew you could depend on them as they did on you. But newcomers – it took a long time before you could trust them the same way.

'What are you wanting down Trinidad Street, then?' Tom asked.

Will fumed with impatience. What did it matter? She was the prettiest thing he'd seen since he didn't know when and she was going his way.

Then snatches of half-forgotten conversations between the O'Donaghue brothers floated to the top of his mind.

'I know who you are,' he cried. 'You're the O'-Donaghues' cousin. Second cousin, or third cousin once removed. What's y'name now? Siobhan. That's it – Siobhan. Come to stop with them.'

He grinned at her in triumph. Relief flooded her sweet face. She became animated. A dimple appeared in one soft cheek.

'That's right! How did you be after knowing that?'

'Mates of mine, aren't they? Work with me, me and my dad, down the West Indias. Mates and neighbours. We all live down Trinidad Street. Come on, now, let me carry your bundle. It's not far.'

With only a slight hesitation, she handed over her entire worldly goods, which Will slung over his shoulder. Tom walked silently, hands in pockets. Will could feel his disapproval, but ignored it. What was the harm in helping the girl along? She was going to be a neighbour. She was practically one of them already.

Siobhan, now she felt safe, poured out her tale. 'I'm real thankful you came along. There was no one to meet me off the boat. I don't know what happened to me cousins. Said they'd be there, so they did. Said London was after being a big wicked city for a girl to be wandering about in. They were right and all, for it's five or more men have come up to me since I've been trying to find my way and it wasn't my soul they were after, neither.'

Contempt rang in her voice. She certainly wasn't a complete pushover, Will realized, and the knowledge made her all the more desirable. Now that she trusted them, there was confidence in the way she moved, the way she looked at him with those great cornflower eyes.

'They should've been there to meet you,' he agreed. 'Shouldn't leave a pretty girl like you wandering around London by yourself. There're some bad blokes about, 'specially down the Highway.' A sudden dreadful thought struck him. Anything could have happened to her down there. A lovely thing like her. 'You didn't come along there, did you?'

'I don't remember,' Siobhan admitted. 'Seems like I've been walking for ever. It's all so big.'

'It *is* big. You can walk for miles and not come to the end of it. Where're you from? Country place?'

She told him about home, about a little village where nothing ever happened, about working in the big house to save money for her fare, about her dream of living with her cousins in the big city where there was lots of life, always something going on.

Will watched the play of expression on her face, the way her lips moved. She had a full, soft mouth.

'Plenty of that all right,' he told her. 'Just down our street there's always something. You must let me take you out, show you around.'

Alongside them, almost jostled off the narrow pavement, his father snorted in disgust.

'Best be getting a move on,' he said heavily. 'Your Maisie'll be wondering where you got to.'

Will could have throttled him. She'd find out soon enough. But just for now it was fun to play at being free and single again.

'Maisie?' Siobhan asked.

'My missus,' Will admitted.

'In the family way,' his father added, just to kick any last ghost of a hope into kingdom come. 'Six months gone. Going to make me a grandpa, she is.'

Siobhan glanced up at Will, and there was a dangerous spark in her blue eyes.

'Well, aren't you just the one?' she said.

They turned into Trinidad Street and stopped outside the O'Donaghues'. Will banged on the door.

'Hey, Pat, got a surprise for you,' he yelled.

Clodagh O'Donaghue, heavily pregnant, wrenched it open.

'Will you shut your row, Will Johnson!' She caught sight of Siobhan and stopped short. 'And who...? Mary, mother of God, it's not Siobhan, is it?'

'It is too. And you'd be my aunty Clodagh?'

'Oh, my poor child, what happened? Come along in, do. What are you doing here today?'

48

There had been some mistake over the dates. Tom and Will were swept into the front parlour as the entire O'Donaghue clan, including a pale-faced Declan, appeared to welcome the newcomer. They all vied to make her feel one of the family, giving her tea, bringing dry shoes, asking after aunts and cousins. Will felt left out, yet loath to leave. Tom pulled at his arm.

'C'mon. Leave 'em to it.'

Reluctantly, Will agreed.

''Bye, Siobhan,' he called above the noise in the tiny crowded house.

For a long moment their eyes met. There was pride in hers, and challenge.

'Goodbye now, and thank ye,' was all she said, yet he had an uncomfortable feeling she had the measure of him, whereas he had everything to learn about her. All he knew was that she was the most desirable thing he had ever met.

'Nice cuppa tea, that's what we all need.'

Alma looked round her little kitchen with satisfaction. No matter how hard the day, no matter how many problems there were, it always gave her a thrill of pleasure to come home. Her own home, a proper house with its own front door, its own kitchen, its own back yard. Small, yes, and crowded, what with her own two great boys and now Will and Maisie lodging, but still hers. After years of the three of them living in one or two rooms in tenement buildings or lodging with relatives whose homes were already full to the seams, she didn't care that the windows didn't fit, the roof leaked, the back wall bulged. It was hers. She

49

had a door key and a real rent book of her own.

She filled the kettle, set it on the range and took a peek at herself in the glass over the mantelpiece. Gawd, she looked a fright. Decent work was on the short side at the moment and she'd had to go ship scrubbing. Her nose! It was bright red. That was what came of having a quick one on the way home. Well, she deserved a little drink, the state those cabins were left in. She took out a comb and tried to tidy her hair up. She was proud of her hair. It didn't show the hard life she'd led.

Long and thick and dark as a girl's in a shampoo poster it was, and hardly a thread of grey to be seen even though she was all of thirty-six. It needed taking down and doing all over again, really, but there was no time for that now, not with all this crowd waiting for her.

'There we are,' she said, forcing cheerfulness into her voice. 'Now then, you kids sit at the table. I got a bit of paper round here somewhere, so you can do some drawing. And Milly, you come here by the fire. Maisie, you take your little brother and change his trousers before he makes wet patches everywhere. There's an old pair of Gerry's in the cupboard. They're too big by far but they'll have to do. I'll give you a drop of hot water out of the kettle in a minute.'

She searched in the drawer by the sink and found a couple of pieces of blue paper that had once held tea and a stub of pencil.

'You'll have to share that,' she said, handing it to Florrie. The girl took it with a whispered thanks.

Alma sighed. All she really wanted was to sit down with her feet up and a cigarette and recover from the day, but here were all these little ones wanting mothering. It was a bad job all round. Milly had married a right bleeding bully in that Archie. Nearly all men knocked their wives about a bit, but not like Archie. He was real vicious, he was. And now they were all suffering. It was worst for those poor kids. Her own boys had known hunger and bare feet, but they'd never seen her beaten up like that in front of their eyes.

'There, there, dearie,' she said, hugging Florrie to her corseted body. 'It's all right now. Aunty Alma'll see to it.'

Florrie nodded. The beginnings of a wan smile twitched the corners of her mouth. Alma liked Florrie. She was a brave little thing, but not strong. Her face wasn't round like a child's should be, but bony and pointed. There was always a peaky look to her, even in the summer, even when work was good and they were being fed properly.

'There's my girl. That Ellen Johnson sat with you, did she?'

Another nod.

'She's a good girl, Ellen. Like her mum. I like Martha Johnson. Doesn't look down on a body, like some I could name.'

It took all her efforts to see to her sister and the children. It wasn't till she sat down herself that she noticed Maisie's mournful look. Flushed from the fug in the tiny room, she had slumped down beside the others, one arm supporting her head, the other curled defensively round her swelling belly.

Alma wound herself up for one more dose of sympathy. Really, you'd think this was the only baby ever to be born on God's earth. She was over the sickness now, there were no other little ones to care for – she ought to be blooming. Alma never flopped around like this when she was carrying. Loved every minute of it, she had. Especially when the baby moved. She used to get her hands under her skirts when no one was looking and stand with them spread over the bulge so she could feel the baby from the outside and the inside, fluttering about. That was lovely, that was. Made her feel powerful, as if she was the centre of the whole world.

But Maisie was not like that. Carrying babies didn't agree with her.

'You feeling bad, dearie?'

A shake of the head.

'Tired?'

'Mm.' Sigh.

Alma glanced over at her sister. This was Milly's job, helping her daughter through her first pregnancy. But there, Milly was in no fit state. She was sitting staring into her teacup, her hands still shaking. She used to annoy Alma, the way she just took it all. Asked for it, really. But there it was, you couldn't change people, and she was her sister. When all was said and done, you had to stick by your family.

'Well, cheer up, dearie. Will'll be home soon. Don't want him to see you moping around like this, do you? You ought to be happy, you ought. Fine husband, new baby coming, home of your own soon, I shouldn't wonder. Lots of girls are jealous of you, that I do happen to know. Lot of girls would've liked to have got your Will.'

'I know.' Maisie sighed again and pushed a

strand of hair back from her face.

Alma felt a spurt of irritation. She was just like her mother at that age; watery, that was it. No go in her. And look what happened to Milly. Not that Will was like Archie Turner, but it never did any good to droop around a man like that.

'Come on now, Maisie, pull y'self together,' she said. 'Give your hair a comb, tidy y'self up. Is that blouse still clean under that apron? Then take the apron off before Will gets in. You look nice in that blouse, you do. Brighten up a bit! You get your Will to take you out. Enjoy y'self while you can.'

'Mm.' The girl drifted over to the glass, but stopped to look down at her mother. She bent down awkwardly to touch her arm, then as Milly grasped her hand, took the cup from her and knelt down, the pair of them holding hands, two heads bowed together.

They looked so alike. Maisie was the image of Milly at that age. Milly had been pretty once, but it had long gone. Maisie ought to make more of an effort. That Will was all right, but he was wild. *She'd* make an effort for a husband like that. Her own had been taken from her in an accident when the boys were babies. There had been plenty of men in the years between but none had married her.

The front door opened, sending a whistling draught through the house. Alma's heart leapt. Gerry! Her darling boy, in from his job at the corner shop for his tea. His bright head appeared round the kitchen door, his wide cheerful mouth, his shrewd eyes that creased up so that when he smiled his whole face joined in. She drank him in, her baby, her great chick.

He took in the scene at a glance.

'Room for a small one?' he asked.

'Come in, darling. 'Course there is. Good day?'

'Grand.'

Excitement vibrated from him, charging up Alma's drained resources, stirring the air of doom with the fresh wind of opportunity.

''Evening, Maisie, Aunty Milly, kids.'

A weak smile from Maisie, nothing from Milly, but the children responded to his bright enthusiasm. They knew him of old. Something always happened when Gerry was around – something exciting. They latched on to him with a desperate eagerness.

'You got anything, Gerry?' Ida asked, bright with expectancy.

He grinned back at her, a teasing smile dancing in his eyes.

'Have I got something? What makes you think I might've got something?'

The little girl squirmed in her seat. 'Tell us, Gerry. Show us. Go on. Bet you have.'

Gerry let them plead with him for a while, laughing, keeping them in suspense. Alma knew – she could tell by the glow about him – that he'd done something clever and maybe foolish. At last his own pleasure with himself would let him keep them guessing no longer.

'Just you wait! Just you wait till you see these.' He disappeared briefly into the parlour and came back holding an apple box that seemed to be full of screws of newspaper. He placed it carefully on the kitchen table. Alma and the children leaned forward, Ida and Johnny squeaking with excitement, Florrie's pinched little face eager.

'What is it, Gerry? What is it?'

With the true salesman's cunning, he did not let them see straight away.

'This was a real piece of luck. And old Rooney didn't see it. He just did not see it.' He sucked in his cheeks, tucked in his chin in imitation of his boss. 'Load of rubbish, boy. What d'you want that stuff for? Throwing good money away.'

The children giggled. It was Mr Rooney to the life. Alma looked at him with a pride that glowed and warmed and wound around her heart. He was a one, her Gerry. Sixteen years old and that bright. He'd have a shop of his own one day, she was sure of that.

'But I could see a bargain when it jumped up and hit me. There was this man, you see, with a load on a cart, selling round all the shops. Got 'em from some factory what's gone bankrupt. Now I can guess what you're thinking: you're thinking that if he's been round all the shops, they'll all have 'em in already and nobody'll want to buy 'em off of me.' He paused to look at his mother, but such a point had not even approached her mind. It made her prouder still that he should be two jumps ahead of her like that. Without waiting for an answer, he went on. 'But you see, these are the seconds, the bits and bobs. I got 'em real cheap and I can sell 'em much cheaper than the shops.'

'But what are they?' Florrie begged.

All three children's eyes were round with anticipation; their noses crept ever nearer to the mysterious heap of newspaper. Soft footfalls crossed the room and Maisie leaned over her aunty's shoulder, unable to resist the lure of the amazing bargain. Johnny's fingers reached out, snatched at a loose corner. Gerry smacked him, but lightly.

'Wait for it!'

He took the top bundle from the pile and unwrapped it slowly, carefully, as if it were the Star of India.

'Now, here, ladies and gentlemen – gentle*man* – we have a rare chance for you to buy, at a quite unbeatable and unrepeatable price, a most beautiful little portrait in the finest porcelain of – Her glorious Majesty the Queen of England!'

With a flourish, he took off the last layer, to reveal a china figurine about four inches high in black dress and a white widow's cap, dumpy and jowled, unmistakably Victoria though the crudely painted expression was a good deal more cheerful than most of her photographs showed her.

'Er – stupid!' Johnny sat back in disgust, sinking his scowling face into his two fists.

But the females, to a woman, were enchanted.

'Will you look at that!'

'Just like her, see – got her to a T.'

'Innit pretty?'

Gerry looked round at their faces with a broad smile of satisfaction.

'You got any others? They all the same?' asked Alma.

'No, no, they're not all the same. There's' – he scrabbled around, produced another bundle, and unwrapped it before them – 'His Royal Highness the Prince of Wales. Good old Teddy. And' – another search, another parcel – 'Her Royal Highness the beautiful Princess Alexandra, God bless her, *and*' – a last dip into the box – 'His Royal Highness's famous Derby winner, Persimmon. Now, Johnny, I think you'll like that one, eh?'

'Horse.' The little boy took the model in one grubby hand and stroked it lovingly with a finger.

'I like the Princess,' Ida said, reaching out to touch.

'So do I,' said Florrie.

'I like the Prince. He's a jolly old cove.' Alma smiled at the portly figure. That was just the sort of man she always fell for: generous, gregarious, all set for a good time. Unfortunately, like the Prince, they were also usually married.

'I thank you one and all. You have just proved what I was sure of when I bought this lot. Ladies love a bit of china to put on the mantelpiece. Old Rooney thought they were rubbish, but I looked at them and I saw all the houses along this street, all with their knick-knacks over the fireplace. So I bought them.'

Suspicion and a tug of fear pulled at Alma.

'What with?' she asked. Debt had sat on her shoulder for so many years. The deals with the tally-man, the trips to the pawn shop, the moonlight flits, all were a regular feature of her life. Only since the boys had gone to work had it lifted.

Gerry, wrapping up his treasures and laying them safely away, told her not to worry. 'I got Old Rooney to advance me the next two weeks' wages.'

'Gerry!'

He gave her a brief hug. 'I know, I know – where's my keep coming from? Just hold out till tomorrow, Ma. I'll go down Chrisp Street market and sell the lot. You see if I don't! Treat you all to fish and chips tomorrow night.'

The three children groaned with desire at the thought.

But Alma was uneasy. 'Chrisp Street? You ain't got a licence, Gerry.'

'No, nor likely to get one neither. Anyway, who wants one for one box of goods? I'll take a lookout – Jack Johnson, he's sharp enough.'

'He's only a kid. Take your brother,' Alma urged. If they were both together, they'd look after each other.

A wariness entered Gerry's face. Alma was about to draw breath to ask why when it was gone, and she was not sure whether she had seen it at all.

'You know Charlie,' he said carelessly. 'Always got something on. He'll be far too busy to come and act lookout for me. No, young Jack Johnson'll do fine. He's always ready to earn a bob.' He carried the box back into the parlour where it could not be tripped over. 'Tea ready, Ma? I got to be back at the shop. Old Rooney only give me half an hour seeing as I'm not going in tomorrow. Mustn't be late or he might change his mind.'

With a jolt, Alma realized that there was a big problem, big enough to put the dislike between her two sons right out of her mind for the moment. Milly and her kids couldn't be sent home yet, so that meant four extra mouths to feed. Four! Though Milly herself wouldn't eat much and Johnny was only little, still there simply wasn't enough to go round.

'What we got, Maisie?' she asked. Oh, the joy of being able to say that, to come in from work and have a dinner cooked. Maisie might be a wet blanket at times, but she wasn't a bad little housekeeper.

'Pea soup and rice pudding.'

Alma thought quickly. Good thing it wasn't fish or sausages. Soup you could share out. Water it down a bit and all.

'Give Gerry his, and the nippers. Rest of us can eat when Will and Charlie come in.' Maisie looked bothered. Alma drew her aside, so that Milly might not notice the embarrassment she and her family had caused. 'Put a drop of water in it and give 'em a small bowlful, and use up all the bread. I'll send out Florrie for some more before the men get in.'

Hot and green, with little bits of bacon floating in it, the soup was served into a variety of bowls. Nearly a whole loaf of bread was cut into hunks and placed in the middle of the scrubbed deal table. The three little ones and Gerry wolfed it down in a couple of minutes. The rice pudding was brought out.

'Give 'em the lot,' Alma whispered to Maisie. 'Florrie can get a bit of jam to put on the bread for the rest of us.'

Milly touched Alma's arm. 'I'm a lot of trouble for you,' she murmured.

'No, dearie.' She bent and put an arm round the bowed shoulders. 'What's a family for, for Gawd's sake? You're my sister, ain't you? You done enough for me in your time. All them clothes you passed on for the boys. All them times you put us up when we was turned out. What's a drop of soup and a warm by the fire?'

The extra expense would mean no night out at the pub tonight. That was her drinking money gone. But there was that sailor she met today. He said he'd buy her one if she went to the Ferry. Alma turned the suggestion over in her mind. She had vowed there'd be no more sailors. They were all the same, expected a girl to give everything for a drink or two. But this one was different: an older man, a widower – or so he said – and not out on the town with the rest of the crew. They'd talked together for an hour or more as she scrubbed out those cabins. She'd hardly noticed her back and her knees and her arms because they'd both been joking around and he'd told her all about things that had happened on the last voyage. Albert, that was his name. Bert. Yes, she would go. After all, what was the harm? It'd give him an eyeful when he saw her all done up in her best togs. The weariness of the day fell from her with the expectation.

First Charlie then Will came in, both of them accepting the roomful of Turners without comment. Charlie ate and went straight out again, saying he had to see a man about a dog. Maisie watched as Will washed, went upstairs, then came down dressed up for an evening out.

'Going down the Puncheon with the lads,' he said carelessly. Then, seeing Maisie's beaten-spaniel expression, he added, 'I 'spect you'd like to stay with your mum. Ta-ta!'

Alma could have swung at him. That was no way to treat the girl. She'd have a word with Martha Johnson about her son, so she would. Maisie's face crumpled. Silent tears slid down her cheeks. Sighing, Alma said goodbye to her evening out.

Milly and the kids couldn't go back till they were sure the old man was spark out, and now Maisie was in no state to cheer them up.

Archie bloody Turner had a lot to be blamed for, she thought as she looked around at the sorry little family. There were times when having no man at all seemed a whole lot better than being saddled with a pig like him.

'There, there,' she said to Maisie, putting an arm around her shoulders. 'They're no use crying over, any of 'em. Always let you down in the end. You're lucky you got your family.'

But Maisie only cried the harder. 'I love him so much,' she sobbed.

'I know, dearie, I know. Treat you like dirt, they do, but still you can't help loving 'em. That's just the way it is.'

3

Saturday night and the air was warm and stale. It had been a sultry day and the heat had soaked into the buildings and the streets. Now the bricks and the cobbles were breathing it out, air that had been used a thousand times, heavy with smuts and smoke. Children still played out in the long summer twilight, the boys at cricket with a stick and a rag ball, the girls crouching on the kerbstones absorbed in jacks or cat's cradle. It was too warm for skipping or hopscotch. Women leaned in the doorways, arms folded across their stomachs, gossiping. Old people sat on the pavement on kitchen chairs, the women knitting or mending, the men with their pipes, watching with critical eyes the goings-on of the younger folk. They all stared, silent and suspicious, as the strangers went by. The group of young men felt the hostility and put a swagger into their walk. They were way out of their territory, but they were not going to let these people intimidate them.

At the end of the street, light streamed from the open doors and windows of the pub, turning the day into evening. Men lingered outside with their drinks, leaning against the dark shiny tiles, laughing and joking. Children waited hopefully for ginger beer. The group of young men glanced up at the sign then shouldered their way through the locals and went in.

The air in the pub was filled with smoke despite the open windows. The ceiling was yellow with it. The place was packed; a dense swell of voices rose from the crowd. Men in their Saturday-night best, their caps on the back of their heads and jackets unbuttoned in the heat, cradled their pints to their chests. Women done up to the nines in tight shiny dresses in bright colours sipped at gin or port and lemon. They were packed into the benches, jammed on to the chairs, standing shoulder to shoulder in between. Somewhere out of sight a piano jangled.

The group from Trinidad Street stood just inside the door and took it all in, Harry and his two cousins Gerry and Charlie, and Will, at twenty-two the oldest by five or six years.

'Popular place,' Harry commented.

'Lot of Irish,' Will said.

You could cut the brogue with a knife.

'That's why they brought her here, ain't it? Brought her here because it's an Irish pub. Harp of Erin. Stands to reason she'll go down a treat amongst her own people, seeing as she sings all Irish songs. Gives 'em what they want to hear.' Gerry always had all the answers.

Charlie hunched his shoulders in impatience. 'Are we drinking or not?' he asked.

They threaded their way to the bar.

The long mahogany counter was awash with beer. Gaslight gleamed and flashed off the glasses and mirrors. Sweating barmaids laboured to keep up with the demand. Throats were dry with the heat and a week's wages were burning holes in pockets.

They bought their beers and eased their way out, then stood in a tight defensive group. They weren't on Dog Island now. This was Poplar, practically foreign ground.

Gerry looked at the crowd, cheerful, laughing, out for a good night's spree. He saw people ready to spend, wanting to spend, people who'd laboured and sweated all week and wanted a good time. There was money to be made here, money eager and waiting to come into his hands.

Harry was gazing at the women.

'I dunno what Ma O'Donaghue would say to some of these,' he said. 'She wouldn't let her Theresa out dressed like that.'

Will followed his glance. A girl quite close to them was smiling up into the face of a big navvy. Her canary-yellow dress strained across her full

63

breasts, its ruffles quivering with the quick rise and fall of her breathing. Her face was nothing much to look at, sharp and flushed in the steamy fug with beads of sweat standing out on her forehead, but her elaborate hairstyle and low-cut dress held the promise of things to come. They drew the eye like a magnet.

'You can bet she's not Irish. They don't let their girls flaunt themselves like that,' Will said, taking on the role of older and more experienced man. His eyes ranged over the heads, searching for familiar faces. He did not expect to spot Siobhan, since she was small enough to be hidden in the crowd, but the O'Donaghues might be sighted.

'Can't see them anywhere,' he said.

'They ought to be here by now. I saw them set off before us,' Harry said.

'Maybe they called for some others on the way.'

Already someone was singing over by the unseen piano, a boozy voice belting out a bawdy song. A few others joined in until it disintegrated raggedly into raucous laughter. It was too early yet. They were not ready.

Will felt hemmed in, pinned down. Frustration began to build inside him. She must be here somewhere. All these loud voices masking hers, all these broad shoulders hiding her. If he knew where she was he could make towards her, but just pushing around the pub searching would be asking for trouble. He glared about him, hating the red faces, the sweating backs. They were fencing him off from her.

'…Will?'

'Eh?' He realized Harry was talking to him.

'Your dad getting work all right now?'

'Oh.' It was difficult to turn his attention to family matters. 'Yeah, well, it's summer, ain't it? More around now. But it ain't easy, ain't easy for no one, getting work as a casual, and he ain't a young man no more.'

'Got his pride too, your dad. Wouldn't take anything.'

'Oh no, not Dad. He's a sugar man, not a dock rat. Only works the sugar boats. And that Alf Grant's put the word out. There's plenty of foremen won't take him on now 'cos they heard he's a troublemaker.'

'Must be hard for your family.'

'But you know my mum. She don't complain. And everyone mucks in, earning this and that.'

'So Ellen's still going to the Central in September, is she?'

'Far as I know. Bloody stupid idea, if you ask me.'

Gerry interrupted them. 'You sure this is the place?'

'Yeah, yeah. Harp of Erin. That's what Pat O'Donaghue said.'

He had been full of it, Pat O'Donaghue, boasting to anyone who'd listen how his little cousin had the sweetest voice on God's earth, how they'd gone out of a Saturday night and she'd taken them all by storm, made strong men cry and had them all cheering and bawling for more, raising the roof, stamping on the floor.

'Why don't she sing down at the Rum Puncheon, then?' Will had asked.

'It's not a singing pub, is it?' Pat pointed out.

'And you lot wouldn't appreciate it, anyway. It's not your common music hall stuff she does, it's the real thing. Proper songs. Irish songs.'

'Don't mean to say we wouldn't like to hear 'em,' Will said.

What he meant was *he* wanted to hear her. He didn't care what she was singing. She could sing in Chinese if she wanted. He just wanted to be there.

'She's something special, is our Siobhan,' Pat said.

Will knew it. He'd known it from the moment he saw her. But getting close to her was another thing. She was surrounded by the O'Donaghues. He hung about each morning just to see her go off to work with her cousin Theresa, who had got her a job at Morton's. The clothes that had marked her out as fresh off the boat had gone within the fortnight. She was dressed like all the others now, but still you could pick her out at a hundred yards. Like Pat said, she was special. The set of her head, the way she walked, that air of pride. They all wanted to get to meet her, all the men. But at first when she went out of an evening, it was up to some club at the Catholic church with the other Irish girls. Once summer came and the light evenings it was better. She would put on her best clothes and parade with a gaggle of friends, like all the other girls, glancing at the boys who gathered on the corners to whistle at them.

She went out with some of them. Will watched them with sick jealousy clutching at his guts, lads of Gerry's age, or older men. None of them lasted for long, and she was safe enough. Ma O'Donaghue saw to that. She had to be in by ten o'clock. One minute past and Pat and Declan'd be out looking for her, and whoever was with her would live to regret it. She was safe, but safe from him as well. With the entire O'Donaghue clan looking on, he could do nothing more than pass the odd friendly word with her, like any other neighbour.

There was a stir amongst the crowd. Will looked towards the door, and there they were: Brian O'Donaghue, Pat and Declan, and some cousins of theirs, all talking in loud voices, swaggering, making an entrance. Will craned his head. She must be with them. They wouldn't be acting like that otherwise, drawing attention to themselves. Then he saw her dark head, a straw hat crowned with daisies perched on top.

'They're here,' Harry said.

'I know.'

'Looks grand, doesn't she?'

'Yeah.'

All four of them followed her with their eyes as, encircled by her bodyguard of male relatives, she made her way across the room. A stool was found for her at the bar. A drink appeared instantly, as if by magic. She perched daintily with a glass in her hand, parrying remarks from the men around her.

'I wouldn't mind a bit of that,' Charlie said.

'You and the rest of us,' Gerry told him.

'Nothing to stop you asking her out,' Harry said.

'Nothing to stop her saying no,' added Gerry.

Charlie stood firm. 'Who says she'd say no? Why would she say no to me? I could show her a good time.'

'You! You don't know how to treat a girl.'

67

'And you do?'

Will listened to them wrangling and felt old and tied down with unwanted responsibilities. His drink tasted sour in his mouth.

He kept looking at Siobhan, waiting for her to look his way. The O'Donaghues were all round her but they were letting others into the charmed circle. He started to edge his way forward.

She was sitting with one leg crossed over the other, easy, confident. Nobody would believe she was just sixteen years old and in the country no more than a few months. And yet there was nothing of the brassiness of the satin-clad girls about her. She was giving nothing away. You had to earn what you wanted from Siobhan.

He was about six feet away now. He could hear her laugh as she listened to something one of the men was saying. Some crass fool blundered in and tried to buy her a drink. She froze him off with a couple of words loaded with contempt. Will felt almost sorry for the poor sod. If she were ever to talk to him like that, he would shrivel up inside.

Then she saw him. Those blue eyes met his and for a moment she stared coolly at him, taking him in, summing him up. Helpless, Will smiled. That knowing expression flicked over her face, then, miraculously, she smiled back. Will could have shouted and yelled his triumph. There was something there. She knew it. She acknowledged it.

But then the smile changed. She turned to Brian and nodded towards Will.

'Just look who's turned up.'

The O'Donaghues drew him in. With difficulty he ignored Siobhan, and spoke to Pat.

'After all you said, mate, I had to come and see what all the fuss was about. Way you put it, I couldn't keep away. Others are here, too. Harry, the Billinghams – oi! Over here. Come on.' He raised a hand with difficulty, trying to get his friends' attention. They saw him, registered surprise and came over.

The group swelled. Will talked to the men – work, football, the price of beer. He hardly looked at Siobhan, perched on her stool, easily fending off the Billinghams' attempts at impressing her. But he was aware of her all the time, a presence at his side, a force that tugged at every sinew and nerve ending.

Over in the corner a heavy chord was struck and held. Those nearby fell silent but a groundswell of conversation carried on at the other end of the room. Siobhan looked over but made no attempt to move. A thin man with a ravaged face and wild ginger whiskers was standing to attention by the piano. His friends cheered him on from a safe distance.

'Come along now, Con.'

'Give us your best, will ye?'

He leaned over and said something to the pianist, who played an introduction. The men roared. They knew it. This was the stuff.

Will listened with only half an ear. The songs were unknown to him: marching songs, full of challenge and triumph. The audience was belting out the choruses. Slowly the spirit of them filtered through to him. He found his foot tapping to the rhythm, the brave words bubbling up. He joined in, hesitantly at first, then louder.

We're all off to Dublin in the green, in the green...

'Going off to fight for Mother Ireland, are you?' Gerry was grinning.

'What?'

'D'you know what that is you're singing? That's a rebel song, that is. IRA. They come over here and make a bob or two but they don't want us over there. Mind you' – he leant forward and produced something from his pocket – 'I've made a bob or two out of them this evening. Want one for your Maisie? Only thruppence. I've got two left. You can have 'em both for fourpence, seeing as you're a mate.'

Will looked. Gerry was holding out a couple of ladies' handkerchiefs, dainty white with a little green shamrock embroidered in one corner.

'Gone like a house afire with this lot, these have.'

'Don't tell me – they're real Irish linen.' Will knew Gerry's bargains of old.

Gerry grinned. You didn't do your neighbours.

'Take one,' he said. 'Give it to Maisie. She could do with some cheering up.'

With a jolt of guilt, Will put it in his pocket. He did not want to be reminded of boring old Maisie. But at least he did not have much to fear from Gerry in the way of competition, since he was far too busy turning a penny. Charlie was more interested in drinking and staring and making remarks than actually making a play for Siobhan. But Harry – he might well try it. He looked at Harry, trying to size him up as a rival, and was reassured. After all, Harry was only a bit older than Siobhan herself. She would think of him as a boy, whereas Will was a young man.

70

The people were calling for Siobhan.

'Where's herself? Where's the little songbird?'

He could look at her now with safety. Everyone was looking at her. She was swept across to the piano and a chair found for her to stand on. Head and shoulders above the crowd, she stood with not a trace of self-consciousness, a small commanding figure in a modest green dress, her black curls caught up under the pretty straw hat. She was not smiling. Her sweet face was composed, waiting. A hush fell over the rowdy bar, spreading from Siobhan across the packed bodies to the doors and the drinkers outside. And now they were waiting for her. She held them, confident. Then she nodded to the pianist.

She started with the familiar ones. 'Danny Boy', 'Rose of Tralee'. Will knew them. He listened in silence, ignored Harry's murmured comments, and joined in the thunderous applause. Then came a couple of songs he had not heard before, tales of unrequited love that curled round his heart and became part of the ache there. She was singing of how it was, she was singing to him. She knew. She understood. Will was standing alone in the packed bar. This time the applause broke over him like a wave, leaving him vaguely disorientated. She was speaking, and yet he did not seem to be understanding what she said. She seemed to be announcing the next song, for there was an indrawn breath of expectation all around him.

The words meant nothing, as she was singing in Irish, but still the song wove its magic. The lilting voice, clear and sweet as a peat-brown stream, played up and down the spine, brushed the hairs

71

of the neck, insinuated into the secret depths. It told of a country wild and beautiful, of a nation subjugated for generations but still upright and proud in heart and soul.

The room was caught in total silence, rapt. Tears ran unashamedly down hardened faces.

The song ended. For one moment, two, the silence held. Then the clapping began and rose to a roar. Feet stamped, mugs banged on tables, voices cried for more.

Siobhan stood smiling amongst it all, a fragile flower drinking the adulation. She shook her head, stepped down and began to walk slowly from the room, surrounded by her menfolk, impeded by her admirers. Will followed, drawn irresistibly. He had to try to possess some of what he had glimpsed. It was more now than simply wanting the girl; he wanted the force behind the song, the power, the emotion, the promise.

He followed the O'Donaghues blindly as they walked through the streets of Poplar. He had no idea where they were going, no thought for the others. It was only when they turned into another pub that he realized they had left the O'-Donaghue relatives and the rest of the Trinidad Street group behind at the Harp of Erin.

'Is she going to sing again?' he asked Brian.

'No – no, we come here for a snatch of peace and quiet. Can't hear y'self think in the Harp.'

Will had just enough presence of mind to offer to buy a round of drinks. He put Siobhan's port and lemon into her hand. She accepted it with a speculative look.

'What d'you think of our little songbird, then?'

Pat asked.

'She's amazing – I never guessed she could sing like that.' Will forced himself not to look at her, but he was very aware of her listening to his words.

'No more did we, till we heard her one evening.'

'She ought to be on the halls. She'd be a star turn.'

He felt rather than heard Siobhan's intake of breath and knew he had put his finger on something.

Brian was looking disapproving. 'What, and have her up on a stage with any Tom, Dick and Harry in London with the price of a seat in his pocket staring at her? Wouldn't be proper.'

'She'd make a fortune,' Will said.

'Fortune be damned. 'Tis no way for a respectable girl to make a living.'

Pat and Declan nodded in agreement.

Will stole a sideways glance at Siobhan. She was sitting looking into her drink, saying nothing, but there was a mutinous set to her full lips.

'You let her sing this evening,' he pointed out.

'That was different. That was hardly more than doing a turn at a ceilidh. You must see the difference, lad. You wouldn't be wanting your sister or your wife going on the stage in a music hall, now would you?'

Will most certainly would not. But Siobhan was waiting for him to speak on her behalf.

'They ain't got the talent. Siobhan has. Anyone could see that. Those people in the Harp this evening, they'd have done anything for her. They'd have done murder for her if she'd asked.'

He would do murder for her himself right now

if she asked.

'She's not going on the stage, and that's that,' Brian said.

'Well, I think it's a shameful waste,' Will told him.

He did not know how he got through the rest of the evening. He tried to act normally, to talk to Pat and Declan and Brian as if nothing had happened, and all the while he was aching to get Siobhan to himself. The pale skin of her forearm with its down of silky hairs, the soft curve of her body beneath her green cotton dress nearly choked him with desire. He had to get to talk to her. Not that he knew what he could say.

His chance came on the way home. Declan had run into a friend and gone off to another pub. Pat and Brian were walking ahead, talking over some family matter. Will fell in beside Siobhan.

'I meant what I said earlier – about you going on the halls,' he said. 'You'd be grand.'

'So they all say.' She took the compliment as nothing more than the truth. 'But you heard them, they won't be letting me anywhere near a theatre.'

'Do you have to have their say-so?'

'They're my family.'

Will understood that. Family was what protected you from the world. Family was strength. Without it you were nothing, no one.

'Maybe they'll come round. Give them time.'

'Sure, and maybe not.' She sounded bitter.

'Do you ever get away from them?' Will was visited by inspiration. He looked ahead. Pat and Brian were laughing over something. They couldn't hear him. 'I could take you to the Empire, to see what you're aiming for.'

For fully five seconds she was silent. Their feet clattered on the paving stones, hers a quick tap-tap, his a steady clump. He did not know how he kept walking. He did not dare look at her. His heart seemed to stop. He could not breathe.

'Sure,' she said at last, as if he'd merely offered her a drink, 'I'd like that.'

They reached the swing bridge over the entrance to the West India dock. Siobhan stopped in the middle and looked out over the Thames. It was dark and the night still and sultry. A stink of waste, natural and man-made, rose off the brown waters. The tide was low and moonlight shone on the grey flanks of mud. On the river, rows of small ships were moored; lamps, red and green and yellow, glowed where lighters were still plying down on the falling tide. Someone was sculling a skiff out to a waiting barge, the oars creaking as he moved.

Siobhan gripped the rail. Will could feel the heat and the tension of her.

'Dirty,' she said. 'Dirty river, filthy city. But exciting.'

His arms ached to hold her, his hands to touch.

'You're exciting,' he told her. 'You're the most exciting girl I've ever met. I've never known anyone like you.'

'I know.' She was half-turned towards him now, but he could not see her face, only the gleam of her teeth as she smiled. He caught the animal force in her, knew she was tempted, that she wanted him too. He reached out to brush the soft bare skin of her arm, but she whisked away, laughing – a low laugh that set him alight.

'I'm Siobhan O'Donaghue and I'm one on my own. There's no one else like me,' she said, and ran to catch up with the others.

Away to the west, lightning flickered, followed by the first warning rumble of the coming storm.

The women were sitting out on the doorsteps. The little houses were too stuffy to stay indoors, and tempers frayed if large families were on top of each other all the time. The men went up to the pub, to drink or meet for some club; the Rabbit Club, the Pigeon Society – any excuse would do. Sometimes the women went too, but more often they stayed on the doorsteps, mending, keeping an eye on the children, gossiping. Ellen heard them as she squatted on the kerb with Florrie Turner, playing fivestones or arranging the paper dolls they cut out and made into families.

'You seen how that Maisie Johnson dresses that baby o' hers? It'll catch its death o' cold. Hardly a stitch on it, poor little mite.'

'Poor little mite, my eye! Great bonny boy he is, doing lovely. Go down with heatstroke, he would, if she dressed him up like you said.'

'His mum'd do a bit more lovely if her old man was home more often.'

'I don't know what you mean.'

'Go on, don't come that one with me. Never home, he ain't.'

'No more ain't your old man, come to that.'

'At least I know where mine is.'

'If you're saying what I think you are, it's a flaming lie. Will Johnson's gone over the Harp of

Erin with the rest of the boys.'

'Yes, and to see who, might I ask? That flighty little Irish madam, that's who. And when he isn't listening to her sing he's out with her down the East Ferry Road.'

'That's another flaming lie an' all. Clodagh O'Donaghue wouldn't let no girl o' hers down the East Ferry Road with no one, and 'specially not with a bloke what's married. Only fast girls go down there. Just 'cos she jilted your Jimmy, you got your knife into her.'

'Huh. She did no such thing. He didn't want a girl like her. And I tell you another thing, too. It don't surprise me one little bit, the way that Will's behaving. Always was on the wild side. I was never happy when he was walking out with my Dot. If it hadn't been that Siobhan it'd be someone else. He only married Maisie because she was in the family way. You can say what you like, but I know what I know.'

Ellen's ears burned. She bent over the game, avoiding Florrie's eyes, pretending she had not heard. Her long curtain of brown hair hid her face. But as she tried to toss the pebble and pick up the next one, her hand shook and she dropped both.

'My go,' Florrie said.

Ellen's attention wandered. She looked up the street to the Billinghams' house. There was nobody outside their door. Alma was out somewhere with her latest man, while Will, Gerry and Charlie, if her overhearings were to be believed, were over in Poplar at the Harp of Erin. Maisie was inside.

'Coming to see Tommy, Aunty Florrie?'

Florrie said nothing. Her thin hand was steady

six inches above the pavement, two pebbles balanced on the back. Nimbly she tossed them up, grabbed a third from the ground and caught all three.

'I won. Yeah, all right, Aunty Ellen.'

The novelty of the new relationship had not yet worn off. They adored Maisie's baby, vying to be allowed to hold him, play with him or take him for walks in the rickety old pram passed down through the Johnson family since Will was a baby. He was a happy little soul, now that he had got over the collicky stage, always ready with a smile for his serious young aunts.

'Maisie?' Florrie stopped outside the door of number forty and rapped on it with her knuckles. 'Maisie? Can we come in?'

There was no answer. The girls looked at each other. Two doors along, a canary in a cage on the bottom windowsill was singing its heart out. Down the other end of the street there was a yell of 'Out!' from the boys playing rounders.

'She must be in,' Ellen said. She was conscious of eyes upon her back watching to see what happened.

'Come on,' Florrie decided, and pushed open the door. Nobody in Trinidad Street would even think of locking a front door. Ellen followed her in.

The little house was quiet, the air stale and oppressive. The girls made their way through the little front parlour on tiptoe, subdued by the stillness. They pushed open the kitchen door and stood staring.

The back door and the window were closed. Little Tommy was asleep in his pram. By the smell of him, he was dirty. Maisie was sitting at the table, with her back to them. Her head was in her hands and she made no sign that she'd heard them. Nonplussed, the two girls looked at each other again.

'Maisie?' Florrie stepped forward. 'Maisie? You all right?'

No answer. Ellen went to one side of her, Florrie the other. They both put an arm round her shoulders, but whatever they said to her, they got little reaction. In the end they gave up, simply asking if they could take Tommy out. This Maisie did agree to.

The two girls manoeuvred the pram and the sleeping baby out into the street.

'What's up with her, then?' Granny Hobbs asked, with a nod of the head to indicate Maisie.

'Nothing,' Florrie lied loyally.

'She's just tired. Wants a rest,' Ellen elaborated. She turned to Florrie. 'Let's take him for a walk. We could go down the river.'

They marched the length of the street, defying the curious stares, but as they reached the West Ferry Road, Florrie rounded on Ellen.

'It's all your Will's fault.'

'What?'

'You heard. It's all your Will's fault. Everyone's talking about it. Poor Maisie can't hold her head up.'

'Florrie! I thought we was friends.'

'I can't be friends with someone whose brother treats my sister like that.'

'She ought to tidy herself up a bit.'

They were still arguing when Harry found them.

'What's all this about, then?'

79

They both looked up, surprised into momentary silence. Ellen's insides gave a funny twist, making her feel almost sick. Harry was straight in from work and he smelt of boats, a combination of tar and bilgewater and old rope. His face and neck and forearms were tanned, and his hair where it curled out from under his cap was bleached almost blond from the sun.

'Well?' he asked.

'It's our Maisie,' Florrie blurted out. 'You should see her, Harry! She's been crying and she don't want to do nothing.'

'Where's Will?'

'Gone up Poplar to the Harp of Erin.'

'Ah.' Anger filled his face, hardening his eyes.

A fear took hold of Ellen. 'Harry, it's not–'

'Not what? Not what I think? 'Course it is. Why else'd he be up there? I saw him the night we first went over. Couldn't keep his eyes off of her, he couldn't. Well, not any longer. I'm putting a stop to this.'

'Oh, Harry, Will don't mean it, I'm sure he don't. Leave it be, please. We don't want no trouble.' She clutched at his sleeve, pleading, but he shook her off.

'Look here, kid.' He took her by the shoulders and looked into her eyes, trying to make her see his point of view. 'There's trouble already, and I'm going to put a stop to it. I like you, I like your family. You're all right. But nobody treats my sister like that and gets away with it, see?'

Ellen nodded. She knew there was nothing she could do. Events had to take their course. She stood miserably watching Harry turn the corner into Trinidad Street. Tommy woke up and began to cry. Florrie grasped the handle of the pram.

'I'm going to take him back and change him,' she said, and flounced off after her brother. Ellen followed slowly.

The whole street seemed to know that something was up. Nobody said anything, but the air was charged with expectancy. Twilight faded imperceptibly into night, children were called in and sent to bed, kitchen chairs were fetched inside, but still some of the women hung about on the doorsteps, waiting for something to happen.

Upstairs in the back bedroom, Ellen leaned out under the sash window looking out into the back yard. Behind her, Daisy and Jack were fast asleep, but she could not even lie down. She crept out on to the top step of the stairs and listened. Mum was still downstairs, Dad was not yet in from his meeting at the Radical Club over in Cubitt Town. She slid into her parents' room and leaned her head against the glass there, straining to see out. Fear clawed at her – fear for her brother, coming back all unsuspecting; fear for Harry, who was younger and lighter. And mixed with it was guilt. If she had not suggested going to see Maisie then all this might not have happened. Somebody, Will or Harry or probably both of them, was going to get hurt, and it was all her fault. Gnawing her knuckles, she wished desperately she could turn back time, could change it all, while slowly the minutes ticked by. She tried to pray, making bargains with God. *Let them be all right and I'll be good forever. I'll even give up my place at Millwall Central, if You can just stop them.*

81

She saw her father coming home, clumping wearily, his hands in his pockets. Perhaps he would go out, perhaps he would stop them. She listened as downstairs her parents were talking, her mother's voice anxious, her father's dismissive. Any hope that Ellen had had withered away. Her dad was going to do nothing. She knew why. To him it was unimportant, a silly spat. She heard his words floating up the stairs.

'Let 'em sort it out between themselves, silly young sods.'

That was that. It was going to happen, and there was nothing she could do but wait.

Harry waited by the swing bridge. Now that it had come to it, he was glad. It had been brewing for far too long, ever since that first night they went over to the Harp of Erin. He leaned on the rail, looking out over the river, his river. After two years' apprenticeship up under the many bridges, down in and out of the labyrinth of docks and creeks, he knew all its moods and loved most of them. Still and calm like tonight, breezy and choppy, dark and angry, each condition had its own challenges, its own pleasures, even if it was only a warm cabin after a cold and difficult trip. He felt sorry for men like his father and Will, stuck in mindless labouring jobs on the docks. On a lighter, you were your own man, responsible for the boat and her cargo. People respected a lighterman.

He tried to assess his chances. Will was older than him, and heavier, but Harry had surprise on his side, and that counted for a lot. It all depended on who was with him. If Will was actually with

Siobhan, then he'd get him, give him something to really remember. But he doubted if that would be the case. The O'Donaghues wouldn't let them walk back together. If Will was with the O'Donaghues, then it was going to be tricky, for they might well come in on Will's side to defend Siobhan's honour. If he was just with Gerry and Charlie, it was all right. Gerry and Charlie would keep out of it and see there was a fair fight. If they were all together in a bunch, it might be a big fight, for Gerry and Charlie would come in with him, seeing as they were his cousins. He hunched his shoulders and felt the strength in his arms. Two years of helping control wooden barges laden with upwards of seventy tons of cargo, using nothing but oars, had developed him beyond his years, and his time as leader of the Trinidad Street gang had sharpened his appetite for a fight. He was looking forward to taking on Will Johnson.

Drunks rolled homewards over the bridge, weaving through gangs of young men and strolling prostitutes. Harry ignored them all. He kept his mind on Will and Siobhan and Maisie, fuelling his anger. He heard them coming. There were a lot of them, walking home together in a large loose bunch, relaxed from a good night out, half drunk, laughing and calling out to each other as they went along. They were behaving decently, since they had a girl with them, not like a gang of men out on their own. None of them took any notice of him, standing still and silent in the dark. As they passed under the street light he picked them out. His cousins, Pat and Declan O'Donaghue with Siobhan between them holding on to their arms, Brian with a couple of the older men. And in the rear, with his hands in his pockets, by himself, Will.

Harry's hands curled into fists. Perfect. He could jump him and have him on the floor before he knew what was happening. But that was not the way he planned it. Will had to know exactly what was happening, and why. He waited until Will had gone past, then stepped out of the shadows.

'Will! Will Johnson. I want a word with you.'

Will stopped and turned. Harry saw recognition in his face, surprise, the start of understanding.

'Do you now? What makes you think I want to talk to you?'

Will's voice was harsh and Harry could tell that he was in a dangerous mood, but decided he was not going to let that stop him.

'You been playing away from home,' Harry said, attacking with his moral supremacy. 'You been upsetting my sister. I don't like that.'

'Yeah?' Will was unmoved. 'So what are you going to do about it?'

In the background, Harry sensed the others turning back and coming to Will's defence.

'Leave it, leave it. This is family business,' Gerry called out.

There was a growl of understanding.

He moved fast then, getting in two before Will could react. Will had been drinking, while Harry was stone-cold sober. Will rolled with the blows, but came back. He was spoiling for a fight. Harry took one on his arm, another on his shoulder. His fist found Will's cheek, then a crashing blow he did not see coming slammed into the side of his head, making his skull ring. He staggered. Behind him and around him, there were shouts and jeers. He fended off the pounding while his sight cleared.

'Had enough, boy?'

Will's face leered at him, lips stretched in a mirthless grin. Harry lunged forward, taking him off guard. His knuckles crunched right into the smiling mouth, grating on the teeth. With a spurt of fierce pleasure he followed with one to the ear and dodged back, laughing as Will landed harmless swipes to his shoulders. That was it, he had it, he had the measure of it. Dart in, leap back. He had speed and agility. Will couldn't follow him. The cheers rang round.

One eye was blurred and there was a drumming in his head, a draining pain in his left arm that made it agony to lift. But Will was failing, his punches were going wild. Hardly thinking, Harry worked on the old tricks, his body remembering fights gone by. He backed down, ducking his head. Will came forward, a shambling mass of frustrated anger, Harry darted in, up. One feeble hit with his left, then a splintering punch with his right, dead on the side of the jaw. Will's head snapped back; he staggered, crumpled at the knees and collapsed. Harry stood over him, chest heaving, heart pounding, the breath rasping into his lungs. For a moment he did not feel the pain.

'Remember that, you bastard,' he said. The words came with difficulty. His mouth was not working properly.

Will said nothing. He got slowly to his feet. The others were closing in, holding him up. Harry felt hands on his arms, heard voices close to his ears.

85

'Well done, mate.'

'Come on now, you got him.'

'He won't forget that in a hurry.'

He was borne along in a daze of pain, riding on triumph. No, Will would not forget that in a hurry.

There was a new respect for Harry in the street after that. He felt it as he hobbled to work, his eye closed and swollen, his muscles stiff, his bruises aching with every step. He saw it in people's eyes, heard it in the way they spoke to him. He had battled for his sister. He had stood up for his family. He had passed the last hurdle into manhood.

Only when he met Ellen Johnson did he feel a jolt of regret. She was sitting on her front doorstep, reading a book. She looked up as he passed, with such reproach in her hazel eyes that he had to stop.

''Lo, Ellen,' he said.

She bit her lip. At first he thought she was not going to speak to him.

'You never had to do it,' she blurted out.

'I did, Ellen. I had to stop him.'

She looked down at her book again. 'I don't like people getting hurt,' she said.

'It was the only way.'

She slammed the book shut and jumped up, tears in her eyes.

'I hate you, Harry Turner. You're a big bully,' she shouted, and whisked indoors, banging the door behind her.

Harry stood for a moment staring at the worn brown paint. Maisie had been just the same. She had railed at him for hurting Will. He shrugged and set off for work. Women!

PART II

1901–2

1

'He'd better blooming well get himself crowned this time,' Martha Johnson said.

'You can't have appendicitis twice,' Ellen told her. She paused in her task of spreading margarine on the bread her mother was slicing. 'Is that all right?'

Martha looked. 'Bit too thick. Scrape some off or there won't be enough to go round. All this food! Be dreadful if it all went to waste. Appendicitis. Nobody ever had that when I was a kid.'

'P'raps only kings get it,' Daisy suggested.

All three surveyed the loaves, the ham, the margarine. The Johnson household was in charge of sandwich making for the coronation party. Other families were providing pork pies, beef pies, pickles, buns, jellied eels. Whisky, gin, beer, ginger beer and lemonade were lined up. The whole street had been saving up for the party for weeks. In the Johnson household, like many others, it had not been easy. With Tom no longer a preference man and up against Alf Grant's prejudice, they all had to take jobs, even the children, to get the money together. But this morning all the effort to put their share towards the party seemed worthwhile. Everything had been thought of. Gerry had come up with yards of red, white and blue ribbon for everyone to trim their hats with, windows and mantelpieces were decorated with

Union Jacks and pictures of the new King and Queen cut out of the newspapers. A couple of the men were organizing races for the children, with sweets for prizes, and in the evening there was going to be dancing. There was something for everyone.

The last sandwich was cut and put on to a plate. Martha looked at the piles with satisfaction.

'Well done, you girls. Damp a couple of tea-cloths and put 'em over the top to keep 'em fresh. Damp, mind, not wringing wet. Then you can go and get changed. And don't rush about,' she added, as they leapt to do as they were asked; 'we got a long day ahead of us.'

Martha was pregnant again after a gap of several years. She hoped she would carry this one, but at forty-three the strain was telling on her.

The girls ignored her warning. A wash to get the food off their hands, then they rushed upstairs to get into their new dresses, acquired after great deliberation from second-hand stalls in the market. Daisy's was yellow taffeta, faded, thin, and a lot less full in the skirt than when they bought it, since Martha had had to take torn sections out and regather it, but still a party dress. Some child in the West End had once worn it with layers of petticoats and black patent leather shoes. Daisy had to make do with her ordinary boots, but still she loved the dress with a single-minded passion. It was the most beautiful thing she had ever owned.

Ellen took her dress down from the hooks behind the door. It was not as bright and partyish as Daisy's, but it was something even better, it was her first real grown-up gown with a skirt right down to the floor, as befitted someone who was now fourteen years old. She slid it over her head, got Daisy to do up the dozens of tiny buttons down the back, smoothed the blue sprigged poplin over her body. Her mother had taken it in, taken it up, and now it fitted perfectly, showing her high breasts and neat waist. She puffed out the full tops of the sleeves, twirled round so the skirt flared out. It was beautiful. She tied red, white and blue ribbons in her sister's hair and sent her off to show their mother, then set about the difficult task of pinning her own hair up on top. She had been practising this in secret for weeks. The result was nearly as good as she hoped for. She surveyed the effect in the mirror in her parents' room. A young woman stared back at her, face solemn, eyes bright with suppressed excitement. She gazed for a long time, trying to make her mind up – was this a pretty young woman, one the boys would want to dance with? Slowly a smile lifted the corners of her lips, spread over her face and reached the hazel eyes. She laughed out loud. Yes, she was pretty. And she was going to a party. She spun round and ran downstairs.

The men were taking furniture out into the street. Her father stopped in the parlour, two wooden chairs in his arms.

'Who's this come to visit us?' he asked. 'Blimey, it's Ellen! I shall have to watch it now, there'll be queues of lads at the door.'

Ellen blushed. Her father very rarely joked like this. He was a serious man, her dad, with his union work and his dream of a better life, not one to tease his daughter. She hardly knew how to take it.

'Is it all right?' she asked.

Martha came in from the kitchen. 'Turn round,' she said, and as Ellen turned, 'Yes, very nice. Lovely. Come up a treat, that dress has.' Jack came running in to find the parlour blocked with people. He glanced at Ellen.

'You look stupid,' he said, and went to fetch another chair.

Martha gave him a playful cuff round the head. The group broke up, laughing. Ellen lingered by the window, looking out. The chairs and tables were being set out at one end of the street, leaving space for the races at the other. Already people were beginning to gather. Old folk were sitting watching and telling everyone what to do, children were racing around shrieking, some of the girls, now that the food preparation was done, were coming out and eyeing each other's finery. Ellen saw Florrie Turner emerge carrying her little sister. She took a deep breath and went out.

The races started about midday, when everyone had finally assembled. There was running, skipping, three-legged, relays. Jack won the boys' running, two small O'Donaghues the wheelbarrow, Ida Turner dragged little Tommy to victory in the toddlers' race. There were yells of triumph, tears of disappointment. Children in red, white and blue ribbons ran about clutching sticky bags of boiled sweets, their cheeks bulging. Ellen watched and cheered and clapped, glad to be out of it. Races were for kids. She was a grown-up now and she did not have to be subjected to the humiliation of coming last.

But the beer was being passed around and everyone was getting excited.

'Mums' race!' somebody yelled. 'Let's have a mums' race!'

The cry was taken up. Mothers old and young were shoved into line, protesting. But once started, they ran with a will. Alma lumbered over the winning line just in front.

'Won by a tit,' joked some racing expert.

There was a boys' tug-of-war, then it was the men's turn. Sleeves rolled up, caps on the backs of their heads, brawny dockers and labourers and lightermen heaved and sweated, their boots skidding on the cobbles. The women yelled encouragement, the children jumped up and down screaming. Ellen abandoned her new dignity and shrieked with the rest. Her father and brother, Harry and the O'Donaghues were all on one side with half a dozen others. Shoulder to shoulder they pulled, their faces contorted with effort. Pat's foot slipped, he fell and took two others with him, the whole team was dragged forward. Their supporters groaned and jeered.

'Get up, get up! Pull!' Ellen yelled. 'Pull, Harry!'

They struggled up, made a desperate effort and regained the lost ground just in time. The spectators reached fever pitch. Frightened babies screamed. Inch by inch the Johnsons' team crept back, dragging their rivals with them. For minutes it hung in the balance, then the others seemed to tire. One of them slipped and they were heaved over the line, everyone ending in a heap on the road.

The victors were swamped with ecstatic supporters, the vanquished helped to their feet and led to the beer table. In the mêlée, Ellen saw Maisie fling her arms round Will and the pair of them hug each other, her mum kissing her dad, the O'Donaghues surrounded by family and girl-friends. Pushed this way and that by the celebrating crowd, she found the person she was seeking. People were clapping Harry on the back and congratulating him. She made to join them, but then stopped short, for there was Siobhan O'Donaghue by his side, and she was looking up into his face. A surge of jealousy, sick and bitter, possessed her. Siobhan was pretty, Siobhan could sing, Siobhan had all the boys after her. Ellen stood fixed to the spot, jostled by rowdy neighbours, staring at them. She could not tear her eyes away. Siobhan was smiling up at him. It was not a smile such as family or friends might exchange, but Ellen recognized it. It was a teasing smile, charged with invitation, but still holding back. Ellen knew, with an instinct that came with her developing body, that few men would be able to resist it. When Siobhan looked at them like that, they were hooked.

'Come on, Ellen, don't hang about here all day. We're all having a drink.'

Theresa O'Donaghue linked arms with her and pulled her along the street with the flow heading for the drinks table.

Once away from Harry and Siobhan she said in Ellen's ear, 'Makes you sick, don't she? She's been through all the men in this street and all the decent ones at work, and now she's decided to have a go at Harry. He's been ignoring her this year past. She can't bear that.'

94

Ellen looked at her, startled, recognizing a jealousy as painful as her own, but deeper and more corrosive.

'Don't you like her?' she asked. 'She's your cousin.'

'More's the pity. It was a black day when she arrived in our house. I've got to share a bed with her. I wish she'd get herself married and move out.'

The O'Donaghues stood in an entirely new light. As a family they had always been one of the tightest knit in a community of close families. Ellen had never before known them to break ranks and admit to tensions within. She imagined having to live with Siobhan in her house, and the reasons became much clearer.

'It must be difficult,' she said.

'Difficult! You don't say. I have to see her up to her tricks morning, noon and night. And the rest of 'em think she's wonderful. Even Mum. She thinks she's such a nice girl, a pleasure to have around the place. I can't stand it.'

Ellen knew what she was trying to do. She wanted Ellen on her side, someone to form a 'we hate Siobhan' gang, like what happened at school sometimes. But however jealous she was of Siobhan right at that moment, she did want to line herself up with Theresa. Ellen was embarrassed. Everyone round them was laughing and joking, and here was Theresa pouring out her dislike of her cousin. She tried to edge away, but Theresa still had hold of her arm.

'Watcha, girls! What's all the long faces for, then?'

Gerry was standing in front of them, beer glass in hand. Ellen smiled at him in relief and he stepped back in pretended surprise, jolting the group behind him.

'It's Ellen Johnson. Stone me, I never recognized you. What a transformation! Here, let me get you a drink. What are you having – gin? Port?'

Ellen smiled and shook her head.

'Not ginger beer? Not now you're a young lady. Here, I know, I'll do you a big lemonade with a little bit of gin. How's that? Just the ticket. And what about you, Theresa? Can't have all this gloom on the big day. You going to dance with me later? I been waiting for a chance to ask you, but you always got all others round you...'

They were swept up in his patter and glasses were pushed into their hands. Ellen sipped, and decided she didn't much like the smell that gin gave to a drink. She tried not to listen too much to Theresa, still talking in her ear, and looked about, not sure quite what to do. The children were still racing around, playing and shouting, but she was no longer one of them. The married folk were chatting amongst themselves, many of the women with babies on their hips. But she was certainly not one of them. The young people were in groups, the boys openly eyeing the girls. The girls were pretending to ignore them but shooting covert glances to see who was looking at them, and breaking into spurts of laughter. The problem was, they were all at work and she was fourteen and still at school. She was not quite one of them any more, and it made her feel uneasy.

Then Vi from across the street spotted her and

called her over.

''Lo, Ellen, you're looking nice. Where you get that dress from, then?'

With relief, Ellen joined them and was drawn into their discussion of clothes and boys, and who was walking out with who, and who they hoped to dance with. The others teased and patronized her, but she hardly minded that. It was all right. She was accepted into the world of young women. She listened and learned, and watched Siobhan hanging on to Harry's arm. With the strength of the others round her, she could even cope with that better. None of them liked Siobhan.

There was a call for food, and the women disappeared into the houses. Children were sent out with plates and cutlery, then victuals were carried out to where, in the middle of the road in an uneven row, stood tables of different heights and widths but all scrubbed so clean you could eat straight off them. Bowls of eels wobbling in jelly, piles of neatly cut sandwiches, raised pork pies divided into slices, peas swimming in bright green liquor, and buns shiny with sugar were set down. Bottles of beer and lemonade and ginger beer were brought over from the stock of drinks. The crowd gathered closer. Children's hands were slapped as they reached out to the irresistible feast. The last plate and glass was arranged. Of one accord, the whole street sat down to eat.

Everyone had made an effort to dress up for the big day. Suits had been taken out of pawn for the men, collars and ties put on, boots shined. The women had bought or borrowed or altered dresses and trimmed up their hats. Everyone

97

wore red, white and blue. The men had favours in their buttonholes, the women ribbons and rosettes on their hats, the girls bows in their hair. Even the prams were decorated. And all along the street, front windows were adorned with flags and pictures. Trinidad Street was part of the British Empire and proud of it.

When the eating was grinding to a halt and everyone was leaning back and loosening tongues and belts, Tom stood up and made a speech. They all listened and commented and shouted out. He was a good one for speeches, was Tom, as long as he did not go on too long. He talked about the great Empire and how they, the working people, were the most important part of it. They cheered their approval.

'And today,' he concluded, 'the King is being crowned monarch of our country. Ladies and gentlemen, I give you a toast – King Edward the Seventh, may his reign be long and happy, for him and for us.'

Everyone struggled to their feet. Glasses were raised.

'King Edward the Seventh, God bless him!' they chorused.

The late afternoon drifted by in a happy haze of drink and laughter. Babies cried or slept in their prams, toddlers played under the tables, children ran about throwing paper and snatching ribbons, groups formed over the remains of the feast. Then as the food went down, they all began to feel the need for something different. It was too early yet for dancing, the eating was more or less over, but none of them wanted to get up and start clearing away.

'Give us a song, Georgie,' somebody called.

The cry was taken up. 'Yeah, come on, Georgie. Good old Georgie.'

A small man in a checked cap and a bright yellow tie stood up, grinning with embarrassment. But it did not take much more encouragement to get him going.

'All right, all right. What'll it be, then?'

Suggestions were shouted out, argued over. Georgie cleared his throat and started with 'Daisy Belle' and soon everyone was swaying and joining in with the choruses.

When he had run through his repertoire, someone else tried to recite a monologue but got lost in the middle. Amongst good-natured barracking, he sat down. A group of girls who had been whispering fiercely amongst themselves stood up and volunteered to perform. They sang 'Rule Britannia!', which they had learnt at school especially for the coronation. Some of the boys insisted on singing 'Rule Britannia, too tanners make a bob', which resulted in a hand-to-hand fight until parents pulled the protagonists apart and calmed them down.

'Where's Siobhan?' the men started to shout. 'Let's hear Siobhan.'

Smiling sweetly, Siobhan rose to her feet. Her black curls were pinned up under a straw boater trimmed with red, white and blue ribbons, and more ribbons decorated her delicate organdie dress. She looked young and pretty and innocent with her great blue eyes and her little round face. Even the matrons whose sons had been jilted and daughters had been deserted in favour of her softened a little. You could not believe ill of a girl who looked like that.

Siobhan judged her audience well. She was not singing for an all-Irish crowd now, but a group of Londoners in patriotic mood. Instead, she chose popular music-hall numbers and brought tears to the eyes as her clear voice soared to the rooftops in lilting melodies and sentimental words, then got them all going with a cracking rendition of 'My Old Man Said Follow the Van'. Only the unmarried girls sat stony-faced and unmoved. The audience cheered and clapped and shouted for more; but with the guile of a born performer, she left them wanting.

Nobody felt up to following that. Siobhan was definitely top of the bill. Chairs were pushed back and people got slowly to their feet, agreeing that so far it was the best party they had ever been to. The remains of the food were cleared to one side, plates and glasses and cutlery taken indoors. The women and children washed up, the men rearranged the tables and chairs in groups in a rough rectangle. Babies were changed and fed, everyone freshened up and drifted back into the street for the next part of the entertainment.

Harry ran a wet comb through his hair. However much he tried to flatten it into fashionable sleekness, the wiry curls always sprang back. He gave up, turning his attention to tying the bow tie he had bought especially for the occasion. That was more successful. He stepped back to look in the tarnished mirror over the kitchen range, and nodded with satisfaction. The grey suit his cousin

Gerry had put him on to fitted pretty well now his mother had done a few alterations.

His father drifted through from visiting the privy, holding a bottle by the neck.

'Blimey,' he commented. 'Getting too bloody posh to live with us, you are.'

Harry ignored him. His father was drunk, had been since midday, but there was little danger from him today, not with the whole street looking on. Besides, Harry was now a grown man of nineteen. If need be, he could deal with his father.

Florrie came in to peek at herself in the mirror and stopped short at the sight of him.

'Coo, you look a real toff,' she said.

Harry grinned and tweaked her nose. 'You look pretty yourself, little 'un.'

'I'm not a little 'un,' she said, offended. 'I'll be leaving school next year.'

'Only joking. You look a real corker, honest.'

Mollified, Florrie studied her appearance. 'You going to dance with Siobhan, then?'

'Might do.'

'She likes you.'

Harry looked at his sister. She was sharp, was Florrie, and growing up fast.

'What makes you think that?' he asked, though he knew the answer.

'She's been hanging round you all day.'

'Has she really? I never noticed.'

'You going to dance with her, then?' Florrie asked again.

'I'll dance with you, if you like.'

Florrie gave him a hug and he responded, clasping her bony little body, and fear unexpectedly caught at his heart. She was too thin and her skin had a blueish tinge even in the summer. With their mother so often unable to cope, Florrie had to take on responsibilities beyond her strength.

Floating in from outside came the plaintive sound of Tim O'Keefe tuning up his fiddle. Today was a time to forget worries and fears.

'Come on, sis,' Harry said, 'it's starting out there.'

The children were already scampering about, the little girls holding hands and dancing together while the boys looked on and jeered. Loony Mike capered around by himself, singing cheerfully out of tune. Gradually, some of the married couples joined in – Mr and Mrs Johnson, his sister Maisie and Will. He spotted Siobhan sitting amongst the O'Donaghues. She caught his eye then looked away, feigning indifference. Desire stirred within him. You could not see her and not want her when everything about her was so inviting. That soft, full body, that smile seemed to offer everything. But he knew her for what she was – a tease. She would lead a man on until he hardly knew what he was doing, until she had him on a string, then she would clam up. Siobhan was giving nothing away. She was waiting for someone richer than Trinidad Street could offer. Harry caught hold of his sister's hand.

'Come on, Florrie,' he said. 'Let's show 'em how it's done.'

He polka'd over the cobbles with her, then tripped round more sedately with his aunt Alma. Family duty done, he paused to see who everyone else was dancing with. It was then that he noticed

102

Ellen Johnson. She was skipping round in Gerry's arms, face flushed with pleasure, skirts whirling out from her neat waist. Harry watched her, fascinated. He had always thought of her as just a schoolkid, his sister's friend, nothing remarkable. Now he saw her in a new light. She had grown up. She had a tasty figure. With her heart-shaped face and bright smile, she was a very pretty girl.

The tune came to an end with a long-drawn-out chord on Tim's violin. Dancers and watchers clapped. Gerry made an exaggerated bow, Ellen curtseyed in response and they both walked back to the Johnsons' table, laughing. As if pulled by a string, Harry got up and strolled over. Maisie was there, sitting on Will's knee, both of them sharing the same glass. He nodded at them, said a word or two to Tom and Martha, then turned to their daughter.

'Hullo, Ellen. I hardly would've known you if you hadn't been with your family.'

She looked up at him from under the brim of her straw hat. 'That's what they all say,' she told him.

'Right little cracker, ain't she?' Gerry said. He stood beside her chair with a proprietorial air.

'Changed a bit since she wore a tam-o'-shanter,' Harry said.

He saw a softer light come into the hazel eyes as she remembered.

'Like to have the next dance?' he asked, holding out his hand.

Tim, another half-pint safely beneath the belt, struck up again.

'She's dancing with me,' Gerry told him.

Ellen stood up. 'Who says? You never asked.' She took Harry's hand. 'Thanks,' she said.

He put his arm round her waist and it felt right. She was light as a feather as they moved round together, her eyes shining with enjoyment. He was acutely aware of the curves of her body, the slide of her dress beneath his hand as she danced. Most intoxicating of all was her pleasure.

'Ain't it lovely?' she cried. 'Oh, I do love parties. I've never been to anything as good as this.'

'There was the jubilee,' Harry said. 'And weddings. We had a good party for Will and Maisie, remember.'

'That was different. I was only a kid then.'

'You're not a kid now.'

He let go of her with reluctance as the music stopped. They both clapped automatically, but their eyes never left each other's face.

'Have the next one with me?' Harry asked.

They danced the next one, and the one after. Twilight deepened into evening, and people brought lamps and candles from their houses and set them on the tables. Tim O'Keefe, complaining of aching arms and shoulders, stopped for a rest. Harry joined the Johnsons as everyone flopped down for a long drink and polished off the remains of the food. Toddlers who had fallen asleep across chairs or under tables were scooped up and carried in to bed.

Renewed and refreshed, the party hotted up. Old and young made a circle and sang 'Knees up, Mother Brown' and 'Hands, Knees and Bumps-a-Daisy'. Panting and laughing, they called for the hokey cokey and did it three times, faster and faster. The sweat poured down their faces, women screamed and men whistled with excitement. Scarlet in the face, her hair coming down, Alma lifted up her skirts to show white frilly petticoats. Slowly, seductively, she swayed from side to side. The crowd caught its breath and watched, hypnotized. Her throaty voice rolled across the street – 'Ta – ra – ra boom-de-ay, ta-ra-ra boom-de-ay...' With a roar, they all joined in, grannies and children, friends and enemies, married and single, all were caught up with the animal exuberance of the song, swaying, singing, dancing with abandon until at last they were exhausted.

'Oh – oh – I'm going to die–' Ellen collapsed on to her seat, her breasts heaving, her face flushed. Her hat had long since fallen off and her hair was beginning to come down. Harry wanted very much to take her in his arms and kiss her, but not here.

'I'll get you a drink,' he offered.

'Thanks – anything – water.'

He found the last drop of lemonade and she drank it gratefully. He leaned over the table, whispering so that her parents would not hear.

'Come for a walk with me? We could go down to the river.'

She looked at him, puzzled. 'What, now?'

'Yes, now. Just you and me.'

Understanding dawned. Caution and daring warred in her eyes. Then she looked away.

'I can't. Not with the party on.'

'Here, Harry.' Martha was calling to him across the table. She pushed two mugs in his direction. 'Go and see if you can find us something to put in these, there's a good boy.'

Reluctantly, he complied.

When he got back, Ellen had disappeared.

'She's gone out the you-know-where,' Daisy informed him. 'She said she'll be back in a minute.'

Tim O'Keefe had started playing again, a slow melody. Couples were drifting into the dancing area, shuffling around close to one another. The evening was drawing to an end. After the excesses of the group dancing, everyone wanted to pair up. Any pretence at proper steps had ended. They just held on to each other and moved slowly to the rhythm of the tune on the fiddle.

Harry stood watching them with his hands in his pockets, feeling empty and left out. And then Siobhan was at his side. She looked up at him, lips parted, a pulse beating in her neck.

'Aren't you dancing?' Her voice was low and inviting.

'No.'

She swayed nearer. He could feel her breath.

'Don't you want to?'

He did want to. But he also wanted Ellen.

'I'm waiting for someone.'

'If you mean Ellen, then Gerry went off at about the same time.'

He looked wildly about, a sense of betrayal churning within. Gerry was nowhere to be seen. He remembered Gerry's possessiveness earlier in the evening and how he had cut him out. So Gerry had been waiting all this time to get her back. He would sort Gerry out the moment he reappeared. He wasn't going to let his cousin get away with that. But even as he thought it, Siobhan moved slightly. Her breast brushed lightly against his arm, sending a thrill of desire through him. He put an arm round her waist.

'Come on, then, what are we waiting for?' he said.

She kept a slight distance from him at first, holding his shoulders, talking to him. But he could feel the heat of her body through the fine fabric of her dress, the movement of her hips.

The tune ended, but they stayed together waiting for the next. As the fiddle sang again, he caught sight of Gerry sitting down and handing his mother a drink. Over Siobhan's shoulder he looked for Ellen, but could not see her. Siobhan moved closer, sliding her arms round his neck, leaning her body against his. He ran his hands down her back and pressed her tighter. Her black curls brushed against his cheek, faintly scented.

The first he saw of Ellen again, she and Gerry were dancing together. Close by, Will passed him with Maisie draped round him and gazed at Siobhan with undisguised lust. The music, the dancing, the soft body next to his were all building into a burning need. He bent his head slightly to speak in Siobhan's ear.

'There are too many people here. Come away with me?'

She looked up at him, a slight expression of surprise on her face.

'Come away? What sort of girl do you think I am?'

'The most beautiful girl I've ever met. Come with me, Siobhan.'

'They'll all see.'

'No they won't. You go first, pretend you're going out the back. I'll wait around for a bit then meet you.'

And as he knew she would, she agreed.

It was dark in the alleyway behind the houses, with even darker shadows of impenetrable black. Harry groped his way along.

'Siobhan?' he called softly. 'You there, darling?'

He heard a movement up ahead, then as his eyes adjusted, he saw a shape detach itself from the wall.

'Here.'

The soft brogue was unmistakable. He made towards her, senses straining. He caught the scent of her, then his fingers, running along the walls, met her shoulder. He clasped her in his arms, his mouth finding hers.

She responded eagerly at first, her lips opening to his. She was all that those inviting glances and provocative moves had promised. Her arms tightened round him and he could feel and hear the quick rise and fall of her breathing. He ran his hands down her back, over her buttocks, pressing her closer to him, the need rising within him. He felt a slight resistance in her then, a holding back, but that only made her more exciting. He wanted that soft body, his hands guessing at what lay beneath the layers of dress and petticoat.

He propped his shoulders against the wall and pulled her with him so that she was leaning along the length of his body. She sighed and rubbed herself against him, and for a measureless time they seemed to be in harmony, each needing the other, each taking pleasure in the other. He revelled in the soft skin of her neck and shoulders, so silky against his work-hardened hands, but as he tried to reach inside her dress she broke away.

'No – I'm a good girl, I am.' Her voice was sharp with self-righteousness.

'Siobhan!'

He felt sick with the pulsing anger and frustration.

She was moving in the shadows. He guessed she was adjusting her dress, smoothing back her hair. His hands opened and closed. He could easily take hold of her, insist she stayed, but he had enough control left not to. Then pride took over. She was not going to have him on a string.

'I'll go back first. You'd better wait a bit,' he told her.

There was not a tremor in his voice. He was pleased with himself.

'Oh – yes.'

She sounded faintly surprised. He smiled to himself in the darkness, a grim stretching of the mouth. She was expecting him to plead, to bargain, even to get angry and start using his strength. She could deal with all of that and still stay on top. But he had refused to play her game. He had opted out, and she did not know how to react.

'And mind you do wait.'

No answer.

He left her there. One day, he vowed as he made his way back to the street, one day he would have her, but on his terms. Until then, she was not going to whistle at him and have him come running like a dog. When the time came, it would be the other way round.

People were still dancing in the square of tables, but there were fewer of them now. Harry sat down with the rest of his family, who hardly noticed him arrive. His eyes went immediately to Ellen. She was still dancing with Gerry, her head on his shoulder.

All the anger came back. He had ruined his chance with Ellen. His cousin had more sense. Gerry had got in there the moment the opportunity arose. Harry watched them. That was where he should be, not out the back playing Siobhan's games.

The tune came to an end with a long-drawn-out note. The couples drifted back to their tables. Tim O'Keefe sat down. That was it. The Trinidad Street coronation party was over bar the tidying up. The King had been well and truly welcomed to his throne. There were one or two half-hearted attempts at taking things into the houses, but on the whole people were happy to leave them in the street. Nobody was going to come along in the night and steal them.

Harry went across to the Johnsons, who were drifting back to their door.

'Ellen.'

She looked up.

'Oh, it's you.' She spoke with exaggerated unconcern. 'I thought you'd found other things to do.'

Harry glanced at Gerry, who was talking to Martha.

'I thought you did.'

Ellen shrugged. 'Well, we're both all right then, ain't we?'

She turned her back on him and started saying good night to Gerry. She did not speak to him again.

The Johnsons went indoors, Gerry smirked at him and ambled off to his house.

Harry stood in the quiet street, hands in pockets, looking at the closed door of the Johnsons' house.

2

Tom Johnson waited behind the chain. Around and behind him maybe two hundred men jostled and shoved. Work had been slack the last week or so, with berths lying empty in the dock, so once a ship was spotted approaching the lock gates the word flew. Small boys ran to tell fathers, the intricate networks of family and street were alerted, and men who had been idle for days began to converge on the gates.

Thanks to a tip-off from Harry Turner, Tom had been one of the first, dragging Archie along with him.

'What's the point? There's always a hundred there before me,' Archie complained.

'Not today there won't be,' Tom told him. 'Not since your lad's tipped us the wink.'

'I'm getting too old for this caper.'

'You're no bloody older than me, mate, and I don't rely on my missus and kids to support me.'

And just as Tom knew he would, Archie rose to the bait.

'Who says I live off my missus and kids, eh? Who says that?'

'Nobody will if it ain't true.'

Archie was red in the face, glaring at him. 'It ain't my fault if our Harry's working regular, is it? And it ain't my fault if there's no ships in. If there ain't no ships in, I can't work.'

'There's one coming in now,' Tom pointed out. 'So shift y'self. We're wasting time. There's plenty more want that job.'

He finally got Archie moving.

It was Alf Grant's quay. As he waited, Tom tried to assess his chances of being taken on. He had not worked for Grant since the day three years ago when he had lost his preference job. It was a long shot, but there was nothing else going and he had to try it.

'When are you going to send that girl of yours out to work?' Archie asked.

'When she leaves school.'

'Bleeding stupid idea, keeping her on when she's old enough to earn a bob or two. What're you trying to do – set y'self up above the rest of us?'

'I'm trying to do the best for my kids. She's got a head on her shoulders. She deserves a chance.'

Archie grunted. Tom waited, ready to crush him if he dared say anything else. Neighbour or not, he had had enough of Archie. The man had no pride in himself. All the street knew it was Harry who was providing for that household.

The crowd was packing in behind him. He could feel the tension mounting. Men dressed like himself in flat hats and loose trousers, worn jackets and collarless shirts stood looking at the gates in the forbidding wall, men with gaunt cheeks and hollow eyes, all waiting for the foreman to appear with the precious handful of tickets. Waiting at home for them were hungry children and anxious wives. They all needed this day's work. The line at the front shifted and bulged as those at the back tried to get through and the early comers resisted them. Two policemen appeared, to a chorus of mingled cheers and jeers.

Thrusting his hands into his pockets, Tom nursed his anger. It was all wrong, this system. He had been here for two hours now. Those who did not get work would then wait till eleven in the hope of a second call-on, before finally going home empty-handed. They nearly all had grumbling bellies. No wonder the police had turned up.

A drizzling rain began to fall. Autumn brought no glorious change of leaf colour in these nearly treeless streets, only greasy paving stones and a threat of a cold winter. The one advantage in the drop of temperature was that the smells were not so bad – the stink of river and factories not so noticeable once the summer was over. Tom turned up the collar of his jacket. Around him there was a muttering of complaints.

'Where's this ship got to, then? They must've got her tied up by now. What's the delay?' the man next to Tom asked.

'Dunno, mate. P'raps they're just keeping us here to make us all the more grateful for being taken on.'

'You think so?'

'Wouldn't put it past them.' Tom indicated the mass behind them with a jerk of his head. 'See all them? All need work. Some of 'em ain't even dockers. If everyone joined the union, we could make sure only union men got work, then we'd get rid of all of the ragtag and bobtail who come down here as a last resort. Be better for all of us.'

The man shrugged. 'Never got me nothing, unions.'

Tom sighed. This was the attitude that killed all hope of better conditions.

'With all these lined up here, they're never going to give us a rise. They don't have to, because there's plenty as'd work for less,' he explained patiently. 'Tanner an hour's been the rate for twelve years now, but they're not going to put it up just because things cost more, are they?'

'Bastards.' The man's face set into lines of frustration. 'I got three sick kids at home and the wife's expecting again in a couple of weeks. I got to get some money.'

The gates opened. Alf Grant emerged, flanked by a pair of bruisers. The men behind the chain pushed forward. Tom braced his legs, his back. The pressure of bodies behind him was growing. Men had been crushed to death at the call-on before now.

Tom saw Grant's eyes run along the line, meet his for a second, then sheer away. With so many here so eager for anything, the chances of Grant taking him on seemed slim, but still he stared at the man, challenging him to make the choice.

'Hobbs, Jenkins, Green...'

The preference men, the 'Royals', came first. There were still tickets in Grant's hand. The casuals tensed. Now was the crunch. They pressed forward. The chain was cutting into Tom in front while the weight of two hundred men bore down on his back. The blood pounded in his head and his eyes felt as if they were bulging. The crowd swayed and gave, arms waving, legs slipping. Grant went slowly. Fighting to keep upright, Tom tried to see the pattern. He knew a lot of these men and it was not necessarily the youngest and strongest Grant was picking. He sensed something odd going on. Archie was called, and the man on the other side of Tom. Still he bore into Grant with his eyes. There was one ticket left. The foreman came back and stopped in front of him.

'Johnson. Not seen you for a while.'

'Been working elsewhere.'

It was difficult to talk calmly when the breath was being squeezed out of his body.

'Come back to us though, have you?'

'Thought I might give it a try.'

He fooled neither of them. They both knew this was a last resort. Grant gave a mirthless smile.

'Nice of you.' He held the precious metal token just out of reach. 'I'll take you on, but there's to be no trouble. Understood?'

So he wanted to show his power, have Tom Johnson on a string.

'There'll be no trouble if no trouble's needed.'

For a long moment Grant appeared to consider the meaning of this. Then he held out the ticket.

'Just remember,' he warned.

Tom tried very hard not to show his relief. He was not going to give Grant the pleasure of knowing how much he needed that ticket.

'That's all,' Grant said to the unlucky ones. He

turned and walked swiftly back towards the gates.

Pandemonium broke out. Men were shouting and cursing in their disappointment. Just along from Tom, two were fighting over possession of a ticket, while others round them argued the point. Someone behind him grasped Tom by the shoulder.

'Gimme that ticket, mate. I'm desperate. We sold everything. It's going to be the workhouse if I don't bring some money home today.'

He was a small man, thin and round-shouldered. Tom was sure he knew him. He looked into a face deeply etched with lines of worry.

'You know me, mate. Reggie Wilkins. We worked together over the East Indias. Eight kids I got at home. Youngest is just a year old.'

Here was greater need than his. He hesitated. Then Archie joined in.

'Sell you mine.'

'What?' Tom was horrified. He never thought Archie would sink that low. But Wilkins jumped at the chance.

'How much?'

'Two bob.'

'Two bob?' Tom repeated. 'Do you know what that means? That means you'll be working all day for half-a-crown, three bob at the most.'

The police were breaking up the fight. The lucky ones were making their way towards the gates. There was no persuading Wilkins. Half a crown was better than starving. Tom tramped into the docks.

The ship looked normal enough, an old three-

116

master somewhat the worse for wear. Tom looked up at the duty officer standing on the deck watching with his hands behind his back. A huge man with a full grizzled beard, his navy uniform jacket unbuttoned to show a vast expanse of belly, he gazed down impassively at the quayside.

Grant was dividing out the work. Most of the Royals were put down in the hold. That was just as usual. It required skill and stamina to work fast and accurately in cramped conditions. The Royals that were left were set to receive the sets of cargo as it landed on the quay and unpack it. The riff-raff were to do the trucking, taking the stuff into the transit shed or warehouse.

'Johnson.'

Tom looked at the foreman, expecting to be deliberately humiliated by being put with the truckers.

'You're up on the deck.'

Tom nodded, concealing all emotion behind an impassive face. The deckman was the most responsible job of the lot. On him the safety of men and cargo depended. But as he stumped off with the others to their given positions, unease still nagged at him.

It was not until he actually got on deck that he noticed the ship's house flag, an unfamiliar white diamond shape on a black background.

'You're not one of Eastcote's,' he said to the deck officer.

The man glared at him as if he were some lower form of life, not deigning to answer.

'What line are you?' Tom insisted.

'Diamond,' came the reluctant reply. The man

had a strong Glaswegian accent.

'Never heard of it,' Tom said, deliberately offensive in return.

But he knew enough about these small lines to be alarmed: little fly-by-night one-ship outfits with safety records that never bore looking at, willing to go anywhere and pick up anything. God only knew what was awaiting them down in the hold. He felt offended, both personally and on behalf of the others. They were sugar men.

'What you got down there?' he shouted down the hatches.

'Sacks of something bloody awful,' came a disgruntled reply. 'Fishmeal.'

Grumbling, they started getting it into the first set of the day, lifting up the ends of the sacks with their hooks and slipping the rope strop underneath. Tom waved the crane jib over. The truckers cleared the last of yesterday's cargo off the quay. The day's work began. Rising and bending, lifting and slinging, with hardly a moment between one set and the next to run and relieve themselves, the treadmill of labour would have numbed the mind if it had not been for the jokes and the backchat. The rain came steadily down, soaking clothes and chilling backs and shoulders already aching. The stench from the hold seemed to grow worse as the morning progressed.

At midday the truckers were given an hour's dinner break. They were not paid when they were not working, and the stuff could sit on the quay till they got back. The shipworkers were given twenty minutes, as the vessel had to be emptied as fast as possible to be turned round. Every day in the dock was costing her owners money.

Tom walked stiffly down on to the quay. He might just have enough time to get something off a stall before getting back to work. There'd been nothing left in the house to eat this morning after they had their bread and scrape for breakfast, so he had not been able to bring anything with him. On the quay he saw Wilkins, visibly failing.

'You all right, mate?' Tom asked.

'Yeah, 'course. What's the matter? Think I'm not pulling my weight?'

Tom looked at his undernourished frame. He probably had not eaten properly for days.

'Just don't let Grant spot you,' he advised.

By mid-afternoon they had the fishmeal cleared. The rain had still not eased up. If anything, it was coming down harder, a relentless grey curtain that had now soaked them all to the skin, making clothing heavy and clinging, hampering movement. Even the men in the hold were getting wet when they moved the stuff under the hatchway, and the cargo was becoming damp. Tom heard exclamations coming up from below.

'Bloody hell, someone's made a poor job of stowing this lot.'

'Will you look at what's happened to these decks!'

'They're leaking. Look, the dullage has shifted and punctured the sides of the bloody barrels. The stuff's run out on to the deck.'

'Whole bloody ship's leaking. You can smell the rot.'

Tom peered down into the gloom. 'What's up?'

A couple of the men were directly under him,

manhandling some steel barrels into place.

'It's these things. Some of 'em are cracked. You should see what it's done to the deck underneath 'em. Eaten into the timber, it has.'

Already they had the first set assembled. Tom waved the crane up.

'What the hell is it?' he asked, as the load swung over and down on to the quay. 'Some sort of acid?'

'Caustic soda,' someone told him.

'Yeah, make soap out of that, they do. Puts you off washing, don't it?'

It all fell into place. That was it. That was why Grant took on all those most desperate for work. If they wanted the money enough they would be willing to handle stuff that could burn into their hands and damage their eyes. He looked at the sorry specimens toiling down on the quay, then along the dockside at the empty berths. Grant had done his job well. These men knew better than to refuse. What he could not work out was why the foreman had taken him on. He must have known that the promise of no trouble had been no promise at all. The only answer that made any sense was that Grant wanted a dispute just so that he could win. He wanted to make an example of Tom in front of the other men, so that the word would go out round the docks.

As if summoned by thought, Grant appeared. The crane jib was swinging back to take the next set.

'Be careful with them. I don't want any breakages,' he said.

'Why, are they dangerous?' Tom asked, a picture of innocence.

120

Grant shot him a warning look. 'It'll be dangerous for you if they're dropped. You'll be off the job.'

Tom looked at the barrels. They were safe enough when they were sound, but not if they were leaking somewhere. He called down to the men in his gang who were setting about lifting them.

'Wait. This needs to be talked over.'

They looked from him to Grant, uncertain.

'What are you listening to him for? Is he the one who gives out the tickets? I said get them out and be careful, so get on with it.'

One or two men started to lift the barrels but most stood where they were. They knew Tom Johnson. Even if they had not worked with him before, they had heard of him. They knew he talked sense, and that he was on their side.

'Do you know what that is that you're handling?' he asked them.

'Caustic soda,' someone said.

'Yeah, and do you know what it does to you if it gets in your eyes? Blinds you, that's what. You wouldn't be much use to no one if that happened, I can tell you.'

The men stirred and muttered. Those who were handling the barrels let them down again and moved over to the hatchway. Seeing the stoppage, the gangs on the quay paused in the unloading and trucking and looked up at the ship to find out what was going on.

'If you don't drop the bloody things it won't get on your skin, will it?' Grant reasoned. 'I warned you, Johnson: no trouble. You were all taken on to unload this ship. Now get on with it.'

Tom held up a hand. Nobody moved. Nobody spoke.

'Those barrels are unsafe,' he stated.

'Not if they're handled properly,' Grant insisted. 'If you lot are careless, that's your own bloody fault, ain't it?'

'They're leaking. You can see it in the hold, you can see what the stuff's done to the decks.'

'I can't see nothing. Like I said, Johnson, I don't want no trouble from the likes of you. Now listen to me.' He looked around at the assembled men, making sure that those down on the quay were listening as well. 'There's three days' work unloading this ship. Three days' pay. But if you lot want to bugger off, that's fine by me. There's plenty more will do the job. I only have to go outside and there's a queue waiting to take your places. So take your pick – get this lot on to the quay and stacked in the warehouse, or go.'

For a long moment the group hesitated. Then Reggie Wilkins manoeuvred the toe of his truck underneath the nearest barrel, grasped the top and tipped it back with obvious difficulty into the carrying position. A noticeable trickle fell out of the side of the barrel and down his wet trousers.

Others followed. Tom harangued them, pointing out the dire effects of the soda, but they would not listen. They knew Grant was right. There were a hundred others outside willing to earn sixpence an hour if they walked out.

Tom watched them with despair in his heart. He knew the poverty that drove them, knew the cold homes and hungry, unshod children. They had run out of coal for the range three days ago at his house and were living on bread and scrape, with tea from used leaves brewed next door. But they were many and the management were few. If they all united they could win. If they gave in, it would always be like this.

Grant came up to him. A thin smile of triumph stretched his face.

'You working, Johnson, or going?'

Either way the foreman had won, and they both knew it.

'I never walked out on anything,' Tom told him.

Grant's smile grew wider. 'Missus waiting for the pay, is she? Wouldn't like to go home short, would we?'

Tom kept his temper with difficulty. 'I'm staying to see over my mates' interests,' he said, with dignity. 'Because nobody else will, that's for sure.'

'You stay, and you stay on my terms, Johnson. You were taken on to unload this ship, and unload it you will, without any nancy-boy whining about hurting yourself. Understood?'

If he walked off now, no point of principle would have been made and Grant would have succeeded in getting rid of him. He needed the men behind him to make a stand. If he stayed, there was still a chance they would see that they were being exploited, and then he would be here to speak for them. But to stay meant to bow to Grant's demands. His mates would see him give in.

'Understood, Mr Grant.' He forced the words out.

'Good. I knew you'd see it my way in the end.' The foreman's voice was oily with success. 'Now get to work!'

Resentment boiling within him, Tom went back to the hatchway. The others avoided his eyes.

'Sorry, mate,' one muttered to him, 'but I need this money and we wouldn't never have won. Not with all them lot still wanting jobs. I'm a Royal and still I been waiting for work all last week.'

'We win if we stand together,' Tom insisted, but nobody answered.

He waved the crane over. He was not defeated yet, he told himself. He might have lost this battle but the war was still on. He was down but he was not out. But however much he bolstered up his hopes, the setback dragged at his spirits. His whole body felt weary. His wet clothes weighed him down, making each movement an effort.

Looking down in the hold, he saw the men rubbing their eyes, tears running down their faces.

'Don't!' he shouted as one ducked his head to wipe his face on his upper sleeve. 'You'll make it worse. It's on your hands and your clothes where you been lifting. It's burning into you.'

Their sight blurred, the palms of their hands raw, the men worked on. Still the cranes brought ashore more sets of barrels. They piled up on the quayside, threatening heaps of dull rusted steel.

The light was failing fast, but still they carried on working. They were into overtime. Everyone was glad of the extra money, but they were tired. Now was the time when accidents happened through sheer fatigue.

'All fast!' came the shout from the hatchway.

Tom signalled to the crane driver. The set went swinging up and over to the quay. Tom straightened up to watch it, then caught his breath. The load was not made up properly. The strop was slipping out from under the end bottom barrel.

'Look out! Greenacre!' he yelled, using the time-honoured warning for an accident.

The men reaching up to guide the load down had already realized and jumped back. A cascade of barrels tumbled out of the sky, dropping ten, fifteen feet on to the stones of the quay. There was a crunching sound as they hit the ground and a cloud of white dust blew up into the air, leaving the watching men gasping and coughing.

'Anyone hurt?' an anxious voice called up from the hold.

Tom peered through the dust. 'No, no I don't think so, thank God. Bloody awful mess, though.'

'Thank God for that,' the man echoed, relieved. Tom did not have to ask who it was that had secured the set.

Somebody was going to have to clear the broken load away, and Tom knew who that was going to be – Wilkins' gang. It ought to be done with shovels and some sort of protective clothing, something to cover their eyes and mouths, but he knew better than to expect that. They were there to unload the ship, whatever the danger to themselves, for the usual sixpence an hour plus tuppence overtime. He looked at them: a sorry bunch, tired and underfed, with red eyes and blistered hands. But they had pride still, and there was a limit to how much they were willing to be pushed around.

Even as the thoughts went through his head, he saw Grant beckon them over.

'You lot – get these shifted. Any that are broken, put into the waste cart.'

Tom could not stand by and let his mates be exploited.

'Hold it,' he called down to the men inside the ship. 'Grant's making the truckers clear the broken barrels. They could be damaged for life.'

The gangers shrugged. It happened all the time.

'Look at what it's done to you already. Think how it'd be if it really got down inside you,' he said. 'Get inside your guts, it would. Eat you away.'

One man nodded, and made his way to the ladder up to the deck. Slowly, the others followed.

Tom waved to the crane driver to stop, then walked deliberately down on to the quay. He stepped through the assembled gang of truckers. Behind him, he could hear the others going quiet, waiting for what was going to happen next.

'That's dangerous, Mr Grant. If those barrels are split, the stuff's going to go all over these men. They need to shift it with shovels, not their bare hands.'

Grant's face went red with anger. His eyes bulged. The veins in his neck swelled. He jabbed a finger towards Tom.

'Are you refusing to work, Johnson? Because I warned you...'

Tom stood his ground. Grant was blustering because he knew he was in the wrong. He thought he could win just by shouting loud enough. Tom kept his voice reasonable, steady.

'No, Mr Grant, I'm not refusing to work, and neither are these men. I'm just saying as they can't lift the stuff with their bare hands.'

'And I'm saying they bloody will.' He looked beyond Tom to the group of men, his eyes searching for the weakest to pick on. 'You – what's y'name – Wilkins. Take one of them barrels out to the cart.'

Wilkins hesitated. He looked from Grant to Tom.

'Don't do it, Reg,' Tom told him. 'You get that down you and you'll never work again.'

But Grant had a stronger threat. 'You leave that there and you'll never work in this dock again.'

There was a groundswell of muttering.

'Don't do it, Reg.'

'He's bluffing, mate.'

'Don't let him push you around.'

A surge of relief and triumph shot through Tom. They had had enough. They were with him. Now he could get somewhere. He stood watching Reggie Wilkins' face, pitying the man. Grant had picked his victim well. Reg was not a fighter. He was a quiet hero, willing to work all day for half-a-crown rather than let his family starve, ready to endure anything just as long as he was earning. Tom said nothing, letting the rest of the gang do the persuading for him, letting Reg see he had his mates behind him.

Grant could see the tide turning against him.

'Get on with it!' he shouted. 'Don't just stand there gaping like a bleeding idiot, pick the bleeding thing up and take it to the cart.'

Reg Wilkins seemed to shrink. Slowly, avoiding looking at anyone, he trundled his truck over to the heap of bent and damaged barrels. He bent and picked up the nearest one, then tried to straighten up. But the heavy day's work after weeks of inadequate food had nearly done for him. He could not lift it on to the foot of the truck. Mesmerized, the others look on. It was painful, watching his feeble efforts.

'Come on, man, put yer back into it,' Grant shouted.

Wilkins got a fresh grip round the thing. Grunting, he heaved it forward. But his boot, which was coming apart at the toe, caught on a cobblestone. He tripped. Man and barrel fell against the truck and all three crashed down into a broken heap. The barrel split apart and Wilkins landed face first in a heap of caustic soda.

'Get him up!' Tom shouted, running forward himself.

'Water!' someone shouted. 'Put water on him.'

The stuff was already damp from the rain. It was sticking to Wilkin's hair, his face, his clothing. He was shaking, gasping. Tom pulled him clear and laid him on the stones. And then Wilkins began to moan, then scream, writhing on the wet quay. The men looked on, horrified.

'Get him in the dock,' someone yelled.

'No, no, he can't swim.'

A bucket of water was hauled up and thrown over the injured man, but it did not wash the soda off, only accelerated the reaction. It was eating into his skin.

'My eyes! My eyes!' Wilkins cried out in agony, begging them to help him.

'Keep bringing water. Fetch a cart. We must get him to the hospital,' Tom ordered.

A handcart was trundled up. Men with only

one jacket to their name tore them off for a makeshift mattress. Wilkins was carefully picked up and laid down. He thrashed from side to side in a vain attempt to escape the searing pain. A last dousing with water, and a team of volunteers trundled him towards the dock gates. His screams echoed off the high warehouse walls and hung on the air.

Tom looked round at the crowd that had gathered. Men from quays all along the dockside had come running. Now they stood in shocked silence. They had all seen accidents before, but nothing like this.

An angry growl started and grew. The men who had seen it happen knew who to blame. Grant stepped in to stop it before it got out of hand.

'All right, all right, the show's over. Back to work, all of you.'

Nobody shifted.

'Come on, we ain't got all day. Get moving.'

Tom waited for the voices to rise. He knew his mates. They were not going to let this one pass. He walked out into the centre of the gathered men and stood by the remains of the shattered barrels. He raised his hands. The shouts died down. There was an expectant pause. He looked round, gathering them all in with him.

'We're not going back to work, Mr Grant,' he stated.

All around him there was roar of agreement.

Grant waved his arms in anger. 'You lot take no notice of him. This is just to do with this quay. The rest of you get moving – go on, get back to work.'

Still nobody moved.

'This ship is blacked, Mr Grant. Nothing on this ship will be touched until we get double pay and special clothing to shift this cargo.'

From the back of the crowd came a shout of support.

'We're with you, brother. We don't go back to work neither.'

The cry was taken up by men from other quays.

'Nor us.'

'One out, all out.'

Grant tried to shout them down. 'You do that and I'll see you never work again. You go, and there's a hundred more ready to take your places.'

Jeers and boos were all he got in reply.

Tom raised his hands again. Gradually the noise subsided. All along the dockside cranes stopped working and men leaned over ships' sides to see what was going on; some were even now walking over to find out what was happening. Now was the moment.

'Which quays are with us?' he asked.

From the growing mass around him gangers identified themselves.

Tom nodded. There were enough to really put the pressure on. He knew his cause was just.

'Are we all together, brothers?'

A great howl of agreement rose and rolled round the vast dock. Tom was lifted up on its strength and solidarity. He turned to Grant, raising his voice so that everyone knew just what the score was.

'You go tell your masters, Mr Grant: double pay and protective clothing. Until then, nothing on this side of the dock moves.'

Cheers and whistles greeted the ultimatum. Grant's reply was nearly lost in the tumult. But as the crowd parted to let him through, Tom heard the foreman's last threat.

'I'll get you for this, Johnson. I'll make you pay if it's the last thing I do.'

3

'Give me that, Mum. I'll finish it off.'

'No, it's all right. You had all them envelopes to do.'

'I've finished 'em. Come on, give it here.'

Reluctantly, Martha handed the shirt over to Ellen and sagged back in her chair, head back, eyes closed.

Ellen moved the single candle a little closer and carried on stitching the patch to the back. The shirt was so old that it had ripped when one of Jack's friends grabbed it during a game of football.

'It's not going to last much longer, Mum.'

'I know, lovey. But if we can just hold it together till this strike's over we can let it go for rags.' Martha was so tired that her voice slurred as she tried to talk.

'Why don't you go to bed, Mum? It might be ages before Dad's in.'

'Yeah, I know.' But still she sat there, shapeless in the eighth month of her pregnancy, too tired to move.

Ellen wished she could offer a cup of tea, but it was too late now to go next door to boil a kettle. She shivered. The little kitchen was cold. Her father was late and her mother looked dreadful, with dark rings under her eyes. Fighting the eternal battle with dirt, on top of a pregnancy, little money coming in, and now a strike, was almost too much for her. Ellen was frightened. She had never seen her mother look like this before. Always Mum had been strong, even through the bad times like when they all went down with scarlet fever.

'Come on,' she said, standing up, holding out her hands, 'I'll help you up.'

'You're a good girl, Ellen.' With a groan, she let herself be hauled to her feet, but still she hesitated, standing leaning on the table and looking towards the street door. 'He should have been back home by now. I don't like it when he's out late. I don't like the sound of this meeting, either.'

'He'll be all right, Mum. Will's with him, remember. They was going to walk home together.'

'Yeah, I know. I just don't like it, that's all. I wish he was safe home.'

She finally let herself be persuaded up to bed. Ellen sat down again to the mending. A boxful of envelopes sat on the table, a thousand, all neatly addressed in Ellen's sloping hand. She glanced towards them with hatred, both hoping and dreading that there would be another batch next week. It was the best-paid outwork they had got yet – found through Gerry, who had recommended her as a Millwall Central girl with neat writing – but she loathed the evenings of penpushing after a day of it at school and then homework. By the end of the batch she had writer's cramp and her eyes were gritty with fatigue. Not that she would have dreamed of complaining. Always in her mind was the knowledge that she was fourteen years old now and should be out earning her living. If she left school and got a job at a factory, they wouldn't be in quite such a fix now. Guilt gnawed at her when Jack went off at the crack of dawn to his job helping the milkman before going to school, or Daisy came in exhausted from clearing up at the greengrocer's, bearing the meagre basket of damaged vegetables that were her pay. Her little brother and sister were helping. Sitting each evening and most of the weekend addressing envelopes hardly rated comment.

Her father was late. Automatically she went to look at the clock in the parlour, before remembering that it was no longer there. Along with their best clothes, the spare knives and forks, the ornaments and the mirror, it had gone to the pawnshop. Things were very tight at the moment. If this strike really developed into anything, they would be down to living on the odds and ends that her mother and the children brought in.

'It could be the best thing to happen to all of us for years,' Tom had said to them. 'If this revives the union, we could bring the whole West India to a standstill, We got right on our side. That Reggie Wilkins, he took three days dying. They didn't ought to treat us like that. We got to make a stand.'

A fund was being set up for the Wilkins. Families with next to nothing in their own pockets gave what they could and kept the widow and her children out of the workhouse. The papers got hold of the story, but reported it in very different ways. 'Terrible death of docker' trumpeted the *Herald*. But *The Times* reported 'Irresponsible strike by dock labourers over incident of carelessness', and implied that Wilkins had been drunk at the time. In the meantime, valuable cargoes had been lying in ships' holds for four days and the owners were getting restive. Tom was optimistic about winning. The meeting tonight was to keep up the men's enthusiasm.

Ellen finished sewing on the patch. She was achingly tired and there was another day of school, homework, housework and outwork waiting for her tomorrow, but her mother's unease had rubbed off and she could not go to bed. She pulled her shawl closer and prowled round the kitchen. Without the range on, the damp was winning its battle. Black stains were creeping up the walls. She found a cloth under the sink, wetted it and started scrubbing at the plaster.

There was a sound in the doorway behind her. She looked up, startled, and there was her mother, her hair down, a blanket draped over her darned and patched nightdress.

'Mum! You did make me jump. I thought you was in bed.'

'I couldn't sleep, lovey. I'm that worried. I know it's silly, but I am.' Martha stood biting at her lip. 'Look, just run round the corner to Will and Maisie's, will you? See if he's in yet.'

Ellen put down the rag. 'You sit down, and stop worrying. I'll go and ask.'

It was very still outside. Down the entire length

of Trinidad Street just one bedroom window was lit. The single street-lamp was out. Ellen let her eyes adjust to the dark. The night was quiet and clear. There were stars above, and a half-moon low in the sky made the doorways into black shadowy caves. In the distance a train whistle blew, a lonely howl.

Ellen looked up the street, her heart knocking in her chest, wishing that Will and Maisie and the babies still lived at Aunty Alma's. Now that Will was a preference man, they had their own place, with a lodger to help with the rent. It was only round in the next street, but still it was foreign territory. She took a deep breath and scuttled down the road. So far so good, but now she was away from the safety of Trinidad Street. She went round by the Rum Puncheon and into the next street. It looked almost the same, two rows of tiny houses with scrubbed steps and swept pavements, but the difference was behind the closed front doors. She could not knock on any one of these and get refuge if she needed to. They were not her neighbours. She thought of her mum waiting for news and ran the last fifty yards to arrive, panting, on Will and Maisie's doorstep.

She tapped on the front door, not wanting to disturb the quiet of the street. Then, having produced not a sound from inside, she banged louder. 'Will!' she called. 'Maisie! You there?'

After what seemed like forever, the bedroom window creaked and shuddered up and Will's tousled head looked out.

'What the bleeding hell's going on? Who is it?'

'It's me, Ellen. Dad's not home and Mum was

worried. She sent me round to see if you was back.'

'Oh – yeah.'

He sounded confused. Anxiety churned in Ellen's stomach.

'We thought you was coming back together, Will. Where's Dad got to?'

Will leant further out of the window and hissed at her in a stage whisper. 'We – er – we got separated, like. He had people he wanted to talk to. So he – er – he told me to go on. Knew Maisie would be waiting up. You know what she's like. She gets in a state.'

'Ah – I see.'

It sounded plausible enough. It was just the way he said it that made little threads of doubt in her mind.

'But he'll be back soon, will he? Mum's getting in a state and all.'

'Yeah, yeah. Sure to be.'

Not at all reassured, Ellen made her way back. Perhaps he would be there when she arrived. Perhaps it was just Mum getting worried over nothing. She listened as she opened the front door, hoping fervently for the sound of her father's voice telling her mother about the meeting. But there was nothing, only her mother, waiting for news.

'Well? Is he back? What did Maisie say?'

Ellen repeated Will's explanation. Martha pursed her lips.

'I see,' she said. She lumbered over to the kitchen cupboard, produced a bottle from right at the back and tipped a generous measure of clear liquid into a cup. The distinctive smell of gin pricked at Ellen's nose.

'Medicinal,' her mother explained. 'I got to calm my nerves.'

She sat down at the table, nursing the cup.

'You go up, lovey. It's late and you got school tomorrow.'

But Ellen shook her head. 'No. I'm waiting with you.'

The tiredness had dropped from her now, replaced by a nervous energy. She picked up the cleaning rag and attacked the patch of black mould.

Tom left the meeting buoyed up by the sense of solidarity. They were all together in this. Blacklegs had been brought in but the strikers had seen them off despite a large police presence. It ought to send men back into the arms of the union. That was what they needed, a strong union again, like they'd had in '89. With that they could do anything; they would have the strength to defy the owners and the funds to open feeding centres so that the families did not go hungry. They could work with the stevedores and the lightermen to make sure that nothing moved. But without the union they had no base from which to negotiate. That was the first priority, getting the members back.

''Night, Tom – we'll get 'em by the end of the week, eh?'

'Have 'em by the short 'n' curlies, mate. 'Night!'

In ones and twos the group with him, the union faithfuls, the old campaigners from '89, peeled off to go to their own homes. The rest of the Trinidad

Street contingent had left earlier, at the close of the main meeting, but Tom had expected Will to stay till the end and walk back with him. Now that he came to think over the evening, he could not remember seeing him there at all. He had called for him to go there, but Will had said that he had some chores to finish first and would be along later. Maybe the boy had not bothered to come at all. That angered him. To think that a son of his should neglect such an important meeting, and on such a feeble excuse. He had had all day to do jobs about the house, and besides, Maisie was hardly the nagging type who insisted on things being done. Will did exactly as much as he wanted. It was not that at all. He simply had not cared to come. Tom marched along, composing a lecture in his head on the need for working people to stick together.

He needed to concentrate on something. Whenever he stopped thinking, images started up in his mind's eye, vivid pictures of Reg Wilkins writhing in agony on the handcart or, as he had seen him later, in the long white ward of the hospital, dying from the infected acid burns. He could not get the horror of it out of his head. It fuelled his campaign against the bosses. It was not right that men should die like that, and the injustice of it roused him to white-hot anger.

He was nearly home now, passing along the backstreets by factory and storage yards. High walls, pierced by narrow passages or great locked gates, hemmed him in. Odours of horses, oil, chemicals and coal smoke hung on the air. He hardly noticed where he was going, for the way was as familiar as his own back yard. Hands in pockets, he looked only at where he was treading, for it was easy to trip over kerbs or rubbish in the deep pools of shadow in entrances or between streetlights.

The first he saw of the men was a movement out of the corner of his eye. Then he heard a voice saying, 'That's him. Get him.' There was a pounding of boots. He spun round, fists at the ready, just as something hit him across the shoulders.

'I got nothing on me worth taking, nothing at all!' he shouted, but they came at him all the same.

There were four or five of them, all with their faces covered. Contempt for their cowardice flashed through his mind, that so many should set on one man. He lashed out at the nearest, but he had no chance. One of them swung at him with a piece of wood, catching him on the side of the head. Pain exploded in a cascade of red light. The eyes above the protective scarves blurred as the ground came up to meet him.

'Bastards!' he tried to yell at them, but his mouth was not working properly. Only a howl of anger came out.

'Again, again, he's not out yet!'

A vague nagging feeling that he recognized the voice was blotted out as boots crashed into his head. His skull seemed to be cracking. His last sensation was of being grasped by wrist and ankle. Dimly through the pain, from a long way off, he heard mention of the river.

It was a clear, still night on the water. Harry stood

at the bow of the *Edith*, watching as the arches of London Bridge came steadily nearer, black against the gleam of the Thames. The tide here, between Southwark Bridge and London Bridge, was straight and fast, shooting like a millrace.

'Steady,' he called over his shoulder to the boy at the stern. 'Hold her there.'

They were lined up nicely to shoot through, with the ebb tide carrying them along. Fifty feet of wooden barge with one hundred tons of sheet glass in the hold, controlled by just himself and the lad holding thirty-foot oars. The archway loomed up, water swashing round the buttresses with the force of the tide. There was a nasty sideways set to the water here and the lighter had to be held up northwards.

'Pull,' he called to the boy.

The bow swung a little.

'And again – steady.'

They were under the echoing, dripping stone. The bridge slid past them, black as Newgate, making the river beyond shine like silver in contrast.

'Nice work. I won't drop you off at Traitor's Gate after all.'

The boy grinned weakly in response. He had not been long at the job and there was so much to learn.

Steamers for the Continent and the Mediterranean lay up in the tiers, each with its cluster of lighters ready to carry on unloading next morning. Schooners and small craft were moored to the Yarmouth Chains. The *Edith* glided silently past, powered only by the strength of the ebb underneath her. Waiting across the river, over-powering the general smell of tar and smoke and filthy water, came the stink of Billingsgate.

A small paddle steamer came chugging upriver towards them, water foaming from the churning paddle wheels, smoke pouring from her tall funnel. Lights were blazing on the decks and from the portholes, illuminating couples dancing to the music of a piano accordion. The tune came floating over the water above the noise, and Harry and the boy joined in with the song – 'She was only a bird in a gilded cage, a beautiful sight to see...' They were still singing as they passed the Tower and shot Tower Bridge, their voices bouncing and echoing off the structure.

More lighters on late jobs were working in and out of the docks and the myriad wharves and tiers. Harry whistled at each one and exchanged news.

'Where are you bound?'

'Down the Derrick.'

'Got a th'gin to Jack's hole.'

'How's old Moaner Polly?'

'Caught a sidewinder last week and fell in the ditch.'

'Going to the Old Vic Thursday?'

'No, I got a full roadun.'

Out here on the river, using his skill and strength, watching the ever changing moods of tide and weather, meeting his friends and catching up with the state of trade, Harry knew he had the best job in London. The problems on shore faded into the background, easily forgotten. It was only as they swung round the sharp bend of the river into Limehouse Reach and passed the huge frontage of Morton's factory that home concerns niggled at him, for it was at Morton's that Siobhan worked. His mother had told him only yesterday that Maisie was sure Will was still seeing her. As if there wasn't enough for her to worry about, what with Tom Johnson trying to whip up a strike. But if that was so with Will and Siobhan, then he was going to have to do something about it again, and that would not please Ellen. Will Johnson was a fool, and he ought to realize that there was no future in it.

The clock at St Luke's had just chimed midnight as they approached the Torrington Arms. In the silence that followed, voices came from the direction of the barges moored off the yard, and something fell into the water with a heavy splash. Booted feet pounded hurriedly away.

'What was that, Mr Turner?' The boy was straining his eyes in the direction of the splash.

'Dunno, lad, but it sounded a bit suspicious.'

Nothing was ever thrown away that could be sold. Children fought over the right to old newspapers or rags. Even old bits of rope had their buyers. Nobody would dump something large enough to make that sound unless it was on the wrong side of the law.

The moonlight caught on a dark shape surfacing. There was only one thing that looked like that.

'It's a dead 'un,' Harry said. 'They just slung him in the ditch. Quick, get your oar for'ard and bring her head round.'

The boy ran to obey. The barge swung round into the path of the body, drifting nearly sideways with the tide, but she was still moving faster than the wallowing corpse. Harry threw a length of chain over to slow her down and gradually it drew nearer, partially submerged, lapped by the black waves. Flinging himself down on the deck, Harry fished over the side with the boat hook, grappling to get a purchase, until he managed to get the hook under the corpse's belt.

'Got it. Give me a hand up with him,' he called. 'And bring a lamp over. I can't see what I'm doing.'

Reluctantly, the boy came. They hauled the heavy, awkward bulk up the side of the barge, water streaming from his clothes.

'It's all right, he's fresh in,' Harry told him. 'It's when they've been washing around in the water for days that they look nasty. You'll never eat shrimps again when you've seen 'em falling out of a dead 'un's eye sockets.'

But when they heaved the man on deck, it was Harry who cried out in shock.

'My God, it's Tom Johnson. Whatever...?'

He was warm, and blood was seeping from a messy bludgeoned wound on his head. Harry put a hand to his neck.

'He's still alive! We got to get him ashore.'

He turned Tom over on his front and pushed downwards on his back. 'Got to get the water out of him,' he explained to the boy.

Thames water flowed out of Tom's mouth. Harry pushed again, his own heart beating in his chest. There was no response. Another push, and with a rasping sound, Tom began to breathe. Harry looked forward. Ahead of them a line of lighters was moored five abreast at the London Wharf. He muttered a brief thanks and jumped up, grabbing an oar.

'Get her alongside there. We'll tie up and carry him in.'

'But Mr Turner!' The boy was aghast. 'What about our job? We got to get down the Vic–'

'Sod the job. I'm getting him home, or to the hospital. Reckon it might well be the hospital.'

He steered the *Edith* in, and the boy leapt across on to the outer barge and made fast. Harry examined his friend by the lamp's yellow light. There were bruises and lacerations all over his body, but what worried him most was the head wound. He tore his shirt into strips and bound it round Tom's skull.

'And God knows how much more water he got inside of him,' he said. 'We got to be very careful how we carry him.'

Between them, Harry and the boy picked Tom up and lifted him from barge to barge. He moaned as they manhandled him up on to the wharf.

'I wish I knew who done this to him,' Harry said. 'If I ever find out, I'll do them in.'

Will stood in the entrance of the ward, nervously clutching a paper bag of apples. Two rows of beds stood before him, each bed exactly like the next, with polished frame, green cover, sick patient. The brown floor shone and there was a strong smell of carbolic. The sense of rigid order and conformity was intimidating. He was on foreign ground here, ruled over by the nurses in their starched blue and white uniforms who stared icily at the visitors, resenting the intrusion into their territory.

The small crowd of people who had come in with him dispersed amongst the twenty-four beds. They spoke in hushed tones as if they were in church. Will walked slowly down the ward, looking at the ones with no visitors. Some were sitting up looking quite fit, others were quiet and still. He avoided their eyes. Sick people made him uneasy.

He found his father almost at the furthest end. Tom's eyes were closed and he was lying quite still on his back in the neat bed, his head swathed in bandages. What could be seen of his face was grey against the white pillow. Shock kicked Will in the guts. His father looked ten years older.

As he stood staring, his father's eyes flickered open, unfocused and bewildered, blinking at the ceiling lights. Will plucked up courage and stepped forward.

'Dad? Dad, it's me, Will.'

Tom's head did not move, but the eyes swivelled round to find his.

'Son?' His voice was hardly more than a whisper.

Will drew the wooden chair up close to the bed and leaned over. 'How are you, Dad?'

A long pause, then, 'I'll live.'

'That's the spirit, Dad.'

He sought for something to say. Usually he had no difficulty speaking with his father. They had plenty in common. But a barrier of guilt now stood between them. Will cleared his throat.

'Mum sends her love. She'll be over to see you

tomorrow. They're only allowing you one visitor at a time.'

'Yeah.'

'Maisie sends her love, too. And the kids. Everyone's been asking after you. The whole street. They all been in and out making sure Mum's all right and wanting to know how you are. If they ever find out who done this to you they'll tear them apart. They're real mad about it, Dad, I can tell you. Out for blood, they are.'

He was not sure whether his father had heard or not. His eyes had closed again.

'Dad?'

The bloodless lips moved slowly. Will leant forward until his head was nearly level with Tom's.

'The funeral...'

Shock closely followed by fear chased through Will's hollow stomach.

'You're not going to die, Dad. You're on the mend. You're going to get better.'

Impatience lit the tired eyes. 'No, Wilkins – Wilkins' funeral.'

'Oh!' Will almost laughed in relief. Here was something he could say to please his father. 'That's tomorrow. Don't you worry, Dad, it'll be a good do. The collection's something amazing. He'll have the lot – horses, black plumes, everything. A real proper send-off. That's real good news, ain't it, Dad?' he said hopefully. As long as they could keep off the subject of the night of the meeting, he was all right.

He looked for some sign of approval, but still his father seemed agitated. He listened again.

'The men – are they still out?'

This was the other question he had been dreading. But at least he had worked out how to answer it.

'That ship's not moved. Rest of the stuff's still lying there in her hold.'

He prayed that his father would accept this; it was the truth. The ship which had caused all the trouble was still blacked, together with her cargo. But that was not the whole story. The rest of the strike had already collapsed. All through the docks, ships were moving as usual. The news of Tom's brutal treatment, though it had angered dockers all over the Island, had also shown them what happened to agitators. That and sheer need had driven them back.

'You got to have meetings. Keep it going. Marches. Keep their spirits up.'

He had accepted it. Will hastened to keep up the illusion. 'Yeah, I'll tell them, Dad. Meetings.'

'No!' Anger turned the whisper into a full voice. The effect was as shocking as if he had shouted. 'You – you got to do it.' His father's eyes glared at him.

Will gaped back at him. 'Me?'

'You. You got to speak at the funeral. That's the time to get 'em.'

Will was horrified. He could not do that. He did not know how to. That was for the Wilkins family, or if not, for one of the union men.

'I – I can't.'

His father's eyes closed. He was so still that Will thought he had gone to sleep. He was about to creep away when the lips moved one more time.

'Where was you, son?'

The effort of speaking was almost too much for him, the words coming out slowly, slurred at the edges. But Will knew only too well what he meant. The guilt that had been lying heavy on his heart welled up and swamped him. He could not answer. His mouth opened and shut, but no words came. He could not admit to the truth, nor had he the face to lie.

'She's a – good girl – Maisie.'

So he knew. Will held his head in his hands. There was no point trying to explain. His father would never understand. There was no way in which he could describe the effect Siobhan had on him. She only had to look at him and he was lost. If she sent half a smile in his direction, he came running. He was helpless. She led him into a tangle of deceptions, setting up tales to cover their meetings. He could see her enjoying the knots he tied himself in to get away and see her, enjoying the power she had over his life.

'Son?'

He could not meet his father's eyes.

'Yeah,' he muttered at his knees. 'Yeah, she is.'

Maisie was all right. She was a good mother to the kids, she kept the house clean and fed him well, she never argued or nagged. But compared with Siobhan she was colourless.

'You got to speak to them. For me.'

Will did not follow him. 'Who, Dad? Speak to who?'

A nurse came up, stiff and officious in her white starched apron.

'Ten minutes only allowed with this patient. He needs to save his strength.'

A shadow of frustration clouded his father's face. He made a last effort. The words came out quite clearly.

'At the funeral. Promise.'

Understanding dawned. Will was to take his father's place, make speeches to the men, inspire them, lead them to victory. It was a huge burden, and he did not want it. He did not want the responsibility, did not want to pledge the total commitment it would demand.

'Your ten minutes is up. Would you leave now, please.'

Easy enough to obey the woman to put his father off with some half-promise. Will hesitated, tempted. After all, his father was in no state to insist. He could simply walk away. But he could not get away from the consequences. His father was lying there now, weak and helpless, because he had been out with Siobhan when he should have been at the meeting. If they had walked home together, they could have put up a much better fight; it might only have been a matter of bruises and black eyes. It might not have happened at all, for the sort of bullies who would set upon a single man would hesitate to take on two. It was his fault.

He looked at the man in the crisply made bed, at the motionless hump beneath the green cover, at the drawn features and pallid skin. It had been touch and go. If it had not been for Harry's quick action, his father would now be one more body floating down the Thames. Will reached out and touched his arm.

'Don't you worry, Dad. I'll see to it. You just get

yourself better.'

Tom's eyes closed. His face relaxed. He said nothing, but Will was sure he had heard.

The nurse took hold of his arm. 'You're doing him immense harm, tiring him like this. Now go.'

Will ignored her. He bent over the bed. 'I'll let you know how it's all going. 'Bye, Dad.'

He negotiated the miles of brown corridors and emerged at last with vast relief into the noise and bustle of the Mile End Road. The traffic, the dirt and the crowds of people were a tonic after the oppressive atmosphere of the hospital. Will stood for a moment on the steps, and the implications of what he had promised to do finally hit him. He tried to picture himself standing at the graveside, addressing the mourners. All those people looking at him, listening as he struggled to speak. It terrified him.

He began to walk up the road, weighed down by the enormity of it. His father always knew what to say. Perhaps if he just used his father's words. Perhaps he could just convey his father's message to the other union men. That was it. The weight lifted a little. He would tell the other leaders that his father was still fighting from his hospital bed, that he was still with them in spirit. Then they could tell the host of dockers who would be sure to be there at the funeral. Relieved beyond measure, he pushed aside the uncomfortable knowledge that this was not at all what his father expected of him.

Gerry sat back on his heels and stared at the stains on his brother's discarded pair of trousers.

There was river mud and a greenish bit that could be seaweed and a rust-red patch. He was sure none of that had been there the last time he had seen him go out in them, the night Tom Johnson was set upon. He tried to call that evening to mind. They had all had tea together, his mum, Charlie and himself. It was just the three of them at home now that Will and Maisie and their brats had got a place of their own. He tried to recall the conversation. His mum had said she was going out.

'I been asked out for a drink, so I won't be back till late, with a bit of luck. You boys doing anything?'

Gerry had told her that he had to go and see a man about a box of sewing thread before his usual chore of seeing the shop was locked up and the takings secure. Charlie had said nothing.

'What about you, Charlie?' his mother had asked. 'You going out?'

Charlie had shrugged. 'Might do. Might go 'n' see the lads.'

Gerry had only seen his brother's mates from a distance. They went to different pubs, lived different lives. But what he had seen of them he did not like. They were the dregs from Manilla Street and beyond.

His mum had gone out first, then Gerry, leaving Charlie at home by himself. There was no way of knowing when he had left, but he had still been out when Gerry got back. The deal over the sewing thread had not materialized. It had been a wasted evening. He remembered he had been getting ready for bed when his mum came in. You could hear her coming down the road, singing at the top of her voice and laughing. The front door banged open and a draught whipped through.

''Night, darling. It's been lovely. Lovely evening. Best I ever had.'

Half the street must have heard her. She was an embarrassment, his mother.

There was a scuffle on the doorstep. Gerry pulled his trousers back on. He was not having his mother inviting men in with all the neighbours listening. He went downstairs. There she was, propped up against the doorframe, coat all undone, hat askew, giggling helplessly while a skinny sailor with his arms wrapped round her tried to kiss her.

'Thanks for walking her home,' he said in his most repressive voice.

The sailor looked up in alarm.

'You can go now,' Gerry told him.

His mother put an arm round the man's shoulders. She could have made two of him.

'This is my friend. He ain't going home yet. He ain't got no home.'

'Well, he's not staying here,' Gerry insisted.

There was a struggle, and at last Gerry managed to get the door shut with himself and his mother inside and the sailor outside. Always affable, and more so when drunk, she promptly forgot about the sailor and allowed herself to be propelled upstairs to bed. Gerry lay awake, listening to her snores.

It was sometime after that that Charlie had crept in. Gerry was too tired himself by then to even acknowledge having heard him, let alone make any comment, but in the morning he saw the cuts and bruises on his brother's knuckles.

'Been in a fight?' he asked.

Charlie glanced down at his hands. A wary look came into his eyes, swiftly followed by truculence.

'So what if I have?'

'Just wondered.'

'Well, keep your bloody wondering to y'self.'

Gerry shrugged. 'Keep your hair on. I only asked. I'm not your keeper, thank God. If you want to get yourself into fights, that's your funeral.'

'Too right it is. And don't you bloody forget it.'

Nothing unusual in that, and yet...

It was later in the day that he had heard the news about Tom Johnson. Mrs O'Donaghue came into the general store in the West Ferry Road that he looked after for a man who owned a couple of other shops in the area.

'That poor Martha Johnson. I don't know how she's going to manage,' she said, plumping herself down on the rickety wooden chair placed ready for customers.

'Mrs Johnson? What's the matter with her?' Gerry asked.

'''Tis not her, 'tis himself. Have you not heard? 'Tis all over the neighbourhood. Well...' Mrs O'Donaghue settled in for a good tale, elaborating all the gory details. Gerry listened with growing horror. It was a dreadful thing to happen, for Tom and for all the Johnsons. He hadn't much time for Will Johnson, but Tom was a fine sort of bloke and his missus a real brick, while Ellen – he had not forgotten dancing with Ellen at the coronation party. It was only the fact that she was still a schoolgirl that stopped him from asking her out of a Saturday night.

'Who done it? Did he see?' he asked.

'He don't remember nothing. And Harry only heard the splash. But it was a gang, that's for sure. I don't know what the world's coming to, that I don't, when respectable men like Tom Johnson are set upon in the street.'

'Mr Johnson's upset a lot of people,' Gerry reminded her. 'He started this strike. The gov'nors must be happy he's been put out of action.'

'You don't think...?' Mrs O'Donaghue said.

'I wouldn't be surprised,' Gerry said. 'Not that they'd dirty their hands. They'd get someone to do it for them.' And even as he said it the image of his brother's knuckles rose up before his eyes. He had shaken it away. Charlie wouldn't do a thing like that. It was unthinkable. His brother might be a thief and a liar, but he would never set upon a neighbour and leave him for dead. Not Charlie.

But now, kneeling on the floor of the back bedroom they both shared, staring at the pair of trousers he had fished out from under Charlie's bed, he began to wonder.

He was so engrossed that he did not hear the door open.

'Praying?' Charlie asked, heavily sarcastic. Then, 'Here, what you doing with them? They're mine.'

'I know,' Gerry said. He was not even sure whether he wanted to take it any further. Perhaps it was better not to know.

Charlie stormed over and snatched them from him. 'Leave my stuff alone, will you? Don't go sneaking around.'

154

Slowly, Gerry stood up. He felt better when he was not looking up to his brother. There was a dangerous set to Charlie's mouth. When he really lost his temper he could get violent. But something inside Gerry made him persist.

'What's the problem?' he asked. 'Got something to hide?'

Charlie glared at him, facing him out, but when he spoke again he was on the defensive.

''Course not. I just don't like you poking your nose into my business, that's all.'

'Fair enough,' Gerry said carefully. But still he could not let it go at that. Knowing he would regret it, he said, 'You better take them down to Mum to be washed. Looks like they got river mud on 'em. And other things besides.'

That wary look came into Charlie's eyes again, but Gerry's comment did not throw him.

'So? I been working down there, ain't I?'

'Have you? You never said.'

'You never bloody asked. Now shut your face. I'm sick of you and your questions.'

Charlie stood glaring at him, waiting for him to leave. 'Go on, push off.'

Reluctantly, despising himself, Gerry went. He walked slowly down the stairs and paused in the parlour. From the kitchen came the sound of his mother talking. It was Sunday afternoon and too cold for chatting on the doorstep so she had invited somebody in. The choice was a bit limited at the moment, since her performance the other night with the sailor had outraged all the more straightlaced women in the street like Mrs O'Donaghue, but there were still plenty who

155

enjoyed his mother's company and found her drunken fits amusing. Whoever it was, he did not feel like facing them at the moment.

He let himself out of the front door and set off down the street. The kids were still out, those who had not been packed off to Sunday school. Sunday afternoons were the only time some couples had alone together, what with the number of people crammed into each bedroom. A lot of children playing now at shops or football had been conceived on a Sunday afternoon. He passed the Johnsons'. He wanted to stop and ask after Tom, but the burden of suspicion he now carried stopped him.

The West Ferry Road was sunk in its Sunday quiet. Even its rows of small shops could not inspire him today. Usually he felt a lift of hope and ambition, looking at all those little businesses. He was going to own something like that one day – for a start.

He stood in the road, wondering where to go. Then it came to him: the Torrington Stairs. He would go and see where Tom Johnson had been thrown in the river.

Under the overcast sky, the water was grey and sullen. Small waves coated with scum lapped at the foot of the weed-covered steps. A bloated rat floated past, belly up, and revolved slowly in the eddy caused by the steps. Gerry watched with fascination as it went round and round, the four clawed feet stiff above the distended body. Eventually the main current claimed it again and it bobbed away towards the line of sailing barges and lighters moored to the London Wharf.

Gerry sat down at the top of the steps. He and his brother used to come here as boys, mud-larking. When the tide dropped and the black mud with its thin cover of dirty shingle was exposed, there was treasure to be found. Stripped naked in summer or barelegged in winter, they slid and dug in the stinking silt for coins, coal, old rope, bits of canvas, scrap iron, timber offcuts – there was hardly anything they could not find a use or a sale for.

He had learnt about trading then, and screwing good rates from scrap merchants and dealers. But Charlie, what had he learnt? Gerry thought back. Charlie was always happier to let others do the work and pinch their findings from them, or give a pasting to anyone who tried to do the same to him. It had been like that at school. Once, Gerry persuaded a gullible child that his marbles were a fit swap for the pebbles Gerry had found in the alley. Proudly he displayed them to Charlie, boasting about his wonderful possessions. He took them out at every opportunity and gloated over them, gazing for ten minutes at a time at the fascinating whorl of colour within the clear glass. Charlie wanted some too, but there was never enough money in their household for food, let alone luxuries like toys. Then two days later Charlie came home with some marbles. He said he had done a swap as well, but Gerry knew otherwise. Either he had stolen them, or terrified some smaller child into giving them up. He had seen him do it many a time.

'Mum'd tan your hide if she knew,' Gerry told him.

'Yeah, but she ain't going to know, is she?' Charlie answered.

'Who says?'

In reply, Charlie took hold of Gerry's arm and twisted it up behind his back until he squealed out in pain.

'I says,' Charlie hissed in his ear. 'Savvy?'

Gerry nodded. Charlie gave one last wrench. 'You better, or it'll be the worst for you.'

After a while, Gerry learnt to turn a blind eye to his brother's thieving. In exchange, Charlie sometimes handed over a token of favour – an orange or some sweets. Gerry never really liked accepting them. If they had come off a stall, that was a bit better; not like stealing off your mates. But all the same, he rarely ate them, preferring to trade them on. Somehow, that did not seem so bad.

But had Charlie and his gang attacked Tom Johnson? Gerry desperately hoped not. There wasn't much to go on, after all: some bruised knuckles, a pair of dirty trousers. Charlie was always getting into fights, and he might well have been working at one of the wharves. He took up jobs here and there, wherever there might be useful pickings, because he didn't care for the drudgery of regular work.

Gerry considered the consequences if it *was* true. His mother would be heartbroken. The family would be ostracized. They would have to move right away from Trinidad Street. If it was proved, and brought to court, Charlie would be sent down for a very long time, maybe even hanged.

He got up, cold and stiff, and walked briskly back home to get the blood pumping round his body. No, it could not be true. Deliberately he pushed the remaining niggling doubts to the back of his mind as he went past the Johnsons' again.

When he got in, Charlie was in the kitchen with his feet on the table, drinking beer out of a bottle. His mouth stretched in a smile that did not reach his eyes.

'Drink, bruv?' He nodded at the row of bottles ranged along the wooden draining board.

Gerry hesitated, then accepted.

'Don't mind if I do. Thanks.' He helped himself, unscrewed the stopper, sat down on the chair by the range and took a long pull.

Charlie was watching him.

'I could put more o' them your way, if you want 'em.'

'How much?'

'To you, sixpence a dozen. But that's only because you're my brother. See?'

Gerry saw only too clearly. They had been knocked off. And if Charlie had plenty more then it was not just a case of a few bottles out of a pile of crates round the back of a pub. He and his gang must have done a proper break-in job. Slowly, he shook his head.

'Thanks, but no,' he said.

Charlie shrugged. 'Suit y'self. But you're missing a bargain,' he said.

Gerry looked at the bottle, and put it down.

'I'd rather not touch any of your bargains,' he said.

4

The front door banged open.

'Anyone at home?'

The Johnsons looked up, every one of them eager for a break from the grindingly boring task of sewing hooks and eyes on to cards.

'It's Will,' Daisy said.

'We're in the back, love. Come through,' Martha called out.

Will clumped into the kitchen. Despite cheeks red from the cold outside, he looked dejected. His shoulders were hunched and his face doleful.

'Guess what!' he said, slumping down at the table. 'I thought I better come and tell you before you heard it from anyone else. The strike's over. The gov'nors have got blacklegs in to clear that acid.'

He looked from face to face, expecting sympathy, but only Jack was roused to insult the powers-that-be with a couple of choice swearwords. Martha cuffed him round the ear.

'The ship's cleared, is it?' Ellen asked.

'Cleared, turned round, now loading up.'

They were all silent, taking in what this meant.

Martha sighed. 'So who's going to break it to your father?'

None of them wanted the job.

'It'll break his heart,' Ellen said.

'I know, lovey.'

Will began to bluster. 'Well, don't blame me. I did my best. I been going round talking to people, like he said.'

Daisy looked up at him. The ends of her fingers were sore from holding a needle. Her pinafore was grubby because they could not afford to heat water to wash the clothes. She spoke for all of them.

'It's all right for you. You'll be going back to work now. Dad ain't. He's stuck in the hospital, and all because of the blooming strike.'

'Leave off, Daisy. Anyone'd think it was my fault he was in hospital–' Will said, then broke off suddenly.

Nobody looked at him.

In the uncomfortable silence, Will shifted the box of cards around.

'You'd best go and tell Maisie,' Martha advised. 'She'll be glad you'll be working again. It ain't easy managing when you got little ones around.'

Will banged out again.

Wearily, the family returned to work, Jack picking the hooks and eyes out of the box and passing them to each hand as it was held out ready, his mother and sisters sewing them onto the cards. They had been tired and cold and bored to death with the things before Will came in with the news. Now a leaden gloom settled upon them.

'So it was all for nothing,' Daisy said.

'Not to Dad it weren't. It was a matter of principle. Like when he got slung off the preference list. He'll still think it was worth fighting for, even though they have lost,' Ellen said.

Martha said nothing, but the lines round her

161

mouth tightened.

They worked on in silence.

'Can't we stop?' Jack whined. 'I'm tired and I'm starving hungry.'

'So are we all,' Daisy snapped.

'We got to get these done tonight or they'll not let us have any more work,' Martha explained for the tenth time.

'Good,' Jack muttered.

The deft fingers moved, stiff with cold but still functioning. Eyes grew sore and gritty trying to sew by the light of one candle. Ellen sat wrapped in her own thoughts. There were three pages of arithmetic she was supposed to be doing for homework, to be given in tomorrow, but it didn't matter any more. She had long ago gone through all the permutations of calculation she could do with the hooks and eyes – if it took five minutes to make up one card, how long would it take three people to make a thousand? How long would it take if they did not stop at all and how much longer if they slept and ate? Would the time taken to teach Jack to sew be worth it in extra cards or was he more useful passing to the rest of them? How many cards equalled a slice of bread? How many hours of work equalled four ounces of cheese? It had kept her brain going for a while, but after three hours she found her thoughts were just going round and round on one track, always coming back to the same place.

At last, Martha shifted uncomfortably in her seat and glanced at Jack.

'You go up the shop now, son. Take a saucer and get us three farthings' worth of marge. We got just over half a loaf left. That'll do.'

Jack, usually slow in doing any errands, jumped up with alacrity. A trip to the shop was a treat after passing hooks and eyes.

'It's not fair,' Daisy complained. 'He always gets the best jobs. Just because he's a boy.'

'Stop your moaning and take the teapot next door. Ask if we can boil a kettle on their range.'

Delighted, Daisy did as she was told. Going next door meant getting warm in their kitchen. Their dad worked down the foundry, so he was bringing in a wage, pitifully small, but regular.

Ellen and her mother were left alone in the cold room, still sewing.

'Mum?'

Martha put her card down, sensitive to the tone of her daughter's voice.

'What, love?'

'*Was* it all for nothing?'

Martha was silent for a moment, considering.

'Well, like you said, love, your father won't think so. Matter of principle, like.'

'But what do you think?'

'Does it matter? What's done's done. Got to make the best of it.'

'But it does matter. If there was a reason, then it ain't so bad. Even Dad being in hospital ain't so bad.'

Martha pressed her lips together again. She sewed on another couple of hooks.

'That is so, ain't it?' Ellen insisted. It was very important that she sorted it out.

'I dunno, lovey. Don't ask me. All I know is, we got no coal, ain't got enough to eat and we're going to be hard put to keep up the rent on this house.'

'Dad is going to get better, ain't he?'

'So they say up the hospital. Please God they're right.'

'But it's going to take a time, ain't it?'

''Fraid so.'

'And you'll have the baby and him to look after.'

Martha said carefully, 'That's right. So what are you trying to say, lovey?'

'Just that I went and got a job at Maconochie's. I start on Monday.'

'Ellen! What about your schooling?'

'I told them today I was leaving.'

'That's not what I meant. You was supposed to be staying on and getting an office job.'

'I know.' Ellen frowned down at the table. It blurred before her eyes. She tried desperately to keep the catch out of her voice. 'But I can't, can I? Not now. How can I stay on when I'm fourteen and there's Jack and Daisy doing as much to earn as I am? It'll be bad enough as it is. They're only paying me six and sixpence. But it's better than nothing and I can still do the envelopes and anything else we get in when I get home.'

Martha reached out and put a hand over hers.

'Oh, Ellen. I am sorry. I know how much it means to you. But I can't say as how it won't be a weight off my mind. That bit extra'll make all the difference. We'll be able to pay the rent, for a start.'

Ellen nodded, not trusting herself to speak. Her mother did not really understand how much it meant. None of them did. They could not comprehend the pleasure she got from using her head, the escape she found in stories, the satisfaction of adding up a string of numbers and getting the right answer.

'And it's not so bad working there, you know. Lots of girls there from around here. You'll have a few laughs, I'm sure.'

'Yeah.'

How could she explain the sense of failure, of having to admit that, after all, she was just like all the rest? For she could not say to her mother that she had always felt she was different; not better, just different. Going to the Central had confirmed it. There was an escape from the life that everyone in Trinidad Street led. But it had all been a dream. She was going to Maconochie's just like everyone else.

Everyone else was glad.

'I knew you'd see it right, Ellen. You got to do your bit for your family, ain't you?' Aunty Alma said.

'All that book learning. Never did anyone no good. Never did that when I was a girl. Went out to work when I was nine, I did,' Granny Hobbs told her.

'We always knew you was one of us really. You coming up the Girls' Club with us Friday?' Theresa and her friends asked.

It had made them uncomfortable and envious that someone might be doing something better than them. Now she was back on their level and they need not think about a different way of life any more.

But *she* still thought about it. She was thinking

about it as she sat hunched up at the top of the Torrington Stairs one Sunday afternoon early in the new year of 1902. It was a damp, dreary day, no weather to be sitting out, but there was no fire on at home and the place was crowded with people. The four walls had seemed to be closing in on her, the familiar refuge had become a cage. At least here there was space. She sat hugging her legs, her chin resting on her knees, watching the greasy surface of the Thames slide endlessly by.

She jumped and looked round nervously as footsteps approached. It was Harry.

'They said you might be here. Can I sit down?' he asked.

Ellen shrugged. 'Suit y'self.'

Since the day of the coronation party, they had avoided each other. She could not forgive him for going off with Siobhan the moment her back was turned. It still hurt that he had so obviously been waiting to get rid of her.

Harry took that for an invitation and sat beside her.

'Aren't you cold here?'

'No more than anywhere else. I like it here. I like to be by myself sometimes.'

He ignored this none too gentle hint. 'I know what you mean. I like to be by myself out on the river.'

They were both silent for a while, staring at the thick water in which no fish could live. Dead water, for all that it seemed to have a life of its own.

'How are you liking it at Maconochie's?' Harry asked.

'It's all right.' It was a lie. She hated it. Hated the noise, the steam, the smells, the forewoman who seemed to have it in for her. Most of all she hated the grinding boredom of doing the same tiny process over and over again, until her mind seemed to go round in circles like a treadmill.

'It's a bit boring,' she added.

'I can imagine. It'd drive me mad, factory work. Out on the river, you might have bad foremen or foul weather or eighteen hours on the job without a break, but at least on the boat you're master. It's up to you to get the stuff to where you're going whichever way seems best to you.'

Ellen sighed. It sounded like bliss. Room to move, new places, new faces, new challenges. Not like Maconochie's.

'You are lucky,' she said.

'I know.'

The thing that was bothering her most rose once more to the top of her mind.

'Was it all for nothing, do you think?'

'All what?'

'The strike, Dad's accident – everything. All for nothing.'

'No.' Harry was emphatic. He spoke slowly, thinking it out. 'No, it wasn't. It don't matter that the strike collapsed and the ship was turned round. What matters is that someone made a stand. If your dad had just stood by and let those men be exploited without saying a word against it, then he would have lost. That would have been acting like a white slave. As it was, he spoke up for what he knew was right, like a free man. Yeah, that's it. He acted like a free man should.'

167

A great weight rolled off Ellen's soul.

'Yeah,' she said, hardly more than whispering. Then added with conviction, 'Yeah, you're right. That's how it was.'

'He's a good man, your dad. A hero.'

'Yeah.' The trouble was, heroes could be uncomfortable to live with.

She did not notice Harry looking at her sideways, studying her face.

'I was surprised you gave it up,' he said.

'But I couldn't go on, not now,' she said.

'Of course not, but you could study in the evening, couldn't you? Read books, that sort of thing? Not just throw it all over now. But then perhaps you weren't really serious about it.'

'I was – I *am!*'

Harry shrugged. 'Doesn't look much like it to me.'

Ellen was stung. How *could* he say that?

'How am I supposed to study when I'm at work all day and helping Mum in the evening?' she shouted. 'Are you saying I shouldn't help Mum? Fine daughter I'd be!'

Harry was unmoved. 'If you'd really wanted to, you'd've found a way. I think maybe you was finding it all too difficult at school.'

He picked up a piece of slate and tossed it up idly, watching as it turned over in flight before landing back in his hand

Ellen was stung. How could he say that?

'I was not. I was fourth in my class.'

'Why give it up, then?'

'I haven't. I – I'm studying in my spare time,' she lied.

'First I heard of it.'

'Well, that just goes to show you don't know everything, don't it?' Ellen said, and flounced off before he could ask for details.

With a sideways flick, Harry sent the piece of slate skipping over the surface of the water. He smiled to himself, showing his strong white teeth.

The first thing that struck Ellen as she slammed back into the house was the warmth. It wrapped round her like a pair of welcoming arms, soothing all her anger and confusion. She went into the kitchen, where her mother was just making a pot of tea.

'The range is alight!' she exclaimed.

She went over to it, letting the blessed heat sink into her chilled body.

'Ain't it lovely?' Her mother looked happier than Ellen had seen her for weeks. Her face had got back its round look, instead of being strained and haggard.

A lighted range meant hot food, hot water, clean clothes, a bath– Ellen shivered with pleasure at the thought of a bath.

'I put a rice pudding in the oven,' her mother said.

Ellen's stomach growled at the thought. A rice pudding. Heaven!

'But how...?' she began. There had been no coal in the house when she left.

'Harry brought us round a sack. Weren't that kind of him?' her mother explained.

'Harry!' At once all the confusion rolled back.

Daisy was watching her reaction. 'He was

asking for you. Did he find you?'

Ellen nodded.

'Oo. What did he want? What did he say?'

'It's none of your business,' Ellen snapped. She felt perilously near to tears, though she hardly knew why.

'Oo.' Daisy was skipping about, her eyes gleaming at the scent of some gossip. 'You're blushing. You are! Come on, tell us. You're in love with him, ain't you? Ellen's in love with Harry Turner–'

'Shut up!' Ellen shouted at her, and ran upstairs.

She flung herself on the mattress and burst in tears. She hated Harry Turner. He was bossy and interfering and insulting. He had abandoned her for Siobhan. He was kind and thoughtful. He had rescued her father from certain death. She did not know what to make of him. She did not know why he had come to talk to her today, or why she was so upset now. One thing was clear, though. He was wrong about why she gave up school.

'I'll show him,' she muttered, when at last she became a little calmer. 'I'll show him. Finding it too hard, indeed. We'll see about that.'

Ellen went to bed that night pink from a blissful bath in the tin tub in front of the range, her hair clean and shining, and new purpose in her heart. She was going to prove Harry wrong if it was the last thing she did.

But sleep escaped her. She could hear her mother getting up and walking round the front bedroom, and the creak of her bedsprings as she turned in bed. Sometime in the early hours she went to sleep, only to jerk awake again, her heart beating wildly. She listened. All was quiet. Wide awake, she lay staring into the darkness. Beside her in the narrow bed Daisy slept, dead to the world, and a couple of feet away under the window she could just make out the hump under the blankets that was Jack.

Then she heard something that made her blood freeze. From her mother's room came a low groan.

Ellen slid out from under the covers, trying not to wake Daisy. Shivering in the penetrating cold, she felt around for a shawl and hugged it to her shoulders, then carefully eased her way out of the room. With two beds in it, the door could not be fully opened. She tiptoed the two steps across the landing and tapped on her mother's door.

'Mum? You all right?'

There was a pause, then, 'Yeah, yeah. I'm quite all right. You go back to bed.'

Ellen hesitated. 'I thought I heard a noise, Mum. Is there anything wrong?'

'No, no. I'm fine.'

Then it hit her. Of course.

'Mum, is it the baby? Is the baby coming? Can I do anything?'

'Not yet, lovey. It'll be hours yet. I'm just trying to rest while I can.'

Ellen knew what she was going to do, and it certainly was not go back to bed. Since Jack, her mother had had four miscarriages and a stillbirth. She could not bear the thought of another tragedy. This baby was going to live. She padded downstairs to the parlour, felt for her coat and

171

boots and let herself out of the house. Two minutes later she was pounding on the O'Donaghues' door. For what seemed like an age, nothing happened. Then the window was forced slowly up and a tousled head looked out.

'Who is it?' Brian's voice was bleary with sleep.

'It's me, Ellen Johnson. Can Mrs O'Donaghue come, please? My mum's having her baby.'

Brian's head disappeared. There was a muttering from within the house, then he was back.

'The missus says, go on home and she'll be along in ten minutes.'

'Oh thank you, thank you, I'll go right away.'

Relieved, Ellen ran back. Mrs O'Donaghue had no nursing training, but all the women in the street swore by her. When it came to delivering babies, they claimed, she was better than any doctor.

The hours that followed went slowly. Ellen got breakfast for all of them and went upstairs to see how her mother was getting along. Mrs O'Donaghue met her at the bedroom door.

'No need for you to hang around here all day long. It's going to be a slow job. You get off to work and send them kids to school early.'

Ellen tried to argue, but Mrs O'Donaghue's word was the law when it came to these matters.

'You're going to need the money, and you know what'll happen if you take a day off work – they'll give you the sack. There's plenty round here to help me if need be.'

In turn, Ellen chivvied Jack and Daisy out.

'You're too young to stay around. You get off to school and maybe when you get back you'll have a little brother or sister,' she told them.

But she felt like a traitor, closing the door behind her and leaving her mother there.

All the way up the street, the women were scrubbing their doorsteps and sweeping down the strips of pavement in front of their houses. The news had reached them long ago.

'How's your mum coming along, Ellen?'

'What's Mrs O'Donaghue say?'

'Just let me know if there's anything you need.'

'I got some lovely little baby clothes she can have. I'll take 'em over. I won't be needing them for a few months yet.'

'Send them kids up to us for their tea if it's not here by then. They can always spend the night, if you like.'

The reassuring strength of the street was around her. She could see and feel and hear it on all sides. They would not let anything dreadful happen to her mother. But it did not entirely assuage the fear that clutched at her heart. Her mum was getting old to have babies. She was a granny. Anything could happen.

At work, she could not concentrate. She kept dropping the jars she was supposed to be labelling. One slipped right through her fingers and smashed on the floor, a red mess of smelly pickled cabbage and fragments of glass.

The forewoman came snarling over to her. 'Johnson! I told you about that before. That's sixpence off your wages.'

The girls around her sprung to her defence.

'Oh, Mrs Biggs, have a heart. Her mum's having a baby.'

'Yeah, she's that worried. She can't help it.'

The forewoman's grim features softened. 'That right?' she asked.

Ellen nodded. 'Started last night.'

'And her dad's up the hospital,' another girl chipped in.

'All right, all right. Just let me get my violin out. We'll all be in tears in a minute.' Mrs Biggs fixed Ellen with her boiled-gooseberry eyes. 'I'll overlook it this time, but just be more careful for the rest of the day, right?'

'Yes, Mrs Biggs.'

'Yes, Mrs Biggs, no Mrs Biggs,' they all mouthed behind the woman's back, and giggled. But Ellen felt no better and the day seemed to go on for ever.

Released at last, she pushed her way through the hundreds pouring out of the factory gates and ran back through the drizzling rain. She paused at the greengrocer's where Daisy worked after school.

'Daisy!'

Her sister looked up from carrying out a pile of boxes.

'How's Mum? Has she had it?'

Daisy shook her head. She looked peaked and anxious. 'No. Mrs O'Donaghue said it's going to take ages yet. Said I ought to try and bring home something to make a nice pan of soup.'

'Oh – good idea. See you later, Daisy.'

Ellen hurried on, worry gnawing at her guts.

Trinidad Street was practically empty. A couple of little girls were wheeling a pram with two crying babies inside, and a group of boys were playing leapfrog, slipping on the wet cobbles as they landed. Jack broke away from them and ran up to her.

'Mrs O'Donaghue says I'm to go to Jimmy Croft's for tea. Is that right, Ellen?'

Ellen supposed it was. It didn't do to have kids hanging round the house at these times. Mrs O'Donaghue had certainly got things well organized.

'Mind you thank Mrs Croft proper,' she told him.

Jimmy appeared at his side. 'My mum don't mind. She says the more the merrier,' he said.

'Good, thanks.' Ellen left them and sprinted the last twenty yards home.

The place seemed to be full of women. They were all sitting round the kitchen table drinking tea and talking in low voices charged with meaning. They stopped abruptly when Ellen entered.

'How's my mum?'

There was a brief pause. 'Oh, she's coming along fine, dearie. Just going to take a while, that's all.'

The group of heads nodded.

Ellen knew they were lying. 'I want to see her.'

'Not now, dearie. You're too young. Your time'll come soon enough.'

'But she's my mum. I can help her. She needs me.'

'She's got all us here to help her. Been one of us with her all day, there has, and will be all night. She won't never be left on her own; you know that.'

They meant well, she realized, but they were treating her like a kid. She hated every one of

175

them – sitting in her house like a lot of old witches, cackling over their own deliveries while upstairs her mother was in pain.

From above came a cry, hardly recognizable. Ellen's heart contracted in fear. She whisked out of the kitchen, pounded up the stairs and raced into the front bedroom. There she stopped short just inside the door. Her mother was lying on her back on a dishevelled bed. There were no covers on her, her knees were raised and spread, and her nightgown was pulled up to the great swelling belly so that she could see her naked legs, pale and blotched with purple veins, and between them a bulging red wound fringed with hair. Ellen stood and stared, shocked rigid.

'What you doing here? You get off downstairs.'

She had not even seen Mrs O'Donaghue. Now she ignored her. Still gaping in horrified fascination, she forced her frozen limbs to move. Slowly she walked across the cramped room to the head of the bed. Her mother looked years older, her face flushed, her cheeks sunken, her greying hair soaked in sweat. She turned her head as Ellen approached and for a few heart-stopping moments there was no recognition in her glazed eyes.

'Mum?' Ellen's throat was dry. The word came out as a croak.

Her mother's look sharpened. 'Ellen? You didn't ought to be here, love.' The strained whisper was not at all like her mother's usual voice.

'Mum, are you all right?' Even as she said it she knew it was a stupid question.

'I will be, lovey, as soon as–' She broke off, her face contracting in pain.

Instinctively, Ellen clasped the hand that opened and closed on the sheet. The sweating fingers grasped at her, clenching as the pain grew. A low moan broke from her mother's lips, swelling to a cry. Her head thrashed from side to side. Terrified, Ellen could only watch and wait, her hand crushed, expecting every moment that her mother was going to die. Then, just as she thought she could not bear it any longer, the grip on her hand relaxed, the cry died away.

Mrs O'Donaghue mopped her mother's forehead with an old cloth. She fixed Ellen with a look that said clearly *I told you so*.

'Right, you've seen what you come to see, and a lot of good may it do you. Now off you go. You're not doing your ma no good staying here. And while you're about it you can tell them downstairs as I could do with a fresh bowl of water and another nip of gin.'

Dumbly, Ellen nodded. She bent down and kissed her mother's damp cheek.

'Just hold on, Mum. We all love you.'

There was no answer from the exhausted woman on the bed.

The women downstairs took one look at her face and bit back the scolding they were about to give her. Ellen delivered the message. Milly Turner put an arm round her shoulders.

'You come back with me, dearie. Have tea with us. Florrie'd like to have you to chat to.'

Ellen shook her head. 'I'm staying here.'

The women argued and cajoled, but nothing would move her. She could not possibly leave now, not after having seen what her mother was going through.

There was always somebody there. The neighbours she had hated so fiercely earlier were now a lifeline. True to their promise, the women came in and out, seeing to their own families then taking it in turns to relieve Mrs O'Donaghue or sit with Ellen. It seemed to her that as evening turned into night and the hours crept by, the cries upstairs grew more feeble. It was Milly Turner who finally let slip what the problem was.

'It's coming out the wrong way round,' she explained. 'Usually they come head first. It's easier that way, you see.'

Ellen stared at her, trying to take this in. 'You mean – it's stuck?' she asked.

'Well...' Milly looked uncomfortable. 'Not exactly. But it's more difficult. And your mum's not as young as she was.'

Ellen looked up at the ceiling. Fear wound cold fingers round her. Her mother was not going to make it.

Then sometime after midnight there was a long despairing wail from the bedroom. Ellen shot to her feet, her heart pounding. Milly put a hand on her arm.

'Wait,' she said.

An urgency in her voice made Ellen obey. They both listened. Then the bedroom door opened and Mrs O'Donaghue called down, weary but triumphant.

'Will you come up here with plenty of soap and water? We done it. 'Tis a boy.'

Milly hurried to fill a bowl and get fresh cloths. Ellen ran straight upstairs, but Mrs O'Donaghue met her at the door. Her apron was splattered all down the front with blood.

'You're not coming in till she's cleaned up. She's in no fit state. Wait there.' She slammed the door in Ellen's face, only to reappear seconds later with a small bundle wrapped in an old torn sheet. 'Take this downstairs in the warm. You know how to bath a baby, don't you? I got to see to your ma.' She thrust the bundle at Ellen and shouted down to Milly, 'Bring up all the rags you can lay your hands on.'

Slowly, infinitely carefully, Ellen felt her way into the kitchen. There in the light she gazed at the tiny creased face of her new little brother. He was not beautiful. Smears and clots of blood stuck to his skull, his slitty eyes were puffed and closed and his mouth seemed misshapen. But he was a thing of great wonder.

'Ah.' Milly paused to peek at him on her way up. 'Ain't he lovely? Ever so quiet, though. Did Clodagh say he was all right?'

Ellen nodded, not taking her eyes off him. The enormity of the responsibility thrust upon her left her speechless. Not daring to put him down, she put more water to heat on the range and found the only receptacle not in use – the mixing bowl – and the last sliver of soap from the sink, together with a shawl and nightie her mother had made ready. Then, sitting cross-legged on the rag rug in front of the range, she unwrapped the soiled bit of sheet. A whimper came from the little mouth. Ellen wept tears of relief. It was all right. He was truly alive. She lowered him gently into the water, marvelling at the tiny limbs, washed away the blood and unstuck his eyelids. The feeble mew came again, but never grew into a proper cry. Ellen dried and dressed him and sat with him cuddled close to the warmth of her body, stroking the down of fair hair. She could scarcely feel him breathing.

She wished he would open his eyes. Perhaps babies did not at first. She spoke softly to him, telling him all about the family he had been born into, about all the things he was going to do when he was older.

Now that he was clean, she wondered if there was something wrong with his colour. She had never seen a new-born baby before so she could not be sure, but the blueish tinge about his mouth worried her.

Mrs O'Donaghue finally came out of the bedroom and collapsed on to a kitchen chair.

'Give me a cuppa tea, lass. I'm parched.'

The baby still tucked in her arm, Ellen did as she was bid. She was aching to ask about her mother, but somehow the words would not come. She handed the midwife a strong sweet cup of tea and sat cradling the baby, waiting.

Mrs O'Donaghue took several sips, her hands shaking with fatigue.

'That's better.' She put down the cup and rubbed her hands over her face. Then she looked at Ellen. 'She's had a bad time, dear. I done all I can for her and she's sleeping now. She'll probably sleep for several hours. You can give her the babe to nurse when she wakes. I'm going home now. If there's any problems, just send for me.'

Ellen thanked her profusely. Her mother had

survived. There was hope.

In her gratitude, she forgot to ask about the child's odd colour. She was still not sure whether it was normal. She was still wondering when two hours later he died in her arms.

5

Alma took out all four of her best dresses and threw them over the bed. None of them looked right.

'Come up the Ferry tonight. There's someone I want you to meet,' Harry had said.

She had questioned him, but he had refused to say any more, just laughed and looked mysterious.

'You wait and see, Aunty Alma. Just come looking your best.'

So here she was, trying to decide. She held the scarlet satin against herself, smoothing the beautiful shiny fabric. She loved this dress. But the boys hated seeing her in it, and she had to admit it did make her look a bit of a tart. The navy wool was her respectable dress. She wore that if she had to go to church, or to visit her more straight-laced relatives. But that was no good for a night out at the pub. The dress she wore last year for the coronation party was nice: a bright blue poplin spotted with white and pink. Very fetching, that had looked, with all the red, white and blue ribbons. But it was a bit on the flimsy side for the middle of winter. So that left the tan-coloured

181

one that Gerry had bought for her down the market only last month. It was a nice dress. Someone posh up the West End had once worn it, and it had only had maybe a couple of owners since. The only trouble was, it was a bit sober for Alma. She preferred a bit of glitter.

She put on the tan dress, did the buttons up with difficulty with the aid of a buttonhook and pinned on as much costume jewellery as she thought she could get away with – earrings, a couple of necklaces, three brooches and an armful of jangly bangles. That was better. Now she looked as if she was going out on the town. She pinned up her heavy hair and crowned it with her favourite hat, the red velvet with the black feathers. Then she stepped back and looked at herself. Yes, she was all right. Not a bad figure for her age. Her teeth let her down a bit, but nobody had all their teeth. No one would guess to look at her what a tough life she had led.

The Ferry was crowded. It was Saturday night and quite a few men from Trinidad Street had deserted the everyday Rum Puncheon on the corner and ventured just a few streets further.

'Wotcher, Alma! How you doing?'

'Evening, girl. On your own? Come and have a drink with us.'

Alma laughed and joked and gave as good as she got. She felt alive again. One very good thing about the Ferry, that little madam Siobhan O'-Donaghue would not be there. Siobhan always made her feel as old as the hills and blowsy. No man wanted to look at a middle-aged widow, however well preserved, when that one was about.

She spotted Harry at the table on the far side of the bar. He came over, smiling, and brought her a port and lemon. It always amazed her that Milly and Archie had produced such a son. Tall and well made, with muscular arms and shoulders, a keen face and a crop of curly hair, he was one of the most handsome young men in the area – barring her own two boys, of course. And brains to go with it, as well. That was even more surprising. Alma supposed he must be some sort of throwback.

'Where's this person I'm supposed to be meeting, then?' she asked.

'He'll be here, don't worry. How are you?'

They chatted about the street and about the robbery at the grocer's over in Cubitt Town.

'Why a grocer? He ain't got much. Poor little man, they really done him over, so I heard. Up the hospital now, he is.'

'The grocery was only a front. He was a money lender, and a fence. The thieves knew where his stuff was kept.'

'Oh, a money lender.' Alma had had many a brush with them in the past. 'Still, they didn't ought to have hurt him like that. He's an old man.'

Then she dismissed the subject from her head and started in on things closer to home.

'I don't see much of you these days, Harry. You're always out and about. Either you're working or you're up to something with your mates.'

'I like to get around, Aunty Alma. London's a big place, you know. There's music halls and pubs and posh shops and parks. No point in staying here on Dog Island when there's so much more to see.

Some of the people round here' – he gestured at the cheerful Saturday-night crowd – 'they don't leave the place from one week's end to the next. Home, work, drink, all just around the corner. A trip up Chrisp Street with the missus on the Saturday afternoon's about the furthest they go.'

'Yeah.' Alma thought about it. These last few years since she came to live in Trinidad Street, she'd been like that, going only as far as wherever she was working. It was getting so that the land outside the Isle of Dogs was foreign territory to her. Mostly she liked to stay where she knew everybody and they knew her, but now, talking to Harry and thinking about the fun he must have, she was fired with a sense of restlessness.

'It's all very well for you – you're a young lad, and a lighterman. You can do what you like. Different for the likes of me.'

'Ah well.' Harry had that mysterious smile about his eyes again. 'Lightermen are the best, of course. And here's one more.' He stood up and waved, and a stocky man in his forties came over.

It did not take Alma more than a couple of seconds to realize what was going on. She was ready to be highly affronted that her young nephew should set her up like this, but then she looked at his friend and decided she liked what she saw. He had the weathered face of a riverman, creased into lines of good humour, and that same air of independence and authority that Harry wore.

'Come on over, Ernie.' Harry clapped him on the back. 'Aunty, this here's my pal Ernie Foster. Ernie, meet my Aunty Alma, Mrs Billingham.'

'Pleased to meet you,' Ernie said, stretching out

a huge hand. 'I've heard a lot about you from young Harry here.'

'Well, you're a jump ahead of me there, 'cos he ain't said nothing to me about you,' Alma told him. But that old stir of interest and excitement inside told her that she wanted to find out.

She couldn't believe her luck. He was two years a widower, with five children – four married and the youngest, a daughter, still at home and looking after the house for him. He had a perm-anent job, and it was common knowledge that lightermen were well paid. On top of this, he was cheerful, entertaining, a good talker and a listener in his turn. And he liked her. She could tell. His eyes never left her face and he responded to her smallest remark. They talked away nineteen to the dozen, finding similar tastes.

'The halls? Oo, I love the halls,' Alma said. 'I ain't been for months, though. My boy Gerry takes me sometimes. I like Harry Lauder – real scream, he is.'

'You do? So do I! Seen him only last week down the Old Vic. And George Chirwin – you seen him?'

Alma admitted that she had not.

'Oh, you oughta hear him sing "Blind Boy". Wonderful! And I like the girls, of course – Vesta Tilley, what a voice!'

She almost forgot that Harry was there until he stood up.

'I got to go and see a man about a dog,' he said.

Both of them pretended disappointment. Harry bid them goodbye with the air of a man who had been proved right.

The evening flew by. It was gone midnight and

the crowd in the bar was beginning to thin out.

'You fancy a plate of jellied eels, Mrs Billingham?' Ernie asked.

'Why, thank you, Mr Foster. That'd be very nice. Nothing like a plate of jellied eels to help the drinks go down, I always say.'

'Me too. Can't beat 'em.'

It was nearly one o'clock before they arrived back in Trinidad Street. They stopped at Alma's door.

'I ain't enjoyed myself so much in ages,' Ernie told her.

Alma had learnt enough over the years not to give it all away at once. Not when it was important, like this one.

'Yeah, it's been quite nice, ain't it?'

'I was wondering...' He hesitated, looked down.

'Yeah, what?'

'Well, I was wondering if you'd like to come to one of the Sunday League concerts with me. At the Alhambra.'

'Oh.' Alma had to stop herself from jumping at it. She said coolly, 'That'd be nice, one day.'

'How about tomorrow?'

She let herself be persuaded. They parted with a decorous shaking of hands. Alma went inside and leant against the door. Her knees were shaking. She took a long deep breath. A great cry of happiness gathered inside her, welled up and burst from her throat. This was it. She had done it. This was the one.

Gerry closed the door of the shop with a bad-tempered bang. He was tired of running other people's businesses, especially when he knew he could do it so much better himself. And there was an opening, if he could just see the way to grab it, but he needed to raise a loan. He tramped back home, hands in pockets, trying to see a way forward.

'Evening, Gerry.'

He looked up, jolted out of his preoccupation.

'Oh – evening, Ellen.' Automatically, he put on his smile and produced a compliment. 'You're looking as pretty as ever. How's your family?'

'All right. You know – much the same.'

Gerry nodded. Things were not so grand in the Johnson household. Ellen was the only one in regular work, and as a girl, her wages were not half enough to support them. Everyone else did their bit, but it was not the same as having a proper breadwinner. Although Tom was out of hospital and back trying to get work, there was a conspiracy amongst the foremen at the docks. They would take Tom on for maybe two or three days a week, just enough to keep him alive, and keep him under.

'Wouldn't it be better if your dad looked for work elsewhere?'

'Oh no, he'd never do that. That would be giving in. He won't let them beat him.'

'Well, that's that, I suppose.' Gerry would not have gone to such lengths because of a principle. He would have cut his losses and run long ago. Jobs might be short at the West Indias at the moment, but there was other work about. Tom Johnson did not have to wait each day behind the chain for foremen to deliberately overlook him.

They reached her door, but he did not want her to go in yet.

'My mum's having the time of her life at the moment.'

'Yeah.' Ellen's weary face lit with pleasure. 'I heard. Do you like her gentleman friend?'

'He's all right. Well no, I tell a lie. He's straight as a die, salt of the earth. She's crackers about him, and him about her. Takes her out every Saturday and Sunday night he's not working. You should hear her! Expert on the halls now, she is. Knows them all, knows the songs. Well, she always was cheerful, no matter what, but now she's singing away like a linnet all day long.'

'But she's your mum and you don't like her having a gentleman friend?' Ellen said.

Gerry was amazed at her perception. That was it. She had hit the nail right on the head.

'Well – yeah, I suppose so.'

'She deserves some happiness, your mum. That's what my mum says. But what about you, Gerry? You anywhere nearer getting your market stall?'

He could not resist the chance to talk about his own affairs.

'There's a space coming up in the Chrisp Street market. Heard through a pal of mine. Just right for me, and they know I been waiting for Lord knows how long to get a licence. Only problem is raising the wind. No good having a stall what's only half full. You got to have it piled high. Bring the customers in.'

'I see. Yeah, I suppose you're right. Well, I hope you get it, Gerry.' She put her hand on the door.

'Wait...'

188

He had not asked her before. She had so much to cope with, what with her father being ill and her mother poorly after the baby and everything. But that quality of sympathy in her voice drew him on. Here was someone who was really interested in his doings.

'How about you and me going out somewhere? Little trip up to Poplar, see a bit of life?'

'Oh – no.' She shook her head and began to open the door. 'Thanks, Gerry, but I couldn't. I got too much to do.'

'You can't be helping out your family every night. Just once won't do no harm. Do you a lot of good. You look like you need a break, need a bit of taking out of yourself. What do you say, eh? We could take a tram, get you off the Island and see what the rest of the world is doing.'

But she was adamant. 'No, Gerry. I can't. Thanks all the same. 'Night.'

She slipped inside.

Gerry walked slowly up the street to his house. He was not going to accept defeat. He'd ask again. But first he'd find some way to get that stall.

It was just as he was going into his place that he realized exactly why he had not asked her before. It was not just because she was so tied up with her family, but because it was too important. She wasn't just any girl. He would make a success of himself, then he would ask her again. By the time he reached the kitchen, he had Ellen all fitted into his plans for the future.

His mother was chirruping away, blithely out of tune, as she sewed frills on to a blouse.

189

''Lo, darling. Your tea's nearly ready. I just got to finish this.'

He kissed her cheek. 'Going out again, Mum?'

'Yeah, just out for a drink, nothing special.'

'Charlie not in yet?'

'He come in, and he went out again. You know Charlie.'

He did. That was the trouble. His mother had always been blind to Charlie's faults, and Charlie had always taken care that she should not have the opportunity to catch him out. Well, if Gerry was honest, she thought the sun shone out of both their backsides, his and Charlie's. But it had always been Charlie she refused to hear any ill of. It was as if she draped a curtain over everything she did not want to face and simply denied its existence. On top of that, at the moment she was so tied up with her Ernie Foster that she would not have noticed if the roof fell in.

Gerry did not tell her what his brother was up to – not about the stealing or his suspicions that he had worked Tom Johnson over – because if she believed him she would be so disappointed in Charlie, and anyway Charlie would take his revenge. And he did not point out that Charlie had no regular job at all, and when he did work it was for men with very shady reputations, so the money he put into the housekeeping must come from thieving. There were no two ways about it: his brother was a small-time thief and bully, stealing not from the rich, but from the weak and those who had very little more than he did. But if he opened his mother's eyes, she would be heartbroken, and Charlie would do him over. So he said nothing.

Ernie Foster came to call for his mother. Gerry shook hands politely. As they left, he considered once again what it would mean if they got married. His mother would go off and live at Ernie's house, he and Charlie would be left here together and their little family would be broken up. One thing was sure, he was not staying here with his brother. He would get lodgings somewhere. Perhaps the Johnsons would take him in. Certainly they could do with the extra money.

The little house felt very quiet. Once his mother left, the heart went out of it, and he hated being on his own. Gerry decided to go down to the Rum Puncheon for a drink. He was just about to go out of the front door when his brother came in at the back.

'Oi, Gerry!' Charlie dumped a small canvas bag on to the kitchen table with a clatter. 'Got something here'd interest you.'

Instinct told him to leave it alone, but his acquisitive nature got the better of him. One whiff of a deal and he was hooked.

'Yeah?' He acted unconcerned, leaning against the doorframe with his hands in his pockets.

'Yeah. Right up your street, this. Something for you to sell.'

Gerry stayed where he was, though his fingers itched to open the filthy bag.

'You interested or not?' Charlie demanded.

'Might be. Depends.'

Charlie glared at him from under his eyebrows. 'What you see here goes no further than these four walls, right?'

Gerry knew he should leave now, but the temptation was too strong. There was that opening going at Chrisp Street.

'Right.'

His brother opened the bag and tipped it up. On to the table spilled a jumbled collection of cutlery, rings, watches and necklaces. Despite himself, Gerry was drawn forward. He reached out and picked up one of the knives. It was tarnished and dirty, but when he turned it over, there was the hallmark. Real silver. It was the same with the rings, a heavy man's signet, a couple of thin wedding bands and a small dress ring set with pearls and a garnet. All of them were gold. He held one of the watches in his hand, staring at the black Roman numerals. If felt round and satisfyingly heavy. He wound the little knob at the top and the second hand began to turn.

At last he looked at his brother. Charlie was regarding him with a mirthless smile.

'Knew you'd be interested.'

'Where'd you get all this?' Gerry burst out, though he knew the answer: the grocer in Cubitt Town.

Charlie just tapped the side of his nose. 'Ask no questions, my son, get no lies.'

'And you expect me to flog this lot for you? What do you think I am, a bloody fence?'

Again there was that calculating smile from his brother. 'Split it with you. Fifty–fifty.'

Gerry was caught, and he knew it. Here in his hands lay the way forward, his future. Here was money without having to take out a loan, a start for his market stall, a whole barrowload of stock.

In his fertile imagination he could see it already, bright and shiny, with a queue of customers. More than that, he could see Ellen Johnson looking at him with admiration: Gerry Billingham, street trader. She could not help but be impressed.

He tried to close his mind to the stark fact that these were stolen goods. After all, they had been stolen before the man in Cubitt Town got them. They had been passing from hand to hand for weeks, or, more likely, months. They certainly weren't hot any more. His thoughts ran inexorably on, refusing to look at the tricky issues of right and wrong. What else was there to do with them? If he took them back to their last owner, they wouldn't reach the people from whom they had been stolen, and handing them to the police was out of the question. It would bring all sorts of unwanted attention upon them. The last thing he wanted was that. So somebody might as well get something out of them, now that they were here.

But still he hesitated. He had cut a few corners in his time, done a few things that were not strictly legal, but this was quite different. If he did this, he would be no better than his brother. Abruptly, he dropped the stuff back on the table.

'No.'

Charlie reached out and grabbed him by the collar. He pulled Gerry forward until their faces were almost touching.

'What d'you mean, no?'

Then Gerry understood. Now he had seen the stuff, Charlie would not let him just walk away from it. He had to be in with him, or Charlie and his lot would get him. That was the choice, and put like that, he felt there was only one answer.

'What I mean is, fifty–fifty's not enough,' he said. 'I got to slog all over the place selling that lot. Can't take it all at once, can I? It's got to be got rid of piece by piece. It'll take me ages, that will, and every fence in the East End's going to be looking out for it. I'll find myself done over in a dark alley if I'm not careful.'

'Fifty–fifty or nothing.'

Gerry shrugged free and took a step back, flexing his shoulders. He knew where he was now, bargaining, although his brother had an unfair advantage in threat and muscle power. After an acrimonious exchange, they settled on forty-five–fifty-five in his favour.

'We'll keep it out the back in the old rabbit hutch,' Charlie said. 'Mum don't never look in there.'

For the next couple of weeks he spent his precious spare hours ranging the East End. His travels took him to parts he had never been to before, far away from the river and the familiar ground of docklands and Poplar. He ventured into areas where great new tenement blocks were inhabited almost entirely by Jews with hardly a word of English; to streets that might have been lifted out of Dublin; to neighbourhoods that tried desperately to be respectable, with tiny front gardens and lace curtains; to warrens where the courts and alleys were ankle-deep in filth, the windows filled with paper and families lived ten to a room.

Everywhere he went, he sold a piece or two of Charlie's haul, telling plausible tales of family illness, emigration, hard times, to account for the heart-breaking sale of a prized possession. The men he spoke to, hard-eyed and cynical, merely shrugged or spat. They had heard it all before a thousand times. Sometimes it was true, sometimes it was not. It was all the same to them. They took the risk and financed it by giving far less than the item was really worth. Gerry haggled but accepted the principle of the deal. That was the game, and he knew it.

As he travelled he kept his eyes open. For miles and miles there were mean streets of terraced cottages, tenement buildings, factories and workshops, all crowded with people. Everywhere women fought a losing battle with the dirt, scrubbing steps and sweeping pavements. Everywhere there were hordes of children, often ragged and barefoot, the older ones looking after the babies and toddlers. It was a seemingly endless vista of poverty and struggle. But all these people had some money to spend. They had to eat, they had to clothe themselves, they needed pots and pans and plates for their homes. Every neighbourhood had its market. Gerry began to see what he could do. He would start with Chrisp Street, then work out into all these others. Now that he had a start, there was no limit to what he could do.

But when he finally got rid of the last pieces and shared out the proceeds with his brother, he found the rules had changed.

'My pals ain't happy with our arrangement,' he told Gerry. 'They think it should be forty–sixty. To us.'

'We agreed!' Gerry protested. 'You can't go back on a deal like that. I been tramping all over town getting rid of that stuff one bit at a time so's it can't be traced back here. I'm a busy man. There's my time to be taken into consideration.'

Charlie just stared back at him, stony-faced. 'You want to tell that to my pals?' he asked.

Gerry wished he was brave, that he could say yes and take on his brother's gang of roughs, beat them at their own game and make them see who was master. But he had always run from fights. He did not enjoy them like the rest of the boys in the street. If he gave in now, he knew that Charlie had a threat to hold over him for ever more. He even opened his mouth to argue and damn the consequences, but the picture of Tom Johnson walking carefully like an old man, still afflicted with blinding headaches, came vividly to mind. He did not want to end up like that.

'Take it,' he said, trying to act unconcerned though the words seemed to stick in his throat and choke him. 'What the hell! I got what I want out of it.'

'Very sensible,' Charlie agreed.

The whole street came and patronized his stall the day he opened. They came by tram or they made it on foot, but practically everyone who was not housebound was there. They were proud of him. One of their own was going up in the world; not enough to become a source of envy – they would not have liked that – just enough to be able to boast about him to mates at work.

Ellen came, with Daisy and Jack, though her parents stayed at home. She gazed wide-eyed at his display of china and glassware. Tea sets, dishes, platters and tumblers were all carefully banked to show them to advantage.

'You got what you wanted, then?' she said to him. 'I'm pleased. It's nice to see someone doing well.'

He could see that she was clutching at her purse, indecision gnawing at her mind. Money for extras like new tea sets was just not there any more. The Johnsons were selling, not buying. Practically everything that was not essential had gone to the pawnshop. They were sleeping on mattresses on the floor, the bedsteads having long since gone.

Pride filled him as he saw the look on her face. He knew that feeling of everything being out of your reach. He had come a long way since he was a bare-foot urchin hanging around for the stuff that fell in the gutters. He waved an expressive arm at his stall.

'Best display in the whole market, though I say it myself as shouldn't. What do you like best, eh? What's your favourite?'

'Oh – I don't know. It's all so lovely.' There was longing in her voice, a need for something bright and pretty and frivolous. Her eyes ranged along the rows, taking in the roses on the cups, the shine on the glasses, the gloriously clashing colours of the vases.

'I like that jug,' Daisy said, pointing to a ruby-red one at the top of the stall.

'Yeah, it's nice, ain't it?' Gerry agreed, without taking his eyes from Ellen's face.

Jack put his hands in his pockets and started whistling. He was bored.

Ellen's gaze lighted on a teapot. It was white

china with a gold rim and a scatter of violets. He could see that she wanted it, but she gave a little shrug and said, 'I don't know. It's all so nice.'

Gerry reached for the teapot. With an expert twist, he wrapped it in newspaper and handed it to her.

'Compliments of the house.'

'Oh no.' Ellen took a step backwards and put her hands behind her. 'Oh no, you mustn't.'

But Gerry insisted. 'Yes I must. You brought me luck. It was just after I spoke to you about it that I got a break and got the money together. Go on, take it, or the luck might run out and then I'll never speak to you again.'

Ellen laughed at the ridiculous threat. Gerry grabbed one of her hands and placed the teapot in it.

'There, deal done. You can't back out now.'

She flushed and protested, but had to hold it, or it would have dropped to the ground and smashed. Gerry smiled at her, satisfied. She was so pretty when she laughed. She didn't laugh enough... One day he would make her smile just for him.

Towards the end of the day, Charlie turned up.

'Doing well?' he asked, lounging against the upright of the stall, dangerously close to the fragile piles of goods.

'All right,' Gerry said. He was not going to admit to any great success. 'Making a bob or two.'

Charlie leaned across and took a china candlestick off the display.

'My girl'd like this,' he said, shoving it in his pocket.

'You can have it trade,' Gerry told him.

But his brother gave his mirthless grin.

'Oh no, sunshine. I can have it for free. You're one of us now, remember?'

It all faded, the excitement of setting up, the fun of bantering with the women and girls, the satisfaction of feeling the coins slide into his money apron. He was on a level with Charlie, and his brother was never going to let him forget it. And it wasn't even as if Charlie was part of a powerful organization. They were only a gang of roughs, small fry, and he could not get away from them. It took the edge off the pleasure.

Harry saw it all happen.

He and Ernie Foster were both loading Cornish china clay from a schooner moored at the Cherry Garden Tiers. It was a cold March day with squally winds racing across the green waters of the Thames and flinging heavy showers in the face and down the neck. Harry merely turned up his collar. In his heavy melton overcoat, he was almost immune to the weather, and at least the wind was blowing away the whiff of guano being unloaded just downriver at Church Hole.

The river was alive with traffic: sailing barges tacking upriver, their tan sails bellying in the sharp squalls, colliers down from Newcastle, steamers from the Continent belching thick black smoke, and everywhere lighters loading and unloading and carrying the capital's imports and exports to the innumerable wharves and factories along the banks. In amongst them a multitude of rowing boats plied, from the smart Customs cutters and the River Police with their white-bladed oars through the watermen and coal foremen to the old ropies, beer boats and drudgers for recovering coal that had been knocked overboard.

It was going to be a tricky trip today, Harry realized, with the wind so blustery and unpredictable, but the thought only made him smile. He liked a challenge. He knew the river as well as his own home. In many ways it *was* home to him, and the brotherhood of watermen his family. He raised a hand as a friend went by, recognizing the colours on his oars and his distinctive whistle. A series of waves told him that he was bound upalong on a long job.

Ernie's barge was filled first.

'See you at the potteries, mate,' he called to Harry as he cast off.

Harry watched him as he manoeuvred into midstream. He was a master, was Ernie, knew his trade inside out. It was always an education to see how he shaped.

His own barge was filled and the tarpaulins pulled over. At about a hundred yards' distance he followed Ernie under Tower Bridge and London Bridge, the barge now gathering headway and fair galloping along.

It was at Westminster Bridge that it happened. Harry never had liked Westminster since he had had a very close shave with the knife-sharp buttresses there. From his position aft he noticed Ernie just straightening up to shoot the fourth bridge hole. Then he suddenly veered, the archway darkened and through it came a small pleasure steamer in a billow of smoke.

'My God!' Harry cried out. 'What the hell is that idiot doing? They're going to crash!'

The splintering crack could be heard from where they were, but little could be seen through the screen of smoke. One thing was clear, though: neither vessel appeared to be moving.

'Quick!' he shouted to the boy. 'Get that oar forward. We got to see what's happened.'

With the tide under them and two rowing, the barge surged over the water. The bridge loomed up on them just as a heavy shower of rain and hailstones rattled down, pitting the angry surface of the river. Peering ahead, Harry saw Ernie's barge pinned helpless against the buttress, with his apprentice desperately trying to push her off, while the steamer was just beginning to drift broadside out on the far side. Shouts and screams sounded above the general confusion.

'What happened?' he yelled.

Ernie's apprentice looked up. His shrill cry, frantic with fear, came across the shortening gap of water.

'Mr Foster – he's gone in – can't see him!'

'We'll go through number three,' Harry decided. 'Give it her – now!'

The boy pulled as hard as he could and the barge's nose obligingly came round. They shot the arch with just inches to spare, and as they came out the other side, Harry anxiously scanned the water through the heavy veil of the rain.

Nothing.

The seconds dragged by. Nobody could stay under that long and live.

Then there was a dark shape surfacing, wallowing in the choppy waves, trailing a frill of blood.

Harry swallowed down the rush of sick foreboding. Action first. Shouting instructions at the boy, he grabbed the boat hook. Life seemed to be repeating itself; it was Tom Johnson all over again, only this time he did not think he would be in time to save the carcass that only minutes ago had been his friend.

Ernie had been swept under the steamer's propeller. It was impossible to tell whether he had been drowned or had bled to death. Harry took his coat off to cover the gruesome remains, a last gesture to preserve the dignity of a fine man. Blood and water trickled out from underneath and washed under the gunwhales.

The boy, a tough youngster from Bankside, went white about the gills and threw up over the side.

'Most frightfully sorry about that, my man. Anything we can do?'

The pleasure steamer's skipper had her under control again and was coming alongside. It was a miniature thing, almost a toy boat, about twenty-five feet long and six wide at its broadest, all white paint, polished brass and shiny varnish, with a little yellow funnel belching real smoke. From the deck and the cabin portholes peered half a dozen vacuous faces of both sexes, topped with straw boaters and ribbons.

Harry stared with contempt at the young fellow supposedly in charge. He might have known it: some toff who thought skippering a boat on the Thames was like driving his motor car along a road.

'Nothing. He's dead,' he yelled back.

202

He had the small satisfaction of seeing the man's expression change.

'Eoh.' That grating, mincing accent.

'He got cut to ribbons by your propeller.'

The face with its drooping fair moustache grew a shade paler. 'Eoh, I say–'

'You'll be hearing from my company,' Harry added, with such finality that the man dared not say another word. He sheered off and headed back upriver. Harry hoped he was shaken, but doubted it.

The boat's name was branded on his memory. *Ballerina. Teddington.* The bloody idiot had probably never been on tidal waters before. Harry worked out exactly what had happened. Ernie had realized the fool was coming straight at him and veered off, since the heavy lighter would smash the delicate shell of the steamer and sink her with all her passengers. In the resulting crash with the bridge, he had been thrown into the river. Ernie had given his life for a few bored toffs out for a bit of amusement. It made Harry sick with anger.

He looked back. Ernie's apprentice had managed to get his barge off the buttress and she was drifting through at last, swinging round as she emerged until she was broadside to the tide.

'We'll get you on board and the pair of you can take her up to the potteries. I can handle this one single-handed,' Harry said to his boy.

The manoeuvre achieved, he was at last able to take in the full implications of what had happened.

'Oh, God,' he said out loud. 'How am I going to tell Alma?'

The funeral was a corker. Half of Wapping turned out for Ernie. All of Trinidad Street was there to support Alma. Lightermen from riverside communities on both sides of the Thames came to pay their respects to one of the brotherhood.

The young man who had caused the accident sent a wreath and five pounds.

'Blood money,' said Ernie's youngest daughter, and returned it.

She had no need of charity from on high – the watermen looked after their own. With admirable generosity, she kissed Alma and invited her to choose anything of her father's to remember him by. Alma, who had been holding back tears all day, finally broke down and called her the sweetest girl in the world. Gerry and Charlie took an arm each and practically carried her home. She seemed to have shrunk since she heard of the accident.

Ellen was watching Harry. He stood carven-faced through the ceremony in the sooty church and the cramped little city graveyard. The weather had turned suddenly springlike, mocking the sombre occasion. Pale sunlight was still shining late in the afternoon as the Trinidad Street contingent left the large Foster family to their spread of ham and salad. She stole up alongside him as they all walked home, stiff and uncomfortable in their best clothes, with black ribbons on sleeves and hats.

'I know what you're thinking,' she said, surprised at her own boldness in intruding.

'I doubt it.'

'You're thinking you ought never to have

introduced them.'

He looked at her in amazement. 'How did you know that?'

She shrugged. 'Dunno. Just did. But you're wrong, you know. At least she had those times with him, and they were happy times. She wouldn't have not wanted them, even if she lost him in the end. You know what they say, "Better to have loved and lost..."'

'Yeah.' Harry's eyes sought his aunt Alma, who was bowed between her two sons. 'But is that true?'

'It is, it is,' Ellen insisted.

'I hope you're right.'

'I know I am.'

She thought fleetingly of a magical evening dancing on the rough cobbles of Trinidad Street to Tim O'Keefe's fiddle. Harry had probably forgotten it. He'd forgotten her soon enough on the very night. The moment her back was turned, there he was dancing with that Siobhan. Not that it had done Siobhan much good. This at least gave Ellen a sour feeling of satisfaction. Rumour had it that Siobhan would like to go out with him, but he was not interested. Harry did not stay on the Island like the others. He went off to places all over London for his evenings out. Rumour also had it that he had girls all up and down the river. Ellen closed her ears to this one, rumours being what they were.

'Who'd have thought it, that we'd all be in the same boat?' Harry said.

Ellen's heart leapt. She thought he was still talking about love.

'What?' she asked stupidly.

'Four years ago, when you first heard about going to the Central, d'you remember?'

She remembered all right. It was like some distant faded dream, a time when she had hoped for a very different future from the one she was now living.

'Yeah.' She sighed.

'I'd always knew I'd have to support my family, of course. But now look at Gerry, with his stall. And you. I never thought you'd be the family breadwinner.'

'No.' For a moment she was silent, then it all came out before she could stop it. 'Poor Dad. He hates it, hates not being able to support us properly. It makes him feel – small, I suppose. And he's really angry that I had to leave the Central. He was proud of me being there. I tell him it don't matter, that I don't care.'

'But are you still studying? You said you would. I had my doubts.'

'You were wrong, then,' she retorted. 'I can't do work like what we done at school, but I do go and get books from up the Settlement. The ladies there are really nice, they help me choose. I read a book nearly every week, and when I take it back sometimes they say, "What did you think of it?" and I tell them and sometimes we have quite a long talk about it, like the people in the book were real, and why they did things and what they thought and whether it was right or not. I don't tell my dad about it, though. He thinks the Settlement's just a sop to keep the workers in their place.'

Harry looked down at her. There was an odd

206

expression on his face, but at least he wasn't as grim-looking as he had been all through the service. He gave her elbow a brief squeeze.

'You're a brave girl, Ellen,' he said, and walked on to catch up with his mother. She was pregnant again and beginning to droop.

Ellen was left feeling limp with disappointment. Brave little girl. Yes, that was her. Someone to be nice to, hardly different from the schoolgirl whose hat he had once rescued. The sensible part of her knew they had a lot to be grateful to Harry for. If it had not been for his prompt action, her dad would now be dead. And there were the smaller things, too. Often he would turn up on their doorstep with a tin or two of food that just happened to have fallen into his pockets, ham, sometimes, or pineapple – delicious, exotic things that made a wonderful change from the weary round of bread or porridge.

But she did not want to listen to the sensible voice. She wanted Harry to do things for her because she was pretty and fascinating – the qualities Siobhan had that sent the boys wild after her. She did not want to be good old Ellen, the dependable. It was boring, boring, as plain and uninteresting as eating bread and marge every day. She wanted to be ham or pineapple, like Siobhan.

She caught a glimpse of herself in the distorting glass of a shop window: thin, haunted, an alley cat's face beneath a cheap old hat; dress ten years out of date – her mother's, lumpy and loose from hasty refitting and carefully patched, its colour, once navy, now almost completely faded to a variety of washed-out greys; horrible, ugly patched boots, coming apart at the toes yet again. No wonder Harry did not look at her the way she wanted. Tears stung her eyes.

She blinked them away. She would make him notice her as more than just a neighbour. She did not know how, but she would do it. She knew she was cleverer than all those others he was supposed to have. She knew she was a sticker, too. She had kept up her studying, against all the odds. But right at this moment, that was not what she wanted him to see. She wanted him to look at her as a woman, to realize that she had something to give beyond a friendly word.

Looking at Harry's back, straight and strong as he helped his mother along, she knew that she wanted him for her own. One way or another, she had to make him feel the same way.

6

'Things'll be a lot better when I start work,' Jack boasted. 'Four more weeks and I'll be fourteen! No more rotten school. When I leave, I shall never pick up a pen again, not in my whole life.'

'That shows just what a dunce you are, then,' Ellen told him.

'It's not fair. I wish I could leave now. I've got to wait another whole year,' Daisy complained. 'I hate Miss Peebles. She's always on at me, she blames me for everything. It's not my fault that other people keep talking to me, but I always get the blame.'

'Miss Peebles is all right if she thinks you try. She knows you don't,' Ellen said.

'Oh well, it was all right for you. You were teacher's pet.'

'Stop it, the lot of you. Your father'll be in in a minute,' Martha ordered. 'Ellen, get this table clear. Daisy, fetch the plates and spoons, and Jack, move that washing over.'

It was Monday, washing day, but the May weather had failed to oblige. Outside, it was raining, and half-dried sheets and shirts and blouses hung on strings across the ceiling and over the fender by the range. Steam and the smell of vegetable soup thickened the air in the tiny room. Moving from table to sink was an elaborate dance of sidestepping. Once Tom arrived, there was hardly room to move at all.

Looking at her family all squashed round the table, Ellen wondered for the umpteenth time how they would have fitted another one in. People did, of course. They were a very small family compared to most. The O'Donaghues ate in shifts. But a little one toddling around, as he would have been by now, pulling the washing off the fender and banging spoons on the table, though he would have made it much more crowded, would have brightened things up no end. Her mother acted as cheerfully as ever, but it did not quite ring true. It was as if she was just putting on a show. Ellen had occasionally caught her looking at other people's babies with an unguarded expression of grief filling her face.

Sometimes it seemed to her as if they were all

209

in a long dark tunnel with no light at the end. The past was a bright, sun-filled place, in which there was always something nice to eat, her mother laughed and joked and was never tired, and her father was strong and healthy and worked every day. If they had stayed in that place, she would now be thinking about starting to look for an office job, not looking back on a year and a half of fruit-bottling. In that other life, there had always been something nice to look forward to.

'I was talking to a mate today,' Tom said, when they had finished their meagre meal of watery vegetable soup and hunks of bread. 'He says he might be able to get Jack a job at the ropeworks. They need a willing youngster.'

Jack looked mutinous but knew better than to say anything. The ropeworks was not a popular place.

'Mrs Croft told me her cousin said they were looking for boys at Edmonson's,' Martha said.

'I'd like that,' Jack piped up. 'Foundries are good.'

'You know nothing about it. Foundries are very dangerous places, especially for young boys who think they know the lot,' his father told him.

'Jimmy Croft works there and he thinks it's good,' Jack muttered.

'Jimmy Croft'd say anything to impress you, and you're fool enough to believe him. He don't tell you about the injuries they have there. Worst record on the Island.'

Ellen remembered something she had heard. 'Someone at work was saying that her brother got work at that new place near the school – you know, where they make compasses and things for ships. She said they pay well, too. Her brother's getting seven and six a week and he's only fifteen.'

'Coo.' Jack brightened. 'Seven and six! Sounds good. What d'you think, eh, Mum? Dad? I could try there. I could ask.'

'It ain't fair,' Daisy moaned. 'I wish I could leave school.'

They were interrupted by a knock at the door, and Harry clumped into the kitchen. He brought the distinctive smell of boats with him, a curious mixture of salt, hemp and bilgewater. Ellen's heart missed a beat. She stared very hard at the empty soup bowl.

''Lo, all. Am I intruding?'

'No, no, of course not. You're always welcome,' Martha said. 'Come in, sit down. Cup of tea?'

It was a luxury for her to be able to offer tea. Being washday, the range was alight.

'Thanks.'

Ellen studied him covertly from beneath her lashes. As he sat and chatted to the others about work and the weather, she took in his broad shoulders and capable hands, the wiry hair on his chest just visible where his top shirt button was undone. He was growing more handsome as he got older, his wide cheekbones and the firm set to his chin becoming more pronounced, a contrast to his fair curls. A sudden need gripped her, an urge to reach out and touch him, so strong that she had to clasp her hands together in her lap, her nails digging into her palms.

'You'll be fourteen soon, won't you?' he said to Jack. 'Any idea what you're going to do when you leave school?'

The discussion of Jack's future began all over again, without really getting anywhere.

'So you ain't decided yet?'

'No, not really,' Jack admitted.

'How about being a lighterman?'

Longing lit Jack's eyes, only to be suppressed. He sighed.

'You got to be apprenticed to someone for that, ain't you? It was all right for you, your uncle took you on. No lightermen in our family.'

'I'd take you on.'

Jack looked at him warily, afraid to believe in case it was only a joke.

'Really?'

His mother and father were both staring at Harry with hope plain in their faces. The whole family seemed to hold its breath. If it could just be true, if Harry was serious, it would be a turning point in their fortunes.

'Really.'

'Honest? No kidding?'

'Honest. That's what I come to ask. I'm a freeman now, I can take on an apprentice. I thought you might be just the lad for the job.'

Tom leaned across the table and wrung Harry's hand.

'You're a good neighbour, Harry Turner. A good neighbour and a good friend. It'd be the best start the boy could hope to have.'

Tears were standing in Martha's eyes. 'You don't know what this'll mean to us. It's wonderful, just wonderful. I can't hardly believe it.' She gave her son a push on the shoulder. 'Go on, Jack, say thank you. You're a very lucky boy, you are.'

Jack swallowed. He was bright red with excitement. ''You,' he gulped.

'It'll be hard work, mind,' Harry warned him. 'It's not all fun and games. You'll be out in all weathers, you'll sometimes have to work nights or start at five in the morning, and there's so much to learn you'll never know it all.'

'I don't mind. I'll like it, honest,' Jack assured him.

Harry stayed for a while longer, answering questions, telling Jack about what he could expect. When he rose to go, Tom stood up too and gripped his shoulder.

'Thanks again, mate. It's the best thing that's happened to us for a long time. I'm beholden to you for this.'

Harry brushed aside any suggestion of an obligation. 'It's nothing, Mr Johnson. Your Jack's a bright boy and there's a lot I'd do for your family. A lot.'

For a moment his eyes rested on Ellen, only to flick away as hers met them. He was ushered out with the gratitude of the whole family ringing in his ears.

A few days after his fourteenth birthday, Jack was scrubbed and brushed, dressed in clothes acquired by much scrimping and sent off with Harry to Watermen's Hall to be apprenticed. The day after, he started work. He survived the inevitable teasing and practical jokes and took to life on the water like the proverbial duck. Being apprenticed to Harry did not necessarily mean that he always worked under him. Sometimes he was set to rowing the freemen out to their barges or taking the foreman from one wharf to another; sometimes he was mate to whoever needed an extra hand. But Harry often figured in his animated accounts of each day's work. Harry's sayings were repeated as holy writ, his odd words of praise treasured. Ellen listened, taking it all in and trying not to let on that the mention of his name made her stomach tie itself in knots.

Summer crept over the city, and as usual the water supply became unreliable and the river stank. The soft-fruit season meant hours of overtime in temperatures of over a hundred as the currants and berries were jammed and bottled. Ellen came home exhausted each evening, with only a shilling or two extra money at the end of the week as compensation for the twelve- or thirteen-hour days. She had no energy for going out with the other girls, but sat on the front step reading while the children played in the street and the mothers gossiped. She was sitting there one Friday when Gerry came by with a handcart.

''Evening, Ellen.'

She looked up, still living inside the story.

'Mm?'

A group of boys were gathering round the cart, begging to be allowed to play with it. Gerry chased them off.

'I got a favour to ask you,' he said.

'Oh?'

Reluctantly, Ellen put a finger on the page to keep her place and gave him her attention. She had been wary of Gerry ever since the time he had asked her out. She liked him as a friend but had no interest in being anything closer.

Around her, she could feel the sharpening of interest up and down the street. The two women nearest to her stopped even pretending to talk to each other and unashamedly listened.

'Yeah. You see, I got a bit of a problem. There's this place closing down over Newham way and they're selling stuff off, real good stuff, just what I want, but I got to get there tomorrow before it all goes. So I got to have someone to mind the stall for me. I thought of you. You're good with numbers, ain't you? And I know you wouldn't cheat me.'

The prospect of working in the open air, of feeling the sun, talking to people, not being under the eye of the forewoman, was unbearably tempting.

'I got to go and do overtime tomorrow. It's the fruit. We're doing the blackcurrants.'

'I'll pay you better than what Maconochie's do. Three bob for the day. How does that sound to you?'

Ellen gulped. 'Three shillings!' It was a fortune.

Gerry misunderstood her. 'Well, all right, seeing as it's you and I know I can rely on you, three-and-six.'

That clinched it. As long as he understood that this was strictly business.

'You're on,' she said. 'What time do I start?'

The market was wonderful. They set out at the crack of dawn to haul the stock down three flights of stairs from the tiny room Gerry rented off Chrisp Street, and went back and forth with the handcart to his stall. Then it all had to be set out artistically. She enjoyed doing that, and Gerry

215

seemed more than pleased with her efforts. He ran through the prices with her, gave her a money apron, told her all the dodges she was to look out for, then left her in charge.

'Not sure when I'll be back, but it'll be in time to help you pack up. Best of luck!'

'Thanks, and to you.'

She loved the noise and the backchat, the smell of fruit and foreign sausages from the neighbouring stalls, the colour and the ever changing flow of humanity. She developed a line of patter, enjoying persuading people that they really did want the things that they had only stopped to look at. Most of all she liked the responsibility. She was in charge, and it was up to her to sell as much as she could. And if she wanted to sit down and have a cup of tea or chat to someone she knew, then it was entirely up to her. No sergeant major of a forewoman came bearing down on her, demanding to know what she thought she was doing.

By late afternoon the money apron was getting satisfyingly heavy. Mostly it was coppers, but there were odd shillings and half-crowns in there as well. Ellen was tired, but it was not the draining exhaustion of a day doing the same thing over and over again in soaring temperatures. She pottered around replacing things that had been sold, trying to remember just how many of each she had got rid of.

'So it is true, then?'

Ellen started and whirled round. There was Harry, standing staring at her with undisguised anger.

'What's true?' she countered, immediately on

216

the defensive.

'That you're working for Gerry. I didn't believe them when they told me.'

'Why ever not? What's wrong with me working for Gerry? It's a whole lot better than slaving in that factory, I can tell you.'

'So you've given up Maconochie's, have you? Gerry's your boss now?'

'No, of course not. It's just for today.' She could not understand why he was being so aggressive. 'And anyway,' she said, straightening up and thrusting her fists onto her hips, 'what business is it of yours? I can work for who I like. I don't have to ask your permission, thank you very much.'

He ignored this. 'So it's not permanent?' he persisted.

'Might be. D'you want to make something of it?'

'Somebody ought to.'

'Look' – she could not believe this – 'if I want to do a day's work for Gerry, I can, right? I'm helping a neighbour out of a hole and earning myself a bob or two into the bargain. I don't know what you're getting so hot under the collar about.'

He was silent, holding her eyes as if trying to see past the words to what she really meant.

'As long as it's just for today.'

His physical presence made her throat dry and her heart flutter. She wanted to submit, to agree that working for Gerry was foolish, to see his hard gaze soften into a smile. But pride kept her defying him.

'Whether it's today or the rest of my life, it's none of your business, Harry Turner.'

'We'll see about that,' he said, and strode off

into the crowd.

'The cheek! The blooming cheek of it!' she said out loud.

She found her hands were shaking. It spread to her knees. She pulled out the rickety stool from under the stall and sat down.

The woman from the next pitch came over and put a sympathetic arm around her shoulders.

'Your brother, is he?' she asked. 'Think they can run your life for you, don't they?'

'No, no, he's' – she sought to describe the relationship – 'he's a sort of brother-in-law. His sister's married to my brother.'

The woman shrugged. 'So what's he doing up here telling you what to do?' Then she chuckled. 'Here – he must fancy you. Lucky girl! Nice, he is. I'd go for him if I was twenty years younger. I like a man with a nice set of muscles. Mind you, young Gerry's not going to like it much, is he?'

'Like what?'

'You going out with that other feller.'

'But it's none of Gerry's business, either.'

'Oh.' The woman was perplexed. 'I thought you was – so Gerry's some relation of yours, is he?'

'No, he's no relation at all.'

'So he *is* your young man?'

'No, he's just a neighbour.'

'Ah.' A customer was waiting to buy some apples. The stallholder moved over to serve her. 'Well, dearie,' she said over her shoulder to Ellen, 'I suppose you know what you're doing.'

It was at that point Eller noticed a cup was missing from the display. While she and Harry had been arguing, someone had stolen it. Anger welled up again, flooding the churning confusion that Harry had left behind. She held on to it, fed it. Anger was easy and clean-cut; it did not raise difficult questions.

'It's all your fault, Harry Turner,' she muttered out loud. 'Everything was all right till you came along.'

The fun had gone out of the day. She was glad when Gerry reappeared, full of news of his day's dealings and eager to hear how she had got on. He was delighted with her sales, dismissing the stolen cup as one of the hazards of stallholding. She did not tell him the circumstances under which it went. She was called upon to admire the goods he had bought, and together they served the last customers and finally packed everything away and carried it back up to the storeroom.

'That's what I call a good day's work,' Gerry said.

'Yes,' Ellen agreed. She just wished she did not keep hearing Harry's objections over and over again in her head.

The effect of the day did not stop there. When she got to work on Monday, her story of illness on Saturday was patently disbelieved. At the end of the soft-fruit season, the casual workers were laid off, and Ellen along with them. She was judged to be unreliable.

Ellen was horrified. Much as she hated the place, the family needed her income. All the way home, she tried to find words to explain to her parents what had happened. Nothing was good enough. Whichever way she put it, she had got the sack. They would be right back to where they had been before Jack started work, just managing to scrape a living. With all the others who had been laid off also looking for work, jobs would be hard to find. It was going to be back to bread and marge and no hot water again until she managed to find something. She dreaded the look on her mother's face when she told her.

'Well, that's their loss,' Gerry said, when she complained that one day working for him had lost her her job. He did not sound very concerned. In fact, he could hardly hide his satisfaction.

'It's all very well for you to say that. I got no money coming in at the end of the week,' Ellen told him. She had been saving up to get the beds back. Now that would have to wait.

Gerry tried to look worried. He sighed and frowned. Then his face changed.

'I know!' he exclaimed, as if he had only just thought of it, 'why don't you come and work for me full-time? With you doing the stalls and me doing the travelling and the buying, I could really get somewhere with the business.'

'Oh!' The thought of getting out of factory work was overwhelmingly tempting. Even in the winter, even on days when it poured with rain or there was snow on the ground, the market was better than the grind of doing the same small process a thousand times a day. But she hesitated. There was the problem of Gerry himself – and Harry.

'Do you – er – do you think it'd work, like you being the boss and me being paid?' she asked.

'Work? We'd be the best! It worked Saturday, didn't it?'

'Yes.'

But Harry had not liked it.

Harry would have to lump it. She thrust aside the image of him demanding to know whether the job was permanent. He had no right to say what she could do.

'All right,' she said.

Gerry was delighted. His face broke into a massive grin. 'You will? Smackeroo! We'll be a great success, you and me.'

Ellen ignored the warning voice inside that told her there was more to this than a working relationship. She needed the money, the job was better than anything else she could hope to get, and she was not going to let Harry Turner dictate to her.

'You bet,' she said. 'When do I start?'

She saw and heard the rumour and the speculation spreading up and down the street during the next few days. And just to confirm it, her mother gave her a warning. Gerry was all right, he was a decent sort, but Ellen must be careful. She did not like the thought of the two of them in each other's pockets all day long. Ellen shrugged off the gossip and assured her mother that it was just a job, and anyway Gerry was not with her a lot of the time. She was not sure herself what he did, but he was out and around chasing after deals.

'Well, I trust you to be a sensible girl,' Martha said, though she still did not sound too happy.

It was not the neighbours or her mother's suspicion that worried her. For all of the first week she was in a state of nerves expecting Harry to turn up at any minute. She was angry with herself for caring so much about what he thought, and even more angry when she was disappointed

221

by his not appearing. She told herself that it did not matter. But when she saw him waiting at the tram stop on the West Ferry Road, her insides turned to water.

He was waiting for her. He stepped forward and put out a hand to help her down. Once she was on the pavement, he did not let go.

'I'd like a word with you,' he said.

Ellen tried hard to appear indifferent. 'All right. Just don't take too long, will you? My mum'll have my tea ready.'

'We'll go down by the river,' Harry told her.

They both maintained an obstinate silence as they walked down the narrow streets. Anger, resentment and something close to fear was winding up inside Ellen with every step. Of one thing she was certain, she was not giving in to any browbeating.

From a dank alleyway between the high cliffs of warehouses, they emerged on to the riverside. The tide was low, so only the host of smaller craft were moving in the slight evening breeze. The sun, not setting yet but getting low in the sky, lit the water and the grey flanks of the mudbanks with pale gold. But neither of them had eyes for the peaceful scene.

'So?' Ellen said, springing to the attack. 'What's all this about, then?'

'You know perfectly well what it's about. You working for Gerry Billingham, that's what. You told me it was just one day, to help out a neighbour.' He was keeping his voice reasonable, making her sound shrill and aggressive.

'It was – then.'

'And now it's changed?'

'No, I'm just working for him all the time, that's all. And anyway, what is it to you?'

'I don't like seeing you giving up a perfectly good job to work for someone like Gerry.'

That did it.

'Perfectly good job, you call it? I call it a blooming awful job. I hated it. And what's wrong with working for Gerry, I'd like to ask? Gerry's a good bloke, and he's paying me more than what blooming Maconochie's ever did.'

Anger and suspicion tightened in Harry's face. He leaned forward until he was nearly touching her.

'Is he? What for? What's he expecting for this money, then?'

Ellen felt as if she had been kicked in the stomach. So that was it. That was what he thought. Fury at the injustice of it boiled up and erupted in a scream of protest.

'If you mean what I think you mean by that, you can blooming well take it back. What sort of a girl do you think I am?'

'I thought I knew. Now I'm not so sure.'

'Well, I'll tell you what I'm sure about. I'm sure it's none of your business. What I do is up to me. You got no right to come telling me what I can or can't do. Who do you think you are?'

He ignored this. 'I'm only thinking of your own good. Do you know what people are saying in the street?'

'I don't blooming well care.'

For several nerve-stretching seconds they stood just inches apart, breathing heavily, glaring at each other, Harry trying to get her to back down, Ellen defying him. When he spoke, it was with deadly quiet control.

'So it's true, then. They're right when they wonder just what you and Gerry do all day.'

She gasped. She was too hurt and angry now to consider what she was saying.

'If that's what you think, Harry Turner, you go ahead and think it.'

In answer, he reached out and pulled her roughly to him. Ellen tried to resist but she was no match for his strength. His mouth covered hers in a long hard kiss that melted her bones, sending her spinning into a timeless, placeless realm of ecstasy. She was left swaying, breathless, disorientated.

Then he let her go.

'Goodbye, Ellen,' he said, and walked rapidly away without once looking back.

Union membership was at a low ebb. Will found himself recruited into going to meetings with his father, who was trying to rouse the men out of their apathy. It was heavy going. The men could not see that joining the union would do them any good. At times it was painful. They simply did not want to listen. Seeing his father growing desperate, Will was moved to jump up and help him. They made a successful impromptu double act.

For several days afterwards he basked in the afterglow, hearing his father describe how he took the meeting in hand and turned it round, how men had joined because of what he had said. They both of them conveniently forgot the scores who walked away unmoved. He saw pride in his mother's eyes as she listened.

'A real chip off the old block,' she said, hugging his shoulders.

He tried to describe to Maisie what had happened. She looked at him anxiously. She could see it meant a lot to him, but she did not understand.

'Oh,' she said, 'that was nice.'

'It wasn't nice, not nice, it was...' He could not put it into words. He had no way to describe that glimpse of power he had seen.

Maisie bit her lip. The two toddlers were yelling for their tea and the new baby was crying. She found it difficult to concentrate at the best of times.

'I'm sure it was lovely,' she tried. 'If it's what you want.'

He gave up. It was no use talking to her. She had no idea. 'Tea ready, then?' he asked.

With relief she turned to the range. This she could do. 'Yeah, yeah, it's just coming. You sit down, I'll get the plates.'

A week later, his father told him there was another meeting. They were hoping to get support from men in other docks. If even a small group of union men could be formed in each dock, that would make a basis for expansion. Eager now for a second taste of leadership, Will agreed to go, arranging to meet him there as his father was seeing the union leaders first.

'I'll tell them,' his father said. 'I'll tell them my son's coming.'

Will was just walking up the West Ferry Road

when he spotted Siobhan at the tram stop.

She looked breathtaking. With the money she earned from singing in pubs, she had more than the other girls to spend on herself, and it all went on clothes. Now she was wearing a primrose-coloured dress that stood out against the brick and cobble and dust like some exotic flower on a rubbish heap. On her head was a confection of a straw hat with flowers on it, and beneath its brim her cornflower eyes danced in her sweet round face. She was fresh and young and beautiful. She stopped him in his tracks.

He stood staring at her. The man who had addressed a crowd of dockers and swayed them with his words was gone. He was as tongue-tied as a fourteen-year-old. He just waited, desperately hoping that she would notice him, and in noticing, smile. He never knew where he was with Siobhan, though he was well aware that she only looked at him when she had nothing else to do. All the men at Morton's were wild for her. Rumour had it that one of the foremen had asked her out. But she never stayed with any of them for long.

She was gazing along the road, watching for the tram, detached from her grubby surroundings, a different species from the other people at the stop or the passers-by in the street. She made him feel gross, ugly, dirty.

And then she saw him. Her eyes flicked over him, bringing him out in a sweat of longing. Miracle of miracles, she smiled.

Will stepped forward as if pulled by strings. 'Hullo, Siobhan. Not at work?'

She looked down at herself, then around at the

busy street. 'No, I don't think I am.'

He went hot. He hated it when she mocked him. He tried not to let it show.

'Where are you off to, then?'

She smiled up at him, teasing. 'Now that'd be telling, wouldn't it?'

There was an air of barely suppressed excitement about her. She was fair buzzing with it, it made her whole body vibrate.

'It's something special. I can tell.'

'Well, who's the clever one, then?'

Men passing by in the street stopped to look at her. Delivery drivers whistled.

'You shouldn't be going alone, wherever it is,' he said. 'You need someone with you to look after you.'

'Is that so? And I suppose you think it should be you?'

A wonderful possibility opened up in front of him. 'Yes,' he said.

'And what makes you think I'd agree?'

'Because you know I'd protect you.'

A McDougal's van trotted by. The driver flourished his whip. 'Wotcher, darling! Coming my way?'

Siobhan ignored him.

'You see? You do need someone with you.'

The tram was approaching, the two horses straining against the heavy load. Will flagged it down and Siobhan jumped on to the platform. She turned to look down at him.

'You coming, then?' she said.

He was beside her in an instant.

It was only as they passed by the western end of

the docks that he remembered he was supposed to be going to the meeting. But with Siobhan sitting beside him, almost touching him, the meeting did not seem to matter.

She would not tell him where she was going. She kept him guessing, would not say whether he was close or not. They left the tram and caught a bus, Will saying goodbye to the last of his money without a second thought, and finally got off by a small theatre crammed between the shops in the Commercial Road.

Siobhan's excitement had turned to nervous tension. She scanned the red and gold sign outside. *Sullivan's Musical Theatre* it declared.

'I think I need the stage door,' she said. The usual confidence had gone out of her voice.

'So...' Light dawned for Will. 'You're going to do it, then? Go on the stage? I always said you should.'

'I'm going for an audition,' she told him.

'Stage door'll be round the side.' Will took charge, grasped her elbow, propelled her along the filthy alley between Sullivan's and the next building and opened the peeling door. It was so dark inside after the sunny street that neither of them could see.

'We're closed,' came an unwelcoming voice out of the gloom.

'Miss Siobhan O'Donaghue, come for an audition,' Will said loudly.

As his eyes adjusted, he saw an ancient man peering at them from a cubbyhole by the door.

'Another one of 'em. Never learn,' he muttered, whether to himself or to them, Will did not know.

228

He gestured impatiently at the interior of the building. 'Go on up there. Up the stairs, turn left, turn right, second door.'

'Thanking ye kindly,' Siobhan said, but for once her charm failed. The man merely grunted and retreated into his lair.

Naked gaslights showed the way along twisting corridors and up dusty stairs. Their footsteps tapped hollowly on the bare boards. Following the old man's instructions, they found themselves in what felt like a large space, though there were high partitions in front of them and a clutter of ropes, while around their feet were weights and boxes. Strong artificial light flooded through a gap.

Then quite near to them, a piano chord was struck. Will felt Siobhan jump and catch her breath. Just the other side of what Will now realized was a wood and canvas stage flat, a man's voice broke into a patter routine.

'We're backstage,' Siobhan breathed.

Her hands were pressed tightly together beneath her lips, her expression rapt as she listened to the unseen performer. He was nervous. He stumbled over words and lost his place. Without an audience to shout back in the right places, the whole thing sounded feeble. Painfully, he launched into a song that was supposed to follow on with the theme of the routine.

'You can do better than that,' Will whispered in her ear.

She did not answer him.

The song came to an end, dropping into the great dark void beyond the stage. There was a moment or two of silence, then a bored, faintly

Irish voice sounded. 'Right, thanks. We'll let you know. Next!'

Behind them, a door opened.

'Hey, you.'

Siobhan jumped and gasped. Will had never seen her look so unsure. They both turned round to see a harassed-looking young man with a large notebook in his hand standing in the doorway.

'What are you doing here?'

Siobhan took a deep breath. Then she switched on her sweetest smile. 'Sure and I was waiting just to see you.'

Will saw the young man fall beneath her charm; he grew flustered and shifted his notebook from one hand to the other.

'And you are...?'

'Miss Siobhan O'Donaghue and this' – a wave in Will's direction – 'is my brother.'

Will caught breath to protest, but was stopped by a freezing look from Siobhan. The young man nodded at him and turned back to Siobhan.

'Delighted to make your acquaintance, Miss O'Donaghue. Teddy Perkins, assistant stage manager. If you'll just follow me, I'll show you where you ought to be.'

Will realized now why he had been allowed to come along. She wanted it to be known that she was available, but protected. That way she could play the field with safety. And since he himself had said that he ought to look after her, he had brought it upon himself.

Together they followed Teddy Perkins round the back of the stage and into a small room where a dozen or so hopeful artistes were waiting. They were all smoking heavily and eyeing one another. Some evidently knew each other, for they were talking together in loud, confident voices about theatres and fellow performers. Siobhan's new conquest scribbled in his notebook and found her a rickety chair.

'If you'd just sit here, Miss O'Donaghue, I'll see that it won't be too long before you're called. Have you got your music?'

She nodded, and fished into her bag to produce a sheaf of sheet music. As she held it out to him, her hand shook. He thanked her and hurried out, leaving them both to the scrutiny of the other occupants of the room.

A woman with impossibly yellow hair and a brightly painted face smiled at Siobhan. 'This your first audition, dearie?' Her voice was cheerfully throaty.

Siobhan swallowed. 'Of course not.'

She did not sound at all convincing.

The woman laughed. 'Go on, dearie, pull the other one. I wasn't born yesterday, even if you was. You want more than a pretty face to get on in this business, you know. You got to have talent, and you got to work hard, bleedin' hard.'

'I know what hard work is,' Siobhan told her.

'And she's got talent,' Will put in.

'You better watch her, then, mate,' one of the men warned sourly. 'Old Mick Sullivan's got an eye for a pretty little girl.'

'What man ain't?' another woman said. 'More than one way to get on if you're young.'

Everyone had something discouraging to say. Siobhan just sat there trying to look vaguely uninterested, though Will could see by the stiffness of her shoulders that their remarks were getting to her. They were all either younger than he was or on the wrong side of forty, Will noticed. He guessed that Sullivan's was a place for hopefuls or those on their way down.

The painted women was called. The moment the door closed on her, the others discussed her past record. General opinion was that she would fail, since every management in London knew she drank and was unreliable. She reappeared some ten minutes later, calling Mick Sullivan every name under the sun. Then a small man in a checked suit and red tie was called. He did not come back.

'Jimmy's in, then,' someone commented as Teddy Perkins put his head round the door.

'Miss O'Donaghue.'

There was a rumble of annoyance from the others, which Siobhan ignored. Will followed as she swept out.

In the wings, Teddy gave her some hasty instructions. 'Mr Sullivan's up in the dress circle, so look up there. Tell him who you are and what you're going to do. Sing up, and try to imagine there's rows of people out there just dying to see you.'

Siobhan nodded. She was ashen. Even her head was trembling with nerves.

'Pinch your cheeks to bring out the colour,' Teddy advised.

Teeth clenched, she did so. She looked a fraction better.

'Take a deep breath and walk on holding it. That makes your eyes sparkle.'

Her breasts lifted as she took his advice. Will watched her with longing as she stepped out on to the brightly lit stage.

She walked almost to the centre front, moving stiffly like a Dutch doll come to life. She curtseyed to the unseen theatre manager.

'Name?' came a disembodied voice from the darkness.

'Siobhan O'Donaghue. "Waiting At The Church,"' she said, and nodded to the pianist in the pit. Will could hear the shake in her voice.

An opening phrase from the piano and she launched into the song, mercifully hitting the first note correctly. At first she was wobbly, but with every line she gained confidence until she was well into the part, inviting laughter and sympathy from the imaginary audience. Her gestures were a little stiff and her projection weak in places, but Will did not notice. To him, she was a star. He had to stop himself from breaking into rapturous applause as she finished. Giving Mick Sullivan no chance to stop her, she went straight on with 'The Mountains of Mourne'. In direct contrast to the first song, she stood quite still and simply let her clear voice soar into the cavernous space of the empty theatre. Just as she had that first time he heard her at the Harp of Erin, she held Will enchanted.

The last notes died into a profound silence. Then out of the hollow body of the theatre came the manager's voice.

'What did you say your name was?'

'Siobhan O'Donaghue.'

'Right, Miss O'Donaghue, I think we might

233

find a little spot for you. Come up here and see my stage manager.'

She accepted it as nothing less than her due, not even thanking him, and walked smoothly off stage. But once in the wings, the pose crumbled.

'I did it!' she squealed.

Will flung his arms round her and gave her a kiss. 'You were wonderful. Congratulations! I knew you would.'

Teddy Perkins was hovering with his notebook. He showed them where to go and instructed them not to take the first offer, since they always underpaid new artistes. The details of Siobhan's first appearance were arranged, and in a short time they emerged, blinking, into the alleyway by the stage door.

Siobhan looked up into Will's face. She was glowing with the thrill of achievement.

'Isn't it wonderful? I'm going to sing in a real theatre.'

'It's where you should be,' Will told her.

He drew her into his arms and kissed her, properly this time. She responded with a fervour she had never shown before, holding nothing back. Her whole body was buzzing with excitement. He could feel it as she pressed against him, the throb of success pulsing through her veins and transferring itself to him. He kissed her mouth, her neck, the base of her throat and she laughed and shivered with pleasure.

'Siobhan, Siobhan, you're so beautiful, so lovely. You're going to be top of the bill.'

She smiled her contented cat's smile.

'I know,' she said.

7

They took up the front of the circle, a solid wall of supporters. Will was there, along with Harry and the Billinghams and every other young man from Trinidad Street. Some of the older ones were there too, with their wives, and all the O'Donaghues over the age of fifteen, together with their cousins and their partners.

It was a hot evening, and even though Sullivan's was not full the air was thick and soupy. Throughout the auditorium women were already fanning themselves with handkerchiefs and men were mopping streaming faces. Cigarette smoke wafted up from the stalls, along with the smell of cheap scent and sweating bodies. The Trinidad Street contingent ate oranges and sweets and shouted up and down the rows at each other, loud in their sense of owning part of the show. Siobhan was theirs and they were here to tell the world.

'Don't think much of this place,' Harry commented, looking round the theatre. 'Very second-rate, if you ask me. Wooden benches – you wouldn't get people at the Gattis or the Old Vic putting up with wooden benches. And look at the state of the paintwork. They haven't done that over in years. The only thing they've taken any trouble over is the stage, and that's not too wonderful, either.'

'You know all about it, then?' Charlie said.

'I know a decent theatre when I see one,' Harry told him. 'And this ain't it.'

Theresa O'Donaghue, sitting on the other side of Charlie, brightened up considerably at this.

'It's not much of a place, then?' she asked hopefully.

'It's a blooming dump,' Harry told her.

Charlie, annoyed at being talked across, turned his shoulder to Harry and started to talk to Theresa, who became quite animated now that she felt a point had been scored over her hated cousin.

'Pity your mum wouldn't come,' Harry said to Gerry.

'Yeah.' Gerry gave a sigh. 'I tried, but she wouldn't. Said she couldn't face a music hall. Said it'd remind her too much of Ernie.'

'Does she still miss him?'

'Yeah. She tries not to show it, but I reckon she does. He was a good bloke, was Ernie.'

Down in the pit, a lone fiddle was tuning up. Then an accordion sounded a preliminary chord. The piano was swelled to an orchestra of three for the performance. There were a few ragged cheers from the audience, and shouts of 'Get on with it!'

The house lights dimmed, the trio struck up a jolly tune and there were whistles and catcalls from the audience, along with half-hearted applause. Along the row, Clodagh O'Donaghue pursed her lips in disapproval.

'This is a rough place,' she muttered to Brian. 'I don't like it. I don't like the thought of her on the stage at all. It ain't right for a nice young girl, standing up there having all the world stare at her. Wouldn't be quite so bad if it was a res-

236

pectable theatre. But this!' Words failed her, but her expression told just what she thought.

The master of ceremonies swept on to the stage, cheeks red above a luxuriant moustache. He launched into his patter, ignoring some of the hecklers and picking up on others and turning their comments to his advantage. With the skill of an old trouper, he quietened most of the rowdy element and drew them together in expectation of a brilliant show. By the time he introduced the first act, most of them were willing to clap.

The dusty gold curtains were drawn back to reveal a crudely painted backdrop of a row of shops. On to the stage bounced a small man in baggy trousers and a crooked top hat stuck with a comical red flower that nodded with every movement of his head.

''Ello, 'ello, 'ello!' he cried, his voice projecting easily over the noise and the space.

They knew this one.

''Ello, 'ello, 'ello!' some shouted back. The comedian swept off his topper and waved to them.

But others called, 'Goodbye, goodbye, goodbye!' and laughed loudly at their own wit.

Bravely he carried on, singing a short song, telling a couple of jokes and finishing with a chorus. About half of the audience joined in.

Clodagh was incensed. 'I'm not having her up there in front of this lot, nice young girl like her. What'd her mother say if she found out? It's not right.'

'Can't stop it now,' Brian pointed out.

'I'll tell you something, this is the first and last time. Crafty little madam, getting this fixed up behind my back. It won't happen again.'

Brian grunted in agreement. It was no use arguing with his wife, and in any case, he was with her on this. It was all right watching other women up on the stage, but it wasn't the sort of thing you wanted your own flesh and blood doing.

A juggling act came on next, two men in yellow satin breeches and a woman in a matching dress that showed her legs up to her knees. The men in the audience whistled in appreciation. They did not care about the skill of the spinning balls and clubs, they were fully occupied with ogling those shapely calves. The act was a success.

'Disgusting,' said Clodagh.

A man dressed as a policeman marched on and sang about all the sights he saw walking on the beat. His voice failed on a top note.

'Boo!' Charlie called out. 'Get him off!'

The cry was taken up. Soon the man couldn't be heard at all. Desperately, he carried on, sweat pouring down his face. In an act of mercy, the curtains closed. The audience bayed in triumph.

'Good riddance. I hate coppers,' Charlie said. He was really enjoying himself. This was just his sort of entertainment.

The master of ceremonies had a hard time quietening them down. They had tasted blood and they wanted more. Gradually they subsided under his torrent of words, until they were halfway ready to listen.

'And now, a lovely little lady to sing for you. With a voice like a thrush and a face like a flower, all the way from Mother Ireland just for you, let's have a big hand for – Miss Siobhan O'Donaghue!'

The front circle erupted into cheers and applause. The trio played a catchy little tune as the curtains opened. This time the backdrop was columns and flowers. On to the stage stepped Siobhan, a picture of fresh innocence in a huge hat trimmed with flowers and a pale green dress cut just short enough to give an occasional flash of ankle as she moved. The Trinidad Street contingent clapped even more vigorously.

She stood centre front and sent a brilliant smile up at the circle. The trio played a few bars of introduction and she launched into her song, a sweet little ditty in which a girl promises to be true to her sailor sweetheart while he's away. As she reached the chorus, she held up a picture frame and gazed at it, inviting the audience's sympathy.

'All I've got is his little photograph,
Cannot hear his voice
Cannot see him laugh...'

She was beginning to get to them. The catcalls were dying down, and they were listening.

Then came a little dance with the picture held in both hands at arm's length, and another chorus. The audience was starting to join in now that they had picked up the words. Loudly the piano started on a repeat. Not expecting it, Siobhan started in a little late, but hardly anyone noticed. After a long chord to finish, and a sweeping curtsey from Siobhan, her followers in the circle stood up and stamped and cheered and clapped. Less enthusiastically, the rest of the theatre joined in.

'More, more, more!' shouted her supporters.

But the curtains stayed closed and the master of ceremonies reappeared. Siobhan had made her debut.

In his seat in the third row of the circle, Sidney Spruce, theatrical agent, sat back with a pleasurable feeling of excitement. He was not deceived by the cheering just in front of him. He was no fool, he knew the local supporters when he saw them. But the girl he had just seen had talent. She needed plenty of training to use it properly, training that he would be able to see to. She had looks and charm, and a freshness to interest even a jaded palate such as his. Best of all, she was young and, as far as he could ascertain, had no links with the entertainment business. Professionally, he scented a potential money-spinner, which he needed right at the moment, since two of his better clients had recently deserted him for more prestigious agents, while another had only yesterday got himself arrested for assaulting a policeman whilst under the influence of alcohol. It had come just at the wrong time, when his wife was demanding a move to a better house. Which brought him to the personal level. He liked very young, untried girls. They made a pleasant change from the hard-bitten women he usually dealt with, artistes who had trodden the boards for years and had seen all that the world had to throw at them. They made an even pleasanter change from his wife and her constant demands for more and better material comforts. He rolled the image of the girl before his eyes again – the sweet soaring voice, the lovely little face, the delectable figure – and thanked whatever providence had guided him to come to Sullivan's this evening.

He slipped out of his seat and clambered over complaining bodies to the safety of the aisle. In the gents' toilets he preened in front of the smeary mirror. An astute face looked back at him, full-lipped, once almost handsome but now running to seed, with bags under the eyes and the first red threads surfacing on the nose. But his hair was still thick and dark, though receding a little, giving him widow's peaks. He combed it carefully, straightened his bow tie, hitched his jacket up on his narrow shoulders and looked at the full effect. Not bad. Good enough to impress a green young hopeful with stars in her eyes, if past experience was anything to go by. He set off to find someone to fetch her for him.

He waited outside the women's dressing room while young Teddy Perkins went to bring her out. He did not want any of the old troupers warning her about him. When she emerged, he knew that instinct had been right. She was even more stunning close up.

'Miss O'Donaghue?'

'Yes?' She looked him up and down with just a quick flick of the eyes, but took it all in. Her expression remained neutral. She had not placed him straight away.

'Sidney Spruce, theatrical agent. Quite a nice little performance you gave.'

She looked distinctly offended at that. She was obviously a rank amateur, used to the admiration of her family circle.

'Sure and that's kind of you,' she said, with sarcasm.

'You're stiff and your voice needs much more projection and you've no idea of how to handle an audience, but with a lot of polish, you could make something of yourself,' he told her, watching her get more annoyed with every word.

She tossed her head at him, her lovely mouth drooping into a delicious pout.

'I don't need to stand here listening to you. I've people waiting for me.'

So she did not cave in at criticism. So much the better, for she was going to need to be tough.

Spruce gave a shrug. 'Well, if you're happy to play the odd spot at a third-rate venue like this every few months, that's up to you. I only represent professionals, and the best ones at that. Been nice talking to you, Miss – er. Good evening.'

He had hardly taken three steps before she called out. He ignored her, and just as he knew she would, she ran after him.

'Wait, Mr Spruce.'

Her hand was on his arm and she was looking up at him with huge blue eyes, her lips parted. He felt a tug of desire, but kept it well hidden. Now was definitely not the moment.

'Yes?' he said.

'You're an agent? You get work for singers?'

'Singers, yes, and dancers, comics, novelty acts.'

'Could you get work for me?'

'I might. Depends how willing you are to do what I tell you.'

'Oh, I am. I want to be a singer. I want to work in the theatre.'

'Very well.' He pretended to relent, and produced one of his cards. 'Come along and see me sometime and I'll give you a try-out.'

'Oh thank ye, Mr Spruce.' With excitement, her accent became stronger. Then she slid him a sideways glance. 'Ye'll not regret it,' she told him.

She was going to be fun, this one.

Sidney Spruce walked out into the foyer with a spring in his step. Mick Sullivan was there, talking to the box office clerk.

'Wotcher, Sidney. Found anything you like?'

Spruce shook his head in wonderment. 'I don't know how you keep open, Mike. How do you get them in off the streets? You got nothing out there but a bunch of has-beens and amateurs.'

He left Sullivan snorting with annoyance.

Two to four days, he guessed. He was right. She turned up at his office the third day after he saw her perform. He was on the telephone at the time, his newly installed and very expensive toy. He waved her into a seat and carried on talking, taking care not to even glance at her again.

'Right, well, I'll tell you this, you've got a first-rate novelty act there. You ain't never seen nothing like it. When them girls all get on that bicycle, it's a sight for sore eyes. Have 'em coming back for more, night after night, you will. You'll have 'em? Right. You'll not regret it, I tell you. Now, of course, they don't come cheap...'

Buoyed up by the prospect of what was to come, he got an extra half-a-crown out of the man. Then he hung the earpiece on the hook and swung round on his swivel chair to look at her.

'Well now, it's Miss – er?'

'O'Donaghue. You saw me at Sullivan's. You said to come and see you.'

'Oh yes, of course. The little singer. Well, I don't like to disappoint you, my dear, but I think I might have been a bit hasty the other day. I do have rather a lot of singers on my books. All good girls, nice voices and pretty faces, and all looking for work. I'm not sure whether I can really take any more on. Not with things the way they are at the moment.'

'Oh.' Her face fell. 'But you said–'

'I know, I know – trouble with me is, I'm too soft-hearted. Get carried away. But it's a tough business, this. You got to have more than looks and a voice. You got to stand out from the crowd, got to have that something extra. I'm not so sure whether you got what it takes.'

'I have. I know I have.' She jumped up and leant over his cluttered desk. 'Just try me, Mr Spruce. What would you like me to do? Sing? Dance?'

Sidney's mind ran swiftly over half a dozen things he would like her to do. It brought him out in a sweat of anticipation.

'Let's start with a song,' he said, going over to the piano.

He went through the motions, listening, criticizing.

'Open up a bit. Smile! That's it. Turn your shoulder a bit and look sideways, invite them, flirt a little – that's better – now take a handful of skirt and swing it, show a bit of ankle–'

She learnt fast. And she had it – there was no doubt about it – that ability to lead a man into thinking she might just offer him everything. It just needed bringing out. Combined with that freshness and seeming innocence, she could be a knock-out. He almost decided it was worth for-going the personal pleasure and the risk of scaring her off in order to make sure he got her on his books. But then he looked at her once more, at the glimpse of ankle, the slim waist, the full breasts, and his need grew into a pressing pain. He had been looking forward to this for three days now.

He moved to the sofa that filled a large part of the small office, sat back and patted the seat beside him.

'Come and sit down and let's have a little talk,' he invited.

A certain wariness entered her face, but she came, and placed herself at the far end of the sofa.

'Now then,' he said, keeping his voice friendly, almost fatherly. 'Like I said, you're a nice little singer. With my help, you could make a first-rate artiste. If you're prepared to learn from me, do everything I say.'

She nodded, her eyes fixed on his face. She was sitting bolt upright, her hands folded defensively in front of her. He controlled the urge to reach out and put a hand on her knee.

'What did you say your Christian name was?'

'Siobhan.'

'Siobhan – Siobhan...' He rolled it round his mouth. 'Pretty name. Nice. I like it. Tell me a bit about yourself, Siobhan. How old are you? Where do you come from?'

She told him about her family in Ireland, why she had come to England, of her family on the Isle of Dogs – plenty of them, he noted, so she was not alone and unprotected – and her work at Morton's, as well as her singing experience. She became animated, losing her defensive stiffness. Every now and again Sidney put in the odd question, and found that there was no particular young man in her life, nor was she looking to marry yet. By the time she finished, he had a good picture of her background. Except for the army of cousins down on Dog Island, she was ideal.

'All very interesting,' he said. 'Only trouble is, there's lots of girls like you trying to get on the stage. I get dozens of 'em in here every week. I got plenty on my books already. Now, you got talent. With the right training, I could get you work. Thing is, are you going to play ball with me?'

'Sure and I will, Mr Spruce. Didn't I say that? I really want to go on the stage. I want it real bad.'

'That's good,' Sidney said. He moved along the sofa and put a hand on her thigh. She drew in her breath, but did not push him away. 'That's really good. Because, you see, if you want to be one of my girls, the first thing you got to learn is how to please me.'

He slid one arm round her waist, the other round her shoulders, and drew her towards him. She resisted him, anger and obstinacy in her face.

'And what exactly do ye mean by that?' she demanded.

Sidney smiled at her. 'I think you know what I mean.'

He kissed her then, long and hard, forcing her to open her mouth, thrilling to the feel of her breasts against his chest.

246

She pulled away, trying to lean back from him. 'That's enough.'

He looked her straight in the eyes, and said with slow emphasis, 'Siobhan, do you want to go back to work at Morton's for the rest of your days and always be poor, always live in a crowded house, never have anything nice to wear? Or do you want to stand up in the spotlight and have beautiful dresses and hear people clapping and cheering you because they love you? Which do you want, Siobhan?'

She stared back at him. Gradually anger softened into acceptance, and then a knowing light came into her eyes and a smile tugged at her lips.

'You know what I want,' she said.

'Good,' Sidney said. 'Now we both understand each other.'

He kissed her again, and this time she responded, putting her arms round him and kissing him with an expertise that sent his expectations soaring. He pulled her on to his lap, almost groaning with the pleasure of her buttocks on his legs, her soft thigh against his hardness. He cupped her breast with his hand, fondling until he could feel the nipple through the thin fabric. He kissed her throat and found her pulse was racing in time with his. He was torn in an agony of choice, wanting to prolong the pleasure, to spin it out, to experience every step, and yet wanting to have her now. He reached round expertly to undo the tiny buttons all down her back, then slid his hand inside to touch the silky skin above the armour of her corset. A shiver ran across her, and he knew it was not of revulsion. He pulled the dress down just a little, exposing one shoulder, then put his mouth to it, revelling in the taste and scent of her, working down to the top of her breast.

'Ah, Siobhan,' he breathed, 'you're a lovely girl, you are. I think we're going to get on just fine together.'

Reaching down, he gathered up her skirt and explored up her leg, negotiating the maze of petticoats with the skill of a man who has found his way there many times before. His fingers slid over stockings and garters, found warm bare skin and caressed the soft flesh of her inside thigh, and felt her give and open up to his touch.

Then her hand came down on his arm and she pulled abruptly away from him.

'I'm thinking that's far enough,' she said, smoothing the dress back into place on her shoulder with fingers that trembled.

'And I'm thinking we've hardly started,' he told her. He was seized with an overwhelming anger. He turned, tipping her off his lap and on to her back on the sofa, then rolled beside her to hold her down with his weight. He grasped her wrists and pinned them to the arm of the sofa.

'On stage you can tease them as much as you like – promise it all and never give nothing away. But not here, d'you understand? I don't like teasers and I don't play games. You want to be top of the bill – well, this is where it starts.'

Still holding her wrists with one hand, he pulled up her skirts with the other, reached inside her drawers and kneaded and caressed her belly and thighs until she stopped resisting and

248

relaxed and opened to him once more.

'That's right, that's nice,' he whispered. 'You're going to enjoy this. It's going to be the best you ever had.'

He let go of her hands and kissed her as he slid his fingers between her legs. She stiffened at first, but as he gently explored the velvety creases she began to quiver and gasp with pleasure, pressing up to meet him and whimpering with disappointment when he stopped.

'All right, my darling, just hold on. Let's do this properly,' he said, throwing off his jacket and tossing away his tie. 'Let's get this pretty dress off, shall we? Don't want to spoil it.' She sat up to let him pull it over her head, and he drew breath at the sight of her, half-naked and rosy in her underclothes. He undid his trousers and freed himself with a groan of relief, then released the one button that held her drawers, and slowly roused her to moans of desire. He rolled on top of her, seeking an entrance, almost unbearably excited.

'Please,' she whispered, and there was fear in her voice, 'please – I haven't – I never...'

'It's the first time?'

'Yes.' She sounded almost ashamed.

They all said that.

'Don't worry,' he told her. 'This is going to be the most beautiful thing you've ever done.'

He eased into her, gently at first, as she cried out and shrank back in the cushions. He disregarded that. They all liked you to think they were virgins. Desire took over, gripping him with need and pleasure. He thrust into her, hardly noticing her cries of pain, driving harder as her nails dug into his back. Then she began to move beneath him, meeting him with a mounting urgency, until he erupted ecstatically.

She was sobbing and trembling when he drifted reluctantly back to reality. In love with all the world now, he kissed away the tears.

'There now,' he said, his voice husky with satisfaction. 'Didn't I tell you it would be the best you ever had?'

'I – didn't know – it was – like that,' she said.

'Ah well, you're with an expert now. I told you I could teach you a lot, didn't I?'

He shifted to take his weight off her while still staying inside, and talked on contentedly about all he could do for her both in bed and on the stage, until the need for a cigarette impinged on him, together with the realization that there was still business to be done today. He sat up with his back to her and began getting into his clothes.

'Here we are,' he said, handing her her dress. 'Best get moving. Nice to stay here all afternoon, but I got a living to earn. Perhaps we can arrange it better next time.'

'Next time?' she echoed, in a small voice.

He did up all the little buttons for her and gave her bottom a friendly pat.

'Oh yes. You passed the audition all right. I'm going to start looking for bookings for you right away.'

'Oh.' She straightened her hair as best she could at the glass on the wall. Not looking at him, she said, 'It's just – it's a sin, don't you know.'

'Catholic, are you?'

She nodded.

He'd had plenty of them before. All the guilt and the hand-wringing. It was all a lot of rubbish.

'Oh well, you'll have to go to confession, won't you? Nothing to it. Give the old priest a thrill, eh? Do a few Hail Marys or what-have-you and Bob's your uncle, good as new.'

She did not look convinced. He opened the door for her.

'Come back next Wednesday and we'll work on your act, and I'll see a few managers. I know some who owe me a favour. We'll get you up there in the spotlight before you can say box office.'

It was only after she had gone that he noticed the blood on the sofa cushions. So she had not been acting. She was a virgin, or had been until half an hour ago. His satisfaction was complete.

Ellen stood by the stall, wrapping a set of tumblers.

'Look lovely on your dresser, they will,' she said, holding one up to the light before deftly swathing it in newspaper. 'How about a jug to go with them? We got them to match. See? Pretty, ain't it? Got them same oranges painted all round the top. Nice to have the set while you're about it. They're the last. We won't be having no more after these are sold.'

The customer hesitated, turning the jug this way and that while Ellen packed the glasses into her bag. Glancing into the crowd ambling by, she caught sight of Harry. He was standing in the middle of the road with his back to her and there were people milling in between, but Ellen recognized him just by the set of his shoulders.

251

She watched him, unable to tear her eyes away. He was obviously waiting for someone, for there was an air of ill-contained impatience about him. As if drawn by the intensity of her gaze, he turned, and their eyes met. Ellen felt a hot blush rising up her neck and over her cheeks, much to her embarrassment. She nodded at him, stretching a bright smile over her face. It was essential to act normally. After all, they were neighbours.

'Wotcher, Harry. Lovely day,' she called.

''Afternoon, Ellen.' He strolled over.

'I dunno,' the customer was saying. 'I got a jug already. Don't really need no more.'

With difficulty, Ellen switched her attention back.

'But you ain't got one to match, have you?' she pointed out. 'All the nobs up the West End have 'em to match. Water sets, they're called.'

'Oh–' The woman considered the jug once more, indecision showing in her face.

Ellen could feel Harry's presence. It sent butterflies chasing round her stomach.

'Tell you what,' she said. 'I'll knock tuppence off, seeing as you bought the glasses. How about that?'

Satisfied, the customer paid up. Ellen wrapped her purchase and sent her on her way.

'Busy today?' Harry asked.

'Middling. Lots of people, but they're just out for the afternoon. They're not all buying.'

His curly hair was blond from the summer sun and his face tanned, making his eyes seem very blue. For the thousandth time, Ellen regretted the silly quarrel that had made them almost strangers. But she could not back down. She enjoyed this job.

'You enjoy this job, don't you?' he said.

She gaped at him. It was as if he could read her mind. 'Yes,' she managed to say, 'yes, I do.'

'Better than Maconochie's?'

'A million times better,' she agreed.

'And you're good at it, too. I can see that.'

She almost said that Gerry seemed more than pleased with her, but thought better of it.

'Thanks.'

A girl of about her own age came pushing through the crowd, carrying a string bag bulging with potatoes and lettuces. She looked Ellen up and down, trying to place her, then slid her arm possessively through Harry's and gave it a squeeze.

'Got them. That'll keep Mum happy. All I got to buy now is the cheese. Mum likes to go to Smith's.'

Harry stood his ground. 'Yeah, in a minute.'

The girl looked at Ellen again, suspicion tightening her face. 'Friends, are you?' she asked.

'Ellen lives down our street,' Harry explained.

'Oh.' The girl relaxed. 'I'm Vi. Harry and me've been walking out for three weeks. I expect you've known him a bit longer than that.'

'All my life,' Ellen told her. Jealousy clawed at her. Vi was a pretty girl, round and fair, with a dimple that she consciously used when looking at Harry. Ellen's hands twitched. She very much wanted to pull Vi's hair, to wipe that superior air of possession off her silly face.

Vi giggled. 'You must know all sorts of dreadful things about him.'

'Hundreds.'

But she was not giving anything away to this stupid creature. A word from her wide reading came to her: *simpering*. Vi was a simpering miss.

Someone stopped and asked about plates. Almost relieved, Ellen turned her attention away. Yet when Harry bade her goodbye, she felt as if a piece of her had gone with him.

It was halfway through the evening before she got home, but the street was still busy. Being Saturday night, nearly all the unmarried young people were out, and most of the men and some of their wives had gone to the pub, but the young mothers and the elderly and the children were enjoying the fresher air after the hot day. Ellen greeted neighbours as she walked wearily home, and kissed her mother, who was sitting on a kitchen chair outside the front door.

'Had a good day, lovey? You must be tired. There's some tea left for you. I'll get it.'

Ellen put a hand on her shoulder to stop her getting up. 'You'll do no such thing. You sit there and I'll make you a cup and bring it out.'

She washed the day's dust and grime off herself, ate the pie and peas her mother had saved for her, then carried two cups of tea outside and sat on the step drinking it while her mother filled her in on all the latest news about what was going on.

'Maisie's expecting again. Come and told me this morning, she did. Mind you, it wasn't a surprise to me. I suspected it a couple of weeks ago. Tears all over the place. I don't know how she's going to cope. She can't manage now. That little Tommy, he's getting to be a proper little terror.

She don't know how lucky she is, having all healthy babies like that. Next one'll probably be just the same. I'd of loved a bigger family.'

Ellen put a hand on her knee. They both thought of the last little boy, the one she had so dearly wanted.

'Tommy's all right with me,' Ellen said. 'And Florrie. He minds what we say.'

'Well, there you are, then. It's just her. Weak as water.' Martha vented her sorrow on Maisie, listing her inadequacies for some time before conceding that she did try to be a good wife to Will, then going on to the next subject.

'That Theresa O'Donaghue went by a while back, all done up to the nines. Must be going out with some lad.'

'I suppose so. I never heard nothing about it, though. If there is someone, it's a big secret.'

'Yeah. That's true. I ain't heard nothing, neither. Perhaps she's just seeing a bunch of her girl-friends.'

'Mm.' Ellen thought about it. 'She must be. If she was going out with a bloke, she'd want to show off about it, would Theresa.'

She sipped her tea and half listened to her mother, trying to let her body relax after the strenuous day. Usually she found it soothing to sit and hear about everything that was going on, to pass the occasional comment and watch the children playing, but this evening was different. She kept seeing that girl Vi standing holding Harry's arm as if she owned him.

'...very quiet today. You're not sickening for something, are you?'

'No, no. I'm all right. Just tired, that's all.'

'That's the trouble with this job of yours. I know you like it a lot better than Maconochie's, and you get paid better, but it ain't right, young girl like you, working till this hour of a Saturday and too tired to go out and enjoy yourself. You ought to be off walking with a young man. Not that I want to get rid of you, mind. It's nice having you here to talk to. But it ain't natural. All the other girls are out on a nice evening like this. You ought to be parading up and down in you best dress with Florrie Turner.' She hesitated, then added carefully, 'I always thought you and Harry Turner might get together. He seemed very interested in you at one time. Look at the way he got you to carry on with your reading. There's not one man in a thousand would do that.'

It was true. She owed Harry a lot. If *only* she had not had that row with him.

'Yeah, well, I saw him today, up the market. With some girl called Vi.'

'Oh, her.' Martha's tone was scathing. 'You know who she is, don't you? One of them Cades from down Manilla Street. Common lot, they are. Not Harry Turner's type at all. Do you know...' She went on at length about the shortcomings of Vi's family. But somehow it did not make Ellen feel any better. They would be more than glad to get a catch like a Freeman of the Company of Watermen.

The evening faded into darkness and the air grew chilly. Ellen and Martha went in. Daisy came home, arm in arm with a friend and giggling fit to burst, Jack arrived from roaming about with his pals, and Tom from a political meeting in Poplar.

'Found Archie Turner at the corner of the street,' Tom said. 'Dead drunk again. Me and Bill Croft had to carry him home.'

'Oh dear.' Martha looked worried. 'Do you think I ought to just pop across?'

'I shouldn't bother. Spark out, he is. Won't be no trouble to them.'

'All the same, I think I better.'

'I'll go,' Ellen volunteered, and was out of the house before anyone could argue with her.

She slipped across the street and tapped on the Turners' door. 'Hullo? It's me, Ellen.'

There was muttering on the other side, then the door opened. Florrie stood there, as pale and thin as ever. The approach of womanhood had given her hardly any extra curves, just made her face look rather more in tune with her years. Ellen glanced past her into the dimly lit room.

'You all right?' she asked.

'Yeah, yeah. Just listen to him.' There was a world of contempt in her voice.

Ellen listened. Gurgling snores were issuing from somewhere behind her friend, along with the smell of alcohol.

'Bleeding pig,' Florrie said. 'Thanks for coming, though.'

Ellen was about to turn away when she caught sight of Harry coming round the corner. He saw her and broke into a run.

'What's up?' he called from halfway down the street. 'Is he...?'

'No, no, it's all right,' Ellen called back. 'Don't worry.'

Harry stopped by her side on the doorstep. He seemed very large and solid and vibrantly alive.

'He's dead to the world. Mr Johnson and Mr Croft got him home,' Florrie told him.

'Pity,' Harry commented. 'They should've left him where he was.'

'I just come over to make sure,' Ellen explained.

He reached out to squeeze her arm, turning her bones to jelly. But as he moved, a faint whiff of cheap scent came from him. All the jealousy of the afternoon surged back.

'That was real kind of you, Ellen. I appreciate that,' he was saying.

She hardly heard it through the bitterness.

'Don't mention it,' she managed to say, shrugging him off. 'I was only being neighbourly. Hope you had a nice evening. 'Bye.'

She stalked off across the street and let herself into her own home, banging the door behind her.

8

Trinidad Street woke late on a Sunday. The devout amongst the Catholics at the Irish end went to early Mass. The Nonconformists went to their services a little later. But the vast majority, who expected the Church to be there only when they wanted to be married or buried, looked on Sunday as what God intended it for – a day of rest. They needed it, after the labours of the week.

Ellen was the only one up to hear the knock at the door. She had given up trying to sleep and instead had heated some water and washed her hair. Now it hung down her back in a shining brown curtain. She put down her brush and went to answer the door.

On the step was Harry.

He was the last person Ellen expected to see at that hour of the morning. She stood and gaped at him, speechless.

''Morning, Ellen. I came to thank you properly for looking in on my family last night.'

'Oh.' She could not stay angry with him, not when he was standing there with his white smile and his blue eyes. 'That's all right. It was nothing.'

'It meant a lot to me. Can I come in?'

'Er – yeah. Yeah, of course. Come on. I'll put the kettle on.'

She could feel his eyes on her as she moved around, making the tea. It made her clumsy. She tripped on a chair leg and twice nearly dropped things. She was acutely conscious of the fact that she was wearing an old patched blouse and faded skirt, both still damp in places from when she had washed her hair. Why couldn't he come when she was looking nice?

'Is everything all right over at your place this morning?' she asked, carrying the teapot to the table with extra care.

'So far. He's still asleep. He'll be in a foul mood when he gets up, but with a bit of luck he'll be feeling too ill to do much more than lie around groaning. We'll just keep out of his way.'

Ellen nodded. It was not easy keeping out of

anyone's way in these tiny houses.

'Good thing it's a nice morning,' she said.

She sat down opposite him, cradling her cup in her hands and avoided his eyes.

'I bought this for you,' Harry said.

He reached across and placed a little object wrapped in white paper in front of her.

'Oh.' At first she could only stare at it. 'But – what's this for?'

He shrugged. 'Just everything. Aren't you going to open it?'

She picked it up. It was hard and bumpy. Bubbles of excitement began to stir inside her. She glanced up at Harry, smiling, and found that he was smiling back at her, enjoying her surprise. Slowly, prolonging the pleasure, she unwrapped the scrap of paper.

There between her shaking fingers was a brooch, a butterfly about an inch across in a silvery metal with sparkling stones in its wings.

'It's beautiful,' she breathed. 'Just beautiful. But why?'

'Put it on,' Harry said.

She pinned it to her blouse, where it rose and fell with her breathing, like a live thing. She stroked it with her finger.

'It's the prettiest thing I've ever had.'

'I saw it yesterday, at the market, and I knew it was right for you,' Harry explained.

Yesterday, at the market, when he was with that Vi Cade. Her heart twisted in a complex tangle of jealousy and hope.

'Oh yeah?'

'Yeah. It was then that I realized Vi wasn't in

the same class as you. I gave her the old heave-ho last night.'

'Did you now?'

She felt strangely breathless. She fought to keep a huge grin from spreading all over her face.

'I've known it all along, really. There's something about you that makes girls like Vi, and even Siobhan, look – fast, cheap.'

She managed to pretend offence. 'You mean I'm boring?'

'No, not at all. They're boring. There's nothing much to them. But you – I've known you all my life but you still surprise me.'

Ellen fingered the brooch again, watching the stones sparkle as she moved it.

'Like going to work for Gerry, you mean?'

He burst into laughter. 'All right, you win. I was wrong about you and Gerry. He's a good bloke, is Gerry. Wouldn't take advantage of a girl.'

'He asked me if I'd go out with him, but I said no,' Ellen told him. 'I like him as a friend, but not anything else. I told him, if we got to work together, that's how it's going to be.'

Harry reached across the table and covered her small hand with his large one.

'That's that settled. So how about coming down the Island Gardens with me this afternoon, then?'

It took a moment or two for it to sink in. When it did, a great warm wave of joy swept through her. She wanted to jump up, to sing and dance around the room. But with an acting ability worthy of Siobhan, she simply shrugged.

'Yeah, all right. Might as well. Might be quite nice.'

After he had gone, she sang and danced and hugged herself.

Island Gardens, at the very end of the great bend in the Thames that formed the Isle of Dogs, was crowded with people out to enjoy the Sunday afternoon sunshine. The grass was yellowing and worn from hundreds of feet and the trees had a tired, late-summer look to them, but after the drab grey of the factories and the terraced houses, it was a little oasis of green in a leafless brick desert.

Ellen and Harry sat on a bench facing the river and the Greenwich shore opposite. The glorious panorama of the Royal Naval College lay before them, with its classical symmetry of colonnades and twin-domed towers, between which could be seen the white perfection of the Queen's House. Rising up behind the buildings in great steps of grassland and avenues of trees was Greenwich Park, topped by the Royal Observatory.

'Some chap back in history called it "Bella Vista",' Harry said. 'That means beautiful view.'

'He was right there,' Ellen said.

She listened as Harry pointed out the various buildings, sometimes adding comments of her own. They watched the river traffic going by, the pleasure steamers coming and going from Greenwich Pier, the other visitors to the Gardens as they strolled past, everyone done up in their Sunday best. They ate ice cream from the hokey-pokey man. But most of all they talked – of their shared past, of the present, but avoiding the future – until the sun began to dip and the shadows grew long. Harry stood and held out a hand to pull Ellen up, tucking her hand under his arm to keep her close by his side.

'We'll come back next week,' he decided. 'If your mum agrees, we could go over to Greenwich and have a picnic in the park. What do you think of that?'

Ellen thought it was the most wonderful idea in the world.

'Oh...' For a moment she was almost lost for words.

'Don't you think you'll be able to?'

'Yeah – no – I mean, I'm sure my mum'll let me.' She looked across to the park once more. 'Do you know, when I was a little girl, I used to think that Heaven must be like Greenwich Park.'

And it truly would be like Heaven on earth to go there with him.

He smiled down at her. 'I hope it won't be a disappointment, then.'

'Oh no, I'm sure it won't. It will be wonderful. A picnic! I ain't had a picnic for – well, I can't remember. Must've been when I was ten or eleven. Yeah, eleven, when we went to Epping with the Sunday school. That was lovely, but going to Greenwich will be–' She broke off, not wanting him to think she was being forward, like Siobhan or Vi Cade.

'Just you and me, eh? For the day. That's my idea of Heaven.' He touched her cheek with his fingers.

She stood gazing up at him, drowning in his words. 'Me too.'

They caught the Penny Puffer back to North Millwall, sitting jammed together on the dusty bench seat. The carriage was crowded with screaming children, harassed mothers, other courting couples. The air that blew in was hot and laden with smoke. Ellen was intensely aware of Harry there beside her, his arm and his thigh pressed against hers. There was an excitement building between them that grew with the clatter and vibration of the train, quickening Ellen's breath and pulsing through her body. Harry's foot brushed against hers, sending the nerves quivering all the way up her leg. Of one accord, their hands moved to clasp together and his thumb caressed her palm, slowly, sensuously. All the while they spoke together, making stilted remarks about the drab landscape through which they were passing, another conversation altogether was taking place between them, an unspoken need and antici-pation. By the time they got to their station, the tension was almost unbearable.

They walked along the dirty streets, silent now, not needing to talk, Ellen's arm tucked securely under Harry's arm, his long stride shortened to match hers.

They took a short cut through an alleyway. The dank darkness between the tall warehouses was friendly and welcoming after the brassy glare of the street. Harry stopped and folded Ellen into his arms. She sighed with overwhelming pleas-ure. It felt so right, her body close to his, as if her whole life had been leading up to this moment. She raised her face. Her eyes closed as his lips met hers, tender and gentle, kissing her slowly and with infinite skill until she hardly knew who or where she was. Their mouths parted briefly to look with dazed wonder into each other's eyes, before meeting once more with growing strength and urgency, probing and tasting, straining ever closer. Ellen was melting, spinning into a dizzying void where time and place had no meaning and there was only the two of them and this shining newfound joy in each other.

Harry held her head between his hands, tracing along her cheekbones with his thumbs. He smiled down into her eyes.

'Ellen Johnson, you are a most surprising girl,' he said.

'I am?'

'You are too. I always knew you had warmth. What I didn't know was you had – fire.'

Of their own accord, her lips curved into a knowing smile, but she said nothing, just reached up to kiss him again.

For she had not known it herself, until that hour.

It did not take long for the news to get to Gerry. It was up and down the street that very afternoon. Harry Turner and Ellen Johnson had gone off down the Island Gardens together.

He felt sick.

He had always thought that working together would bring them closer. Despite what Ellen had said about it being strictly business, he nursed the belief that one day she would come to see him in a different light. All that he did, all his ambitions, were now centred on her. Where once he had worked to get away from the spectre of poverty, now it was for a neat house, nice furniture, a bunch of kids – and Ellen.

Charlie came slouching into the kitchen to eat before going out for the evening.

'Saw Ellen Johnson and Harry Turner coming along,' he said, leering at Gerry. 'You been well and truly cut out there, bruv. Couldn't get a knife between 'em.'

Gerry said nothing.

'Yeah, you should've got in while you had the chance,' Charlie went on, watching to see the effect his words were having. 'All this time you've had her there working for you. You should've made a move. Easy, no Mum there watching what you 'n' her's getting up to, nice lock-up to take her to. Couldn't be better. You could've had her any time you wanted. Too late now, though. Old Harry's got in there first.'

Gerry tried to shrug it off. 'Wasn't interested. I just pay her to mind my stall. Anyway, she's not that sort of girl.'

Charlie gave his suggestive laugh. 'Go on! They're all that sort of girl once they get going. Quiet ones are the best. You take my word for it, bruv. Best of all are the religious ones. Phew! Get a religious girl and you're made.'

'You best be careful her mum don't find out, then,' Gerry said.

But Charlie was enjoying himself. 'You ever had a virgin? You're not a proper man till you have. Now Ellen Johnson, she's a virgin. Nice girl, brought up proper, too busy minding her family to play around with the boys. Mind you, bet she won't be by the time Harry Turner's had a try at her.'

Gerry stood up. There was a pounding in his ears, a sick jealousy and hatred boiling in his guts. If he did not go out right now, he was going to throw up or hit his brother.

'I'm going down the Puncheon for a drink,' he said.

Charlie's crude laughter pursued him through the door.

At the O'Donaghues', in a back bedroom drenched with the exotic heady scent of florist's roses, Siobhan was holding court.

'...So then I sang my new song and they went wild. Clapping and stamping, they were, and calling out for more. And I curtseyed and I kissed my hands to them – like this – and then the curtain came down, but still they were shouting. They wouldn't stop. I was coming off, but the stage manager, he came rushing out from the wings.

'"Go back," he hisses at me, "go back and give 'em an encore, or they'll tear the place apart."

'So back I go, and the band strikes up the introduction, and there's a great roar from the audience, and when the curtain went up again they were shouting so loud I couldn't start...'

Theresa choked back a scream and pulled her pillow over her head. She was lying with her back to her cousin, pretending to ignore her, but there was no escaping Siobhan. She was sitting up in bed, bright and bursting with life despite a late night, waving her arms about as she talked. Sixteen-year-old Mary sprawled across the foot of the bed, drinking it all in, while little Bridget bounced up and down, caught up in the excitement of the tale. Theresa could not bear it. It was nothing but Siobhan, Siobhan, Siobhan. If she wasn't there herself, they were all talking about her. If Theresa went out anywhere, people did not ask how she was doing, they wanted to hear about Siobhan. She wasn't anything herself, she was just Siobhan's cousin.

'...When I got back to the dressing room, there was this great big basket of roses...'

'Ooh, wonderful.' Mary groaned in vicarious pleasure. 'Who was it from? Who sent it?'

Siobhan grinned. 'Look at the card,' she said.

'Get the card,' Mary told Bridget. The little girl frisked across the room and fetched it. Mary groaned again. *'From a devoted admirer,'* she read aloud.

Theresa could take it no longer. She flung away the pillow and sat up.

'For crying out loud!' she screamed. 'Can't you shut your face? Don't you never talk about no one but yourself? Me, me, me – that's all you ever say.'

Siobhan merely sat looking superior. She did not have to say anything; her loyal followers said it all for her.

'Shut your face y'self,' Mary retorted. 'You're just jealous, that's your trouble.'

'Yeah, you haven't got a basket of roses,' Bridget jeered. 'You're just an old sourpuss.'

'Oh, let her be,' Siobhan said, lazily magnanimous from her pinnacle of beauty and popularity. 'Poor thing. Twenty-two and not wed. Sure and 'tis hard when you're left on the shelf.'

'So who's left on the shelf?' Theresa exploded.

'You're only a few months younger than me and I don't hear no wedding bells ringing.'

Siobhan lay back against the rickety bedhead, a patronizing smile on her beautiful face.

'Ah, but I'm not busting me knickers to catch someone, am I? I'm biding me time. If I wanted to get wed, I could do it tomorrow. That's the difference.'

It was true. That was what twisted Theresa in an agony of jealousy. Siobhan could have anyone she liked, whereas *she* had only a secret on-and-off relationship with Charlie Billingham, and she would not even have that if she did not agree soon to do what he wanted.

Then with a spurt of malicious pleasure, she remembered that Siobhan did not have quite everyone she wanted.

'You can bide your time as much as you like, but you won't get Will Johnson unless Maisie dies. I can just see you taking on all his screaming brats,' she spat. Oh, the satisfaction of it.

'That's a wicked lie, so it is,' Mary said. 'Our Siobhan would never go with a married man.'

'That's right,' Bridget chimed in.

Siobhan merely shrugged. ''Tis all she can think of to say.'

Theresa was consumed with the desire to grab handfuls of that curling black hair and yank it out. She wanted to hear Siobhan cry out in pain and beg for mercy. She wanted to trample on her. But she had one more verbal weapon.

'And you haven't got Harry Turner, neither. He sees you for what you are. He's not interested.'

For just a second or two, Siobhan's face showed

a shadow of the frustration and longing that possessed Theresa. She seized on it.

'Everyone knows you'd like to have Harry Turner. But he hasn't never asked you out. Not once. He'd rather have Ellen Johnson. Just fancy, you being cut out by Ellen Johnson!'

'What do I want with Harry Turner?' Siobhan sniffed.

But Theresa knew that she was putting it on. 'I seen you looking at him. I saw the way you made up to him at the Coronation party.'

'Coronation party! That was years ago. I was only a kid then.'

'Yeah, years ago,' Theresa agreed. 'You wanted him all this time.'

It was the truth and they both knew it. But Siobhan was never going to admit to it.

'You're talking through your hat, so you are. Harry Turner! I'm not looking to live here all me life, you know. There's more to London than Dog Island, believe it or not.'

'Yeah, you never been anywhere. Siobhan has,' Mary said.

Her brief victory swept away, she could not help but rise to the taunt.

'That's a lie and all. My young man takes me all over. He takes me to music halls. And he buys me suppers.'

'Oh yeah? And who is this young man of yours, then?' Mary asked. 'We don't never see him. I don't think there is anyone. You're just making it up.'

'I am not! I just don't want all the old women in Trinidad Street eyeing him up, that's all. You don't keep nothing to yourself round here. You only got to cough and they're all talking about it. That's why I don't bring him back here.'

Mary gave a rude snort. 'I never heard nothing like it. What a load of old cods.'

'It's not! I have got someone!' Theresa screamed, rigid with rage. She hated all of them, hated her sisters for ganging up on her, hated Siobhan for everything. Nobody cared about her.

Siobhan was sitting looking at her with that infuriating superior smile. She waited till the row died down. Then she spoke.

'Prove it.'

There was a brief silence as all three sisters took this in.

'Yeah.' Mary took her up. 'Prove it. Go on. Bet you can't.'

''Course I can,' Theresa retaliated.

It was at that moment that she knew she would have to give in to Charlie. To hold out would be to lose not only him but the only rag of pride she had to clothe herself with. Without a man to boast about, she would be completely swamped by Siobhan.

Theresa managed to hang on to Charlie through the autumn, but she could never be sure of him from one week to the next. Because of the difference in their religions, it all had to be kept a deadly secret. She could never ask him to call for her, and when she went to meet him, he was always late.

That's how it was again one bleak November evening. She stood in the shelter of the shop doorway, trying to shrink right out of sight. She hated the way people stared at her as they walked by, summing her up. It made her feel like a prostitute.

''Evening, darling. All alone?' a passing young man called.

Theresa put her nose in the air and pointedly ignored him. The man laughed and went on.

A group of girls from the church club went by. Theresa flattened herself against the window, praying that they would not see her. But God was not listening to her today. He did not consent to be party to deceit.

'Oh, look, it's Treece. Wotcher, Treece! What you doing here?'

They all clustered round, some half-dozen of them.

'She's waiting for someone. Who're you waiting for, Theresa?'

'She's waiting for her fella, that's what. Who is it, Treece? Is he nice?'

Theresa could not resist that one. 'Yeah, he's ever so nice,' she said.

'He didn't ought to get you to meet him here. Why don't he come and pick you up at home?'

'Bet her mum don't like him, that's why.'

'Who is he, Theresa? Come on, you can tell us. We won't let on.'

But Theresa gave nothing away. Whatever they might promise, she could not trust them not to talk, and then she really would be in trouble. Her mum would never let her out again. As it was, she was taking a huge risk. These were the girls she had told her mother she was going out with this evening.

In the end, they got fed up with questioning her and made off, linking arms and talking loudly amongst themselves.

'Oh well, if she don't want to talk to us, that's her funeral.'

'Let her keep her silly secret. He's probably horrible, anyway.'

'Must be to treat her like that. I wouldn't wait around in the street for any boy, I wouldn't.'

Theresa glared after them. She touched the heavy gold cross that hung round her neck on its piece of string. Charlie had given her that. It was lovely, really heavy against her chest, an expensive gift, not some cheap bit of rubbish from the market. She brushed aside the memory of the manner in which he had given it to her, pulling it out of his pocket and flinging it down at her with one of his dismissive shrugs.

'Here, this is the sort of stuff your lot wears, ain't it? You best look after it. You ain't getting nothing else.'

It was just his way. He must love her really if he gave her something like that.

Harry Turner and Ellen Johnson drifted by arm in arm. There was no danger of their noticing her, they were too wrapped up in each other. Theresa watched them with envy. It was all right for Ellen, her mother liked Harry. She did not have to make up stories and wait in the street. Some people had all the luck. Still, it was good being able to get at Siobhan with the fact that Ellen had Harry. Siobhan hated it. She could pretend not to care, but Theresa knew she was sick about it. She hugged that thought to herself.

When Charlie finally turned up, the evening was half over.

'Had a bit of business to do,' was all he offered in explanation.

Theresa was so pleased just to see him that she did not protest. He was here – that was all that mattered. He was here and he was hers. He had given her an expensive present, so that even Siobhan looked impressed. Siobhan had been jealous of the cross. She did not have anything as nice as that.

Charlie forged up the street with his swift, stiff-legged walk, his hands in his pockets. Theresa had to almost trot to keep up. She threaded an arm through his and tried to slow him down.

'What's the hurry?' she asked. 'Where're we going? Somewhere nice?'

'I need a drink,' he said. He was all tense and excited about something. Theresa could feel it vibrating in the muscles of his arm, but she knew better than to ask him about it, especially if it had to do with his 'business'. Charlie never explained anything he did not want to.

They walked in this fashion for some way before turning in at a pub. They had been there several times before. Nobody from their way went in it, since it was practically in South Millwall, but Charlie could always find some mates hanging around there. Charlie ordered a pint with a whisky chaser, then, as an afterthought, a half of milk stout for Theresa. Theresa stared doubtfully into the thick black liquid. She was none too keen on milk stout. She watched as Charlie downed his pint and threw the chaser after it. He couldn't half drink, could Charlie. Nobody else in the bar was drinking anything as posh as whisky chasers. She forgot about the stout, fiercely glad just to be with Charlie, proud of the way he looked, with that swagger to him, even proud of the way he neglected her, leaving her alone at a table while he laughed and joked with the other men in the bar. After all, that was how a real man behaved. Later, she would have him all to herself. In the meantime, she wanted to grab people by the shoulder, to tell them that she was with Charlie Billingham, to see the respect in their eyes.

As an hour or so ticked by, she could see the tension drop away from him. He became loud and cheerful. Theresa's complacency began to fade. At this rate, the evening would be gone and she had hardly had anything of him. She waited for a lull and risked sidling up to him. She pulled at his sleeve.

'Charlie.'

He whipped round and stared at her as if he had forgotten her existence.

'Who...? Oh, Treece. What you want?'

'Charlie, we been here an awful long time, and my mum'll kill me if I'm back late. You know what she's like.'

Charlie gave a grimace. 'Old witch.'

But he drained his glass and banged it down on the bar, then put his arm round her, his hand sneaking under her arm and pinching her breast.

'Oi, I got to go now,' he shouted to his cronies. 'Me and my girl are going for a walk.'

Theresa blushed scarlet. Half of her was bursting with pride at being identified with him,

275

the other half curled with embarrassment at the loaded suggestiveness of Charlie's voice, the whistles from the other men.

They emerged into the dampness of the autumn night. A fog was beginning to drift in off the river, wrapping the streets in a shroud of grey.

'We better go somewhere a bit sheltered,' Charlie said. 'Bloody weather. I hate winter. Come on.'

He led the way back towards home along the muffled roads until they came to St Luke's. Theresa suppressed a surge of guilt. After all, it was not as if it was a proper church. It was only a Protestant one. They made for the porch, but it was already occupied. Trysting places were few once the summer was over. Cursing under his breath, Charlie dragged her round the churchyard, keeping close under the walls. The first alcove they came to was also taken up with a couple. After stumbling against gravestones, they found a place tucked under one of the buttresses.

'This'll do,' Charlie decided.

He backed her into the corner, leant the weight of his body against her and fastened his mouth on hers. Theresa returned his kiss with desperate eagerness. This was what she had been waiting for. Now she had him to herself. Nobody could distract him now, for she could give him what none of his pals could.

She stood with the rough stones of the wall digging into her back, her legs braced, pretending to enjoy it as he kneaded her breasts and bit her neck, his hips all the while thrusting at her until she could feel his hardness through the layers of her clothes. He struggled with her long skirt and petticoats, his rough fingers demanding against her soft vulnerable flesh, poking and rubbing. His breath was coming in harsh gasps, and she could hear him grunting and cursing with frustration.

'Sod it,' he hissed. 'Why do you have to wear so bloody much? I hate doing it standing up, you can't get it in proper. Come here.'

Taking her by the wrist he pulled her away from the wall and on to the wet grass. Stumbling, Theresa caught her shin against a gravestone and nearly cried out in pain. It was cold and rank-smelling amongst the close-packed graves, but Theresa knew better than to complain. She lay with the chill dew seeping through her shawl and blouse while Charlie thrust into her, waiting for that moment when he cried out then subsided on her, that moment when he always said he loved her. She moved with him as he had taught her to, her arms clasped about him, her eyes tightly shut, glad that it no longer hurt like it had at first. And then, swiftly, it was over, and he was collapsed on top of her, groaning now with pleasure.

Theresa stroked his head tenderly, every nerve straining to hear him whisper her reward.

Nothing.

Still she waited. His breathing was settling into a slow steady rhythm.

'Charlie?' she breathed in his ear. 'Charlie? Darling? You do love me, don't you, Charlie? Say you love me.'

The only reply was a low unmistakable snore.

Misery welled up from the core of her being. She did all this for him because she loved him.

She would give anything and everything just to keep him, but she had nothing but herself, so she gave him that. All she asked in return was the right to call him hers, and a kind word. She lay and sobbed while he slept and grew soft and slipped out of her.

High above them the clock struck the hour. Eleven. Charlie woke up.

Theresa was gripped with panic.

'Eleven! Oh no. Eleven! I thought it was only ten. Jesus, Mary and Joseph, my mum'll kill me. An hour late! She'll keep me in for a month. What am I going to do?'

'Oh, shut your row,' Charlie grumbled.

He got slowly to his feet and started doing up buttons while Theresa frantically sorted out her clothing, all the time gabbling about getting back.

'Come *on*,' she squealed, grabbing at his arm.

Charlie shook her off. 'If you're in such a hurry, you get going,' he said. 'I want to sit here and have a fag.'

Weeping with fear, Theresa hobbled in the direction of the gate. Her petticoats were still all caught up, her blouse half undone, her back soaked to the skin. She blundered into gravestones and twice nearly fell before reaching the road. Once there, she tried to pull herself together. It was dark and foggy, and she could hardly see five yards in front of her face. She took several long, shuddering breaths, did up the buttons and shook out her underwear. She felt very slightly better. She must not get lost. That would be fatal. Which way? Right. She must turn right for the quickest way home. She must remember exactly which street she was in. Still sobbing and whimpering, she put her hand against the wall to steady herself, and trotted into the thick night.

In any other circumstances, she would have been terrified of being knifed, beaten up or worse. But she was so frightened of being late, so taken up with what tale she was going to tell to her mother, that she hardly gave her present safety a thought. The roads seemed to go on for ever. It was like the nightmare where you run and run and get nowhere. From the river she could hear the horns and bells of ships, muffled or weirdly distorted by the fog, so that she could not tell which direction they were coming from.

Just as she had begun to think that she had got lost and was going to be out all night, she saw the bleary glow of light from a corner pub. Like a ship in a storm, she headed towards it. The Rum Puncheon – she had reached Trinidad Street. Relief hit her in the knees, so that her legs nearly crumpled under her.

She did not turn into the street straight away, for now she had to come out with an explanation, and nothing she had thought of so far was going to get past her mother's critical ears. The whole sorry evening flashed before her eyes: the long wait in the shop doorway, the jeers of her girl-friends, sitting in the pub, the performance in the churchyard ... her girlfriends. An inkling of a story came to her. A row – they had had a row. They had wanted to go in this pub but she had not and they had argued about it and she had run away and got lost in the fog. It was pretty feeble, but it would have to do. She had to say something. Her heart thudding in her chest, she ran down the street and in at her own door.

'And where do you think you've been, madam?'

Arms akimbo, her mother was waiting for her. Even in her nightgown with her hair in a plait, she was enough to make strong men quake, small and skinny as she was. She looked like an avenging angel.

'I – I – I'm sorry, Mam, I got lost. It's the fog. You should see it, Mam, it's a real pea-souper. I was so frightened, I couldn't see where I was and then I must've turned the wrong way, and I was all alone 'cos we had this row...' She gabbled on, tears running down her face, making very little sense.

Unimpressed, Clodagh reached out and turned her round, inspecting her back.

'What you done to yourself? You're wet through, and muddy.' She grasped Theresa by the forearms and peered into her face. 'What you been up to? You don't get wet like that walking in the fog.'

Guilt sent a deep blush all over her face. Theresa took refuge in tears. Her mother shook her until her head felt loose on her shoulders.

'That's enough of that! I want the truth out of you. And just you remember the Blessed Virgin is listening to every word you say.'

'There – there – there was this man. In the fog.' Out of nowhere, a feasible story came to her. 'Oh, Mam, it was horrible. He jumped out at me and I fought him, but I tripped and I fell and he had me on my back and there was this puddle, but I managed to get away and I ran and – oh

Mam, I was so glad to get home. I never been so frightened in my life.'

She worked her way into fresh tears, but this time her mother's arms went round her and she was held to her thin bosom and rocked and soothed and stroked like a baby.

'There, there, 'tis all right now, so it is. You're safe home with your own mam.'

Smothering the guilt with relief, she let herself be comforted until the weeping was just an occasional sob.

'Now then.' Her mother held her back a little and looked her in the eye. 'Tell me now, did he hurt you at all? Did he touch you?'

Theresa shook her head emphatically. 'No, no, he never. I got away.'

Clodagh heaved a great sigh. 'All the saints be thanked. Now away up to bed with you and I'll bring you some hot milk.'

And so she got away with it. Or so she thought.

9

Within a fortnight, merely being back an hour late and wet through seemed almost desirable to Theresa, in contrast to the problems that now confronted her.

She did not realize at first that she had been given the push. Charlie quite often stayed away for three or four days at a time. Even though they lived only a few doors away from each other, it was quite possible not to run into him, since they had different patterns to their days. Theresa got up early and worked all day, Charlie came and went at all hours. She still boasted to Siobhan at night about her mysterious young man who took her to wonderful places and bought her expensive presents.

Then he cut her dead in the street. Theresa stood stock-still and stared after him, a terrible cold fear creeping over her. It had happened, what she had lived in terror of all these weeks. He had gone off her. He had grown tired of the fuss she made about getting home on time at night.

'Charlie!' She snapped into action, propelled by overwhelming need. She must convince him that it wouldn't happen again. She was ready to promise anything. 'Charlie. What's up? What's the matter?' She grabbed him by the arm, her fingers clutching at him.

'Nothing.' He tried to get away.

She should have felt relieved, but she did not. There was a closed look about his face.

'When are we going out again, then? Saturday? It was all right last time. My mum never found out.'

She could feel the watching eyes of the street upon her. Within five minutes, one or other of the Irish women would be over at her house, asking her mother was she was doing talking to Charlie Billingham. Then her mother would be on at her about taking up with Protestants. If she got hold of anything like the truth, there would be the devil to pay. But her need to hold on to Charlie was too urgent for caution.

'I got something on Saturday,' Charlie said, and made to get away.

Theresa hung on to him. 'Sunday, then?' she begged recklessly. 'What you doing Sunday?'

'Dunno. I'm sort of tied up.'

'When, then? When we going to see each other?'

'I dunno. P'raps never. Let go, you silly cow. I got to go.'

He prised her fingers off him and strutted off. Theresa stood looking at his retreating back as grey misery slowly filled her.

Somehow she dragged herself through the next few days. It was made a hundred times worse by Siobhan, who sensed something was wrong and kept asking when she was going out with her wonderful man again and why he had left her high and dry on Saturday night and what he was going to buy for her next time. All this while she was getting herself all done up to go out singing or with her latest. Theresa had just enough energy left to save face with some feeble lies, sustained by the thin thread of hope that Charlie was just in a mood and it would all be better in a couple of days.

It was not. By the end of another week, she heard the latest gossip. He had been seen out with some girl from a couple of streets away, a Protestant. So there was no hope left. It was over.

It was all her mother's fault. If she had not been so fussy about who she was with and what time she had to be in, Charlie would not have gone. That was the trouble. It was not that he did not like her. She knew he loved her really. He had said so. She had the gold cross to prove it. She

283

held it tight between her hands so that it made a clear impression on her palms, for an even greater fear had now taken possession of her. He had to love her, for she needed him by her. She was late starting her period.

She had taken no notice at first. She was often three or four days over. But not a week. Never a week. It was too dreadful to contemplate. Each successive day she woke up, praying that today would bring the pain in her back and the blessed dark red stain, almost believing that it would, shutting her mind to the knowledge that it was not going to happen. The week stretched to five. She had to believe it. There was nothing to show, she was not sick, her clothes were if anything looser, since she was hardly eating, but she knew. Inside her was Charlie's baby.

Siobhan was getting ready for an appearance. Clodagh still violently disapproved, but she restricted her control to sending Patrick along as protector.

She sat on the bed they shared, peering into the tarnished mirror and brushing her black curls, and smiling at herself with that cat-that-got-the-cream expression.

Theresa felt physically sick with jealousy. Siobhan had everything – looks, dresses, talent and a lot more freedom than *she* was allowed. She could just imagine what would be said if *she* had wanted to go on the stage. Her mother would have locked her up for a month. She did not realize that her mother had recognized a will and a ruthlessness superior to her own – and seen that if she did not bend, then Siobhan would leave and be lost from their influence for ever.

'You're after looking like a month o' wet Sundays, you are,' Siobhan remarked. She began pinning her hair up, curl by curl, her fingers dexterously tucking each one into place. 'I've heard nothing about this fine young man o' yours lately. Taking you out tonight, is he?'

It was the last straw. Theresa flew at her, hitting and scratching, twining her fingers in that hateful hair and pulling out a satisfying handful. Siobhan screamed and fought back, with tongue as well as hands.

'You bitch! You jealous little bitch! You can't bear it, can you? With your skinny body and your sour face, no man'll ever look at you. You're so plain you turn the milk, you do.'

They rolled over on the bed and fell, struggling, to the floor. Siobhan taunted; Theresa fought silently, hatred fuelling her strength. She took vengeance for every slight, real or imagined, she had suffered since her cousin came to live with them – for Charlie's desertion, for the terrible future that lay before her. She laid it all at Siobhan's door. She clawed, trying to mutilate that loathsome, still-smiling face, but could never quite reach it.

Then the door crashed open and Pat and Declan were there, hauling them apart. The tiny room was crowded with people, all yelling, all demanding what was happening, all appealing for calm. Theresa was beside herself. She hardly knew who was there. She found her voice at last and screamed her hatred, hurling incoherent accusations.

285

A sharp pain on her cheek made her head snap sideways. She caught her breath. Her mother was in front of her, face white, eyes blazing, hand still raised.

'That's enough of that, d'ye hear? I'll not have fighting amongst family. Hold your wicked tongue.'

Theresa gulped. The breath rasped in her chest, then tears of pain and anger and humiliation started. Her mother turned to Siobhan.

'And you can take that expression off your face. I'll thank you to remember that I've taken you in like one of my own. You'd best fix yourself downstairs, then be off out. And no slipping away from your cousin Pat, mind, or it'll be the last time you set foot on that wicked stage.'

Her brothers retreated with Siobhan, leaving only her mother in the room. There was nothing Theresa could say, no way she could explain, however much she craved the comfort of those strong arms. In the end she was left alone in the growing darkness to sob her heart out.

Sometime during the long night the turmoil subsided and narrowed down to one thought that she held on to with the desperation of the drowning clinging to a passing branch. She must see Charlie. Nothing else mattered; she just had to see Charlie, and tell him. With that firmly fixed in her mind, she even managed to fall asleep as Sunday dawned grey and damp above the rooftops.

She knew her courage would fail her if she waited. Feeling empty and lightheaded and not quite in touch with reality, Theresa slipped out of the house as soon as her mother had gone off to

Mass, taking with her those of the younger children who had been confirmed. The street was quiet. Nobody was out. Most of the tattered curtains were still drawn. Cold struck up from the paving stones. Theresa stood before the Billinghams' door with her hand clenched in a fist ready to knock, unable to raise her arm. She did not know how long she stood there, but her body felt stiff from the cold. Then a rattle of a door opposite suddenly shocked her into action. She knocked.

Alma lay in bed staring drearily up at the ceiling. The cracks were getting worse. It needed a good coat of whitewash. She did not care. She did not seem to care about anything much these days. She always woke far too early now, even on Sundays, but had not the energy to get up. The long hours were filled with thoughts that chased themselves round in circles.

She was lonely, that was the beginning and end of it. It was so unfair, the way things worked out. There she was, with her empty heart and her empty bed, she who loved men. She loved their big voices and their rough laughs, their jokes and their promises. She loved their sheer physical presence, large and loud and demanding. She did not even mind their selfishness or their smelly feet; it was all part of having them around the place. She would have made a good wife, she knew that with no false pride. Not like some of them along the street. They all wanted to be married right enough, since nobody wanted to be left a spinster, but they did not actually like men, some of them. They were glad to get them out of the house, wanting only their wages of a Saturday so that the rent could be paid and the food bought. They certainly did not want them in their beds. They submitted to their husbands' demands with resignation or martyred silence because it was the price that had to be paid for protection. They would much rather sleep alone.

Not Alma. She loved having a warm body in bed beside her. She liked the feel of an unshaven cheek, the rough muscular hairiness of a man in contrast to her own round softness. She liked to wake to find an arm thrown across her or a thigh snuggled up against her own. And she revelled in the act of love, losing herself in a glorious welter of passion and fulfilment. She could have been happy in marriage, and she could have made some man happy too.

But it was not to be, not since Ernie went. Her eyes filled with tears at the thought of him. She missed him so much. The first overwhelming pain had subsided, but there remained a dull ache of loss. She loved him still. In the lonely nights she still made love to him, though they had never done it in real life. What they had had was too special. Like a virgin bride she had been saving it for when they were married.

On the other side of the thin wall she heard one of the boys stir and get up. Gerry, she suspected. It was not like Charlie to be up at this time.

A tap at the door and Gerry's head came round. 'Mum? You awake? I got to go out.'

'On a Sunday?' Alma protested. 'What you got to go out on a Sunday for?'

'Going to see a bloke up Petticoat Lane.'

'You'll make yourself ill, you will, always rushing around. You don't never get no rest. Everybody's got to have some time off.'

'Not if they want to make money. Don't grow on trees, you know. And don't you worry about me, Mum. Tough as they come, I am.'

It was no use arguing, since he wasn't going to listen to her.

'You take care,' she said.

He clattered downstairs, moved around in the kitchen for a while, then was gone with a bang of the front door.

She knew what was driving him. It was that Ellen Johnson. She could not forgive Ellen for what she had done to her boy. Since she had taken up with Harry, Gerry had been working like a man possessed. It wasn't right. She could hardly look at Ellen now without wanting to take her by the shoulders and shake her. Turning down her Gerry like that! The girl must be blind.

The anger lifted her out of the depression a little. When it came down to it, there had always been only her and the boys. They were what mattered most in the world. As long as she had them, she was all right.

She must have dozed a little then, for the knock at the door shocked her awake. Her heart banging in her chest, she waited, wondering if she had really heard it. Then the knock came again, more urgently. She dragged a shawl round her shoulders and went downstairs.

On the doorstep was Theresa O'Donaghue. She looked at her, not quite taking her in at first. Then slowly, her brain started to work.

289

'Blimey, it's you, Theresa. What the bleeding hell do you want at this time of the morning? It's Sunday. I'd've thought you'd've known that.'

Theresa swallowed. Her thin face was white and strained. 'I got to see Charlie,' she said.

'Charlie? What you want with him?' Alma stared at her, uncomprehending.

'Please, Mrs Billingham, I got to see him. Can I come in? Please.'

Her voice was edged with desperation. Alma stepped to one side, all the while eyeing her doubtfully.

'Well – all right – I suppose so. But he's in bed. He don't never get up before midday of a Sunday.'

'I'll wait,' Theresa said.

'Oh. Well, you better come through, I suppose.'

A cup of tea seemed essential to life. Alma plodded around, poking the ashes, making up the fire, putting a kettle on to boil. Suspicion gnawed at her. It was not like Theresa O'Donaghue to come calling on a Sunday. She had never done it before. Alma knew that Clodagh did not approve of her – straightlaced old sourpuss that she was.

She finally came and sat opposite Theresa, plonking a cup of sweet tea down in front of the girl. She did not touch it. Neither did she answer any of Alma's questions. They sat in uneasy silence while a clock ticked away on the mantelpiece amongst the samples from Gerry's stall.

'Charlie give me that,' Alma said with pride, indicating the clock with a nod of her head. 'Not many boys give their mums nice presents like that.'

Theresa looked as if she was going to burst into tears, but still she said nothing. Alma gave up on her. She never did have much time for the girl. She went and got herself dressed, spending time over it since she did not have to rush out anywhere.

It was an hour and a half before Charlie made an appearance, his hair sticking up on end and his shirt hanging out, his bony feet bare. When he saw Theresa, suspicion and wariness crossed his face.

'You got a visitor,' Alma told him, unnecessarily. She watched them both with unease in her heart.

'I ain't got nothing to say to you,' Charlie said, avoiding Theresa's eyes.

'But I got something to say to you,' she insisted. She looked at Alma. 'It's private,' she said.

'If you want to talk, you'll have to do it here,' Charlie said stubbornly.

'I can't.'

'All right. Keep it to y'self. I'm going to have a wash. Any warm water, Mum?'

'In the kettle,' Alma said automatically, a slow understanding growing in her mind. Her eyes were on Theresa; they flicked down from her face to her body, assessing. So that was it. Who would have thought it, a cold little madam like her? Without looking at her son, she said, 'I think you better sit down and listen, Charlie. We don't want no slander going on behind our backs, do we?'

'What?'

Uncomprehending, but realizing that something was up, Charlie also looked at Theresa. The girl was visibly wilting.

'Out with it, then,' Alma said.

Theresa's eyes sought Charlie's, pleading. Alma was glad to see that he did not give way.

'Well?' he said.

'I – I–' She struggled to speak, but only disjointed phrases came out. 'Last month – you know – you remember – and now it's – I – six weeks and I never...'

She had guessed right. She turned to her son. 'This right, what she's saying?'

'What?'

She gave a sigh of exasperation. Any girl could put upon him.

'It's a good thing you got me here to look after your interests. She's trying to pin a baby on you, can't you see that? I never knew you and her had anything to do with each other. You never told me. Nobody in the street told me, neither.'

Charlie looked dumbfounded, as well he might. It was obvious that it was the first he had heard of it.

'*What?* No, never. Never had nothing to do with her. Catholic, ain't she? Can you see old Ma O'Donaghue letting her out with me? Not likely.'

Alma nodded. That was true enough, though Clodagh O'Donaghue ought to be glad to have her Charlie taking an interest in one of her girls. A good boy, was her Charlie.

'Just what I thought.' She looked at Theresa, jabbing an angry finger at her. 'You better take your wicked lying tongue somewhere else, you little slut. You can't come in here bold as brass and start saying things like that.'

The girl just sat there. She did not seem to be listening. She was staring at Charlie as if the world was about to end.

She found her voice at last. 'How *can* you?' she cried, cutting through Alma's tirade.

She flew at Charlie, grabbing handfuls of crumpled shirt and pulling him close so that she could shout in his face. 'How *can* you say that? You know I'm not lying. You know it's true. It's yours, yours! What am I going to do? What are you going to do? You got to do something, you got to, you got to...!'

Alma dragged her off. The arms used to scrubbing ships and pulling pints were even stronger than Theresa's despairing rage. There was a ripping sound as Charlie's shirt gave way. Theresa was left with nothing but two handfuls of cotton fabric.

'That's enough. If my boy says it's not his, it's not his. Now out. I'm not having sluts in my house. Out!'

She pushed the sobbing girl out into the street and slammed the door shut behind her.

'Well,' she said, dusting her hands. 'There's a how-de-do. What on earth made her pick on you? You don't hardly see each other in the street, let alone have anything else between you.'

Charlie shrugged. 'Dunno. Think she's mad.'

'Clodagh O'Donaghue's going to be mad when she finds out. No wonder the girl was desperate. I wonder who the father is?'

Charlie shrugged again. 'Could be anyone.'

'Well, it's no one she can name, that's for sure, or she wouldn't have been in here accusing you.

Maybe she's taken up with a married man. Though I can't recall ever seeing Theresa with anyone, that's the funny thing...'

The speculation quite cheered her up. By midday she was ready to step out down the street and have a chat to the other women.

It was all over the street by the end of the week. Some helpful soul told Clodagh O'Donaghue, or rather asked her if it were true, pretending not to believe such a tale. Clodagh denied it and went to confront her daughter.

It was a Thursday evening. The children were out playing in the street, the other working members of the family were not yet home and Siobhan had been sent up to the shop to buy a ha'porth of jam. For once, the house was quiet. There was no hoping someone would interrupt them.

Theresa hung her head. It was no use denying it.

'That cow Mrs Billingham. She had no right going telling everyone.'

'Mrs Billingham? What's Alma Billingham got to do with it? How come she knows before me, your own mother?'

Theresa had no fight left in her. 'Because I went to see Charlie,' she admitted dully.

How she wished now that she hadn't. After all, what good would it have done? She couldn't marry him. He was a Protestant. No priest would marry her to a Protestant. If only she had stopped to think, she might have kept the dreadful secret for another two or three months.

'*Charlie?* Why...? On no – Mary, mother of God

294

help me. You're not telling me Charlie Billingham is...?' Clodagh gasped.

Theresa knew just what was going on in her mind. A baby conceived before the wedding was a sin, but a forgivable one, just so long as the marriage was hurried up a bit. People might count the months on their fingers and make sly remarks, but it happened all the time and would be forgotten after a while. If she had got herself into trouble with a Catholic boy, it could have been patched up. The O'Donaghues would have gone in force to see his family and a match would have been made of it.

But marrying a Protestant in one of their churches was another thing altogether. It did not count as a marriage at all in the eyes of the Catholic Church. It was living in sin. Having the baby with no visible father around was just as bad. Either way the situation was total disgrace, a disaster. The whole family was involved in it.

Her mother sat down hard. Her face was white, the muscles sagging with shock.

'I don't believe it. That a child of mine – that you of all girls – should bring shame like this on all of us...'

Tears rolled down Theresa's cheeks. She flung herself on to her knees and threw her arms round her mother's legs.

'Oh, Mam, Mam, forgive me. I didn't mean to, he made me.'

But she found herself pushed away.

'You wicked girl! I brought you up right, to respect the Church and its holy laws. You know what's right and wrong. There's no excuse. You've brought ruin on us all. How could you do this to us? How could you?'

Theresa huddled on the floor, abject. Beneath her shins the worn oilcloth felt hard and cold as she waited for the final blow to fall.

'And after I've worked my fingers to the bone all these years to see you don't go hungry and you got a clean decent home to live in and neat mended clothes on your back. You had everything we could give you, and this is how you repay us. Think of what this means to your sisters – did you not stop for a moment and consider them? What respectable young man's going to look at them if they've got a whore in the family? And your brothers, and your father and me, how can we ever hold up our heads again? The shame of it!'

Theresa had known all along what the outcome would be. She had seen it happen to two other girls in the Catholic community these last couple of years. For her mother to stand by her would be the same as condoning her behaviour. The whole family would be tainted. There was only one thing that could happen. Through the pounding in her ears she heard heavy footsteps going upstairs and moving about in the back bedroom. All too soon there was the whisk of a draught as the parlour door opened and a thud as a bundle was thrown down beside her.

'There's your things.' Her mother's voice was hard as flint, cold as the winter depths of the Thames, devoid of emotion after the rage and the shock.

Theresa could not move. 'Please, Mam. Don't

do this to me.' She looked up at her mother, desperation in her eyes, but the face that looked back at her was inexorable. She was the rotten limb. She had to be cut off to save the whole body of the family.

Her mother turned away, went to the mantelpiece and tipped the contents of the jar there into her hand. There was a clink of hard-earned coins.

'Take this.' She thrust the small hoard into the pitifully tiny bundle of possessions, avoiding Theresa's eyes. 'I'll not send you out penniless into the world, for all you've brought upon us. Now go, before the men get back.'

And so Theresa stood, stiff at the knees, a blessed sense of unreality wrapping her overburdened emotions. This was not happening to her. She took her jacket off the peg as if it were just a short trip up the road she was set upon, and struggled into it. Her fingers refused to do up the buttons. She picked up the bundle, moved to the door, opened it. She looked back as she stood in the opening, her hand on the latch. Her mother was standing still in the middle of the room, staring at her with an unfathomable depth of grief on her lined face. Neither of them said anything. There was nothing more that could be said.

She walked slowly up the street, looking neither right nor left. She was a ghost now. As far as her family was concerned, she was dead. She did not exist.

At the corner she passed Siobhan carrying a dish of lurid red jam for tea, the tea that she would not be there to share. Siobhan's quick eyes flicked over her, taking in the bundle.

'And where might you be off to?' she asked.

Theresa stared back at her. She seemed a long way off, detached.

'I'm going off to be with my young man,' she said, and the fantasy flowed easily. 'He's got a house in West Ham, a place of his own. He says he's tired of hiding and waiting, he can't live without me any longer. So I'm going to join him. I don't care what Mam says. I want to be rich and I want to be happy, so I'm going. Goodbye.'

For once, Siobhan was silenced.

Theresa walked on, her head held a little higher. She had got one over on Siobhan at last.

PART III

1905–7

1

'I'm going out,' Will called.

Maisie came in from the yard with her arms full of washing off the line.

'Oh.' She hesitated. 'Are you? Where you going, then?'

He could not quite meet her eyes. She had large eyes, soulful – her best feature. When she was flushed, as she was now from battling with the washing, she almost regained the prettiness that had originally attracted him.

'Just out with the boys,' he lied.

The two youngest children, Albert and little Lily, came toddling up to him, pink and clean from their pre-bedtime scrub. Albert hung on to his leg and Lily held her arms up to be picked up. Will bent down and caught her chubby little body between his rough hands. She squealed with pleasure as he swung her high in the air, almost touching the ceiling. He had a soft spot for Lily. She was an appealing little thing, with round face, round eyes, soft baby curls. He kissed her cheek.

'Say goodnight to your dad, then.'

'Ni-night,' she responded obediently.

Albert tugged at his trouser leg. 'Me! Me!'

Will set Lily down and tousled Albert's hair. 'Goodnight, Titch.'

The little boy hit him. 'Not Titch. Albert!'

Will cuffed him lightly round the ear. 'It's Titch until you learn some manners. Say goodnight proper.'

'Go'night,' Albert muttered.

'Goodnight, Albert. Now go to bed.'

The two trotted off up the stairs. Maisie dumped the washing on the kitchen table and pushed a lock of hair back from her forehead.

'Will – send the others in as you go, will you? They'll mind what you say.'

Glad to be let off so lightly, Will agreed.

The two older boys were out playing with the street gang. Will bellowed at them and told them to go in for bed, dusting their backsides for them when they protested.

'And I don't want to hear you been cheeking your mum, neither,' he warned.

Duty done, he set off, but the young voices, the family responsibilities, clung to him.

Once over the bridge and off the Island the guilt began to fall from him. He was away from home. What you did away from home didn't matter. It was quite a long trip to the theatre in Islington. Changing from one crowded bus to another, the sense of freedom grew. He was on new ground. Acres of brick, rows and rows of anonymous streets separated him from the inquisitive eyes of workmates and neighbours. Here, nobody knew him, nobody cared where he was going or who he was with. He felt young and carefree again. By the time he reached the stage door, there was a swagger in his step.

'Mr Will Johnson,' he told the doorkeeper with careless confidence. 'Miss O'Donaghue is expecting me.'

The glory of being able to say that. She had been keeping him at arm's length for a couple of months now. He had been in agony, wondering if she was ever going to let him meet her, especially now that they had made love.

It had been unlike anything he had experienced before, despite the fact that they had had to listen out for Declan, who was on escort duty that night. Hidden behind a basket of theatrical props in a forgotten corner of a theatre, he had discovered that what he had been doing with Maisie all these years was not the half of it.

He could not bear the thought of never doing that again. His need of her consumed him day and night. And tonight he knew that none of her relations was able to pick her up.

A woman in stage make-up answered his knock on the women's dressing-room door. The smell of scent, sweat and greasepaint oozed out round her. She looked Will up and down, took a drag of her cigarette, then called over her shoulder for Siobhan.

'Visitor for you, dearie. Nice bit of muscle on him. Wouldn't mind him myself if you're not interested. Only if he's got money, mind you. I'm not looking at anything without the necessary in his pockets.'

Siobhan appeared, ready for her act, in a dainty pink dress with rows of ruffles round the hem and the low neck and a big picture hat covered with paper flowers.

'Don't touch me,' she snapped as Will reached out for her. 'You'll ruin my costume.'

The painted woman laughed and went back inside, winking at Will as she closed the door. Siobhan glared after her.

'That Doll Sanders is no better than a prostitute. I don't know why she don't go on the streets and have done with it. God, but I hate sharing with the likes of her. These theatre managers are so stingy. They only give you your own room if you're top of the bill.'

Will opened his mouth to say something soothing, but she forestalled him.

'And you're late. I'm on in ten minutes. What took you so long?'

'I'm sorry–' Will began.

The callboy squeezed between them and banged on the men's dressing-room door. 'Mr Rivers! Five minutes, Mr Rivers!'

Siobhan sniffed. 'This place is a shambles, so it is. I'm not playing here again. I told Mr Spruce that, straight.'

'You deserve better,' Will said.

'Don't I know it! Mr Spruce, he's been promising me better billing and classier places for months, years, but nothing ever comes of it. I'm sick of him; he's all talk, that one.'

'Perhaps you ought–' Will began.

'And you're not much better. Always late. Here.' She shoved a crumpled pass into his hand. 'Don't just stand there looking stupid, go and get a standing place out front.'

She whisked back into the dressing-room, leaving him staring at the door. Putting it down to stage nerves, Will did as he was told. As he stumbled his way round the maze of ill-lit corri-

304

dors, he could hear the callboy shouting for Mr Rivers to go on stage and five minutes for Miss O'Donaghue. Anxious not to be too late to see her perform, he ran back and forth, getting more hot and desperate by the minute. At last he opened the right door, found himself in the tawdry splendour of the front-of-house and slipped into the auditorium just as the five-piece band struck up her introductory bars.

And there she was, stepping into the spotlight, fresh and innocent as sweet sixteen in her frilly dress. She had two numbers on the go now, 'My Whistling Postie' and 'The Lights of Old London', both lilting melodies with sentimental words, suited to her style. This time she sang the postman one, getting the audience to whistle an accompaniment to the choruses. To Will's ears it was faultless. He could not understand why it did not stop the show. But inexorably the curtain came down and the next artiste was introduced. The programme ran on smoothly towards the big name at the top of the bill.

Remembering his duties for the evening, Will went back to wait for Siobhan in the corridor. She emerged, still made up, with a light cloak over her costume and thrust a huge hatbox and a valise at Will.

'Come on,' she said, pushing past him and hurrying up the corridor.

Obediently, Will followed. They climbed into a waiting cab and Siobhan gave the name of the next theatre. In the stuffy darkness, Will felt for her hand. At first she snatched it away, but after some pleading on his part, she consented to let him hold it. He praised her performance extravagantly, but it did nothing to improve her temper.

Another venue, another set of dusty corridors and crowded dressing rooms. If anything, it was worse than the last place. The crowd was much rowdier and the seats were nothing but wooden benches. Will looked with distaste at the rows of whistling, catcalling men and their loud women. He could not see them appreciating Siobhan's charms. But she was further up the bill here, only five items from the top. After a couple of risqué comics, she was like a breath of fresh air. They were restive during the first half of the song, but after a while the sentiment started to come home to them, and they listened like lambs.

'You were wonderful, wonderful,' Will told her as she came out once more, this time dressed in her ordinary clothes.

'This is the last time I play here,' she said. 'This place is hardly better than a penny-gaff. I'm worth more than this.'

Carrying the costume, Will was drawn along in her wake. They ended up at a chophouse. Will blenched at the prices on the menu chalked on the wall. A meal here was going to cost a week's wages. But there was no way of backing out now, unless he wanted to lose Siobhan altogether. He tried to push the thought of his four hungry children to the back of his mind, and chose the cheapest dish. Then he listened with a sinking feeling of doom as Siobhan ordered lavishly.

'Performing always makes me ravenous,' she said, tucking into a loaded plate, then taking a long drink of the bottle of wine she had ordered.

Will nodded dumbly. His appetite had deserted him.

She threw him a saucy look. 'And not just for food and drink,' she said.

Will swallowed. She was so unexpected. He never knew what she was going to say next.

'That's good,' he responded, a little belatedly. 'I'm much more hungry for that than for this.' He nodded at the food in front of him.

Then the eternal difficulty reared its head. 'There anywhere we can go? I don't know this part of town.'

'We can get back in that dump. Doorkeeper'll let you in if you slip him a bob. We can use the star dressing room.'

A shilling took Will two hours' hard labour to earn, but the prospect of having her in the privacy of a locked room was worth five times as much.

'Just the job,' he said.

Siobhan talked away between mouthfuls, telling him about fellow artistes, bad audiences, conditions backstage, her opinion of Sidney Spruce. It was all damning, but as the food and drink restored her humour, it changed from a string of complaints into barbed jokes against all concerned. The underlying theme was that she, Miss Siobhan O'Donaghue, was ill-used. Nobody appreciated her talent. She was not getting the pay, conditions, venues or billing that she deserved, and it was everybody's fault but her own.

Will could only nod and agree, watching her full lips and the rise and fall of her breasts as she spoke, and thinking of her soft round body, soon to be his. He sent silent thanks that Pat and

Declan were no longer on constant guard over their cousin. Now that they were both married, their wives did not take kindly to their going out night after night to play chaperon, and their mother was finding it difficult to get menfolk enough to escort her, even within their big family.

'You ought to be top of the bill at the Empire,' he told her, saying no more than what he believed to be the truth.

'Of course I should,' she said. 'I know that, you know that, but does Mr Wonderful Sidney Spruce tell them that? No, he does not.' She poured out the last of the wine and drained it, banging her empty glass down on the table.

Will leant across and took her hands. 'Let's go back to the theatre, eh?' he said.

She gave him a long, considering look, pulled her hands away and sat back in her chair.

'That depends,' she said.

Will's hopes plummeted. It was always the same with Siobhan; nothing was ever straightforward. There was always some catch, some bargaining point.

'Depends on what?' he asked.

She did not answer right away. 'My glass is empty,' she said pointedly, twirling it between her fingers.

For a while he thought she was just delaying things and that another drink or two was all she was waiting for. He watched her drinking the wine, remembering what she looked like partly dressed, what her soft hot body felt like beneath and around him. Under the table, he rubbed his leg against hers, sending shafts of excitement through his nerves. But she drew sharply back.

'Stop that!' she hissed.

He sighed, frustrated and perplexed. He would never understand the workings of her mind.

'What's the matter?' he asked. 'What's up with you?'

'You've been up, that's the trouble.'

For a moment he just stared at her.

'What?'

'What?' she mimicked viciously. 'Going back to the theatre's all very well, but one thing leads to another, don't it? If you want to do it this time, then it's got to be permanent. You got to face up to your responsibilities.'

He stopped on the verge of saying 'What?' again. The gist of what she meant was beginning to sink in, and sending messages of fear around his body.

'Just what are you saying?' he asked slowly.

She did not answer, but just sat there waiting for the penny to drop. Her hand gripped the table top, white-knuckled, and the smile that glittered in her face had not a trace of humour in it.

'You're – you're having a baby.'

'No. I'm having your baby.'

He could not think straight. Images jostled in his mind – Siobhan on stage, Siobhan arm in arm with one of the local boys, Siobhan beneath him, Harry Turner coming at him with fists raised, Lily pink and scrubbed and ready for bed, Maisie's swollen pregnant belly, Mrs O'Donaghue...

'You're joking,' he said, to gain time.

She shook her head very slightly, holding him with her eyes.

'You're a lucky man, Will Johnson. You got me

tied down. Lot of men have wanted to do that. Lot of men would like to keep me to themselves, but you gone and done it.'

There was resentment in her voice. She had not wanted it this way.

He knew what she said was true. He had had to wait his turn so many times. And now he was being offered what he had always wanted. And yet – it was not quite what he had imagined. When he fantasized about owning Siobhan, it was not as part of a family. He had a family already. Siobhan did not fit into the part of housewife and mother. That was Maisie's role. Siobhan was the bright, teasing, carefree one, up in the spotlight, forever just out of reach. He wanted her to stay like that, so that other men would see her there and envy him when she walked out on his arm.

He recalled Maisie when she was in the same position. Half proud, half scared, she had told him she was in the club, and he had known that there was no alternative. He had to marry her. All the street knew they were going out together. If he backed down, his mother and her mother and all the neighbours would have something to say about it. There was no getting away with it.

'But what about your family, the street?' he blurted out. 'We couldn't go there. There's Maisie and the kids – they'd never...'

They would be outcasts.

She cast her eyes to the ceiling. 'The devil take my family, and the street,' she said. 'Use your head, do! We don't go back there. We get a room for tonight, then we find ourselves lodgings. Easy. You find yourself a job, we get a place. Nobody need ever know.'

'But...'

It took his breath away. To just walk out on everything – Maisie, the kids, his job, his family, the street, all the people he knew. It was wiping away his life, his personality. It was one thing to leave them behind for an evening. The sense of freedom had been as good as the effect of two pints on an empty stomach. But to leave them for ever was unthinkable. Without the familiar references, he hardly knew who he was.

'I can't,' he said.

Siobhan did not cry, or rail, or swear. Desperation did not work on her that way. Instead, her full lips parted, showing the tip of her pink tongue. Under the table, her foot travelled slowly, sensuously up his leg until it rested in his crotch just long enough to rouse him. Then it went down the other leg, lingered on his foot, and was gone, leaving him in a fever of desire.

'Coward,' she said.

He wanted her, right now. He wanted to say 'Let's go', and take her to a rooming house and make love to her all night long on a proper bed, and to hell with the consequences. But to do so would be to throw away everything he knew. She was right, he was a coward.

'I–' he began, wavering.

He would never see little Lily again. She would never toddle up to him with her arms raised to be picked up. She would never cling round his legs, giggling. Tommy and Peter and Albert would have no dad to show them how to shoot goals or take them for their first drink.

'I can't. I can't leave them all in the lurch.'

Siobhan went white. Fear, anger and an edge of panic pinched her face, making it look old and ravaged. She was not used to being rejected. Then she recovered herself. She took a deep breath through her nose, held it, then shrugged and stood up.

'You'll regret it,' she said, and walked out without a backward glance.

Will was left staring after her. He wanted to jump up and run to stop her, but his legs were leaden. He could not. He could not just leave everything, even for her. The waiter appeared with the massive bill. Will searched through his pockets and paid it with every last penny.

Somehow, he got out on to the street. He looked up and down, expecting, hoping, to see her small, determined figure lugging her clothes, but there was nothing. It was as if the pavement had swallowed her up. Without making a conscious decision, he set off for the theatre, walking faster and faster until he broke into a run. He pounded on the door but it was all locked up. Not even the stage doorkeeper she had said they could bribe was there. It was then that he finally realized he had lost her. He had made his choice and he was going to have to stick with it. *You'll regret it.* Her words pounded over and over in his head. And as he started on the long walk home, he already did.

Harry walked briskly along Chrisp Street. It was Saturday evening and the crowds in the market were rapidly thinning. Some of the traders were already packing up for the day. Around the fresh-food stalls hopeful knots of the very poor were gathered, waiting to pick up the last of the bruised fruit or off-colour meat at bargain prices. Harry glanced at them and looked away, proud that his mother no longer had to hang around on the chance of getting a bit of food that nobody else wanted. At least his family ate properly now. He shook off the other problems. It was Saturday, he had been paid and he was on his way to meet Ellen. It was time for enjoyment, not worries.

It was going to be a surprise. He had got off earlier than expected and rather than wait for her to come home, he had decided to come up here and take her out straight from work. It would give them that much longer together. The thought of the evening ahead put a spring into his step, despite the gruelling week he had spent at work. Six twelve-hour days on the trot were worth it when there was a night out with Ellen to look forward to. At a flower stall he paused, on the point of buying her a bunch of roses. But on closer inspection the blooms were wilted.

'Not good enough for my girl,' he told the vendor. 'Only the best for her.'

He would save the money and take her somewhere for a slap-up meal, and watch her face as she read the menu, her lip caught in her teeth as she tried to decide between all the delicious treats. He would see the weariness of the day slip from her and a glow come to her cheeks as she ate and relaxed and enjoyed herself. He grinned to himself, almost laughing aloud in anticipation.

As Gerry's stall came into view he stopped, waiting to catch the first sight of her. The handcart was parked in front of it, half loaded. They were packing up. Then he saw her. Her arms were full of newspaper-wrapped bundles and she was smiling, evidently sharing a joke with someone. And as he watched, Gerry appeared, also smiling, and flung an arm round her shoulders, a brief intimate gesture that brought all Harry's suppressed suspicions boiling to the surface. He strode the last few yards, ready to do murder.

'Ellen!'

She jumped, colour rising in her face. Gerry hastily withdrew his arm.

'Harry! I never thought–'

'Yeah, I can see that,' he said. 'Sorry if I'm breaking something up.'

Gerry gave a placatory smile. 'We was only having a bit of a laugh. Between pals, like.'

'If you will come creeping up like that, checking up...' Ellen said.

'I wasn't meaning to come checking up. I was meaning to take you out. But perhaps I ought to come and see what's happening up here more often.'

'Come off it, mate. I wouldn't move in on you. You know that,' Gerry said.

'Blooming well ought to know it,' Ellen added.

Harry looked from one to the other. He wanted to believe them. But Gerry was no fool, he knew a good thing when he saw it, cousin or not.

Under his accusing stare, Gerry shifted and looked away, fiddling with some of his goods.

'Look, er – why don't you two make off now, eh? I can finish the packing up. Go and have a bit of fun.'

Ellen looked awkward. 'Oh, Gerry, I couldn't do that. There's loads to do yet.'

'Don't let me drag you away,' Harry said.

'Don't be so bloody pig-headed,' Gerry told them both. 'Shove off, for God's sake.'

'Oh, well – if you're sure.' Ellen deliberately threw Harry a defiant look and kissed Gerry on the cheek. 'Thanks, gov'nor. You're a real pal.'

Then she tucked her arm into Harry's and smiled up at him. 'So where are we going, then?'

He was so angry he could have shaken her. Playing games with him like this! It was the sort of thing Siobhan did, not Ellen. He strode off down the street, not caring that she had to trot to keep up with him.

'Harry...' She was clinging on to his arm, her face red with exertion. 'Harry, I'd love a drink.'

They were right by a pub. He needed one himself, he realized, and marched in. They sat opposite each other at a small table, not speaking. But by the time he had downed half a pint, he felt a bit better. Across the table, Ellen was looking at him with amusement in her eyes.

'You are stupid, you know.'

'Oh yeah?'

'Yeah, you are. We been all through me working for Gerry, over and over again. You got to trust me, Harry.'

'It ain't that I don't trust you. It's Gerry.' He stopped. It was too difficult to put into words, to explain how he felt when he saw another man touch her. He said, 'It's just that I love you. I want to keep you all to myself.'

She reached across and put a hand over his. 'I

love you too. Don't you see that? And you have got me all to yourself, in that way. Gerry's just work. You wouldn't be jealous of Maconachie's if I was still there, now would you?'

He sighed. She just didn't see it. But when she looked at him like that, with her small hand on his large one, he could not stay angry with her.

'I suppose not,' he said.

Ellen stretched across the table and kissed him on the lips. 'That's better.'

The evening fell into a familiar pattern. They went to a chophouse and gorged themselves on meat pudding and peas, then to a music hall, then walked home along the embankment in the moonlight. Idling along with his arm round Ellen's waist and her head leaning on his shoulder, Harry was practically the happiest man in London.

'If only things could always be like this,' he said. 'You and me and the river and the moon...'

'Mm. It's just lovely, ain't it?'

In the darkness between the pools of lamplight they kissed.

'I love you,' Ellen said, sighing with pleasure.

'I love you too.'

If he could just solve the problem of his family, he could ask her to marry him and be done with the nagging question of Gerry for ever.

It was only a few days later that his mother remarked one teatime that the Masons were moving out of number twenty-four.

'Bloody good riddance,' Archie growled. He was in a foul mood as he had no money left and the Rum Puncheon had refused to put any more on the slate.

Ida said nothing to contradict him, but stared down at her plate, biting her lips. The Masons' daughter was exactly her age and a good friend.

Florrie was more open. 'They're good people, the Masons. It's not at all a good riddance. We shall all miss them.'

Archie stood up and thumped a fist down on the table. 'You shut your trap. You don't know nothing.'

There was an intake of breath round the table as everyone else looked at Harry. Milly's hands closed on her apron.

'No, Harry, please, no,' she whispered under her breath.

Harry sat quite still, holding on to his temper. He waited until he knew he could speak calmly.

'She's got a right to her opinion,' he said, looking straight at his father.

For several long moments, he and Archie glared at each other. Then slowly, Archie sat down and began eating again.

'Where they going to?' Johnny asked.

'Rotherhithe,' Milly said.

'Rotherhithe!'

The children's eyes widened. That was over the water, practically another country.

As the talk resumed along an almost normal path, Harry let his attention drift. If the Masons were going, that meant their house would be empty. Possibly the landlords had not yet relet it. From number twenty-four he could still keep an eye on his family while getting away from his father. He would not be constantly aggravating the situation simply by being there. Best of all, he could ask Ellen to marry him.

'–Harry?'

'Yeah?' He had not even noticed be was being spoken to.

'You said you was going to be up early tomorrow?'

'Yeah, I got a long one upriver.'

It was as if the sun had come out on the future, lighting up the course he was to steer. He would get hold of the rent collector the very next time he came and find out about the house.

Harry was at work when the Masons left, but all those who were at home that day turned out to gawp at the pathetic little collection of household goods as they were loaded on to the cart, and to wish the family well in their new neighbourhood. As the procession of cart, pram and children turned out of the street, those left behind gathered to discuss the departure. General opinion was that the Masons were mad. To move south of the river, and to a rough area like Rotherhithe, when they were nicely established on the Island seemed reckless in the extreme. It served as a point of conversation on the doorsteps and in the Rum Puncheon for days.

They had not been gone twenty-four hours before Harry got hold of the key. He was not really sure why he wanted to look at the place. It was hardly going to be different from any of the others on the street and he knew Mrs Mason to be a proud woman who would leave it spotlessly clean, but it seemed important that he should make absolutely certain before inviting Ellen to come and see it.

It was just as he had imagined it. He stepped into a small front parlour that was already starting to smell damp and musty. Over the fireplace an oval patch of wallpaper where the mirror had been showed a pattern of stripes and flowers in contrast to the faded yellowy-grey blur covering the rest of the room. The tiny fireplace was swept out and the square of oilcloth, too old to move without cracking, was shining. In the kitchen, the range had been blackleaded. Three shelves had been put up in the alcoves with a row of hooks underneath them. He tried to picture Ellen there but it was so still and lifeless that he found it difficult. He had to bring her here. She would breathe the life back into the place, make him see their own things in it, suggest little improvements.

He went up the creaking stairs to the front bed-room. The last of the evening sun was streaming in through the window, adding a friendly touch to the empty space. Once again there were small signs of the previous occupants: patches on the wallpaper – pink flowers on pale blue this time – and marks on the wall and floor where the Masons' bed had been. It was odd standing where all the little Masons had been conceived, but here upstairs it was easier to think of how it might be. He squatted down on the space where he would sleep, his back to the wall, his elbows resting on his knees, imagining he was waiting for Ellen to come upstairs. She'd climb up softly, her tread light, and smile at him as she came in at the door. Then she would undress, asking him to undo all the little fiddly buttons down the back, and he would slide his hands inside as the dress opened out...

At first he thought the footsteps on the stairs were part of his own fantasy. Even when the door of the bedroom opened he thought it was Ellen, come to find him. The last person he expected to see was Siobhan.

'You left the door open, so I let myself in,' she said, by way of a greeting.

He did not get up, but stayed staring up at her, resenting her intrusion.

'You can let yourself out the same way, then,' he told her.

But she did not go. She wandered round the little room, running her fingers along the walls, over the windowsill, casting considering glances at him. There was an animal restlessness about her that held the eye, as if the very clothes on her back were a restraint.

'If you're waiting for Ellen, you'll be here a long time,' she said.

Her skirt brushed his arm as she passed. Despite himself, it sent a shiver of pleasure through his nerves.

'That so?'

'She's got other things to do this evening.'

He said nothing.

'Just like she has most evenings.'

She came to a halt in front of him. She was standing very close, so that the hem of her dress was touching his feet. He found her presence profoundly disturbing, producing a compound of irritation, suspicion and sexual attraction.

'Just what are you trying to say?'

In answer, she sat down on the floor facing him,

her hand resting on his knee, her eyes gazing into his with an expression of compassion and concern.

''Tis time someone told you, Harry,' she said earnestly. 'She's been stringing you along something wicked all this time, so she has, and I can't bear to see it any longer. 'Tis time you opened your eyes.'

He instantly decided that whatever she was going to say, he would not believe a word of it. He knew his Ellen. She was as true as they came. But as he thought it, a worm of doubt wound in under his guard.

'They're wide enough open already,' he said.

'Harry, Harry, the whole street knows. They all know what's going on, but nobody wanted to tell you. Nobody wanted to hurt you, Harry. They all know what she means to you. But it can't go on, Harry, not now you're looking at a place. I am right, ain't I? It is for herself and you?'

'Yeah,' Harry admitted.

She looked so anxious, so innocent, and her voice was so sincere. But she was lying. He was sure she was lying.

She sighed and shook her head, biting her lip in seeming indecision.

'Maybe I'm talking out of turn...'

'Too right you are,' he said, shifting abruptly so that her hand was jerked off his knee.

'Maybe she'll tell you herself once she knows how serious you are.'

'Tell me what?' Harry demanded. 'What is all this about, eh? Just what are you trying to say?'

She shook her head again. 'No, no. I better not.

Best left unsaid. Forget it, forget I ever came here.'

She made to get up, but he caught her by the wrist.

'Tell me.'

Despite all he thought he believed, black suspicion was growing. He had to know what she was hinting at, what everyone else in the street was supposed to know.

'Come on, tell me. You can't leave it at that. Say!'

'Oh, Harry, you must have had some idea, surely? You must have wondered, just a little bit? All that late working? All them odd hours?'

The trouble was, he *had* wondered. Only the other day he had been brought face to face with it. He had never been happy about her working for Gerry. He knew in his head that his cousin was a good bloke, and that Ellen was faithful, but in his heart he had always harboured a dark corner of distrust. What with his own erratic working hours and the demands of the market, Gerry saw a good deal more of Ellen than he did. And there were plenty of opportunities for them to get close.

'No,' he shouted. 'No, never. She'd never do the dirty on me, not Ellen.'

Siobhan reached out and put a hand over his clenched fist. 'Harry – I know 'tis hard, but 'tis best to face it now. If 'tis bad now, it'd be far worse after you were married. *If* she marries you. I may be doing her wrong. I hope so. She may be just stringing the both of you along till she decides which of you is the best bet. Once you ask her, perhaps she'll choose. Have you asked her?'

'It's none of your business!'

'But it is, Harry, it is.'

She moved a little closer, took his other hand and tried to gaze deep into his eyes. Harry refused to look at her, but it did not stop her.

'I'm making it my business because I'm your friend. I'm a better friend to you than all the others. They just let you go on being deceived because they don't want to be the one to tell you. But you got to be told, Harry. Let her go now, before it gets any worse. You know where she is, right now?'

'Packing up the stall,' Harry said. His voice came out harsh and grating.

'It don't take that long to pack the stall up. They'll be in that storeroom of his. He's made it nice and comfortable there, I'll be bound, nice and cosy, all private. Just the two of them to-gether, having a bit of fun...'

It all fitted: the odd remarks people made, the looks, most of all the way Ellen refused to give that job up. If she had really loved him, she would have done what he asked, found herself some-thing else, something where she wasn't working side by side with Gerry all day long. But she hadn't. All the time she had insisted that she kept it on, so that she could be with Gerry.

Siobhan was leaning against him now, her thigh against his. She shifted one hand so that it was resting on his leg, her thumb moving slowly, sen-suously.

'Just the two of them together,' she repeated, 'doing what they been looking forward to all day long.'

All that time he had controlled himself, not gone all the way, because he respected Ellen, because she was worth waiting for, because with her it had to be right. And all that time she had been knocking off with Gerry. The pain and anger possessed him and clouded his judgement.

He wanted to strike out, to hurt as he had been hurt, to destroy, but through that need came another, growing ever more urgent. Siobhan was touching him, her sure hands teasing, rousing, her voice close to his ear, husky and low.

'Forget her, Harry. You don't need her any more. I'm here, I can give you what you want.'

He could feel the heat of her, smell the animal muskiness. He looked at her properly for the first time. All that little-girl innocence that she put on was gone. The eyes that looked back at him were knowing, the lips parted in invitation. As he took it in, she sat back on her heels, still holding his gaze, and began to undo the buttons of her blouse one by one. Slowly the soft pink flesh was revealed, the fold of her camisole over the lush curve of her breasts. Harry's fingers were drawn irresistibly towards her, and as they touched her warm skin he was set on an inevitable path. Her head arched back, she purred with pleasure as he explored her body and eased off the blouse. With one impatient movement, she pulled the camisole over her head and flung it to the floor, then launched into his arms, her lips meeting his in a passionate kiss.

'You know we were meant, we were always meant,' she gasped between shuddering breaths. 'You and me, we'll be good. You know you've always wanted me.'

Part of him always had. The other part hated her for shattering his world.

'Yeah, and you've always wanted me.'

They rolled over and over, each seeking mastery, each trying to lead, to take possession of the other. Shedding clothes, they kissed and touched and explored, tongues and lips and hands moving, sweat and breath mingling in a desperate attempt to gain control by pleasure. But Harry had the black anger and pain on his side, and he held her at last beneath him, teasing and retreating, until she was moaning and writhing in an agony of unfulfilled expectation. He pulled back, panting, and studied her as she lay there spread out. Deliberately, he ran the tips of his fingers over her, circling her belly, her thighs, approaching but never quite touching the centre of pleasure. She cried out, her hands pulling him towards her with the strength of desperation, her body arching to meet his.

'Please, please, now!'

'You want me?' His lips stretched in a mirthless smile.

'Yes, yes.'

Her fingers were digging into his buttocks, trying to force him into her.

'Now, please, now—'

He waited a few seconds longer, then gave her what she wanted.

2

Ellen got off the tram in the West Ferry Road and walked wearily towards home. It had been a long day and she was even more tired than usual, despite the fact that Gerry had sent her off early.

'I'll finish off here,' he said, as she tripped carrying a box to the cart. 'You look all in. Why don't you get off home?'

She smiled in relief. 'Thanks, Gerry. You're the best gov'nor in the street.'

'I know,' he said gruffly, not looking at her. 'Go on before I change my mind. I'll clear up.'

She did not see him stand and stare after her as she walked away.

As she turned the corner into Trinidad Street her eyes automatically sought Harry's house. They would be going out tonight, as usual. Sometimes she worried about how things were going. She knew he loved her, and she loved him passionately, they were happy in each other's company and had grown ever closer over the last two years; but he had never given even a hint of anything further. People had been teasing her for some time, asking when she was going to marry him and what she was waiting for, until she was beginning to wonder if he really was serious about her, or whether she was only a rather longer-standing girlfriend than usual.

People called out to her as she passed.

''Evening, Mrs Croft, 'lo Elsie,' she answered absently.

Their curious glances were lost on her, the significant looks and the elbowings. It was Granny Hobbs who stopped her.

'Seeing your young man this evening, are you?'

'Yeah, that's right. When I've had my tea.'

'Think maybe you ought to look in on him before then, girl.'

'What do you mean?' Ellen frowned, not understanding.

Old Mr Bright sidled up. 'You go on home, Ellen. Don't listen to nothing she says.'

Granny Hobbs rounded on him. 'Shut your trap, you silly old fool. The girl's got a right to know what's going on.'

'What's going on? What do you mean?' Ellen looked from one face to the other.

'Best go and find out.' Granny Hobbs folded her skinny arms across her chest and gave a meaningful nod.

The hairs on the back of Ellen's neck prickled. She looked wildly up and down the street. Everyone seemed to be staring her way. Her mother was at the door, looking out for her. Over at the Turners' the door was shut and the windows blank. No clue there.

'What is it? What's happened?' she cried. 'Tell me!'

'You ought to go and look for yourself, girl. Go along to the Masons' old place. See who's there and who they're with,' Granny Hobbs advised.

She set off at the run, her heart thudding in her chest.

327

'Ellen!' Her mother tried to stop her, catching at her arm, but she brushed her off. Her legs felt like lead and there was a terrible pain in her heart. Going in at the door of number twenty-four, her feet rang loud in the empty spaces. Nobody was in the parlour, nobody was in the kitchen, but above the pounding of blood in her ears came the sound of rhythmic movement from up the stairs. She climbed up, each step a mountain, the noise of gasping breath and animal moans getting ever louder as she drew near. She pushed at the bedroom door and stood stock-still. There on the floor amongst a scatter of discarded clothing, two people were locked in passion. Siobhan and–

'Harry!'

She thought she screamed his name, but no sound came out. She stood frozen with horror, watching as their excitement mounted ever higher and burst at last in a climax of mutual ecstasy.

Their release unleashed her fury.

'You traitor, you bastard, you whore!'

Beside herself, she picked up his abandoned boots and hurled them at the half-naked, slippery bodies. They both started and looked at her, bemused, satiated. Then Siobhan's lips parted in a smile of deep satisfaction, while shock slowly spread across Harry's face.

'Ellen!'

'Yeah, Ellen. Ellen, the girl you was going out with, remember? The girl you said you loved. Loved! Liar! How could you? How *could* you?'

She caught hold of the heavy leather belt lying by her feet and swung it wildly, bringing the buckle down first on his back, then on Siobhan's arm.

Red weals appeared, giving her a sense of triumph. She flicked the belt back again, ready to inflict another blow. Siobhan screamed, covering her face. Harry half rose and snatched it from her.

'Ellen, stop it.'

'I shan't, I shan't,' she yelled.

Cheated of her weapon, she took to kicking them, hitching up her skirt and lashing out with her heavy working boots.

'I hate you, I'll hate you both for ever!'

Harry grasped first one then the other ankle, holding her with an iron grip so that she was quite unable to move.

'Let me go!' she screamed at him, pounding at his naked back with her fists. 'Let me go!'

Then, quite suddenly, her voice broke and tears ran uncontrollably down her face. Harry released her.

Choking with rage and unbearable pain, she turned and ran down the stairs and out into the street.

It was the talk of the street for weeks. Somehow, Ellen kept her head high and ignored the looks and the sudden silences. Not that the neighbours were against her. Far from it. She was the injured party and had all their sympathy, but sympathy is close to pity and that she could not bear. There was respect, too, for the way she had laid into the guilty couple.

'You didn't half give it 'em, girl. Good for you,' Granny Hobbs commented.

There was nothing like a fight for entertainment. Of course, it would have been better if it had spilled out on to the street, where everyone could have had a look.

There was a certain amount of disapproval of Harry's part in the affair. He and Ellen had been going out for a long time and it had been expected that they would get married. But it was tempered with acceptance. After all, they were not actually engaged, and men were men.

The full weight of moral outrage was reserved for Siobhan. Going into empty houses with other people's young men was just not right. Siobhan kept a cool silence and took to staying away from home as much as possible. It was not so much the street, though that was bad enough, it was her aunt's attitude that kept her away. After the shame of Theresa's fall from grace, Clodagh could not stand the prospect of another of her flock going to the bad. Life at number twelve was one long lecture for Siobhan, who merely said 'Yes' and 'No' and gave no sign of attending properly to a word said, much to Clodagh's fury and frustration.

All three of them kept the secret of what had actually happened that day. As far as the street knew, Siobhan and Harry were caught kissing. That was quite enough to account for a major row between Harry and Ellen. For their own different but urgent reasons, none of them wanted the truth to be known. Things were bad enough as it was.

Harry did try to explain to Ellen, but she was not willing to listen. The attempt at a reconciliation blew up into another row, after which they refused to speak to each other.

'You're being stupid and pig-headed,' Martha told her daughter. 'You got to make allowances.

One slip! You don't throw a man over for one slip. Not a good man like Harry Turner. It's not as if you was even going to get married. Now next time you see him, you just unbend a bit. At least look at him. Do something. You do want him back, don't you?'

'What, and wonder whether he's going to run to her whenever I'm not there?'

Tears that she managed to hold in check in public spilled over. Ellen broke away and fled upstairs.

Martha sighed. It was the same every time she tried to talk to the girl. She knew her daughter was desperately unhappy and still loved Harry, but she could not break through that stubbornness. She did not know what to do for the best. Other women along the street assured her complacently that it would all come out in the wash, but Martha was not so sure. When Ellen made her mind up, she was the very devil to shift.

The one person who never said a word about it all was Gerry. Up at the market, Ellen could escape from the constant speculation, make an attempt at being as cheerful as usual for the sake of trade and pretend to the outside world that everything was all right. Gerry talked to her about his deals, about characters at the market, about his plans for the future. Neither Harry nor Siobhan was ever mentioned. It was as if they did not exist. It was balm to Ellen's battered heart, giving her a chance to rest and recuperate. They took to going for a drink after packing up, so that by the time Ellen got home in the evening she ate a very late tea and went straight to bed. The fact that Gerry relied on her gave her something to get up for when morning dragged round again.

It was six weeks or so after the fateful day that Siobhan stopped Harry in the street.

'I got to talk to you,' she told him.

'I don't think there's anything to talk about,' he said, making to pass on.

But she caught him by the sleeve. There was none of the usual challenge in her face today, just a deadly earnestness.

'Oh but there is, and 'tis very important,' she insisted. 'Do you want me to spill it here in the street or shall we go somewhere quiet?'

Something in her voice stopped him from brushing her off.

'All right, all right. I'll meet you down by the river in half an hour. By Tyson's quay.'

He deliberately arrived late, expecting her to do the same since she was so adept at playing games, but found to his surprise that she was there before him.

It was a dull autumn day with a hint of drizzle in the air, the sort of day that reduced all colours to shades of grey – light grey sky, steel-grey water, dark grey buildings, brown-grey mud. She stood on the weed-infested piece of ground beside the quay, with the panorama of the river behind her – a bright figure in green and yellow against the monochrome background.

Harry stopped short, looking at her. Whatever it was she was up to, he decided he was not playing. But even as he thought it, he remembered that that was what he had thought last time.

'Well?' he said.

She stood for a moment, holding herself aloof.

332

'There's no need to take that tone with me,' she told him. 'You're responsible for this just as much as I am.'

'Responsible for what?' he asked, while half a dozen possibilities flashed through his mind.

'For our baby.'

For several seconds, he stared at her. It had been said in a such a matter-of-fact way that it did not fully sink in.

'Our *what?*'

'Our baby. Yours and mine.'

'But...' He snatched at the obvious way out: 'Are you sure?'

'Of course I'm sure. I've missed twice.'

'But what makes you think it's mine?'

She gave him a cold look. 'You're not suggesting I've been with anyone else, I hope?'

That was just what he was suggesting.

'Come off it. I wasn't born yesterday. You never learnt tricks like that without a bit of practice.'

She looked mortally offended. 'I don't know what you're talking about. I was taken advantage of, I was. I went to speak to you, one neighbour to another, and before I knew what was happening, you had my skirts over my head.'

Her outraged tone grated on him. He spoke to her as he would never dream of speaking to a woman.

'Balls. You were no bloody virgin. I know it and you know it, so don't try that one on me.'

It was no use, though, since he had no proof. He stared back at her with loathing as the implications of what she was saying became plain. They were both of them unmarried, and the whole street knew they had been together. Maybe they did not know what had happened that time, but Siobhan would soon make it clear to everyone, and then he would be made to take up his responsibilities. He was trapped. There was only one thing he could do. He was going to have to marry her.

'Pity there were so many people got to know about it. From your point of view, that is. You might have been able to wriggle out of it otherwise,' Siobhan said.

'I'm not trying to wriggle out of it,' he said.

She smiled then, a hint of the old teasing challenge back in her eyes.

'There's no need to look so put out. There's a lot of men as would be very glad to be in your shoes, Harry Turner. Very glad indeed.'

'Like my stupid brother-in-law, you mean?' he said bitterly.

'Will? Oh, he would never make the grade. I have very high standards, I have. Not many men are good enough for me.'

And not many women were good enough for him. She certainly wasn't.

'You set this up, didn't you?' he accused.

She was a good actress, he had to give her that. She looked a picture of pained innocence.

'I did not! I might remind you that I have a career on the stage. I don't have to go forcing men to marry me just to get a roof over my head.'

'Well, you can forget about your precious career now,' Harry told her with grim satisfaction. 'I'm not having no woman of mine prancing around showing her legs off to all and sundry. You'll stay in the home where you should be and have my tea ready on the table when I come in.'

'Yes, sir.' She gave a mocking little bob.

With a swift movement, he snatched her waist and pulled her close.

'You'd better believe it,' he said. 'You've walked on stage for the last time. If you want me to give this baby a name, it's on my terms. Got it?'

For several seconds she tried to hold out on him, looking up into his face with an irritating smile on her lips, but slowly her expression changed, her eyes slid away, her shoulders slumped.

'Got it?' he repeated.

'Yes,' she agreed, in a small, sullen voice.

It was very small compensation for what he had taken on.

Outwardly, everything went on as usual. Ellen did not need her mother's advice to keep her pride and act like she did not care; she had already decided on that course. However much she wanted to put her head under the bedclothes and give up on the world, she managed somehow to get up and get dressed. Everything seemed a huge effort, even lifting a brush to do her hair properly. It was a great temptation just to bundle it up any old how.

'That's right,' her mother approved, fussing round her, straightening her collar, brushing her shoulders. 'Never let yourself go. Once you do that, you're finished. Got your hat? That's it, put it on right. Needs something doing to it, that does. Treat y'self to a bit of ribbon or something, fancy it up.'

Grim-faced, Ellen jabbed a large pin through the hat to anchor it to her head.

'I'll not bother with ribbon, I'll get another blooming hat,' she said.

Martha gave her a brief hug. 'That's my girl. Off you go, now. Chin up!'

Outside, kids were off to early-morning jobs, a couple of men on early turn were setting out to work, and Loony Mike was scrubbing his mother's doorstep with a sulky indifference that was going to earn him a clip round the ear when she saw it. The main rush to the factories had not yet started, for which Ellen was grateful. She did not want to talk to anyone. Gerry came out of his door, dapper as usual, with a bright red scarf knotted round his throat, a cheerful smile on his round face.

'Wotcher, Ellen! Nice day for it.'

'Yeah, lovely.'

The first lie of the day.

'Got to go over Hoxton way later, see a bloke about some stuff. You be all right to carry on on your own?'

'Yeah, fine.'

It was all right at the market. Nobody there knew that Harry Turner was about to marry Siobhan O'Donaghue. Nobody commented archly on the swiftness of the arrangements, the sour look on Clodagh O'Donaghue's face, the wrangling over whether it was going to be a Catholic or a Protestant ceremony. Nobody there discussed the likelihood of the couple's happiness. She was able to keep the mask on at work. It was going back to Trinidad Street again that was the hard part.

Street life was always in full flood when she got

home. The craze at the moment was for swinging round the lamp post. Someone's dad had brought home a length of old rope, and an older boy had shinned up the post and tied an end to the cross-piece. For once, both boys and girls were playing together, taking it in turns to run, grab the free end and swirl round with screams of excitement.

Involuntarily Ellen stopped short at the corner, looking at the kids. A few weeks ago, when she was happy, she would have run and joined in, raising shouts and whistles from the onlookers. But not now.

Gerry scuffed at a cobblestone with his toe. 'What you doing tonight then, Ellen?'

'Dunno. Read a book, I expect. I got one to finish. Due back tomorrow.' Though at the moment even fiction was losing its magical power to transport her into other worlds.

'How about you and me going out somewhere? We could go up West if you like, see how the other half live.'

'Oh, I dunno, Gerry. I'm too tired.'

'Go on, do you good. Have a change.'

Along at number twelve, the door opened and the priest appeared, accompanied by Mrs O'-Donaghue. Ellen came to a snap decision.

'All right,' she said. 'You're on.'

Sidney Spruce was spitting feathers.

'No artiste of mine has ever, *ever* failed to turn up for an engagement, not in all the years I been in the business. You know why? Because I only work with professionals, that's why – artistes who got the stage in their blood, artistes who'll go on even if they got a broken leg, artistes who know what side their bread's buttered. They don't not turn up just because they don't feel like it. There's paying audiences out there, girl – people what've slaved all week to go to the hall for a good night out, people what've been looking forward to seeing all the acts, and you, you go and let them down. You can't do that if you want to stay in the business.'

Siobhan was not even bothering to look him in the face. She stood there with a hand on her hip and an insolent twist to her mouth, waiting for him to finish.

'I don't,' she said.

But Sidney did not hear her. He was in full flood now.

'Hours I spent on the telephone, clearing up after you. Hours! Smoothing them down, buttering them up, convincing them you was a good bet for next week. Sweated blood, I have, keeping your engagement open for you. Anyone else would've given up on you, given you the push. D'you know where you'd be then? Out, that's where – out in the cold. People'd soon get to know why I dumped you, and nobody else'd take you on. If you're unreliable, they don't want to know. You'd hear nothing but the sound of doors slammed in your face. And that'd be the end of your stage career. It'd be back to the factory for you, seven till six, six days a week, just like all the other East End girls.'

He paused for a few seconds, expecting to provoke some sort of response from her. Remorse, tears, promises of good behaviour, gratitude for his continuing interest – anything would do. He had not exaggerated very much when he said he had sweated blood to keep her spot open. It had taken a lot of very persuasive talking on his part and a calling-in of favours he would have preferred to keep on ice for more important deals. All he asked in return was something back from the girl, proof that she appreciated the trouble she had caused and the effort he had taken. But there was nothing.

'Well, that's where you're wrong,' she said calmly.

'What?' He thought he had not heard her correctly.

With exaggerated patience, she repeated, 'Well, that's where you're wrong.'

'What d'you mean, that's where I'm wrong? What have you been up to behind my back? You gone and signed up with somebody else? You can't do that, you're on my books, you belong to me.'

'I don't belong to nobody – yet,' she flashed back at him. She studied her nails, first one way, then the other. 'As it so happens, I'm getting married.'

'You're *what*? You can't be. You're joking.'

'I'm not.'

'But why?' As soon as it was out of his mouth, he realized it was a silly question. She was getting married for the money. Some fool with more money than sense had fallen for that innocent-little-girl act and she had been holding out on him until the day was set. It was the oldest trick in the book.

'How old is he?' he asked cynically. 'In his

sixties? Nice dicky heart? Leave you a rich widow in a few years, eh? Very nice too. I hope I get invited to the wedding, seeing as you'd never have met if it wasn't for me.'

'Wrong again.' She showed her even white teeth in a mirthless smile. 'He's my age, strong and handsome.'

'So why ain't you carrying on working? Don't stop most artistes.'

'He don't want me to. Besides, I'm expecting.'

To his own surprise, Sidney experienced a slight feeling of shock, of betrayal. He knew he had been the first, and he was inordinately proud of it.

'But – I thought – you said I was the only one.'

'You are,' she told him. 'But what use is that to me when I'm up the bloody spout? Can't come to you with it, can I? You're not going to leave that wife of yours and give the kid a name, are you? I got to do something about it myself, so I have.'

'So it is mine?' he insisted. He had to know; it was very important to him.

'Of course it's yours. It's all your fault – everything's your fault. I was a virgin before I met you. Now look what's happened – and I know you won't lift a finger to help.'

He saw everything fragmented before him: their intimate little meetings stopping for ever, her earning potential disappearing. And just when everything was going so nicely, too. He had taught her everything he knew in the way of sexual tricks and hinted that he liked something new every now and again, and sure enough she came up with new ideas to amuse and titillate him. She was quite a nice little asset on the income side, too. Not a top earner – far from it – but he was hoping to arrange a provincial tour for her that could well establish her name. But not any more, not now she had dropped this bombshell.

Then he gathered his wits together. Ever the survivor, he was a quick thinker.

'So you're cuckooing this kid on some poor sod, are you?'

'He's not a poor sod, he's a strong man. He'll look after me proper.'

'Yeah, make you cook and clean and clear up for him, and give you a new baby every year. You'll have lost your figure and half your teeth by the time you're thirty. Wonderful prospect!'

He could see by the look in her eyes that this had gone home, but she was not admitting it.

'I suppose you've got something better to offer, have you?' she said sarcastically.

Now it was his turn to play for time. He took a cigar out of his case, rolled it between his fingers, sniffed it, cut off the end and lit it. He took a satisfying puff.

'As a matter of fact, yes.'

Siobhan said nothing. She simply looked sceptical.

'How about a tour of the Midlands – Leicester, Nottingham, Derby, the Potteries, Birmingham? Get your name known, get some experience of different places, different audiences, then see about a nice summer season at the seaside. Clacton, maybe, or Yarmouth, or Skeggie. Might even get you Blackpool or Brighton. Set you all up ready to come back to the Smoke as a top performer. What d'you think?'

There was undisguised longing in her face now, followed by a childish anger and disappointment at having such a treat snatched away.

'I can't, can I, you stupid bastard. Not with this kid.'

He had got her.

'Get rid of it.' Sidney shrugged. 'Then I'll start on setting the tour up. I've only got to do a bit of telephoning, pull a few strings, and we're halfway there.'

'Get rid of it?' she repeated.

'Yeah. You must've thought of it, surely?'

'Yeah, but...' She bit her lip.

The hardened artiste had gone, leaving the little Irish girl straight off the boat. For a moment he thought she was going to go all religious on him. But no, she was only thinking of herself.

'You hear all these stories. Girls bleeding to death,' she objected.

'No – old wives' tales. All put about to scare you girls off.'

Hope lit in her face. 'Is it possible then – I mean, safely?'

'How far gone are you?'

'Three months, maybe more.'

'Safe as houses,' he lied. 'Put you in touch with someone, if you like. Mind you, it'll have to be quick, soon as possible. And it's not cheap, but I'll stake you for it. Nothing but the best for my artistes.'

She was staring into nothing, thinking. He could practically see all the pros and cons running round in her head.

'And after, you'll fix this tour up for me?'

'It's a promise.'

Still she hesitated. 'I can't go back. I can't tell him.'

'Don't then,' Sidney told her. 'Once you got the – problem seen to, you can go into lodgings, then off round the Midlands. Easy.'

Her expression cleared. She gave a decisive nod.

'Right. I'll do it.'

By the time she left the room, twenty minutes later, it was all arranged.

3

It was unseasonably warm for March, and the women were out on their doorsteps.

'Mary O'Donaghue as was is expecting,' Milly Turner said, nodding down towards number twelve.

'She never is! Blimey, these Irish. At it like rabbits,' Ethel Croft commented.

Alma Billingham settled her hands comfortably over her stomach and prepared for a nice long gossip.

'Well, at least they got the wedding ring on first. More than can be said for Theresa. And just look at Siobhan,' she put in.

They all shook their heads in pious disapproval.

'That Siobhan was a wild one. Right little

stirrer. Mind you, I wasn't surprised when she made off. It was Theresa what shocked me. I'd never have thought she was one to play around,' Ethel said.

Alma bridled at what she fancied were prim looks from the others.

'And it weren't my Charlie, so there's no need to take that expression. He never had nothing to do with her. It was her tried to pin it on him. Not that Clodagh O'Donaghue believes it. She ain't so much as looked at me, let alone spoke to me, since the day that girl left.'

'Clodagh ain't never been the same woman since Theresa went. Really knocked the stuffing out of her, that did,' Milly added.

'Well, it would, wouldn't it? Bad enough for anyone to have your daughter shame you like that, but it's worse for them Catholics. Burn in Hell for it, they do, or so they believe. Daughters! Dunno what girls are coming to these days. Nothing but a big worry. You're lucky you ain't got none, Alma,' Ethel said with a superiority that belied the words.

'Sons are bad enough,' Alma replied.

Milly sighed. 'Don't I know it!'

'Your Gerry's doing all right, though,' Ethel pointed out.

'Yeah – not so bad. Well, tell you the truth, he's doing very nicely.' Alma could not resist the chance to boast. Her other little chick was reaching out. 'Going to open a little shop, he is, on the West Ferry Road. Household goods, like the stalls, only they'll have to be a bit over market prices, on account of the overheads.'

The other two women looked impressed.

'Don't it worry you, Alma, him taking on all that credit? He must be doing it all on tick, surely? Keep me awake at night, it would.'

'No, not any more, it don't. Used to. But he's got his head screwed on, has my Gerry. Ain't never got into trouble yet. Just you wait! He'll be a big man round here by the time he's thirty.'

Ethel gave a sly smile. 'Reckon young Ellen Johnson's got her head screwed on an' all. Stuck to your Gerry like glue, ain't she?'

'Ellen's a good girl,' Alma maintained. 'Not afraid of work, neither, and honest as the day's long. I'll not hear a word against her.'

Milly looked sceptical. She said nothing in the presence of two such strong personalities, but she had her own opinion of Ellen Johnson, born of Ellen's treatment of her son. She was nothing but a gold-digger, giving up on Harry at the first excuse and hanging on to Gerry Billingham and his money for all she was worth. What made it worse was that Gerry was her sister's son. Once, she would have been glad of a daughter-in-law like Ellen; now she felt distinctly cool towards the whole Johnson family. If it wasn't Ellen, it was Will. She had found her Maisie the other day in floods of tears. She'd been clearing out the cupboard in the bedroom and come across a pile of music-hall posters hidden right at the back. Every one of them had Siobhan O'Donaghue's name on it. No, she did not trust the Johnsons. As if summoned by her feeling, Martha could be seen coming out of number thirty-two with a bucket and brush. She saw the group of women, nodded, put down her cleaning things and made to come over.

'I got things I got to do indoors,' Milly said, and shuffled off.

'I see she's got bruises on her again,' Alma commented.

'Well, they all do it, don't they? Wouldn't know my old man loved me if he didn't give me a black eye every now and again,' Ethel said.

'Oh yeah, they all do it, but not like what hers does. He half kills her. Mind you, she does ask for it. She may be my sister, but I have to say it. It's that hangdog look of hers what does it.'

Martha joined them.

'Nice day. Thought I'd do a bit of spring cleaning. Get them curtains down.'

'Getting ready for a wedding, eh?' Ethel asked.

'What?'

'Your Ellen and Alma's Gerry. 'Bout time they tied the knot, ain't it?'

Martha bristled. 'What you trying to say? That they got to? My Ellen's not like that O'Donaghue lot.'

'No, no. Don't be so blooming touchy. I just thought they'd been going together for long enough to make their minds up, that's all. It's no more than anyone else is saying.'

If she did but know it, it was just what Gerry himself was thinking. He had realized that Ellen was the one for him practically since the coronation party, when she was only fourteen. The problem was Ellen herself. Her attitude towards him had never changed. She was a good friend and a first-rate helper, willing to work hard, able

346

to discuss his business dealing with a sharp understanding, seemingly happy to share his free time. On the face of it, they were ideally suited. But still he hesitated. Despite their close association and all the evenings out, their friendship was still just that. She kept a certain distance. She never made the first move. She did not let him take more than a swift kiss on the doorstep before parting.

It was their joint future he was thinking of as he showed her the shop on the West Ferry Road.

'Seems a nice enough place,' she commented. 'Decent size and everything. Needs a good clean, but it's nothing a few buckets of soap and water can't do. And the back room comes with it, does it?'

'Yeah, that's the real beauty of it. A proper stockroom. So if I see a real bargain, I can buy the stuff and store it until I can sell it again.'

And there was the flat upstairs. At the moment, it was occupied by a middle-aged couple who sub-let the two rooms up in the attic to a family with four children, but they might be persuaded to move on, in which case the accommodation would be ideal for himself and Ellen and their children. If he could just attain that dream, he would be a happy man.

'That'd be handy,' Ellen was saying.

She was wandering around, peering at the shelves, poking under the counter, generally getting the feel of the place. Gerry could just see her there, a nice white apron on, serving behind the counter. It was just right for her.

'What I was thinking was...' he began.

'Mm?' Ellen was looking in the cramped display space of the shop window, wrinkling her nose up at the cemetery of dead flies and the little heaps of flaked paint and dirt. 'This needs more than soap, it needs a good going-over with something stronger – Lysol, maybe – to get it really clean. I know we're not selling food, but a place does need to smell nice. Puts me off shopping in a place if it's rancid.'

'Yeah, yeah, you're right there, we'll do that. Look, Ellen – what I thought was, you could be in charge of the shop–'

'Me?' Ellen stopped short in her tour of the premises to give him her full attention. 'But this is what you always wanted, ain't it, to be boss of your own place?'

It had been, but his ambitions had moved on since then.

'Yeah, but I'm best at doing the deals, getting the stuff. And it'd be much nicer for you here than in the market, out in all weathers. I don't like it when you have to stand all day in the rain or the fog. It ain't right. You'd be nice and snug here, whatever it was like outside. Yeah, this is the place for you, and I'll go out and about just like I am now.'

'Well...' She was biting her lip, considering.

He knew just what was going through her mind. Gossip on the street already assumed that since they were in each other's pockets all day, they must be carrying on together. If she took the shop on, pressure for them to get married would be almost irresistible. Which was what Gerry was counting on.

'I dunno, Gerry. I like the market, all the people passing and the other traders to talk to. It's like one big happy family. It'd be lonely here.'

'You could always sit and read here, if there was no one in the shop,' he said slyly, knowing her strange passion for sticking her nose in a book.

'Yeah, I suppose so. No, I don't think so, Gerry, if it's all the same to you. I think I'll stick with the stall.'

He argued for a long time, but he could not shift her. It did not occur to him that, in his capacity of employer, he might tell her to take it or leave it. Perhaps he was afraid that she might leave it. All his customary self-confidence failed him when it came to believing in their relationship. But he did not give up altogether. Come the winter, or even the height of summer if it got really stinking hot, she might yet be glad of an indoor job. In the meantime, there was stock to be bought for his new venture.

It was the talk of the street for weeks. Nobody from their part of the world had ever risen to the heights of shopkeeper before. They all went to admire the place when it opened and were without exception impressed. They told their workmates about it, boasting that this bloke in their street had opened that new place on the West Ferry Road, taking some of the reflected glory upon themselves. Those who could afford it bought things; more did not; but nearly all shared the opinion that Gerry Billingham had really overreached himself this time.

Gerry himself tried to close his eyes to it. It would all work out right, he reasoned. Everyone worked on tick – that was how it was done. Once people started buying at his shop on a regular basis, he would be all right. There was nothing to worry about.

Towards the end of July, he heard of a bargain he could not resist: a consignment of kettles being knocked down at a giveaway price to whoever had the readies.

'But we got a huge load of stuff here already,' Ellen argued, when he told her about it.

'Not kettles, we ain't. We're real short on kettles.'

'I don't like it, Gerry. Things are ever so slow at the moment. People don't seem to be buying.'

'They will, they will. Give 'em time.'

Time was just what he did not have, and well he knew it. The interest on the loan he had taken out was mounting up and he had not paid for half the stock he was selling now. But the kettles would do it. The profit on them would save him.

'You got to speculate to accumulate,' he said grandly.

Ellen sighed. 'You're the boss. But I still think you're going to get your fingers burnt.'

'Not me, sunshine. I'm going to be a rich man. Just you wait and see!'

He had always believed that, and people had always been prophesying his downfall. So far, he had proved them all wrong.

Three months later, even he was getting worried.

'Gerry, I can't sell any more of these blooming kettles,' Ellen told him. 'They're rubbish. People keep bringing them back and complaining. It's getting us a bad name.'

'Tell 'em they got 'em cheap, and what do they expect for that money,' Gerry said.

'I can't look them in the face and say that. They're not just cheap, they're rubbish. They go into holes the moment you put them on the range.'

He knew it. People had come into the shop with the same complaint and it was obvious that they were not just trying it on. The kettles were still in their original shiny condition, just a little blackened round the base from their one use, and leaking water. He had to admit it, he had been well and truly done.

'The bastard must have shown me a couple of good 'uns. I didn't check the rest,' he said. He should have known better.

'What you going to do with 'em, Gerry? They're littering the place up here. You can't move for flaming kettles.'

'I dunno.' For once, he was stumped. 'Sell 'em on to some other mug, I suppose.'

But it would have to be somewhere well out of his territory – south of the river, maybe, or even out of London altogether. He did not want any comebacks. While he thought on that one, he had a pair of unwelcome visitors. They came into the shop just as he was shutting up one evening, a smallish, ferret-like man and a huge bloke with a slab face and hands big enough to crush rocks. Gerry did not need to be told what their line was. The moment he saw them his guts crawled. But, ever the optimist, he tried to brazen it out.

'Evening, gents. What can I do for you?'

The little man came and leant on the counter.

'Plenty, my son, plenty.'

His companion wandered round the cramped space. Gerry wanted to tell him to standstill. He was so big and clumsy-looking that Gerry was afraid he would knock something over.

'Nervous?' the first man asked. 'Nothing to be nervous about, as long as you got the money.'

'What money?' Gerry asked, playing for time.

The man tutted and shook his head in mock sorrow. 'Dear me, that won't do at all. No good playing stupid with me. Nor with Mr Praed, neither. He don't like people playing around, Mr Praed don't.'

So it was Praed who had sent them. There were two people Gerry owed the most money to, and he was one of them.

'Oh, that money,' he said. 'That's coming. I got a lot of bad debts, I have. Lot of money owing to me. You know how it is, the sods hold on to it. I can't get it out of them. But it's coming. I'll have it ready by next week.'

'Next week's not good enough. Mr Praed don't like being kept waiting. He's tired of waiting for you. Ain't that right, Jimmy?'

The bruiser ambled over to the counter. 'That's right,' he agreed, staring at Gerry as if he were a troublesome fly that needed swatting.

'I – I'll see what I can do,' Gerry promised.

The small man tutted again. He picked up a little china figure from the counter, a pretty girl in a pink dress with bright yellow hair.

'Nice,' he commented. He gave it to his large sidekick. 'Much too nice to be lying around. Could get broken.'

Unwisely, Gerry tried to snatch it back. Jimmy merely held it up out of his reach, then deliberately opened his fingers and let it drop to the floor. It shattered into several pieces. Gerry winced.

The small man sighed and shook his head. 'Dear, dear. What a pity. That's the trouble with Jimmy here, you see. He don't know his own strength. And he's not even roused at the moment. If he was roused...' He let Gerry's imagination fill in the end of the sentence.

Gerry opened his mouth, but nothing came out. There was a terrible sick feeling in the pit of his stomach. He did not have the money and he did not know where he could raise some. All he had – all he had was a brother who acted much the same as these two. In his desperation, he grabbed hold of this dubious lifebelt.

'I wouldn't let him loose if I was you,' he said, trying to inject the same quiet menace into his voice that had just been used on him. 'Your Jimmy's not the only one who can get nasty. You heard of Charlie Billingham? Same name as me, see? Funny, ain't it? Could be because he's my brother. And you know how it is – blood's thicker than water. A hard man, my brother. He don't like it if he hears I been pushed around.'

His eyes flicked nervously from one face to another, hoping, praying, that he might see even a shadow of the fear that was turning his legs to pieces of chewed string. To his utter consternation, both men burst out laughing.

'Charlie Billingham? That's a joke! Ain't that a joke, Jimmy?'

'Yeah.'

'Charlie Billingham hard? He's about as hard as a rotten banana.'

He caught Jimmy's eye and indicated Gerry with a jerk of the head. Jimmy stretched over the counter, grabbed Gerry by the lapels and lifted him off his feet. Gerry found himself eyeball to eyeball with the bruiser. The broken nose and red veins loomed before him in horrible detail. His breath, tainted by his blackened teeth, wafted up Gerry's nostrils and down his throat. Gerry though his last hour had come. Then, just as quickly, he was back on his feet again. He had to hold on to the counter to keep upright.

The small man bared his teeth in a mocking grin.

'Friday. That's when Mr Praed wants his money. Friday, first thing. Or else me and Jimmy here'll have to come and pay you another little visit.'

Gerry swallowed, and nodded. 'R–right,' he managed to squeak.

'Remember.'

The two left the shop, setting the bell jingling. For a moment, Gerry stood staring at the space they had just vacated. Then he bolted out the back and was violently sick.

Ellen watched with increasing concern as Gerry ran round chasing his tail in an effort to keep one step ahead of his creditors. His normally cheerful face became drawn, with lines of tension about the eyes and mouth, making him look older than his twenty-five years. She admired the way his fertile imagination kept coming up with new schemes to

354

shuffle around what little money he had, but though he did not confide details, she could see that it was just a continuous train of emergency measures. Nothing was bringing in enough new money to get him out of the downward spiral.

She doubled her efforts at the stall, trying to shift as much as she could, but though it helped, it was not enough. One afternoon, two men came asking for him. She recognized them at once from Gerry's description: Praed's bruiser and his bear-leader.

'He ain't here,' she said, staring the small one straight in the eye though her heart knocked against her ribs.

'Well, tell us where he is then, darling.'

'Ain't he at the shop?' she asked brightly.

'Would I be asking you if he was?'

'If he ain't there I dunno where he is,' Ellen said.

The weaselly man gave an unpleasant smile. 'You take my tip, darling. Get out while you got the chance.'

Ellen did not tell Gerry about their visit. He had enough to worry about.

'Trouble is, everyone's avoiding me now they think I'm going under,' he said, as they packed up.

'You've not gone under yet,' Ellen pointed out.

'No.' Gerry gave a smile, a travesty of his usual grin. 'No, I'm still swimming. Just.'

She tactfully did not mention the kettles. That piece of bad judgement was what had really started it off, but it was a taboo subject between them. They had been gathered up and sold for a song to a dealer in the wilds of Southwark.

'Thing is, though,' he said, 'I reckon I'm going to have to give up the shop.'

'Oh, Gerry!'

She knew how much it meant to him. The shop was what he had been aiming at for all these years, ever since he was just a kid working at old Rooney's after school.

'I can't pay the rent. In fact, I ain't paid it for weeks. There was always someone breathing down my neck. Well, you know that. But now the rent man's on to me.'

'Oh, Gerry, that's terrible. Ain't there no way you can hang on to it? Hold him off for a bit?'

Sadly, he shook his head. 'I tried, girl. But I'm going to have to let it go.'

All one Sunday, they toiled to clear the shop out. It was depressing work. Only a short while ago they had laboured to clean it up and bring stock in and arrange everything on the shelves and in the window. It had been a big new adventure then, and their energy seemed boundless. Now it was all a terrible effort, draining them of even the ability to speak. Ellen tried to keep up a flow of chatter for a while, and Gerry gamely attempted to respond, but in the end they lapsed into silence. Back and forth they trudged with the handcart, taking what was left of the goods to be stored in Gerry's bedroom until it could be transported up to Poplar to be sold on the stall.

In the street, the girls were squatting on the kerb playing cat's cradle, the boys were flicking cigarette cards, the old folk sat on chairs outside their doors, and some of the mothers were gossiping, arms folded, shoulders leant against the wall. Ellen could feel their eyes upon her and knew what they were thinking, what they were saying once her back was turned. There was sympathy for Gerry in his plight, but there was also a strong element of 'I told you so'. They were even rather satisfied that he had failed, since it proved that he was no richer or cleverer than anyone else in the street, after all. Ellen wanted to shout at their smug faces, to point out that at least he had tried, at least he saw something beyond the hand-to-mouth existence that they all took for granted.

At last it was all done, and they took a final look around the empty premises. Gerry's shoulders were slumped, his voice flat and toneless.

'I better take the key round the landlord's office and stick it through the door.'

Ellen had never heard him sound so defeated. On impulse, she reached out and put an arm round his waist.

'It's not the end yet, you know, Gerry. You still got the stall, you still got loads of stock. You'll bounce back, I know you will.'

In answer, he held her close, hugging her to him with a fierce strength, burying his face in her neck.

'You're the best, Ellen,' he said, his voice muffled against her skin. 'You're the very best. I love you.'

The words jolted through her heart. She wished she could say what he wanted her to, that she loved him, but she could not. She liked him, he was a good pal and she was very fond of him.

But love – that was something different, that was what she had felt for Harry, what she still felt for Harry. When they were together, the whole world had been a brighter place and she had lived on a higher level where everything was new and sparkling and full of wonderful opportunities. Even a simple walk to the shops or a drink in a pub had been an exciting expedition when Harry was by her side. It was not the same with Gerry.

'You're a real pal, Gerry,' she said lamely. To gloss over the lack of passion, she rushed on, 'This is only a little setback, I'm sure of it. You'll get what you want one day. You've always got what you wanted, ain't you?'

'Not everything,' he said bleakly.

Ellen knew very well what he meant. 'Nobody ever gets everything,' she said, with feeling.

'No, I s'pose not.' He released her, making a visible effort to act as if everything was all right. 'I'll take this key back, then. See you tomorrow.'

Ellen was left feeling that she had failed him.

Quitting the shop eased the difficulties for a while, but it did not solve them. Gerry still seemed to spend a lot of time either placating people or avoiding them. Late one Saturday he appeared at the market, breathless and harried, and demanded all the money that had been taken so far. As Ellen emptied out her apron into his hands, he kept glancing over his shoulder as if expecting someone to pounce on him.

'What is it?' Ellen asked. 'What's up? Who's after you?'

'It's that bloody Praed again. He's out to get me.'

'Praed? I thought you'd settled with him.'

'Only part of it, enough to get him off my back. Now he wants the rest. With interest.'

'Oh, Gerry.' With shaking fingers, she scraped out every last farthing. 'Will that be enough? Will he be satisfied with that?'

'I flaming well hope so.'

Gerry stuffed it in his pockets and made off through the crowd.

Ellen packed up the stall on her own that day. One of the other stall holders helped her to pull the cart back to the store. She hung around for a while, expecting Gerry to come, but he did not. In the end she locked up and took the tram back to the Island, worry gnawing at her. Praed had a nasty reputation. The other market traders thought that Gerry had been foolish to get mixed up with him.

She did not go directly home, but stopped off at the Billinghams'. Alma was busy getting tea ready.

'No, love, I ain't seen hide nor hair of him all day,' she said in answer to Ellen's anxious enquiry. 'I thought he was up the stall with you.'

'No.' Ellen did not know whether to tell Alma what she knew. Best not to worry her, she decided. She handed over the last of the day's takings. 'He might need this. I think he's a bit short at the moment.'

Alma sighed. 'Too true he is, lovey. I'll give it him when he comes in. Staying for a cuppa?'

'My mum's expecting me, thanks. But would you ask him to step along and let me know he's back, when he does turn up?'

Alma followed her to the door. She gave Ellen a quick kiss on the cheek.

'Don't you worry, I'll make sure he does.'

But Ellen hardly heard her. Harry had just come out of number forty-seven and was walking down the street. He was all dressed up for Saturday night in a navy suit and stiff collar, a bowler hat at a rakish angle on his blond curls. Ellen found herself gaping at him. As he drew level with her, their eyes met and she felt a hot flush rising up her neck. He gave a curt nod.

''Evening, Aunt Alma, Ellen.'

''Evening,' Ellen answered, equally coldly.

Alma watched his retreating back. 'Hmph. Bet I know where he's off to, him and all his mates. To watch that Siobhan doing her act.'

'*What?*'

'Oh yeah, haven't you heard? She's back. Large as life and twice as natural. Not staying here no more, of course. But she's playing in London, at the Gattis. That's where they're all off to, all the young lightermen. They always goes to the Gattis.'

Ellen felt as if she had been kicked in the stomach. All this time, despite the fact that she and Harry were hardly on speaking terms, she had nursed a secret hope that one day they might make it up. Not that she would ever make the first move. As the injured party, she felt that was not her place. Her mother had hinted that maybe Harry considered himself the injured party, what with her going out with Gerry. Ellen did not see this at all. She was just good pals with Gerry. That was altogether different from what Harry had got up to with Siobhan. Why, if she had not disappeared into the blue like that, they would have been married with a baby, possibly two by now. It was not the same at all. And so things had stayed in a stalemate, with both of them too stiff-necked to give an inch. Now she suddenly saw it all in a different light. It was not just an interlude, however long, before they got together again. It was over. Harry worked long hours during the week and went out spending freely on Saturday night and Sunday. He had a full life. And now he was off to see Siobhan perform. She walked slowly home, her heart full.

It was a subdued Gerry who finally turned up at gone nine o'clock. Ellen flew into the front parlour the moment she heard his knock on the door.

'What happened?' she demanded. 'You all right? He didn't beat you up, did he?'

'No, no, I'm all right. I done it. Paid him off.'

It was said with such conviction that Ellen believed him. She was not to know that it had been done with borrowed money.

'That's good. That's real relief. You mean Praed's right off your back now?'

'Yeah. All paid up.' Only there was a new loan to pay back now.

'That's real good news, Gerry. The best I heard for ages. Oh – by the way, I left the last of today's takings with your mum.'

'Yeah, thanks, she gave it to me. You took your wages out of it, I hope?'

'No,' Ellen admitted. 'I didn't know how pushed you were.'

Gerry reached out and pulled her to him, kissing her on the lips. 'You're one in a million, Ellen. When I'm out of this mess – and I'm over the worst now – will you marry me?'

Ellen stared at him, not knowing what to say. He flushed, as if the question had been just as unexpected to him.

'What d'you say, Ellen? Will you? I never had the courage to ask you before, but you stuck by me through all this, and that must mean I'm more than just a neighbour to you.'

'Oh, you are, Gerry. And anyway, I couldn't have walked out when you was in trouble, now could I? It's just...'

It was just that he was not Harry. When Harry came upon a crisis, you could rely on him to know just what to do. There would be no fuss and bother, he would calmly take command, and people would do as he asked them because they respected him. Gerry was clever, and fun to be with, but when it came down to it, Harry was a rock, whereas Gerry was built on sand.

But she could not tell him that in so many words.

'You know I've always loved you, Ellen. For years, ever since you was just a kid. These last months, I couldn't have hung on if it hadn't been for you. I'd've gone under, honest I would, but I kept going, 'cos I had you to think about. It's all been for you. And I can build it up again, I know I can, if I got you with me.'

A rock could stand up to the storms of life. Harry didn't need her. He had more than proved that. You could even take away his job, his family, his friends, and he would still be strong. She looked at Gerry, at his kind face, his anxious eyes. Gerry loved her. More than that, he needed her.

'I dunno, Gerry, I can't make my mind up just like that.'

'You don't have to,' he assured her. 'Not right away. I'm not asking that. I'm not asking you to marry me now, not with things like what they are. Oh no, it's got to be done proper, when I'm back on my feet again and I can afford to rent us a place of our own. Look – I'll ask you again in six months. How about that? In six months, you can give me an answer, yes or no. That sound all right to you?'

Relieved at being let off the hook, Ellen agreed.

It was less than six months later that a house unexpectedly fell vacant in Trinidad Street.

'Do nicely for you and Gerry,' Martha remarked, as she stood ironing sheets. 'Mind you, I dunno what you young people are coming to these days, needing a whole place of your own before you get wed. When me and your dad got married we just had a back bedroom at his parents' place. All you need to start with. Still, you could have a couple of lodgers to help with the rent, like. Always someone needing a room.'

'Mum!' Ellen was horrified. 'I always thought you was on my side.'

'Your side? Of course I'm on your side, lovey. What on earth do you mean?'

'I mean about marrying Gerry. Everyone expects me to, but I ain't said nothing, now have I?'

Martha gave an indulgent laugh. 'You don't need to, do you? It's plain as the nose on your face that you're only keeping the poor sod hanging about. You've had long enough to make your mind up, God knows.'

'I know.' Ellen sighed. 'Trouble is, I can't make my mind up, and that's a fact.'

Martha sat down and gave her daughter her whole attention. 'You're not still carrying a torch for Harry Turner, are you?' she asked shrewdly.

'Well...'

'I thought as much. Trouble with you, my girl, you believe all them books you keep reading. All very nice, I'm sure, but you got to live in the real world, ain't you? If you wanted Harry, you should've gone and made it up with him ages ago, like what I told you to, not gone on working with Gerry and going out with him in the evenings. That's not fair to anyone, now is it? Least of all Gerry. He's all right, he is. Bit on the fly side but his heart's in the right place. You could go a lot further and fare a lot worse than Gerry. You think about it, or you might find that chance slipping through your fingers and all.'

'I do think about it. I lie awake at night thinking about it. But it don't seem to do no good.'

'Well, I'll tell you something what might get your brain working. That Siobhan's come back.'

As always, the very sound of her name gave Ellen a sick feeling. And it was mentioned quite often now she had returned from her tour.

'I know. She's doing the London halls again.'

'No, I don't mean just back in London, I mean back here, in Trinidad Street.'

'She's never!'

Dismay was followed rapidly by anger. She had never forgiven Siobhan, and she never would. While she was out of sight, Ellen managed to keep her more or less out of mind, but here in the street she was nothing less than a threat to everyone, and especially to Ellen.

'You mean she's staying? What does Mrs O'Donaghue say to that? She's not stopping with them again, is she?'

'I dunno, love. She only come this afternoon. Just turned up out of the blue, all dressed up to the nines' – she paused for effect – 'in a cab.'

'A *cab?*'

'First time I ever saw one down our street. Caused quite a stir, it did.'

'Yeah, I bet it did.'

If Siobhan had come back for Harry, Ellen could not bear it. If he were to marry anyone else she could accept it, with great difficulty, as long as she was good enough for him. But not Siobhan.

'If she so much as looks at Harry, I'll tear her eyes out,' she said. And she meant it.

It was ten days later that she actually saw Siobhan again. She was at the door of the now vacant house – number forty-five, right next to the Turners'. Fuelled with the darkest suspicion, Ellen marched over the road to accost her.

'Didn't think we'd see the likes of you back here again,' she said.

'Oh? Why ever not? This is where my family is.' Siobhan gave her a look of innocent surprise.

Ellen felt as if her head was about to burst. 'Moving back in then, are you? I'd've thought you was used to flasher places than this by now. Can't see you sharing with all the O'Donaghues again.'

'I don't need to share with them,' Siobhan told her with a patronizing smile. 'I've a few bob of my own now, and, as you say, I'm used to something better. But family's family, after all.' She opened a gloved hand to reveal a sturdy door-key. 'I'm thinking of taking this place.'

'You're *what?*'

The words were out of her mouth before she could stop them. She flushed, furious at herself for sounding at a disadvantage.

'I thought it might be quite nice,' Siobhan was saying, obviously enjoying herself. 'The stage is such a strange life. People come and go, you see too much of them for a short while then nothing at all for months. It's best to keep a hold of your old friends, don't you think?'

'Well, you can't have this house,' Ellen heard herself saying. 'It's spoken for already.'

'That's not what they said at the landlord's office.' For the first time, Siobhan looked slightly put out.

'You must've been talking to the wrong person.'

'How come you know more about it than they do?'

''Cos I'm the one what's taking it.' She did not know what had made her say it. It just seemed the only way to keep Siobhan out.

'You? You and who else?' The smile became pure poison. 'You and Harry?'

If she hoped to wound, she succeeded. But Ellen was not going to let her know that.

'Harry?' she said, as if it were some sick joke. 'Oh no, you done me a favour there, Siobhan. I'm real grateful to you. It's not Harry, it's Gerry. Me and Gerry are moving in here – it's all fixed. So you better let me have that key.'

To her deep satisfaction, Siobhan was silenced. She held out her hand, and Siobhan placed the key in it.

'Thanks,' she said, and walked off home without a backward glance.

4

'Funny,' Maisie said, sticking a pin through her hat to anchor it to her hair, 'I never thought Ellen would go and marry Gerry. I always thought her and our Harry would get together in the end.'

Will grunted. He was fed up with this wedding before it even started. People seemed to have talked of nothing else for the past month.

Maisie carried on regardless. There were very few high spots in her life and she was out to make the most of this one.

'My mum thinks she's only doing it for his money,' she said.

'Your mum would,' Will snapped.

He was knotting a tie under his one and only stiff collar and he knew it was going to give him gip.

Downstairs Albert and Lily started scrapping, and Tommy, with all the authority of eight years, was telling them off. Maisie sighed and wailed down the stairs.

'Leave off, you lot, you'll wake the baby.'

If they heard her at all, the children took no notice.

'I'll be bloody glad when this is over,' Will muttered, still trying to get his tie looking right. 'Go and shut them kids up, for God's sake.'

Maisie sighed again and left the bedroom. Will looked morosely at his reflection in the tarnished mirror. Nothing about this wedding pleased him. It was because of his stupid sister that Siobhan was not after all going to come back to Trinidad Street. And Harry bloody Turner was still free, which meant he could still end up with Siobhan after all. There was not even the remotest chance of Siobhan turning up for the ceremony, since the O'Donaghues were still on the outs with the Billinghams. The only saving grace of the day was the opportunity to get totally pissed in the pub in the evening.

The noise downstairs seemed to be increasing. Peter had joined in with the row. Will swore and wrenched his tie into place. Times like this, he could not think why it was he had not gone with Siobhan that night. In fact, there was not a day when he did not regret it.

At the Turners' house, the atmosphere was hardly any better. Archie Turner disliked weddings on principle, Milly, Johnny and even little Bob were such partisans for Harry that they did not want to go at all, but had to because Maisie was married to a Johnson and Gerry was their cousin. Florrie and Ida had mixed feelings, but did not admit to them. Both of them felt that their brother had been slighted, but they were looking forward to the social side of the day. After all, there was nothing like one wedding for bringing on another, and they each had their eye on one or other of the young male guests.

'If you ask me, Harry's far better off without her,' Ida said, as she and Florrie tweaked at each other's dresses and made last-minute adjustments to their hair.

Florrie smoothed her skirt over her narrow hips. 'I dunno,' she said. 'I still wish Ellen was marrying him. She's been my friend ever since I can remember. It would've been nice.'

'Can't see how you can stay friends with her.'

Florrie did not answer. Sharp in her mind's eye was the picture of her younger self on a winter's evening in the street, rigid and burning with murderous hatred while Ida and Johnny clung to her, cold and frightened. Ellen had been there, trying to help, trying to give comfort. You did not turn your back on friendships like that.

'How do I look?' she asked, changing the subject.

'Nice,' Ida said loyally. 'I've always liked that dress. Suits you.'

'Mm,' Florrie said. She looked down at herself and wished she had an hourglass figure like that Siobhan O'Donaghue instead of a skinny body hardly different from her brother Johnny's. Men did like something to get hold of. 'You look lovely,' she said.

Ida smirked. Like her mother and Maisie, she had a surface prettiness that was now coming into its short flowering. She had great hopes of this wedding. She had fancied Jack Johnson for ages and this was a good chance to catch his eye.

Down in the kitchen, Harry was also getting ready, with such an air of aggressive isolation about him that the entire family gave him a wide berth, insofar as that was possible in a tiny house inhabited by seven people. With meticulous care, he slicked down his blond curls, tied his narrow blue and red tie and brushed the shoulders of his navy suit. He tried not to think of the reason for all this careful preparation. It was just his cousin, getting married. That was all. He had a well-built wall about his emotions now, and he was not going to let anyone see it breached today. He had not been at home when the confrontation between Ellen and Siobhan had taken place next door, but naturally there had been plenty of kind people ready to fill him in with the details. So Siobhan had done Ellen a favour by coming to the Masons' place that day. Fine. If that was the way she saw it, then it was a favour to him too. Gerry was welcome to her.

At number forty, Alma was already close to tears. She was still in an old dress with her hair in a plait down her back, and she was twitching around the kitchen in a state of high nervous tension, picking things up and putting them down.

'I still can't see why you can't come and live here,' she said.

Gerry sighed. They had been through this a dozen times or more.

'Mum, I know there's room enough here, but I

370

just wanted us to have a place of our own.' He cast about for something new to say, something that would really convince her. 'It's like proving I've *got* somewhere, that I've made it.'

'But everyone knows you got somewhere. Who else round here has got a market stall? I just don't see why you got to move out.'

'*Mum*, I'm only going across the road!'

Ellen had sagely said that his mum was bound to feel like that, since she was losing her baby.

'Baby!' Gerry had cried, laughing. 'I'm twenty-five!'

'You're still her youngest, though, and the youngest of only two. Of course she doesn't want you to go.'

'That's just stupid,' Gerry had said.

But now he remembered what she had said and with an effort at patience, put his arm round his mother.

'I'm only going across the road, Mum. I'll see you every day, don't worry. And you know what they say: you're not losing a son, you're gaining a daughter.'

'Yeah.' Alma looked unconvinced. 'But–'

'No buts. You go and get your glad rags on. Don't want them Johnsons outshining us, do we?'

'No, no, of course not.' His mother went off upstairs.

Gerry stood looking after her. There was one very good reason for moving out that he had not brought up: Charlie. He did not want Charlie listening to every movement on his wedding night or any other night. He could just see his

371

brother grinning at him in the morning and leering at Ellen, making suggestive remarks and drawing him on one side to ask how Ellen was.

What was making it much worse was the fact that he was not at all confident about the part he had to play tonight. It was not a thing he could get advice about. He could not possibly admit to his mates that he was still a virgin and ask them for a few tips.

He stood in the small kitchen, dressed in brand-new clothes from top to toe, on the day he had been planning for years, and broke out in a cold sweat. What if he wasn't up to scratch?

A few houses away at the Johnsons, it was Tom who was expressing the doubts.

'I dunno,' he said to his wife. 'I'd've been a whole lot happier if it was Harry Turner.'

'There's nothing wrong with young Gerry,' Martha said, just a trifle too emphatically.

'I know there ain't nothing wrong with him. He's just not the man Harry is, that's all.'

'There's plenty of girls as'd like to be in our Ellen's shoes today, I can tell you.'

'Yeah, yeah, I know that an' all. But be honest, Martha. You know our Ellen. Who do you think she ought to be marrying? Who's best for her, eh?'

Martha came and sat heavily on the bed beside him. She did not answer directly.

'Trouble with our Ellen is, she's stubborn as a mule. Got it into her head that she weren't going to make the first move after that to-do with Harry and Siobhan, and look where it's got her. Harry thinks she don't care, and he's got other interests all over the place, so Gerry steps in. And after all, love, he worships the ground she stands on, that's plain.'

'Oh yeah, I agree. And that's a good start. But there's more to a good marriage than that, ain't there? You got to stick at it, through thick and thin. You know all about that, eh, love?' Tom put his arms round his wife and drew her close, smiling into her eyes. 'You've had enough to put up with all these years, ain't you? But you been good to me all that time. The best, you are.'

Martha leant her head into his neck and returned his squeeze.

'I got the best an' all,' she replied. She looked up at him and planted a kiss on his lips. 'I tell you something, if our Ellen's half as happy as what we been, she's a lucky girl.'

The other side of the thin wall, Daisy and Ellen were getting ready. Daisy was in a fine state of excitement.

'This is going to be the best party we had for ages,' she declared, positively skipping round the room. 'There's been too much doom and gloom lately. All bad news. I'm really going to enjoy myself today.'

Ellen smiled at her. 'Good, I'm glad,' she said.

At seventeen, Daisy had grown into a big, bonny girl with a generous figure, a high colour, abundant energy and an argumentative streak.

'What about you? Looking forward to it? Nervous?' Daisy asked.

'Yes,' Ellen said.

She was nervous. She had jumped into this because of Siobhan and now she could not back out without hurting poor Gerry. Not that she wanted to back out. She was very fond of Gerry. It was just that – she stopped short, refusing even to admit it to herself. But inside she knew that this was second best.

Daisy gave a chuckle. 'So you're not getting him the way Maisie did, or Mary O'Donaghue?'

'No, I'm not,' Ellen said emphatically.

'You've not tried him out, then?'

'Daisy! What do you know about it?'

'More than what you do, by the sound of it.' Her sister bounced on the bed, laughing.

Ellen shook a finger at her. 'You just be careful, miss, or *you'll* be ending up like Maisie and Mary.'

She did wonder about the wedding night. She had been dying to do it with Harry. With Gerry she was not at all sure. But that was part of being married, so she going to have to accept it.

'I wish it was all over,' she said suddenly.

It was the truth. Once it was done, there was no going back. She could throw herself into her new life.

'Blimey, what a waste!' Daisy said. 'It's your day, remember. Enjoy it while you got the chance.'

Ellen nodded.

Daisy glanced at her, then with sudden perception came over and gave her a hug. Ellen clutched her back with a desperate fierceness. She needed very much to have someone to hold on to.

'You'll be all right, honest you will,' Daisy said.

'I hope so,' said Ellen.

For a long minute Harry's name hung in the air between them, but neither felt strong enough to speak it.

All of the street that was not on the outs with the Billinghams – which was roughly all the non-Irish – turned out to see Gerry and Ellen married at St Luke's. General opinion was that he looked real smart, just like a toff. Everyone else had got their best clothes out of pawn, and maybe bought a new tie or retrimmed a hat, but Gerry was actually dressed in all new things. They were most impressed.

Ellen, it was agreed, had always been a pretty girl. Today, in a red and navy dress and a hat fluttering with artificial red roses, she looked a proper picture. A lot of people remarked that she looked a bit pale, others that you couldn't exactly call her blooming or blushing, but then, as yet others pointed out, if she wasn't now, she would be tomorrow.

After the service, the two families and as many of their relatives as could be fitted in went back to the Johnsons' for tea. Everybody caught up with family news and eyed up the opposite side. The bride was kissed and the groom shaken by the hand. Bottles of beer were opened and the atmosphere became increasingly jolly. As noses grew red and faces shone, both sides decided that the other family was mostly all right, not a bad lot at all, until the whole party spilled out of doors and went up to the Rum Puncheon.

They came in in a big noisy group, laughing and calling to each other, some already singing. Inside, quite a crowd from Trinidad Street had already gathered and were lining up the drinks. A cheer went up as Ellen and Gerry came through the doors, together with a ragged chorus of 'Here Comes the Bride'. Gerry, elated, bowed and ceremoniously led his new wife to the seat that was hastily placed for her. Laughing, Ellen sat down and took the glass that was thrust into her hand.

They were all well away now. Maisie was leaning against Will, misty-eyed, living her wedding all over again, while Will had recovered from his bad temper and was cheerful and expansive with drink. Martha and Tom stood smiling and drawing strength from the sheer force of all the goodwill around them. The young people were sorting themselves out, some still making the first tentative steps towards getting into pairs, others, like Ida Turner, firmly in control. Her arm was so tightly linked with Jack Johnson's that you could hardly have got a knife between them. Someone started singing and they all joined in, swaying in time to 'Daisy Belle' and joyfully belting out the top notes.

Alma was better now that she was in the centre of a big happy crowd. It did not take much to bring out the optimistic side of her personality, and with a mixture of beer and port flowing potently round her system, she was on top of the world. Everything was fine. It was the best thing that had happened for years. She came round behind the newly-weds and flung an arm round each of them.

'Here's my lovely boy, and my lovely girl,' she gushed, shouting above the noise and kissing them both. And to Gerry, 'What's all this, you standing here like a lemon? Sit her on your knee, why don't you? You're married now, y'know! Her mum can't stop you!'

Gerry laughed and pulled Ellen up, then sat on her chair and settled her on his knee, his arm around her waist. Cheers and whistles broke out all round. It was at that moment that there was a shifting in the densely packed crowd, and Ellen caught sight of Harry.

He was leaning on the bar, nursing a pint, a small still island of silence amongst the hilarity, his normally open and cheerful features contracted and dark. He looked utterly unapproachable.

Ellen stared, unable to tear her eyes away. She could feel Gerry's arm round her, Gerry's legs beneath hers, and she knew with a deadly certainty that she was in the wrong place. As if drawn by the intensity of her gaze, Harry looked up and met her eyes. Time and place lost meaning. There were just the two of them, one at each end of a short dark tunnel. Ellen wanted to get up, to run down the tunnel, to reach the light at the other end. But her legs would not move. She was fixed to the spot. She tried to say his name, she cried it out inside her, but nothing came out. Then someone blundered between them with his hands full of spilling pints and the spell was broken. When she looked again, Harry was gone.

The gathering that had been so warm and friendly and jolly now palled. She looked around at the red, sweating faces, at hair slipping out of its pins and ties askew and she no longer felt part of the crowd. The mouths, gaping, drinking, were wet and loose, the eyes avid. The noise was terrible, a discordant row battering her eardrums.

She wanted very much to go away, to be some-where cool and dark and utterly quiet, to be alone. To cry. But there was no escaping now. She had made her decision and there was no going back. She was tied.

The evening seemed to go on for ever. The en-tire repertoire of the street's songs was gone through and started again. Alma was on the table, doing a spirited performance of 'Knees up, Mother Brown' to shrieks of laughter from the rest of the pub. If anyone had been sober enough, they could have counted the layers of her underwear.

Gerry pulled Ellen closer and said into her ear, 'You want to go now?'

'Yes,' Ellen said, with feeling.

Half a second later she realized what this meant, and regretted it. Gerry gave her a squeeze and heaved her off his knee.

'We'll try and creep out,' he said.

No chance of that. The street was out to enjoy itself, and seeing off the bride and groom was an important part of the sport.

'Aye-aye, look who's slipping out!'

'Where're you two off to then, as if we didn't know?'

A passageway to the door was formed, with densely packed bodies on either side – a gauntlet of racy remarks, jokes, advice, back-slapping, handshaking and kissing to be run before they could leave the pub. Ellen found herself facing her mother. She flung her arms round her and for a brief moment they hugged each other fiercely.

'Oh, Mum.'

Martha kissed her forehead. 'You'll be all right,

lovey. Just do what comes natural.'

Her father was shaking Gerry's hand, squeezing his shoulder. 'Take care of her, son.'

'I will, Mr Johnson, I will.'

Gerry put a protective arm round her shoulder and they braved the last few feet to the door, emerging into the chill of the evening. Still they were not free, for a straggle of merrymakers followed them right to the door of their new home.

'Pick her up, pick her up!'

'Carry her over the threshold!'

Laughing, Gerry complied, staggering slightly as he lifted her up the step.

Then the door was closed behind them and at last they were alone. Ellen shivered. The house felt cold after the fug of the pub. Gerry took her in his arms and kissed her long and tenderly.

'Just us now, eh, love?'

'Yeah.'

'Happy?'

'Oh yeah – very.'

'Good. 'Cos I am. Happiest bloke in the world.'

She was acutely aware of being right next door to the Turners. They were so thin, the walls between these houses, you could hear a cough or the scrape of a chair. When it was quiet, you could hear voices. It was quiet now, with all of the street still celebrating their wedding. All except Harry. He had left the pub. He could be right next door now, on the other side of the wall.

An hour or so later, Ellen lay on her marriage bed, staring up into the darkness of the ceiling. Gerry lay asleep, sprawled partly across her, still damp with sweat. She lay perfectly still, not wanting to disturb him and start all that up all over again. She felt bruised and battered and profoundly disappointed. It was not Gerry's fault, she supposed. Judging by the gasps and cries, he had reached whatever it was that this was all in aid of. She had glimpsed it often, with Harry...

The gates of memory opened. She had meant to keep them closed. It was all past now, after all. But she could not help it. It all came flooding back, the pressure of his mouth on hers, the eager questing of lips and tongues, the burning need of two young bodies separated only by the frustrating layers of clothing. She had wanted him so sweetly, so desperately, wanted to be swallowed up, to be lost, to become part of him.

It had not been like that tonight. She had been left unmoved. As Gerry's breathing deepened and slowed, she stared up into the blackness, tears gathering into the corners of her eyes and running silently down her face.

PART IV

1908–9

1

Ellen sat up in bed and settled the baby against her bent knees.

'Jessica,' she said softly, 'Jessica.'

The infant gazed back at her with unfocused blue eyes.

Tenderly, Ellen unwrapped the worn shawl that had served each new Johnson. Her daughter's tiny hands and arms emerged, pink and perfect. Ellen placed a finger in her palm and thrilled at the tight hold, the delicate fingernails, pale and polished as the inside of a seashell. She freed the rest of the baby's body, marvelling all over again at the miracle she had wrought. This tiny creature with the rosebud mouth and the rounded knees and miniature toes was hers. She had made her.

As she watched, the round face crumpled and grew red. A thin wail rose rapidly to a demanding cry. Ellen's breasts, already painfully engorged, ached unbearably in response. She lifted the baby up, supporting the heavy head with one hand.

'Are you hungry, then?' she asked. 'Don't fret, it's coming.'

With nimble fingers she undid the buttons of her nightdress, exposing a breast. She settled the baby in the crook of her arm and watched the little head turn unerringly towards her and latch onto the nipple. She tensed against the first excruciating working of the hard gums on her sore flesh, then gradually relaxed as the baby's powerful sucking released the accumulated pressure. It sent waves of pleasure tingling right through her body from her nipples to the tips of her toes.

It was wonderful, wonderful. Her very own perfect baby, and she was the only one in the whole world who could give her exactly what she needed. She bent over so that her cheek rested on the baby's head, feeling the soft fluff of hair and the hard, warm skull. A wave of pure joy rose in her. Her own baby, someone she could love with passion and intensity, without reservation. Someone of her own.

Gerry came in to the room.

'I'm off then.'

'Mm.' Ellen did not look up.

'It might be quite a long day. I got to go and see a bloke this evening. You'll be all right, won't you? You don't mind?'

'What? Oh – no, that's all right.'

Ellen managed to tear her attention away. She focused with difficulty on her husband as he stood by the bed, gazing down at them. There was such undisguised love and anxiety in his face that a twinge of guilt broke through her absorption.

'I mean,' he was saying, 'I don't like leaving you both for too long.'

'We'll be fine. We're not exactly on our own, are we? There's my mum and your mum just over the road. They're sure to look in.'

'Yeah. Yeah, of course. They'll keep an eye on you. It's just – I don't like leaving you that long.'

It was a great yawning plea for some gesture on her part. Ellen gently parted the baby's clamping jaws from one breast and transferred her to the other, smiling as she did so.

'That's it – it's just as good that side.'

Then she looked again at Gerry. She sometimes felt he was almost as demanding as the baby, and not half so appealing.

'Don't worry,' she said. 'We'll still be here when you come back.'

Still he hesitated, fussing over odd details, spinning out the time. Ellen answered him in monosyllables, waiting for him to go. Finally, he went. Ellen heard the front door close behind him and settled back with a sigh of relief. She only had to get the two lodgers off to work and then it was just the two of them, herself and Jessica. That was how she liked it.

The baby changed and sleeping soundly in the crib, Ellen got herself ready for the day as the kettle boiled and the porridge reheated on the range. The lodgers, a ship-repairer and a metal-worker, appeared just in time to bolt down their breakfast, grab the bread and cheese Ellen had made for them and disappear out of the door. She was glad to see the back of them. They were no trouble and they contributed a good deal to the family income, but she resented their presence. They were one more nuisance to come between herself and Jessica. But now at last the house was hers. She ran upstairs to check on the baby, putting her hand under the covers to feel the minute rise and fall of her chest. It was all right; she was still breathing. She slept so soundly that sometimes Ellen almost believed she had died. She stood gazing down at the closed little face.

Perfect. She could sit and just look at her all day, given the chance. But there were jobs to be done; shirts needing ironing, floors needing scrubbing, yet more washing for the baby, quite apart from the shopping and the cooking and the daily chore of scrubbing the step and the sill and sweeping down the pavement. And then this afternoon she had promised to look after Maisie's younger ones while Maisie turned out their back bedroom.

Downstairs on the range a bucket of water was heating. Ellen tied on a sacking apron, found the scrubbing brush and heaved the bucket out through the parlour to the front door, pausing on the way to look at herself in the mirror. She nodded at the reflection. Not bad. She told herself that she was hurrying to get the job done before Jessica woke again, but inside she knew there was another reason. If she got out there early enough, she might catch Harry on his way to work.

Out in the street, several other women were already busy with their steps. Some had got as far as doing the pavement. People were hurrying off to work, some still munching at doorsteps of bread. Older children were coming back from early-morning jobs. Ellen waved to her sister Daisy, who was on her way to Maconochie's, and exchanged brief enquiries about their families.

She had just plumped the bucket down and plunged in the brush when the Turners' door opened. Ellen's heart turned over. She stared with intense concentration at the stone step.

''Bye, Mum. See you tonight!'

Ida came bounding out. Unbidden, disappointment gripped Ellen.

''Lo, Ellen. You're at it early.'

'Got a lot to do.'

'Oo, you old married women! Got to rush. I'm late.'

Off she ran, shouting to a friend at the end of the road. Ellen marvelled at her cheerfulness. She had never gone to a day's work at the factory so eagerly.

''Morning, Ellen.'

This time it was Florrie. Ellen smiled up with real pleasure.

''Lo, love.'

'How's the baby?'

'Oh, she's lovely – you must come and see–'

'I will, I will, but not now. Ellen?'

'Yeah?'

'Pop in and see my mum during the day, would you?'

''Course. She not well?'

'Oh – well – the usual. You know.'

'Yeah. Right.'

She had been kept awake last night by the shouting and crashing next door.

'Thanks a million, Ellen. 'Bye!'

Ellen sat back on her heels and watched her friend hurry up the road. Florrie was still too thin. Today she looked as if the wind would blow her away. Ellen was so engaged with worrying about her that she did not see the next person come out of the Turners'.

''Morning, Ellen.'

She jumped, the blood pumping into her face.

'Oh – Harry – good morning.'

He was gone, tramping down the street with his

hands thrust into the pockets of his heavy melton overcoat, his back uncompromisingly turned. She had not even caught a glimpse of his face. Unaccountably angry with both him and herself, she attacked the step as if the dirt on it were a personal affront.

It was later on in the morning, when she had just finished feeding the baby again, that her mother let herself in at the front door.

'Coo-ee! Ellen?'

'In the back, Mum.'

'Ah.' Martha swooped down on Jessica and took her in her arms. 'How's my little darling today, then?'

Jessica gave a windy grimace and belched delicately. Both women laughed.

'Ah, ain't she just the dearest little thing? And to think you wanted to leave her with me and go on working at that stall.'

Ellen smiled at such blind foolishness and got up to put the kettle on. 'Yeah, daft, weren't I? But that was before she was born, remember.'

It had been the subject of many a fierce argument between Gerry and herself. Gerry, who had seen his mother work herself ragged to provide for himself and Charlie, was determined that his wife should not have to do that, that his child should have a mum at home to care for it. Ellen was equally determined not to give up the fun and challenge of the stall. They were still rowing about it when she went into labour. It was Jessica herself who resolved the situation. Ellen could no more bear to leave her than to cut off a piece of herself.

She smiled at her mother, who was crooning at

the baby. Martha had taken on a new lease of life since the birth of her grandchild. It was not as if Jessica was the first, for there were all Maisie's, but as she put it herself, your son's children belong more to the other granny. Jessica was hers. She healed all but a small part of the wound left by the little boy who had died, and finally reconciled her to the fact that there would be no more.

They drank their tea and discussed the doings of the street – Daisy's latest young man, Jack's on-and-off relationship with Ida Turner, the tragedy of Mary O'Donaghue's crippled son.

'I was thinking, last night,' Martha said, when they had exhausted the possibilities of their neighbours' lives. 'I was lying awake, and I got thinking, and I had this idea. Wouldn't it be nice if we all went on a trip in the summer? We ain't been on an outing since you was, what–?'

'Six,' Ellen said. 'I was six and Will was at work and Jack and Daisy was just little 'uns. We went to Southend on the steamer. Oh, I remember that, all right.'

'Yeah, it was lovely, weren't it? One of the best days of my life. And what I thought was, why don't we do it again?'

'What, all of us? All the family? You lot and me and Gerry and Jessica, and Will and Maisie and their lot – oh, and I expect Gerry's mum'd want to come too.'

'Oh yeah, everybody, all the family. We'd have to save up. It's not going to be easy for Will, but if they start now, putting something away each week ... and I can help a bit. We're all right now all you kids are off our hands or working. What d'you think?'

'I think it's a wonderful idea!' Ellen's imagination took fire. She saw sparkling blue waves, thrashing paddle wheels, Jessica waving at the seagulls, herself with the wind in her hair. And Southend! The pier and the bands and the beach and the candy floss. 'Oh yes. Oh, Mum, you are a clever old thing. I'll start saving right away. And I can help Will and Maisie out a bit, you know, on the quiet. And I suppose Jack and Daisy might want to take whoever they're going out with along with them...'

Once started, the idea gathered size like a snowball rolling down a mountainside. Just as Ellen predicted, Alma was game, then Maisie wanted her family along, so the Turners were added, and then the Crofts, since both Florrie and Daisy were going out with Croft boys, and before they knew where they were, half the street was included. Even the Catholics began to take an interest, despite the fact that the Billinghams were in on it. It was thought that a trip would do Mary O'Donaghue-as-was the world of good, so she and her family were added, and then Pat and Declan and their wives and families wanted to come along until, wonder of wonders, Brian said one day that he and Clodagh were thinking of joining in.

'Well,' Martha said, relating this to Ellen, 'I never thought I'd see the day. It'll be worth it, just for that. I've always liked Clodagh O'Donaghue, and I never wanted to be on the outs with her, especially over something what that Charlie may or may not have done. I know Alma thinks he's God's little white lamb, but between you and me, I wouldn't be surprised if it *was* him what got her Theresa in the family way.'

'Yeah, I wouldn't be surprised, neither,' Ellen agreed, 'but don't never say it to Alma's face.'

The question she really wanted to ask, the one that hung on her lips begging to be answered, was the one she could not speak – not even to her mother. Least of all to her mother. Her mother believed she was over it, believed she was happy with her home and her husband and her baby. She could never admit otherwise, not to her mother. She knew very well what the answer would be: *Don't be such a fool, forget all about it, don't play with fire, count your blessings*, above all, *don't act like your stupid brother.* And of course it was all so very true. She knew she should be happy with what she had. She *was* happy with what she had. So she said nothing, and listened out for clues.

It was Florrie who provided the answer. She was chatting to Ellen about the outing one Sunday afternoon, saying how she had almost got her fare saved.

'...and me and Ida are putting some by for little Bob, but we ain't telling my mum, so's there'll be some over, like, for spending. Ain't no good going on an outing if you can't buy a drink or two and an ice cream and go on the rides, now is it?'

'Are all your family going?' Ellen asked. The words sounded so pointed that she had to cover her tracks, to modify them. 'Even your dad?'

'Yeah, him an' all.' Florrie's bright face twisted in contempt and loathing. 'My mum'd catch it if he was left behind. I expect we'll have to carry him home.'

Ellen gave a sympathetic nod. 'So you'll be a big party,' she said.

'Yeah.' Florrie gave a little shake to her shoulders, as if dismissing her father. 'Yeah, it's going to be good, ain't it? Best thing we all done for ages.'

Her opinion was shared by the entire street. It was the first topic of conversation. Every misfortune was measured by it. Someone had lost a job, or was ill, or suffered an accident – would they still be able to come on the trip? Mothers used it to threaten children into good behaviour – *pack that up or you won't go on the trip*. Not going became a real fear. It was Harry who thought of the back-up fund. He walked into the Rum Puncheon one evening and plumped an empty sweet jar on the bar.

'What's that, then, Harry?'

'He's brought his own pot with him – he don't like the way they wash 'em up here.'

'It's in case he gets caught short!'

Harry joined in the general shout of laughter at this.

'Go on then, Harry boy, what's it for?'

'It's for the trip, for emergencies, like. We all put in what we can, then if anyone's in a fix at the last minute and can't pay for their ticket, we get it out of this. That way, no one gets left out.'

They all looked at the jar with awe, as if a genie might billow out of it.

'Blimey, Harry, that's a blinder of an idea.'

'A real corker.'

Harry dug in his pocket and produced a handful of loose change.

'That's to start it off,' he said, letting it slide off

his fingers with a loud clatter.

Of course, they all had to follow suit. From then on, the jar sat on the bar, challenging everyone's generosity, reminding them that they might be the ones who needed a subsidy. The cash tinkled in, pennies and ha'pennies, even farthings, but over the weeks it mounted up, rising to the top, until the landlord had to change some of the coppers into silver to stop it all from flooding over.

And then Clodagh O'Donaghue dropped the bombshell.

Martha came straight over to Ellen's to chew it over with her.

'Have you heard? Have you heard who says she's coming on the outing with us?' She was so incensed she did not even ask after her favourite grandchild.

'No, who?' Ellen bustled about, filling the kettle, fetching teacups.

'That Siobhan O'Donaghue.'

'*What?*'

'That little Irish slut.'

Ellen had never heard her mother use such strong terms before. She put the cups down on the table and stared at her.

'How did she get to hear about it?'

'The O'Donaghues told her, I suppose. She still sees them from time to time.'

It was dreadful. Her whole day would be ruined if Siobhan came.

'Tell them she can't come.'

'I can't do that, now can I?' Martha sighed.

'I don't see why not. It's your trip. You thought of it.'

'But it don't belong to me. It's everyone's. It's the street's trip.'

'She don't live here no more. She's got no right.'

If Siobhan came along and made up to Harry ... but she could not say this out loud. She had no rights over Harry any more. She was a married woman, a mother. She tried a different tack.

'What's poor Maisie going to feel?'

'Don't you fret,' her mother said grimly. 'I'll have a good talking to that son of mine before we go.'

But the pleasure had gone out of the anticipation. Whenever she planned what she would wear, she knew that Siobhan would be there, looking ten times more stunning. Whenever she thought about what they might do, she knew that Siobhan would take it up and turn it round to her own ends. The thought of her was like a grain of sand in her mind, rubbing and rubbing, producing not a pearl, but a great painful blister. Just to make it more irritating, Gerry thought Siobhan would make a useful addition to the party.

'It's not every street can take a music-hall artiste on an outing with them,' he said. 'I don't know what you're so worked up about. There's sure to be singing. She can lead us all. It'll be good.'

'Huh,' Ellen said. 'You're just like all the rest. You just want her there so you can give her the eye.'

Gerry was appalled. He reached over and pulled her into his arms.

'Oh, sweetheart, no. That's not it. You got me all wrong there. There'll never be anyone for me but you. You know that. There never has been anyone else for me. I've always loved you.'

Guilt nagged at her. He was so sweet, so kind, such a devoted husband and a doting father. She could not want for anything better. She hugged him back.

'I know, love, I know. I'm just being crochety. Take no notice of me.'

'And you love me too, don't you?'

The trickle of guilt turned into a flood. She kissed him. 'Of course I do, you old silly.'

And she meant it.

They all assembled on Fresh Wharf in the shadow of the Monument, a loud gathering of people in their best clothes, all talking at the tops of their voices and out to get every last ounce of pleasure from the day. Mothers stood with babies on their hips, grabbing at toddlers as they made a break for freedom; older children ran about shrieking while their fathers, self-conscious at being with the whole family, either ignored them or made heavy-handed efforts at discipline. Young people stood in strictly segregated groups and eyed each other from the safety of the herd. The few old folk shook their heads and told anyone who cared to listen that it had all been different in their day.

Alongside was the steamer, *their* steamer, *Clacton Belle*, long and slim and elegant with her black hull, gleaming white superstructure and tall yellow funnel. They waited in the 'fore cabin queue, the cheaper one, but, as they all told each other, it was so much healthier than saloon class. They were all dressed for the day in their best, in many cases the same clothes that had come out for every wedding and knees-up for the last five years or more, fresh out of pawn with maybe a new scarf or a bunch of flowers on a hat. Not everyone had made it, in the end. One family of children was down with a summer fever that everyone hoped was not diphtheria, Granny Hobbs, after years of perfect health, had succumbed to an ulcerated leg, and one of the fathers had had an accident at work. The rest of his family was there, though, thanks to Harry's emergency fund, and there were plans to bring back rock and picture postcards for those forced to stay at home. Only one of the trippers was unaccounted for.

'Where's that blooming Siobhan, then?' Alma asked, craning her head to see if she had missed the girl in the crowd.

Milly gave a little shrug. 'Suits me if she don't turn up. She's done enough mischief to my family to last a lifetime.'

Alma looked at her in amazement. For Milly, that was a strong speech.

'Blimey, girl, you're speaking your mind at last. Keep it up,' she said.

Milly went pink and nodded.

'It's this trip, ain't it?' Alma said. 'Even the thought of a bit of sea air puts new heart into you.'

She certainly felt a new woman herself today. With her best red dress and her new shawl shouting with bright pink and yellow roses and her hat with the waving blue and purple feathers (only slightly bent) she knew she looked a picture. Nobody, she decided, would think she was over forty. Who knew what might happen on the trip? She looked over the passengers who weren't from their party. There were plenty of men but it was difficult to make out whether they were with someone or not. Then her eye fell on Gerry and Ellen, and she experienced the familiar contradictory mix of emotions. There was little Jessica, looking over Ellen's shoulder, her clear eyes round beneath a frilly sunbonnet.

'Ah, the little love,' she said out loud. She adored that child.

But at the same time came the nasty jolt: a granny. She was a granny. She was old, a has-been. She might as well give up on her own life now and just live through her children and grandchildren. It gave her a dreadful sinking feeling, as if she was being dragged down into a muddy pit.

'No,' she said.

'What?' Milly asked.

'Nothing – just it's going to be a fine old day, ain't it? A real beano. Like we used to have when we was girls.'

Nothing was going to spoil today for her. She still had her figure, and plenty of it. She still had quite a lot of her teeth. And she still knew how to have a good time.

'There she is,' Milly said.

There was a stir in the Trinidad Street contingent as others spotted her as well: Siobhan O'Donaghue, dressed all in white.

'White! Think of the washing!' Milly gasped.

'Don't you tell me she's a blooming virgin,' Alma said sourly. 'I think we all know better than that. Beats me why that Clodagh O'Donaghue lets her back into the bosom of the family, what with her high principles and all.'

'Ain't nothing proved, is there?' Milly said. 'First she was going to marry our Harry, then she made off. Nothing but his word and hers. No baby.'

Siobhan certainly looked like a princess as she moved towards them. The crowd naturally parted to let her through. Alma was suddenly struck with total discontent over her own dress, for Siobhan's spoke Fashion. It was cut in the latest soft line with the higher waist and the wide kimono sleeves, making Alma realize that hers was out of date. The pure white cotton was trimmed with a wide band of broderie anglaise all the way down the front, and there was a single pink rose pinned to her breast to match the pink roses and white veiling on her straw hat. She looked fresh and young and, it had to be admitted, virginal; a ripe luscious strawberry, ready to be picked.

'Bloody hell,' Alma muttered. 'Will you look at their faces? Can't hardly keep from slobbering.'

Every man's eye was upon her.

'Well, that's the end of any chances them girls had for the day. Your Florrie and your Ida ain't going to be too pleased, are they?'

'They're younger,' Milly pointed out.

But there was no such comfort for Alma, a forty-four-year-old granny. The young lads whom Florrie and Ida admired might not dare to aspire to Siobhan, but the older men certainly did.

'Oh, sod it,' she said. 'When are they letting us on this blooming boat? I could do with a drink.'

As if by magic, the crowd began to move forward. Up the gangway they went, laughing and chattering, to spill out on to the deck. Alma's naturally cheerful spirits began to rise again.

After all, a trip was a trip, to be enjoyed. Blow that blooming Siobhan.

'Come on,' she said, grabbing her sister's arm. 'Round the other side and find a nice sheltered place by the cabins, and some deckchairs. We can make a little camp, and then anyone who wants can go strolling round the deck or whatever and we'll all know where to find each other.'

The others fell in with her. Milly and Maisie and a selection of Maisie's children, Gerry and Ellen with Jessica, Tom and Martha Johnson all sat down in a broad semicircle with their bags and coats and paraphernalia, testing the deckchairs, looking about for offspring, assuring each other that this was the life. Archie disappeared straight into the bar. Will fiddled around with the deck-chairs, sat down, stood up, looked around, a picture of indecision. Alma soon sorted him out.

'Why don't you go and help your dad-in-law with the drinks? Mine's a port and lemon. What you having, Maisie love?'

Will had no choice but to comply. But such was the goodwill engendered by the day that when he came out again twenty minutes later, Archie was still with him, and what was more, he was bearing drinks for all the family. Milly went quite scarlet with pleasure.

The young people were off at once to explore the boat and see who else was on it, while the older children gathered on the sponsons above the paddle wheels, peering over into the murky Thames for the first stirrings of action. The volume of smoke pouring out of the funnel increased, the ship's officers shouted orders and the deckhands let go the lines. Simultaneously, the siren tooted and the children shrieked 'We're off!' With a shudder, the great steam engines woke into life and the paddle wheels began to turn, only slowly here in the crowded river, but magnificent in churning cream and brown water.

Alma settled back in her deckchair and watched the teeming wharves and warehouses of the south side slip by. With the infuriating Siobhan pushed temporarily out of mind, a breeze just beginning to touch her face, and a nice fresh port and lemon in her hand, all was well with her world. She raised her glass.

'Here's to us!' she cried.

One of the deckhands turned and grinned at her.

Up on the top deck, Siobhan was holding court. She was sitting just forward of the funnel with her old escort of Pat and Declan on either side and a cluster of males old and young all around her. The novelty of seeing their own river bank from the new perspective of the water was lost on them. They saw nothing of the historic sights slipping by on either side. All they wanted was to get a little of this fascinating creature, to breathe the same air, to catch her eye. Not only the Trinidad Street crowd, but other men on the boat could not keep away. Siobhan's perfectly controlled figure and exquisite face were quite apart from the more natural and well-known attractions of their own women.

Harry leant his back against the rail and looked at them, then at the cluster of disgruntled young girls gathered at the other side of the deck. His unmarried sisters were looking in Siobhan's direction with faces as sour as lemons, and it did not take a genius to discover why. Both Jack Johnson and Jimmy Croft were caught up in the fringes of Siobhan's admirers. Jack he decided to leave to his fate. He was only a lad and, besides, having Maisie married to a Johnson was enough. He did not need any more ties with that family. Jimmy was a different matter. Florrie did not say much, but Harry got the impression that she was really in love with him, and if there was one person he did not want to see hurt, it was Florrie. He knew that, like himself, she was not the sort to fall in and out of love easily. There was a quiet deep passion hidden inside her frail-looking body that she very rarely revealed. He strolled over to the edge of the group and stood alongside Jimmy Croft.

'Do yourself a favour, mate – give it a miss,' he said.

'What?' Jimmy only half looked at him. He did not want to be distracted.

'All you stand to get from that is burnt fingers.'

'Oh, come on, Harry. I mean, look at her – you know what I mean. After all, you and her was–'

'Listen, mate,' Harry said. 'You ever had a nice shiny apple, all rosy red skin and not a spot on it, and bitten into it and found yourself looking at half a maggot?'

He had all his friend's attention now. Jimmy was gaping at him, the expression in his eyes gradually changing as the meaning of this little parable slowly sank in. An involuntary twitch of revulsion pulled at his mouth.

Harry let him get on with his own thought processes.

'Me, I'm going over to our girls,' he said casually. 'Reckon they'll welcome a bit of the old chat.'

He broke into the group at the forward rail and put an arm round his sister Ida's waist.

'Enjoying it, are you? There's old Dog Island. Looks different from the water, don't it? Which of you girls works at Maconochie's? I wave to you lot when I go past here, but none of you ever waves back. Too blooming stuck up, that's what you are.'

He was beginning to raise a few smiles. He worked a little harder, telling them how all the lightermen knew that the prettiest girls were hidden away behind the prisonlike walls of the great factory, and how he'd nearly collided with other boats many a time when they were out on the quay eating their dinners at midday.

'And here's the dear old Island Gardens coming up,' he pointed out. 'See the trees, and the dome of the tunnel? How many of you got happy memories of the Gardens?'

It was out before he could stop himself. Some of his own happiest memories were of afternoons spent under those plane trees, but they were not ones he cared to take out and look at these days.

With relief, he found that he was getting a reaction.

'–Wouldn't mind going down that tunnel with you any day, Harry.'

'When you going to take me ship-spotting, eh?'

He flirted with all of them, showing them places of interest along the river bank, telling them tales of funny incidents and close shaves amongst the watermen. Their giggles and retorts kept him afloat.

He became aware of another male presence, a rival for all this undivided attention: Jimmy Croft.

'Wotcher, Jim!'

And if the fool did not go for Florrie, he did not deserve her. He kept up the act, letting events take their course, trying not even to glance at them. But out of the corner of his eye he saw Jim in between two of the younger girls and Daisy Johnson. Daisy was looking up at him sideways with a come-hither smile, saying something. Bloody Johnsons. Florrie was standing to one side, ignoring him. He wanted to shout out to her, to give her the hint: *Just show him a sign, girl. Not a lot, not all over him, just a little signal, like.* But she was too far away and he had his own part to sustain.

Down the river the paddle boat steamed, cutting her way between great iron cargo vessels, grubby little coasters, stately sailing ships with brightly painted figureheads, flocks of barges and lighters and tugs. Past the acres of brick where hundreds of thousands of people lived out their lives in cramped houses and treeless streets, past the forests of smoking chimneys and the bleak factories, went the *Clacton Belle*, a bright little oasis of pleasure, filled with people escaping from the treadmill. On the decks and in the cabins they strolled about and flirted, laughed and joked, smoked, ate and drank and watched the everyday world slip by them. Some of them, the lucky ones, were on their way for a whole week's pleasure at Clacton or Walton or even as far afield as Yarmouth. Others, like the Trinidad Street party, had only the one day. But all were out to wring every second of fun from the voyage.

Once they were into the lower reaches, and the houses retreated and marshes opened out at the sides of the river, Harry made some excuses and eased away from the gang. It was a mixed group now, still more young women than young men, but a whole lot jollier than when he had first joined it.

'Come straight back,' the girls called out to him.

'Yeah, yeah,' he said, but he left them to it.

He went down to the main deck to join the rest of his family. He bought them a round of drinks and made sure his father was not yet the worse for wear, but the togetherness of the married couples and the demands of their small children made him feel excluded. He made his way down to the lower decks and for a while watched the engines working; it was a different world, of steam and oil, shining brass and huge pumping steel pistons. Some of the Trinidad Street boys were there, so he explained to them how coal and water were transformed into the power to push the *Belle* along. They jumped up and down, excited by the sheer raw energy, and admired the engineers crawling unprotected among all that moving machinery with oilcans and rags. He left them running backwards and forwards over the hump above the driving shaft, and went up on deck again. He was leaning over, watching the hypnotic curve of the bow wave forever falling over into the green water when a figure in white joined him at the rail.

'All alone?'

'Looks like it.' He did not look at her.

'Where have all your admirers gone?'

'Same place as yours,' he countered.

She placed a hand on his arm, a white-gloved hand. In spite of himself, he felt a stirring of interest.

'They're a bunch of jackasses,' she said.

Her fingers moved on his arm in a mere suggestion of a caress. To counteract it, he answered more sharply than was necessary.

'Well, I'm better off than you, then. My friends are a good lot of girls – nice girls, the sort that'd stick by you when you're in a hole.'

She gave a merry little laugh at that. 'My, you're the grumpy one, so you are. I didn't think you were the kind to harbour grudges, Harry Turner.'

'I'm not.'

'That's all right, then.'

She threaded her arm through his and leant against him. The body beneath the virginal white was as full and promising as ever. He had to fight against the natural reaction to pull her closer.

'So we're still friends?'

That saved him.

'Wrong.' He placed her hand back on the rail and put a good foot of clear space between them. 'We never was friends. Just – lovers. Briefly.'

She was silenced. He stole a quick glance sideways and saw that her mouth was set in a hard line.

'I take it there never was a baby,' he said.

'There was a baby.' She sounded devoid of emotion. 'I lost it. Miscarried. You know what a miscarriage is?'

He knew that well enough. His mother had suffered from several, often after his father had knocked her about.

'Yeah.'

There was a plaintive sniff beside him. 'It does something to you, losing a child. You're never the same person again.' Her voice was thick with unshed tears.

But he did not even have to fight against it. He knew her for what she was.

'Very convenient for you, losing it just when you thought you might have to leave the stage. Would have been a wrench for you, wouldn't it, giving up all these – jackasses dying for a word from you.'

'You're very cruel.' It was a near sob this time. 'You can't understand how I feel. No man could.'

'What I can't understand is why you came on this trip. You must have plenty of young toffs ready to take you out, so long as you hold out the promise to pay them.'

'What the devil do you mean by that? What are you saying?' The pose of bereft mother was abandoned. Real anger sparked off her tongue.

Harry ignored her questions, letting the jibe sink in. He carried on with his train of thought.

'All I can think of is that you want to show off, let everyone get an eyeful of you. You don't want your family to know you've really gone the way of your poor cousin Theresa, do you? So you put on this pretty dress and these white gloves and you act pure as the driven snow in front of them and all the rest of the street. Well, maybe you'll fool your family, because they want to be fooled –

'specially your aunt Clodagh. But the rest of us know you for what you are. We may not dress like the people you go around with now, and we don't talk posh, but we're not stupid. We know a whore when we see one.'

He left her at the rail and went up to the top deck, where the air was fresher.

The banks of the river grew steadily further apart. Farmland and distant woods and churches replaced the relentless brick. They passed the new docks at Tilbury and the ancient town of Gravesend and now there were fleets of little fishing boats moored in the shallows. On the skyline to the south was the ridge of the North Downs, to the north lay the Essex marshes, bounded by the Langdon Hills. Past the walls of Canvey Island, the estuary opened up. There were real waves, and the steamer lifted just a little to them, as if they were really at sea. The girls squealed in pretended fear and clutched whoever was handy, the men braced their legs and looked sturdy and heroic, the children ran madly about or had to be pulled down off the rails, where they were playing at dares. Hats had to be held in the wind and unguarded newspapers fluttered overboard. A sense of adventure invaded the boat. They were travellers, battling with the elements. They waved to passing shipping as if they too were bound for the other side of the world. People spoke to complete strangers and instant friendships were struck up.

'There it is!' cried someone with sharp eyes.

Ahead of them, crouching on the water, a long black line ending in the low dark blob: Southend Pier, the longest in the world. A crowd gathered at the forward rail to watch it get closer. Gradually the blob grew into a definite shape. Decks and buildings could be made out. Colours grew distinct, and now they could see the roofs and windows of the theatre and the tea rooms and the shelters. Flags fluttered from mastheads, there were lines of people sitting in deckchairs along the rails, and over the water came the sound of music. A band! A band was playing! The pier came closer still, and figures could be made out fishing and strolling and playing at deck quoits. And they were an attraction themselves. People were standing watching the *Belle* come in. The Trinidad Street contingent gathered themselves together, collecting up children and bags, straightening hats and scarves. As the boat came alongside they congregated behind a restraining chain, waiting to be let ashore. The warps were thrown and made fast, the paddles stopped, the gangways set up. A deckhand unfastened the chain and they all surged forward. They were here. They had reached Southend.

2

They funnelled down the gangway and on to the pierhead, passed the queue of people waiting to get on and the fringe of spectators, and then gathered in small groups to decide just what they were going to do next. Some wanted to stay on the pier and listen to the band, others wanted to head straight for the beach, and a third group were keen to get to the donkey rides and amusements. Numerous children complained of being hungry, and gradually a consensus emerged.

'Time to eat! Dinner,' the mums declared. It was well gone twelve, getting on for one.

A couple of families went up to the sundeck and started getting out the sandwiches. Most headed for the trams. They would eat when they got to the shore.

And what a wonderful scene it was when they got there. The smells! The usual town reek of steam, oil and horses was overlaid by a wonderful mix of beer, frying chips, candy floss, cockles and shrimps, and the unique seaweedy whiff of Southend mud. For of course the tide was out. It wouldn't have been Southend if the water had been in. And there laid out before them were all the pleasures they had ever dreamed of: rows of slot machines, innumerable pubs and teashops and foodstalls, boat trips, donkeys, Punch and Judy, pierrots – and beyond the noise and colour, peaceful gardens and a pretty bandstand ... something for everyone.

In the cheerful mêlée, nobody from Trinidad Street noticed a tawdry figure standing outside one of the pubs, with a hand poised on her hip and a grubby pink feather boa wafting across shamelessly exposed breasts. But she noticed *them*, and the professionally inviting smile on her face faded into horror. She left her pitch and began to stalk them, always keeping the crowds between herself and them, a silent observer of their carefree fun.

The combined Johnson, Turner and Billingham families, their young people gathered once more under the wing, marched off the pier and spilled immediately on to the grubby shingle of the beach, the children yelling with delight. It was a difficult operation finding enough room amongst the packed bodies, but they managed it at last, with a few black looks from people already established.

'Florrie, where's Florrie?' the cry went up.

She was discovered picking her way towards them, pink to the ears with suppressed joy.

'Meeting him later, are you?' Harry asked.

Florrie nodded, speechless, and dived into the anonymity of the family group.

Where was Siobhan? That was more to the point, Will thought. He had been well and truly tied down during the boat trip, with the added frustration of seeing her approach Harry and get the brush-off. He could not fathom Harry. If he were as free as Harry was, he would not be treating her like that. But he was stuck with the whole family, and it was getting him down. It was bad enough having Maisie and his own five children around. To have all Maisie's lot, and his family, and the Billinghams as well, was just too much. He sat munching squashed jam sandwiches, glaring resentfully at all the people enjoying themselves, especially men his own age who were unencumbered by kids and sported striped jackets and boaters and moustaches, free to eye up the girls and have a good time. He looked down at his own clothes. He had quite fancied himself this morning, before setting off. But now he realized that the trousers were bagging at the knees, that the jacket was too long in the arms and far too dark for a jolly day out at the seaside, that his boots were workman's boots, however well mended and polished. He had no chance at all, compared with those others. By his feet, Lily dropped her sandwich and wailed, Peter laughed at her and Tommy hit him, so Peter hit him back and pushed into Albert, who also dropped his sandwich and attacked both of them, screaming. Will cuffed all three boys round the ears and bellowed at them to shut up or else. They obeyed, but looked at him sulkily, lower lips stuck out.

A couple of yards away, Charlie Billingham was lounging back on one elbow as he ate. Will suddenly saw a way out. Charlie was not going to stick around with the women and children all afternoon. Neither was Harry or young Jack, for that matter, but he did not want them along. When the party started breaking up after the food was gone, he would tag along with Charlie.

'Oi, mate,' he said, calling behind the backs of the womenfolk. 'You going off along the front later?'

'Yeah, might. Why?'

'Thought I'd come along of you.'

Charlie did not look overpleased. 'Suit y'self,' he said.

It was good enough for Will.

The last thing Charlie wanted was someone tagging along with him, but it was convenient for him to have Will at his side while he got away. When the sandwiches were eaten and the teatrays taken back to the café, he chose a moment when

411

everyone else was busy sorting themselves out to beckon Will with a jerk of the head.

'You coming, then?'

Will scrambled to his feet and they made their way up the beach, threading their way between the deckchairs and children and up on to the promenade. Here Charlie paused a moment, taking it in.

Will dug him with his elbow and nodded in the direction of a group of pretty girls.

'Get an eyeful of that. Nice, eh?'

'Yeah.'

But Charlie was not looking at them. It was the sight of all these people with spare cash in their pockets that held his imagination. Every single person had spending money about them, and none of them was looking after it. The thought of it filled him with an excitement that chasing girls had never given him. His acquisitive greed was too deep to be denied.

'Come on,' he said, plunging into the crowd.

His eyes flicked this way and that. Ahead of him was a bulging pocket with the corner of a leather wallet peeping over the top. Easy, so easy. But he was all too aware of Will at his shoulder and breathing down his neck. He spotted a row of machines lined up by a candy-floss stall.

'*What the Butler Saw*,' he said. 'Fancy a look?'

'Yeah, why not?' Will grinned.

They both put pennies in and peered into the eyeshields as they turned the handles. Charlie waited till he heard a chuckle coming from Will, and then a whistle. Silently he slid away.

It was a wonder he did not feel the waves of

hatred emanating from the woman watching him from round the corner of the stall. So venomous was the expression on her face that it made a small icy hole in the jolly heat of the day, casting a chill on anyone who caught sight of it.

Back on the beach, all Will and Maisie's children, and Bob Turner, were paddling in puddles in the mud. The young people had gone off in a group, together with Jimmy Croft, who had Florrie's arm through his. Archie had disappeared in the direction of the nearest pub and Milly was peacefully dozing in her deckchair, mouth open and hat askew.

Ellen sat with Jessica lying across her lap. She had just fed and changed her, and the baby was gurgling happily, playing with her fingers and toes.

'Ah, the lamb,' Martha cooed. 'You give her to me, lovey. She'll be quite happy. You two go off and enjoy yourselves. Go on. No need to sit around with us old 'uns all afternoon.'

'That's real kind of you, Mum,' Gerry said, before Ellen could object. He held out his hands and pulled her up. 'Come on, we'll see the sights. How about the pierrots? You ever seen them?'

Ellen found herself escorted off the beach.

Alma was left amongst the older women. Milly was still asleep. Maisie was distracted by keeping tags on where all her children had gone, and Martha was playing with Jessica. A restless dissatisfaction crept over her. Never mind Gerry and Ellen, she didn't want to stay here with the old 'uns either. Why, Maisie was older in spirit than she was. She wanted to be out there where it was all going on, having a rare old time, not

413

sitting in a deckchair. She wanted a man to stroll arm in arm with and to have a drink at one of the pubs. It was all right when you were young, you always had a pal or two to go off with and eye up the boys. At her age, it was different. You couldn't just go out and pick up strangers.

'Them boys, they never listen to a word I say. I wish their dad was here. He'd give 'em what for. But he's gone and sloped off and left me,' Maisie complained.

'Oh, leave 'em be, they're doing no harm. They're having a lovely time,' Alma told her. 'Nothing like a nice game of mud pies.'

'But they got their best clothes on! They'll ruin 'em.'

'It'll wash. Comes off easy, Southend mud. Not like the stuff at home.'

Then inspiration hit her. The two grannies were happy to sit there, and Maisie needed a break every bit as much as Ellen.

'Here, Martha,' she said. 'You can keep an eye on Maisie's bunch, can't you? Here's your Will gone off and left her all on her tod. I reckon her and me ought to walk about a bit, see some of the sights.'

'Oh – I dunno – I didn't ought to...' Maisie looked almost frightened of having her maternal duties so suddenly lifted from her shoulders.

Martha took it all in her stride. 'That's right, dearie. You and Alma go and have a look round. Shame to come all this way and not see anything.'

'But Will–'

'If he comes back, I'll hold on to him till you

arrive,' his mother promised.

It took a little more persuasion, but in the end Maisie gave in. She wasn't the companion Alma would have chosen, but she was a whole lot better than nothing.

'Oo, it does seem funny not having no kids. Do you think they're all right?' she kept saying.

Alma reassured her, pointed things out to her and bought her a candy floss. Gradually Maisie relaxed and Alma could enjoy herself. She gave herself up to the noise, the colours, the crowds. The boisterous good nature of it all exactly chimed with her personality. She was happy just to be part of it.

'Oh, a steam organ,' she cried, catching Maisie by the elbow. 'I love them. Come and have a look.'

It was a magnificent machine, carved and painted and glittering with a mosaic of mirrors, its pipes glowing red and gold. On a little platform at the front a group of carved figures as large as children tootled trumpets and banged drums in time with the music. Alma watched, entranced, as a rousing version of 'My Old Man Said Follow the Van' rolled around them.

She was not sure what distracted her and made her look amongst the crowd gathered round the organ, but when she did, she at once caught sight of her son. He was a little along from her, at the far edge. She was about to shout his name, to push her way through to him, when a shifting of people brought not just his head but his whole body into view. It was then that she saw it happen. His hand came out of his pocket, slid into the pocket of the man in front of him and then

415

back into his own, all in one smooth movement.

Alma stood transfixed, his name dying in her throat. She could not believe what she had seen. Not her Charlie. He hadn't really done that. He was still standing there, staring up at the organ like all the others, a picture of innocence. No, she hadn't seen it. What was more, she was going to make sure she hadn't. She was going to confront him, right now, and put her mind at rest. She nudged Maisie with her elbow.

'There's Charlie! Look, I'm just going to say hullo.'

'Where?' Maisie asked, shouting above the racket of the organ. But by that time he was gone.

'I dunno.' Alma was confused. 'He was there a minute ago, I know he was.' Her head was spinning and she felt slightly sick.

'You all right, Aunty Alma? You look a bit queer.'

That was it. She wasn't feeling herself. She was seeing things.

'P'raps you got a touch of the sun. Why don't we have a nice cup of tea?'

Alma felt she needed a brandy more than tea, but for once in her life she let Maisie take charge.

'Yeah. P'raps you're right. Yeah, a nice cup of tea,' she said, and staggered to the nearest tea stall.

And a little way behind her in the swirling crowd, the woman in the pink boa saw it all, and smiled malevolently at her confusion.

Gerry and Ellen had also strolled under the pier and along the promenade by the amusements. Ellen would have preferred to go the other way,

416

by the cliff gardens, but Gerry was so eager, so full of it all, that she had not the heart to object. The souvenir stands drew him like a magnet.

'Here, look at this,' he kept saying. 'Ain't that pretty? What a corker! They must make a mint here.'

Ellen found herself admiring plaster donkeys, ashtrays, combs, ringholders, eggtimers, plates with pictures of the pier on them ... all with *a present from Southend* written somewhere. Gerry was like a child in a sweet shop.

'Must find out where they get these from. I could sell these. What d'you think? Go down a bomb.'

Ellen was sceptical. 'What would you have on them, then? *A present from Poplar?* Don't quite sound the same, somehow.'

'No,' Gerry had to admit, 'maybe not. But them eggtimers are nice. People'd go for them.'

Gerry found the owner of a shop and got into a long conversation about suppliers and customers and the problems of the retail trade. Ellen wandered round fingering the stock. Then she saw something that made her heart stand still. There in a display cabinet were black velvet trays of rings and brooches, and in amongst them was a little butterfly of silvery metal with coloured sparkling stones set in the wings. Ellen stood and stared at it. It was exactly like the one Harry had given her, his peacemaking gift. She never wore hers now, but she had it still, hidden away at the bottom of a drawer. Suddenly she could not stand all this poking around any more.

'I'm going outside for a breath of air,' she said

417

to Gerry, and plunged out of the door without waiting for his reply.

All the world was enjoying itself, eating, drinking, going on rides, parading up and down. It was all too noisy, too crowded. Children were screaming, men shouting, trams and buses blowing their horns. A hurdy-gurdy man was playing nearby, whilst on the other side of the promenade the steam organ was blasting out its tunes. The two lots of music produced a discord that was hard to bear. Without stopping to think, Ellen started to walk back towards the pier. She had to get away from all this. She needed some peace and quiet.

She had just reached the place where the pier passed over the promenade when she noticed her bootlace had come undone. She moved to one side to do it up, and as she straightened up again, someone seemed to step back into the deep shadows, guiltily, as if avoiding her. She peered, her heart beating with sudden suspicion, then realized it was a woman and relaxed. She was a prostitute, by the look of her, and keeping stony still in the protecting shade of the broad structure above them. Then as Ellen's eyes adjusted, recognition dawned and her mouth dropped open. The woman, seeing she was cornered, tried to make a run for it, but Ellen was too quick for her.

'Theresa! Oh, Theresa, it is you, ain't it? You gave me such a shock!' And before she could escape, Ellen put both arms round her and kissed her cheek.

'Blimey, you're the last person I thought I'd meet here. What...' Then the words dried up, for it was all too obvious what Theresa was doing here in Southend. She was earning her living.

'I just came down for the day,' Theresa lied breathlessly.

'So have we,' Ellen said, swallowing the untruth in an effort to hang on to her. There were so many things she wanted to ask, yet she did not know how to start. She fell back on the trite and tested. 'How – how are you, Theresa? You – er – you look well.'

'I'm all right. And you? I can see you're all hunky-dory. Married, are you?'

'Yeah – I got a little girl now. Jessica. She's lovely.'

Theresa's painted face took on an expression of deep and bitter jealousy. 'Well, it's all right for some, ain't it? Good girls like you can keep their babies. They got men to look after them. Me, I had a little girl and all, but I had to leave her at the workhouse.'

'Oh, Theresa–' Ellen's arms dropped to her sides at the sheer horror of it. 'Oh, I'm so sorry.' But even as she said it, she could not imagine how anyone, even in Theresa's circumstances, could bring herself to do such a thing.

Theresa backed away.

'Keep your pity – I don't want it,' she spat. But then her hand shot out and she gripped Ellen's arm so tight that she gasped with pain. 'But promise me one thing, Ellen Johnson...'

'Anything!' Ellen assured her.

'Don't you breathe a word, not a word, about seeing me here today. You hear me?'

Ellen nodded.

Theresa gave her a shake. 'How do I know you'll stick to it?'

Ellen looked at her, at the thick make-up, the revealing dress. Only the truth was going to convince her.

'I wouldn't upset them all by letting them know what you came to,' she said.

Theresa glared at her, considering this, then she let go. 'No, I don't suppose you would. Always were too bloody sugar-sweet.'

And she made off into the brassy sunshine, disappearing almost instantly amongst the promenading trippers.

Ellen was left shaking, hardly able to take it all in. Poor Theresa, to have come to that – it did not bear thinking about. It was only a few steps to the beach where her family was, but at the rails she hesitated. She ought to join them. But that meant explanations, and she could not explain how she felt. She was tight and keyed up, her nerves still jumping from the scene she had been through. She certainly could not tell them about Theresa, and neither could she easily explain why she had run out on Gerry. She hadn't even got enough self-possession at the moment to lie. She walked on. The cliffs were just over the road, a green haven. Perhaps there she could sit by herself and sort her thoughts out a bit.

'Hullo, Ellen.'

She started; a hand flew to her face.

'Harry! You made me jump.'

Like her, he was on his own. Also like her, there was an air of isolation about him. She knew that he did not feel part of all this jollity either.

'Looking for Gerry?'

'Well, not really. That is, he's back there some-where, looking at things. It all just got a bit noisy, that's all.'

'Ah.'

He was standing looking down at her, his expression unreadable. She found her eyes drawn irresistibly to his.

'I thought, perhaps I'd go and climb up to the gardens. It's nice there. At least, it looks nice. Quiet, like. I thought so when we was coming down the pier, I thought...' She was gabbling, talking rubbish. Under his steady gaze, she found the words running out. 'So that's where I'm going,' she ended lamely.

All thought of Theresa had gone right out of her head, as if the brief meeting had never been. There was just her and Harry, reaching out blindly across the great gap that divided them.

'Mind if I come too?'

At first, she was not sure whether she had really heard him say that. But he was standing waiting for a reply. It was true: he *had* said it. For an endless moment she felt as if she were balanced on a knife edge. She knew that this was a turning point, that whatever she decided would have momentous consequences. All the reasons why she should refuse him rushed into her head. She brushed them aside and smiled up at him. She felt lightheaded with excitement.

'Why not?'

They crossed over the busy road and started to climb a gravelled pathway up the steep cliffs. The grass was yellowing and the bushes and trees were dusty from the long summer, but still it was green and restful. The gardens were still in the process of being laid out, but there were green painted benches already placed here and there. They wandered along, not touching, not speaking, gradually getting higher. The noise of the promenade had faded now. Sparrows could be heard chirping in the trees. They arrived at a bench surrounded by young laurels and a mock orange blossom bush.

'Would you like to sit down?' Harry asked.

Ellen nodded. 'I am a bit tired.'

They sat well apart, Ellen with her hands in her lap, Harry with his elbows hooked over the back of the bench and his legs stretched out in front of him. They both gazed at the view. There below them lay the beach and the pier, the cloud shadows chasing over the shining mudflats, the brightly coloured crowds of people. Down there were their families, real life, complications, but up here they were out of it all.

'Nice, ain't it?' Ellen said. 'Peaceful. Don't often get a chance to just sit and look, at home. Not a lot to look at, really. Not like here.'

'There's Island Gardens,' Harry said.

'Yeah, there's that.'

They were both silent. The happy hours spent at Island Gardens or across the river in Greenwich Park shimmered between them. A time of innocence, gone for ever.

'I saw you talking to Siobhan on the boat,' Ellen blurted out, and immediately regretted it.

'Her – she's poison, that one.'

'I...' Ellen opened her mouth and shut it again.

'That's what I think, too. So do most people in the street. The women, anyway.'

'They're right.'

Ellen could feel the vibration of his fingers tapping on the bench. She wanted to say something but was afraid it might come out wrong. The rules were all changed between them now. She was married to Gerry.

'She's greedy,' Harry said. 'Greedy for whatever she can get – men, money, admiration. Doesn't care how she gets things.'

'I know.'

A silence grew, and into it came a realization. She should have known that, when she found them together that dreadful day. She should have made allowances.

'I–' she began.

'It was–' Harry said at the same time. They both stopped.

'Go on.'

'No, you.'

She waited.

'It was the stupidest thing I ever done in my life, letting her stay that day,' Harry said. 'I don't know why I did.' He paused, getting his thoughts in order.

Ellen waited, hardly daring to breathe.

'When – when I said she was poison, that wasn't quite right. She's more like – you know, people who drink, I mean really drink, the ones who can't do without it. It's like being that way. You know you shouldn't, and it won't do you any good, but you can't stop yourself. That's how it is with her. But I never liked her as a person, or even as a woman. Not like with you. It was quite different with you.'

'I see,' Ellen said.

But she didn't. She just saw that he found Siobhan more attractive than her.

They were both gazing unseeing at the panorama, neither risking looking at the other. Revelations were easier that way.

'There was a baby, so she said.'

'*What?*'

'She told me, about six weeks after. That's why I had to ask her to marry me. At least I was spared that. She disappeared right after.'

'Oh.' Ellen could hardly take this one in. It was a total surprise. 'But what happened? I mean, she didn't have it?'

'She lost it. Miscarried. Least, that's what she said. That's what she was telling me today, on the boat.'

'Oh.' Despite herself, a shadow of sympathy crept in. She thought of losing Jessica. 'Poor thing.'

'Ha!' Harry gave a snort of derision. 'Poor thing, my foot! She never wanted a baby. She was off the moment she got rid of it, wasn't she?'

'Yes, she was,' Ellen agreed, and was profoundly glad.

Behind her she could sense Harry's arm on the seat back. His fingers brushed her neck, sending fiery threads of pleasure through her. She stared very hard at her hands, gripped together in her lap.

'There ain't a day goes by when I don't regret that time with her,' Harry said.

Ellen's throat was very tight. 'It was my fault

and all. I didn't ought to have gone off with Gerry right away. I should have given you a chance.'

Harry's arm wrapped round her shoulders. She turned to look at him then. For a timeless space they gazed deep into each other's eyes, then slowly, inevitably, their bodies drew together, their lips met. In that long melting kiss they rediscovered the joy and tenderness they had once known, held on to it, made time stand still.

'You know I still love you,' Harry said.

In answer Ellen slid her hand round his neck, running her fingers into his close curls. She pulled his head down so that his mouth found hers again. There was no more talk of Siobhan or Gerry from then on, just a blissful reawakening of everything they had once been to each other. For a while they forgot about the rest of the world. There was just the two of them, cut off from real life.

It was the tingling in her breasts as the milk came in that called Ellen back to her responsibilities.

'I got to go,' she said, stricken. 'Jess'll be hungry. Oh, Harry, what are we going to do? I can't leave you now. I love you.'

'Ain't nothing we can do. You're married to Gerry now.' His voice was flat with finality.

'Yes,' she whispered.

He held her face in his hands and gave her one last tender kiss. 'Come on.'

They walked back through the gardens until they were close to the pier.

'You go down that way and come along like you been the other side all along,' Harry said 'I'll wait here a while then walk in from this way.'

Ellen nodded, fighting back the tears. Already the magical afternoon was being tarnished by this deception.

'Be brave.' Harry squeezed her arm.

'I'll try.'

She turned and walked unsteadily away, not daring to look back.

It was a rowdy party that travelled back on the *Clacton Belle* that evening. Everybody told everybody else where they had been and what they had done, all talking and nobody listening. There was a permanent queue for the bar, and those who still had money left bought rounds for those who hadn't. Several children were sick with excitement and too much sticky food.

The couples who had paired off during the day wandered out on to the lamplit decks and watched the lights of the shore passing by. Toddlers fell asleep in their mothers' laps or curled up on the deck. In the packed, smoky forecabin, Alma started the singing. Red in the face, cheerfully tipsy, she raised her loud and surprisingly tuneful voice in a chorus of 'I Do Like to Be Beside the Seaside'. Before she was two lines into the song, everyone else had joined in. Between them, they knew enough songs to carry them halfway home, and when they had run through the lot, they started again. What with the noise and the alcoholic haze, no one noticed that both Harry and Ellen were exceedingly quiet.

3

Outwardly, everything went on as before. People worked long and hard, ate poorly and made love to forget these things. Young people fell in and out of love, babies were born, babies and old people died of natural causes. There were accidents, one fatal and two crippling, the usual run of illnesses, one miscarriage – Maisie's – and one wedding.

When people got together at the Rum Puncheon or on the doorsteps, talk often turned to the trip to Southend. Every detail was gone over time and time again, and the conclusion was always reached that it had been the best day out ever, even though for some individuals it had been more of a trial than a pleasure. (Nobody was going to admit that they had not enjoyed it when everyone else seemed to have had such a good time). Even so, there were no moves towards planning another one, since many of them were still paying off debts from scraping the fare and spending money together last year.

Ellen became pregnant again and in the early autumn gave birth to a boy, Edward, named after Gerry's long-dead father and known from the first as Teddy. The breach between Billinghams and O'Donaghues was healed well enough for Ellen to be able to ask Clodagh to assist at the birth. The only person who was not pleased about all this was Jessica, who found herself ousted from her position as only, adored baby. She let her displeasure be known by throwing temper tantrums and attempting to hit the baby, until appeased by the rag doll that her father brought home one day. This unfortunate toy, alternately loved and abused, soaked up much of her jealousy.

Next door, Harry still lived uneasily with his family. Many a time he thought about moving out. There were plenty of people more than willing to take him in as a lodger. But he knew that his money was needed and he feared for his mother's safety if he left. His father had now given up all pretence of supporting his family. Even Johnny, still at school but selling papers in the streets morning and evening, was adding his pittance to the household, along with Florrie and Ida. Archie worked only enough to supply his drinking habits.

'Good thing,' Florrie commented sourly. 'He'll drink himself to death all the sooner. It's the only way she'll ever get rid of him.'

'If I don't kill him first,' Harry said, before he could stop himself.

Brother and sister looked at each other.

'It frightens me sometimes. I could do it,' Harry admitted.

'I'd help you finish him off,' Florrie said.

They were silent, half horrified, half elated by the relief of confession. Both knew without saying that it was a secret of the deepest kind between them.

'Why do we care so much? There's plenty more like him. Their families manage,' Harry said.

'Because we're us,' Florrie said, which was

probably as near to the truth as anyone would get.

More than ever, Harry was out of the house. His work demanded long hours, sometimes with early starts, sometimes requiring him to be away all night on a trip upriver. Saturday night was always music-hall night with a bunch of friends. But on Sundays he was part of the street again, and could hardly miss seeing Ellen out with her babies or talking to the other women. When they met they spoke only briefly, avoiding each other's eyes. It was difficult to keep up the pretence of being nothing more than neighbours.

He watched her covertly, concerned for her welfare, yet in one corner of his heart hoping she was not happy with Gerry. She always looked well enough. Looking after a home, a husband, two lodgers and two children was a heavy task, but she was young and strong and Gerry was a good provider. They ate better than most in the street and always had enough for fuel for fires and cooking. To a partial observer like Harry, though, there was a difference in her. The light had gone out of her, the warmth and sparkle that he had once known. Only when she was holding one of the children did it come back, that glow of possessive love. In the night he found himself listening, almost hoping for the sound of raised voices, ready to rush in and defend her. But Gerry would never dream of laying hands on his wife and all Harry ever heard was the wail of hungry infants – Gerry's children.

One Saturday night not long after the birth of Teddy, Harry was out as usual with half a dozen of his friends. He had almost not gone with them that evening, for the hall they had chosen had Siobhan on the bill and he had no desire to go and see her perform. The others all went on at him to come, and in the end, as the alternative was an evening in the Rum Puncheon watching his father get drunk, he agreed.

'Wouldn't mind a bit of that,' one of them commented as Siobhan came on to the stage.

'Yeah, she can ring my bell any day.'

They whistled and clapped as she curtseyed to the audience, and fell silent as she began her song. It was another of the sentimental little ditties that she specialized in. She had her act down to a fine art now, teasing, smiling, seeming to be inviting them in, then backing off with a whisk of the skirt and a melting glance over the shoulder.

'Fancy once living in the same street as that. You ever get a chance, Harry boy?'

'No,' he lied. He had never told any of them anything of what had happened. 'She wasn't interested in the likes of me. Had her eyes on the stage-door Johnnies even then.'

He watched her move, heard her sing. The whole act was so typical of her it left a bad taste in his mouth.

After the show, they all went off for a drink in a nearby pub. It was a foggy October night, cold and cheerless. The street lights made faint yellow haloes in the grey but did little to illuminate the streets. Harry was a little behind the others, feeling out of tune with his friends' jokes and laughter. All around him swirled the cheerful audience from the hall, calling out to each other, singing snatches of the songs. Usually he was part of it, bright and happy from the entertainment, ready to down a pint and have a sing. Tonight he felt set apart.

'Oi, Harry! You coming? We nearly lost you.'

'You go on,' he called. 'I'll be with you.'

They were swallowed up in half a minute, lost in the sooty blanket of fog. Harry decided to make for the bus stop. He just was not in the mood for it tonight. He crossed the road, dodging between hansoms and buses, carriages and motor cars. The smell of the fumes hung in the stagnant air, catching at his throat. As he walked along close to the shopfronts, hands in pockets, minding his own business, a female figure stepped out of a doorway in front of him.

'All alone, darling? Want some company?'

He stared at the prostitute in the red feathered hat and yellow fringed shawl. Her pudgy face was painted into a semblance of youth and her mouth was smiling, but the eyes were predatory.

'No thanks.'

He was about to step round her when a pull of familiarity made him look again, more closely. And as he did so, he saw that she too had recognized him. She whipped round and began to run down the street.

'Theresa!'

He chased after and caught her easily. He gripped her arm.

'Theresa, stop, please.'

'Let go of me! Let go!'

There was an agony of shame in her voice. She

431

tried to wrench her arm away, her head turned to the side so that she would not have to look him in the face.

'I only want to help, Theresa. I won't tell anyone, I promise. They'll never know.'

'No, no!'

She was twisting and fighting, kicking at his legs. The hard toe of her boot connected with his shin. He got hold of her other arm and gave her a shake.

'Stop it. Shut up and listen.'

Abruptly, she did just that, though she still did not meet his eye.

'Look, we can't talk out in the street like this. Is there somewhere we can go?'

She must have a place where she took people, but he did not want to go there. He had never been in a brothel in his life and he was not going to start now.

'A pub,' he suggested.

He had temporarily lost his bearings in the fog. He dragged her along till he saw the bleary glow of lamplight spilling out into the night. Anywhere would do, so long as his friends were not there. The sign was unfamiliar. It would do.

It was crowded and smoky inside. He hung on to Theresa, fearing she would make a run for it if he left her while he fetched the drinks.

'Gin?' he asked, and she nodded.

He managed to find a corner table just as its occupants got up to leave and shoved Theresa on to the bench seat and squeezed in beside her.

'Here.' He pushed the gin, a large one, in front of her and she downed half of it at a gulp.

'Better?'

She nodded again.

He took a pull at his pint and decided that he would do the talking first. He started telling her what had happened in the street since she left – the births, the deaths, the marriages. She was listening, he was sure, but she gave no sign of it. She just stared at her drink, and occasionally took a sip. It was half an hour before Harry paused for breath.

'Another?' he asked, and took a chance this time, going up himself to get the glasses refilled.

'Ta.' Theresa took a sip and fiddled with the glass. Harry waited. 'I never thought Ellen'd marry Gerry,' she said at last.

'No, well – that's how it goes, ain't it? Things never do turn out like you wanted, do they?'

She shook her head. 'They didn't turn out right with my young man.'

Treading carefully, he said, 'West Ham, wasn't it, that he lived?'

'Yeah.' She sighed. 'Only it went all wrong.'

He had no idea whether she was telling the truth. It hardly mattered. The fact of it was that now she was a common prostitute picking men up off the street.

'Look, Theresa,' he said, 'I know you. I know you didn't choose to do this. I want to help in some way. Couldn't you get a proper job? There must be something...'

She gave a bitter laugh. 'You must be joking. Who'd take me on?'

'Plenty of people. You don't need references. You could get a factory job.'

She shook her head. 'They'd take one look at me and they'd know.'

'You could buy some different clothes, do your hair plain.'

'No, no, it wouldn't work.'

'Well then, there's places you can go. I've read about them. Refuges for women – like you. They take them in and help them, find them decent employment.'

It was as if he had turned a switch. She began to talk.

'Yeah, yeah, I know. I been to a couple. They delouse you and the doctor comes and does horrible things to you and they give you bloody awful dresses to wear and make you scrub floors and do laundry and sew. And all the time they preach at you. Then they get you a job as a skivvy. Place where they put me, everyone knew where I come from. The women wouldn't talk to me and the men all wanted it for free. I left after a week. I was better off on the streets.'

'But you went back, another time,' Harry persisted.

'Only because I was ill. I knew they'd look after me better than what they do in the hospital. Not throw me out the moment they stitched me up.'

'But surely you don't want to keep on the way you are?'

In answer, Theresa drained her glass and pushed it towards him. He took the hint and bought another. The gin was having no noticeable effect on her at all. He guessed that she drank heavily most of the time.

'I could help you,' he said.

'Oh yeah? How?'

'I could find you somewhere to live, some decent lodgings with nice people. Not on Dog Island – I know you won't want to go back there – but somewhere else. I got friends all up and down the river. I could lend you some money if you needed it, so you could get some new clothes and things, and then you could get a factory job.'

Theresa looked sceptical. 'So what's so bleeding wonderful about a factory job? On your feet for twelve or more hours a day, too hot or too cold, horrible smells all round, and some bleeding dragon of a forewoman breathing down your neck and fining you the moment you open your mouth. And what for? Twelve, thirteen bob a week, if you're lucky. D'you know what I earn?'

Harry shook his head.

'Five, ten bob a night. A *night!* Last week, this bloke give me half a sov. Half a sov for half an hour, just for being nice to him. Said he'd come back again, too. Easy. You don't get money like that in no bleeding factory.'

'You don't get a dose of the clap in a factory, neither,' Harry retorted. 'And what's going to happen to you when you get old? You won't be able to work this pitch much longer. Younger girls are coming in all the time.'

'Dunno. Don't think about it.' Theresa shrugged.

Harry could see that he had to be brutal. 'You'll be down the Highway doing it for fourpence, that's what. And you won't even be working on your back. Fourpence for a quick one up against the wall with some drunken sailor, that's all you'll be fit for. If you live that long.'

She was unmoved. 'My glass is empty,' she said.

Harry ignored her. 'You can't go on like this.'

'So? I'll die young. I don't care. Ain't nothing much to live for.'

'Let me help you.'

'You can smash that Charlie for me.'

'What?' The sudden vehement hatred after the dull apathy shocked him.

'That bastard Charlie Billingham. It was him what did for me.'

He did not follow her. 'Charlie? But I thought … the bloke in West Ham?'

She shrugged. 'Weren't no bloke in West Ham. I just made that up for that bleeding bitch Siobhan. She believed it and all.' She gave a harsh laugh. 'She's playing across the road there. Did you know that?' Her face was contorted with jealousy.

'She may be up there on the stage, but she's just the same as you,' Harry said gently.

'What?' For the first time, she looked right at him.

'She does what you do, only she's not so honest about it. She doesn't so much sell it as bargain with it, but it all comes to the same thing.'

'Oh.'

She sat silent for a long while, frowning at the glass. Harry took it away, filled it up, replaced it.

'I'm glad you told me that.'

'It makes it better, does it?'

'Sort of – yeah, yeah, I suppose it does.'

He gave it one last try. 'It's not too late, you know, Theresa.'

She sighed. All the fight had gone out of her.

She was just a tired, worn woman with a grotesque layer of face paint.

'Wouldn't you like to give it up?'

Longing came into her eyes. She was far away, looking at somewhere quite different from the scruffy pub. Harry wondered if it was Trinidad Street in the days before Siobhan came along.

'We had some fun, didn't we, when we was kids?' he said.

'Kids! Blimey, sometimes I wonder if I was ever a kid. It's like – like that was someone else.'

He put a hand over hers. 'Give it a try, eh? You could do it, you know. You could break out. I'd help.'

But she shook her head.

'No. I'd never stick at it. I seen other girls try. But they always come back. Ain't worth the effort.'

She defeated him. He had nothing to say in the face of such fatalism.

'Well, is there *anything* I can do?'

With a spark of life at last, she flashed him a grin. 'You can give me some of that money you was on about. After all, you owe me. I been wasting good time sitting here jawing with you. I could've earned another half-sov.'

Harry dug in his pockets. It would all be wasted, he realized. She would probably stay here and drink it. But reasoning had failed, and he could see no other way to help. He took out all that he had, all his spending money for the week, picked out some coppers for his fare home and pushed the rest across the beer-puddled table. Theresa reached out, but he kept his hand over it.

'Promise me you'll go to a doctor to find out if

you're clean.'

She pouted and half turned away from him. 'Promise!'

'I hate doctors. They poke around inside of you.'

'Better than going down with a dose.' He began to draw the money towards himself.

'All right, all right. I promise.'

'Good.' He took his hand away. In a trice, the assorted silver was out of sight.

'You got to promise something too,' she said.

'Oh, what?'

'Never to breathe a word about me to anyone. Not a word. You promise that?'

He agreed. She seemed to relax a little, trusting his word.

'You always round this way?' he asked.

'Yeah. On and off.'

'I'll come back, and if you change your mind, if you want to make a new start, I'll help you. You've only got to ask.'

'Yeah, right.'

There seemed to be no more to say. He stood up and hesitated, looking down at her, wishing he had the words to change her.

''Bye then, Theresa, and – God bless.'

''Bye, Harry. You know something?'

'What?'

'Ellen was a fool not to marry you.'

He left.

During the journey home and all through the next week, he felt that he had handled it badly, that he could have done more. He had never liked Theresa much, she was too hard-edged and quick to find fault, but that was not the point.

She was part of his childhood. He had teased her and pulled her hair as a boy, speculated about her as an adolescent. Her mother had helped his through births and miscarriages. It was terrible to think that a girl he had grown up with was out on the streets of London selling her body to any man who came along.

For the life of him, though, he could not think what else he could have done or said. She seemed sunk in her present existence, not even wanting to get out. He wished there was someone he could discuss it with, but he was bound by the promise he had given not to tell anyone. He knew that once the news was out it would be all up and down the street and chewed over for weeks. The only person he could safely share it with, who could be trusted to keep it to herself and perhaps give some good advice, was Ellen. But he never got to have long conversations with Ellen these days. It was just as he had said to Theresa, things never did turn out the way you wanted. It was easy enough to say, difficult to accept. Certainly he had not accepted it.

Ellen drew back the curtain to look out into the street. A thick yellow cowl of fog enveloped the world. She could not see the houses on the opposite side, except for one faint smear of light in someone's bedroom window. Further down the road, the feeble glow from the streetlamp made another point of reference, but apart from that there was nothing to prove that the street was there at all. She fought back a quiver of irrational fear. She was alone in the house except for the babies. It was Saturday night and Gerry was out seeing someone about a not-to-be-missed bargain, and the lodgers were down at the Rum Puncheon. She looked at the ground outside. The line of the kerb could just be made out, which gave her an immense sense of relief. It was all right, she was still anchored to the earth. Without that friendly stretch of pavement that she knew so well, swept daily and scrubbed weekly, she might have been adrift in the universe. The prospect frightened her. She was used to living with people all around her. Being without them made her feel unprotected, prey to any danger that might come prowling through the fog.

She went back to the warmth of the kitchen, but even here she was not completely at ease. The range did not seem to be drawing properly. She could not settle to anything. There was a pile of mending that needed doing, and for the first time in eighteen months or so she had been to the Settlement and borrowed some books, but even the new world waiting inside the cloth covers could not hold her. She kept running upstairs to check on little Teddy, putting a hand on his chest to make sure he was still breathing, and tucking his tiny hands under the covers when he fought himself free of the shawl that swaddled him. But she knew it was not really him she was anxious about. She told herself it was the fog. It was enough to make anyone nervous, especially when they were on their own. That was not true either. Fog had never really worried her before. She just felt a vague unease, a sense of something wrong, and the fact that she could not put her finger on it made it worse.

The time went slowly by, measured out by the tick of the clock on the mantelpiece – a massive piece in funereal black mock marble, with pillars on either side of the face, that Gerry had picked up cheap somewhere. Ellen never had liked it, but he had been so delighted with it that she hadn't had the heart to tell him to take it away again.

'Gives the place a bit of class,' he had said.

Ellen thought it depressing. She had dressed up the rest of the mantelpiece with the brightest pieces from the stall to counteract it.

At about half-past ten, when she had just put the baby down after his feed, there was a scrape and a thump on the front door. Ellen jumped up, her heart beating wildly. She was halfway across the parlour when the door flew open and banged against the wall and a dark figure stumbled into the room. She bit back a scream.

'What the...? Where the bleeding...?' a slurred voice demanded.

It was Archie, rolling drunk.

Ellen took a deep breath, then regretted it. The smell of him filled the air. 'Not here, Mr Turner. Wrong house.'

He stood swaying, trying to focus on her. 'Ellen? Ellen Johnson?'

'You're in the wrong house, Mr Turner. Try next door.'

'Bloody Johnsons. Always putting their noses where they're not wanted.'

The fear was pulsing strongly now, but she tried hard not to show it. She repeated the words yet again, keeping her voice as steady and calm as she could make it.

'Go next door, Mr Turner. This is my house. You're in the wrong house.'

She sent a silent prayer that he would comply. Archie might be undersized, but she knew how vicious and totally unpredictable he was when drunk.

'Wrong house, wrong house? What you mean, wrong?'

He stopped as it finally got through to him that the door was the other way round from his own. Abruptly, he turned and stumbled out again. Ellen slammed the door and shot the bolts, something she had never done before. The men would just have to knock and identify themselves before she opened it to them. She went back into the warmth of the kitchen and collapsed into her chair, her knees shaking. She looked at her hands and found they were trembling. Then she heard the sound of falling furniture next door, and her own distress was overlaid by worry about poor Milly.

It had been a nice quiet evening at the Turners'. Both girls went out with their young men, Johnny went down to the Crofts' and Bob was packed off to bed by eight. Milly was able to do a bit of mending, make a pot of tea all to herself and doze in front of the range with nobody making any demands upon her. It was as good as a holiday. Promptly at ten, Ida and Florrie came home, escorted to the door, as was proper. Soon after, Johnny came back. They chatted for a while about their various evenings, then began drifting off to bed. All was still well on the surface, but Milly was

442

beginning to get the familiar crawling sensation of Saturday-night fear. Sometime soon, Archie would be home.

'Come on, get a move on,' she nagged at Florrie, who was lingering in front of the range.

She did not want any of them up when he arrived. It only made it worse. She prayed that Harry would be good and late. It was often past midnight by the time he got back, but what with the fog, he might come home earlier. Florrie disappeared upstairs and Milly began to get ready for bed. Perhaps if she was up there when he arrived, he would take it out on her in that way instead of hitting her. Trouble was, he was usually incapable of doing it when he was drunk, and that made him angrier, so he still ended up hitting her.

In the early days when they were first married, and for quite a few years afterwards, she had taken a certain pride in her bruises. After all, it only went to prove that he loved her. But as time went by, childbirth, miscarriages and sheer hard work weakened her and the attacks became more vicious. It was no longer a case of a couple of punches and some bad language. He would fling her against the wall, throw furniture, kick her when she was down. The pride degenerated into a dogged endurance. That was the way he was. She simply accepted it.

She had just put her foot on the stair when she heard the Billinghams' door bang open. She stood still, listening. A couple of minutes later it slammed shut and her own flew open. She wanted to run upstairs, but could not. She just stood there, waiting.

Archie staggered across the parlour, knocked into a chair, picked it up and threw it aside. It broke. Milly whimpered.

'What are you staring at?' Archie demanded.

She shook her head, speechless.

'Wassermatter? Cat got your tongue?'

In two staggering steps he was across the room and grabbing at her. She cowered back against the stairs, but he just reached out and got hold of a handful of blouse, and jerked her up till her face was only a couple of inches from his. His contorted features swam before her. His breath made her faint.

'Wassermatter, eh? Eh?' he was shouting.

She tried to answer. Her lips moved, but nothing came out. Whatever she did was wrong. If she said something, he was sure to take exception to it. If she stayed silent, he did not like that either.

'Stupid bleeding cow. All your fault. You brought it all on me, didn't you? Eh? Didn't you?'

Sweat broke out all over her. She could feel it standing on her forehead. Her body was clammy with it. The blood was thudding in her ears so loudly that she could no longer think. Hardly knowing what she did, she nodded.

'Thass right. Proud of it. All your fault.'

He had hold of her shoulders and was shaking her. She fell back against the stairs and her head hit the riser with a crack, but there was no merciful loss of consciousness. She let out a wail. It was, her one defence. Once, she had bitten back the screams for fear of upsetting the children. Now she screamed and cried out from the first, for this was what he wanted. He liked to hear her.

The sooner he knew he was really hurting her, the sooner it was over.

'What you doing down there? Get up! Lazy bleeding cow.'

He dragged her on to her feet, hit her so that she staggered sideways into the kitchen, hit her again as she grabbed at the table, and kicked her as she slid down on to the floor. The world shattered into jagged red points of pain. She was gasping and wailing and weeping.

'Stop it! Stop it!'

Just when she thought it was bad, it became worse. Through a haze she could see Florrie, a blur of white with two pinpoints of black fury in her eyes and her teeth bared like a tigress.

'You leave her alone, you coward, you bully! Leave her alone!'

For just a moment Archie hesitated, then he swung round on his daughter with a roar of fury.

'No, no!' Milly screamed.

There was something in Florrie's hand. She raised it in threat.

'That's right, hit me,' she challenged him. 'Go on, hit me. Just you try it.'

He stopped in mid-flight, then turned back and lashed out at Milly again, the toe of his boot crashing into her ribs. She moaned.

Above her there was a movement, a flash of white, a crack. This time it was Archie who yelped.

'You bitch!'

She saw his arm move to strike his daughter, but there was another crack first, and then he was falling, falling. He collapsed across her, knocking the breath out of her, leaving her pinned and gasping.

445

The silence was worse than the noise. Ellen could stay still no longer. She had to go and see if there was anything she could do. First she ran up to check on the babies, drawing strength from their peaceful sleep, then she slipped next door.

A frozen tableau met her eyes. Ida, Johnny and Bob were crowded in the kitchen doorway with their backs to her, as if not daring to move any further. Beyond them came the whooping sound of someone who had been winded trying to catch their breath, and there was the unmistakable choking smell of singeing hair hanging in the air. Nobody moved.

Ellen swallowed. 'Is – is there anything...?' Her voice came out as a croak.

Ida turned to look at her. Her mouth hung open in shock. 'It's our dad,' she whispered.

Ellen walked forward and the three parted to let her through. There stood Florrie, like an avenging angel in her white nightgown, her hair flowing loose down her back, and her eyes wide and staring. Even as Ellen looked at her, the flush drained out of her face to leave it ashen. In her hand was a broken chair leg, the end clotted with blood and hairs.

'Florrie, what...?' But as she spoke, she knew. She looked down on the floor. The noise came from Milly, pinned beneath her husband. But it was Archie that everyone was staring at. It was his hair that was scorching. He lay across Milly, his back on the fender, his head against the range. His jaw sagged, and his eyes were half open and rolled up into his head so that only the whites showed. His chest was quite still.

One thing was clear to Ellen: somebody had to do something, and as everyone else was in a state of shock, it had to be her.

'Get him off your mum. Let her breathe proper,' she decided.

She bent down and started tugging at Archie's ankles. Nobody else moved, so she looked up and said quite sharply, 'Come on, lend a hand.'

Ida and Johnny reluctantly joined her. Ellen left them to the feet while she steeled herself to lift Archie's bloody head up so that it did not drag over Milly. Between them, they pulled him clear and dropped him on the floor. Ellen shuddered. She held her hands fastidiously away from herself.

'Now help your mum up,' she said. 'Get her a drink of water, or something.'

While the three younger ones did that, she looked at Florrie, who was still standing in silence with the chair leg in her hand.

'Give me that,' she said, and with swift decision thrust it into the range. The fire blazed up merrily.

'Now...' She cast about the room, not quite sure what to do next. One thing was certain, the truth must never come out. She was not going to see her best friend hanged.

Milly, hunched on a chair, was crying and moaning. The noise grated on Ellen's nerves. She could not think straight.

Florrie's lips moved. 'I killed him,' she whispered. 'I killed him. He's dead.'

Milly's wails rose hysterically. Ellen closed her eyes briefly. She could not bear the sound of it.

'Look, it was an accident – we all know that – a

dreadful accident. He hit his head on the range,' she said loudly. 'That's what happened. It wasn't Florrie.'

Bob, Ida and Johnny all nodded. Milly sobbed.

'Oh, for God's sake!' Ellen yelled. The others gaped at her. 'Why don't you get her to bed? She'll be better off there. Get her to bed and – and put cold compresses on the cuts and bruises. Yes, that's best.'

Once again the three younger ones did as they were bid. They were more than happy to accept Ellen as the leader, and doing something useful made them feel better. As they escorted their mother upstairs, Florrie and Ellen were left staring at each other over Archie's body.

'It was an accident, Florrie,' Ellen repeated.

Slowly, Florrie nodded. 'I'm glad he's dead,' she said. Her voice was toneless.

Neither of them knew quite what to do next. Ellen had an idea that they ought to call in the police, but the very thought of it terrified her. Once they arrived, her friend could be carted off in handcuffs. The front door rattled, and they both started. Ellen bit back a scream. She half expected to see a burly policeman come in. Both girls went limp with relief when they saw that it was Harry.

'What the hell's–' He broke off, taking in the scene.

'I hit him. He's dead,' Florrie explained in the same flat voice.

'It was the range, it was that what killed him, not Florrie,' Ellen put in.

Between them, interrupting, contradicting, they explained what had happened. Harry ran his hands through his hair, until it stood up on end.

'Bloody hell,' he said. 'What're we going to do?'

'It wasn't Florrie,' Ellen repeated vehemently.

'Yeah, I know that, you know that, but are the police going to believe it?' Harry asked.

Neither girl could answer him. Despite the warmth of the room, Ellen felt cold.

Out of nowhere, the solution came to her.

'We could throw him in the river.'

There was a long silence as all three of them considered this.

'Yeah,' Harry said slowly, working it out as he went along. 'It's a real pea-souper out there. Can't see your hand in front of your face, hardly. He could've lost his way and been set on. We could say he never come home. We could go to the police tomorrow morning and report him missing, all worried-like. So long as we all stick to it–' He broke off as an important point struck him. 'Noise! It must've made one hell of a row. Someone would've heard. You heard, Ellen.'

'But there's nobody else in, except the babies. The men are all out.'

'Right.' Harry nodded. 'And Granny Pierce next door never hears nothing. She wouldn't hear if the Day of Judgement arrived.'

'There's Mum,' Florrie said.

'Ah.' That was a problem.

'Could you get her to agree to it?' Ellen asked.

Neither Harry nor Florrie was sure.

'You never know with her. She might break down if they ask her questions,' Harry said. 'But then, she'd do the same if we just said it wasn't Florrie's fault. She could come out with the fact that she hit him. No, we got to do it your way, Ellen. It's the river.'

Bob, Ida and Johnny came creeping in, their faces showing how glad they were that their big brother was back. Harry briefly explained what had been decided upon.

'It's the only way,' he said. 'Are we all agreed? Because we all got to be together in this.'

He looked from Ellen to his brothers and sisters. They all nodded.

'Good.' He glanced at the clock. 'We got to get moving – they'll all be rolling home from the Puncheon any minute. You go back next door, Ellen. Just act like nothing happened. You never heard nothing, it's been quiet all evening. Right?'

'Right.'

'You get me a bit of sheet or an old shirt or something, Ida, to wrap his head up in. You and me, Johnny, will take him down to the river. The rest of you better clean up all this mess and get rid of what's left of that chair. And somebody's got to get it into Mum's head that he never came home tonight. Everyone know what they're doing?'

Silently they got to work.

Ellen left them to it. She let herself in at the front door and stood in the parlour, listening to the scrabblings and shufflings going on at the Turners', her heart still beating nineteen to the dozen. Her hands were shaking. She looked at them and realized that they were stained with Archie's dried blood. Her stomach lurched in revulsion. Just in time she ran to the scullery and hung over the sink, retching and groaning as if to bring up all the badness in a wicked world.

4

It was four days before they fished Archie out of the river; four days in which all the Turners and Ellen had time to wonder if they had done the right thing. The Sunday was the worst. Harry went to the police in the morning and reported his father missing. They did not seem overly concerned. People went missing all the time and most reappeared after a couple of days. Fully grown men were able to take care of themselves. Particulars were taken and Harry was told to inform them when he turned up again.

Meanwhile the others waited at home, trying to keep Milly calm. It was decided that she should stay in bed until the latest lot of bruises had faded, since they had to keep up the fiction that he had not been home at all. Bob was allowed out in the street to play, after being made to repeat the story three times over. Johnny sloped off with his friends. The girls were left with their mother.

Next door, Ellen fidgeted around, trying to act as if nothing had happened but wondering all the while how soon she could go in and see how they all were. In the end she hid the last of the tea, pretended great annoyance at not having remembered to buy any and shot out of the front door to borrow some.

Ida greeted her with cries of relief. 'Oh, Ellen, am I glad to see you! Ain't it horrible? I didn't

451

sleep a wink last night.'

'Neither did I. Is everything all right? How's your mum?'

Ida cast a glance towards the ceiling and dropped her voice. 'Ever so poorly. She just keeps crying and saying how she's been a wicked woman and now she's being punished. We dunno what to do with her, Ellen. I mean, it wasn't like it was her what hit him. My mum's not wicked. All she ever done was try to look after all of us proper. I dunno what she means.'

No more did Ellen. 'I suppose she's just upset. What about Florrie? How's she?'

'Oh, well, you know our Florrie. She don't say a lot.'

Ellen knew only too well. 'Tell her I'm here, Ida.'

Florrie had that all too familiar frozen look about her. Ellen put an arm around her shoulders.

'You mustn't blame yourself, love. It wasn't you what killed him, I know it wasn't.'

Florrie turned a hard little face towards her. Her eyes were steely. 'Yes it was. I done it, and I'm glad.'

It sent a chill through Ellen's body.

'I don't believe that, and neither do you, not really. And you're never, ever to say it to anyone else. The important thing is that we all stick to the story. We're all in it together now.'

'That's the only thing I'm sorry for. I never wanted to drag all you lot into it. But not for hitting him. I'm not sorry for that.'

Ellen did not know what to say. In all the years they had been friends, she had always felt inadequate when faced with Florrie's problems.

'Well, if there's anything I can do, you know I'm always there next door,' she said. It sounded very feeble to her ears.

'Thanks, Ellen. You're the best pal anyone ever had.'

Warmth stole briefly across Florrie's face. She returned her hug.

When Harry returned, they debated what should be done about Milly.

'Do you think she'll stick to the story?' Ellen asked.

'God, I hope so. If she don't, we're all sunk,' Harry said.

'What are we going to say to the neighbours? It'll look funny if we don't say nothing, and once it's out they'll all be over here. They'll see she's odd. I mean, you can't miss it. She's acting ever so strange,' Ida said.

'Aunty Alma'll be over here anyway. She always does of a Sunday,' Florrie reminded her.

'Yeah, and you won't keep her out of Mum's bedroom.'

'You'll have to say...' Ellen was thinking aloud. 'You'll have to say that she was so upset your dad never come home that she went and fell down the stairs.'

The others looked at her.

'That's it! They'll swallow that, all right. And it's only natural that she's still funny now, 'cos he's still not come back,' Ida said. 'You are clever, Ellen.'

'And Ellen can tell the neighbours, too. If you don't mind?' Harry said.

Ellen shook her head.

'Then it looks natural. She's come in here now–'

'To borrow some tea,' Ellen told him.

'To borrow some tea. Give her a bit now, Florrie, so's we don't forget. Then we tell her all about Dad not coming home, and she tells her lot and anyone else she runs into.'

'I think one of you better go over and tell your aunt Alma,' Ellen said. 'After all, you'd do that, wouldn't you? You wouldn't just sit in here by yourselves, worrying. First thing you'd do is go and see her. And Maisie too – you better go round and see her.'

And so the story spread. By midday most of the street knew. The Turners' house was filled with sympathizers. Florrie slipped next door and volunteered to take Ellen's babies for a walk. Ellen, recognizing her friend's need to get away, tucked them up in the pram.

'Take as long as you like. I only just fed Teddy so he won't need another one for three or four hours.'

'Thanks, Ellen.' Florrie gave a tight smile.

Her knuckles were white on the handle as she marched off down the road. It was a long Sunday afternoon for Ellen, wondering how Milly was holding out next door and listening to first Gerry then Alma speculating as to where Archie might be.

Milly was the weak link. All the rest, even Bob, realized exactly what the price of truth would be. But Milly was unpredictable. Harry stopped outside the door as he set off for work on Monday morning. Ellen was scrubbing the step.

'Ellen?' He glanced up and down the street. Other women were already cleaning, people were going out. 'Can you pop in and see to my mum sometime? She's still – you know...'

'Yeah, right.' Ellen knew exactly what he meant. She sat back on her heels and looked up at him. 'Don't worry, Harry. I'll see she's all right.'

She did not feel as confident as she sounded. The moment Gerry and the lodgers were out of the house, she went next door. Milly was still in bed. This roused twinges of alarm. Usually they had difficulty in getting her to lie down; she dragged herself around, getting the family off in the morning, however badly Archie had beaten her.

'You feeling poorly, Mrs Turner?' she asked. 'Like me to make you a cup of tea?'

'I don't want nothing.' Her voice was totally expressionless.

'Well, how you feeling? It's cold up here. How about coming down into the kitchen? Florrie made the range up before she went and it's burning nicely now.'

'No – no – I couldn't.'

'But it's much warmer downstairs.'

'I couldn't – not there. Not in there...' Milly's chin trembled.

Ellen began to understand. 'You got to come down sometime, Mrs Turner. You can't stay up here for ever. Come on, now. It won't be so bad once you done it. Get it over with, eh?'

'No.' Tears began to course down her cheeks. Milly made no attempt to wipe them. She just lay there, weeping.

'Oh, Mrs Turner, don't take on. I know it's dreadful but...'

But what? But it's a good thing he won't be coming back to knock you around any more? Somehow, Ellen knew that this was not how Mrs Turner saw it.

'But crying ain't going to make it any better,' she substituted.

Nothing she could say seemed to make any difference. Milly refused to move, refused to eat or drink. Ellen did not know what to do. She was relieved when she heard the front door open and Maisie calling up from below. She left Milly in the charge of her daughter, but spent the rest of the morning worrying. Supposing Milly told Maisie what had really happened? Maisie, of course, would say nothing to endanger her sister, but Ellen was sure that the fewer the people knew the truth, the easier it would be to keep the secret. She went back next door again in the afternoon, to find Milly much the same.

'You do know we mustn't tell anyone, don't you, Mrs Turner?' she said. 'He never come home Saturday night. You must remember that.'

Once again the tears stood in Milly's eyes.

'It's all my fault, all my fault,' she said. 'It wouldn't never have happened if it weren't for me. He'd be alive now.'

'But it ain't your fault, Mrs Turner. It was just a dreadful accident.'

'I'm a wicked woman. It happened because of me.'

It was fixed in her mind. Milly was not listening to reason, and Ellen ran out of arguments.

She still had not faced the kitchen when the news came that a body matching Archie's description had been found. By great good fortune, it was evening and Harry was home. He persuaded the policeman that his mother was too ill to get up, and went to identify the body. Even though he had seen drowned people before, even though he had hated his father, it still made him feel sick. He took one glance at the bloated features with the empty eye sockets and looked away.

'That's him,' he said.

'Looks like someone done him over. Lots of nasty blows to the head. Would he have had anything worth taking about him when he went out?'

'He had his drinking money,' Harry said.

'Argumentative sort of bloke, was he?'

'He was when he'd had a few.'

'Ah – well. Can't release the body yet, Mr Turner. We got to send it for a post-mortem. Unnatural death, like. Have to be an inquest.'

Harry nodded, outwardly taking it calmly, though an unreasoning fear shot through him. An inquest. They might find something, some sign. It might all come out. If they started questioning his mother, she would never hold out.

Somehow, they all lived through the days that followed. Now that Archie had been found, Milly could openly mourn his death. The women in the street came in and comforted her, and she was at last coaxed downstairs. Florrie was grateful for this. It was one small burden less. She slipped in and out of the house like a shadow, sharing the housework and cooking with Ida after the long day's work, trying to keep the household afloat.

457

She made herself as inconspicuous as possible, so that nobody would think to include her in their sympathy or ask what she thought had happened on the night of her father's death.

Florrie put food on the table for the others, and watched them persuade her mother to eat, but was unable to swallow more than a mouthful or two herself. Food seemed to choke her. The little that she did get down lay heavy in her stomach, giving her pains. The days were bad enough, but the nights were worse. She stayed awake while the events of Saturday night revolved over and over again in her mind.

'I'm glad,' she said to herself, repeating it like a charm against the horrors of the darkness. 'I'm glad he's dead. He deserved to die.'

When she did sleep, nightmares pursued her. She was back in the kitchen again, with the chair leg in her hand, but her father snatched it from her and beat her mother to death and then started on all the others until there was just him and herself amid the bleeding bodies, then he came towards her... Or her family was sitting in the kitchen when she came in, and as one they all stood up and pointed at her, until she had to turn and run out into a foggy and featureless night, but wherever she went, people appeared out of the gloom, pointing at her with a stony absence of forgiveness until she knew there was nowhere she could go, no one she could turn to...

She woke, sweating and crying out, to be comforted by Ida. But once her sister had gone back to sleep again, she was terrified of the same nightmares recurring. She did not know what was worse, the dreams or her own night thoughts.

Most of all, Florrie was haunted by her mother. That was when the remorse and the guilt gripped her, when she was confronted by a face blank with grief, and heard the way her mother blamed herself, and saw her inability to do anything but sit and stare into space. Every night she resolved to speak to her, to tell her she was sorry, to try to get through the invisible barrier that her mother had put up between herself and the world. Every morning the words dried in her throat. She could not do it.

Without realizing it, she spoke less and less to anyone, shrinking within herself as her already slight body grew thinner still.

'Florrie?'

She flinched as if she had been struck. Her nerves were raw.

'Florrie, you look really poorly. Are you eating properly?'

It was Ellen, her kind face creased with concern.

'I'm all right.'

'You're not all right. You're ill. You got to keep your strength up, Florrie. You'll fade away.'

She shook her head. She even found it difficult to talk to Ellen.

'Jimmy Croft was speaking to me yesterday. He says he's real worried and can't get a word out of you. I told him you was all shook up about your dad and your mum and everything, and he's got to be patient with you. But you can't keep him waiting for ever.'

She wanted to go to Jimmy. She wanted to feel his arms round her, to give in to all the raging emotions that she kept pent up so tight inside her, to cry and cry on his shoulder. But she was afraid, afraid she might say something.

'I can't go out. Not at the moment.'

'After the inquest, then. Once you got that over with, you must pick up the threads again.'

'I don't know.' She could not imagine life ever being normal again.

'You must, Florrie. Don't let him slip away. Don't make the mistake I did. He's a good bloke, is Jimmy. He loves you, and I know you love him. Don't mess it up. You'll regret it all your life if you do.'

Slowly the words sank into her brain, the sense of them trickled down and connected. A little of the fog of fear, guilt and defiance that surrounded her cleared. She looked at her friend and for the first time since the night of her father's death, considered something outside herself and her family.

'Do you regret marrying Gerry?'

She saw Ellen bite her lip, saw loyalty and caution war with truth.

'I regret not marrying your Harry.'

'Oh.' It opened up a whole new way of looking at things. 'I never thought...'

Ellen gripped her arm. 'So don't do the same yourself, see? Promise me?'

Slowly, she nodded.

'You'll start going out with him again after the inquest?'

'Yeah.'

But first there was the inquest to get through. Perhaps it would all come out. Perhaps she would be sent to prison. Perhaps she would hang.

'We'll give him a good send-off, Mum,' Harry said. 'You just name it – black horses, plumes, ham tea... Anything you like.'

Milly shook her head. 'The expense.'

'Never mind the expense. I can afford it. You just say what you want, Mum, and you can have it.'

'I don't know. I can't think.'

'Come on, you'd feel better if you tried to think about it. What d'you think he'd've liked, eh?'

Harry was at his wits' end. The inquest was over; his sister was safe and his mother no longer had to fear either questioning from the police or her husband coming home to beat her up, and yet still the family was reeling from the effect of his father's death. His mother in particular seemed to be getting worse instead of better. She was unable to do anything. The girls had to nag her even to wash herself, and forcibly took her clothes away from her and gave her clean ones. She was locked away from them in a grey wilderness. Harry had some inkling why. It was the same terrible burden that he carried, a knowledge that the truth had been hidden, making him a party to the death. Even though he was convinced that what they had done was for the best, still he had to cope with a constant feeling of guilt and deception dragging at him like a stone. For his mother it was worse. She still held on to the idea that it was her fault. More than that, she actually appeared to be missing his father. This Harry could not comprehend.

So he pinned his hopes on a good funeral. Everyone said that funerals were great healers. It was worth taking out his precious savings if it helped his mother, and if he was honest, the thought of spending on his father salved a little of his own guilt as well.

The girls helped with the preparations, Maisie and Alma rallied round, and Ellen came in from next door. It was the best funeral the street had seen for a long time, gaining unmixed approval from everyone. But still the most they could get Milly to do was get dressed and actually attend. For the rest, she just sat and let it all go on around her.

'I don't know what to do with her,' Harry confessed to his aunt.

'She's grieving, believe it or not. You'll have to let her get over it in her own way,' Alma told him.

But as the weeks went by, nothing changed. If anything, she seemed to withdraw further into herself. Harry felt helpless. It was like navigating though fog; there were no points of reference. When his father was alive, he had worried about his mother, but at least he had felt he could do something in defending her from the worst of his father's excesses. Now there was nothing. He could not reach her.

He wished there was someone he could really talk to about it. Alma was a brick, but she did not know the whole story. He could not speak to Florrie since it was she who had set the whole thing off and he did not want to heap any more on her head. The obvious choice was Ellen. He longed for her wisdom, her reassurance. Often it seemed to him that if he could just hold her in his arms again, the whole problem would be eased.

But she was cut off from him. He stuck by what he had said in the gardens at Southend. She was married to Gerry, and that was an end to it. When they met on the doorstep or in the street, Ellen would promise to look in on his mother, and he would thank her. They were neighbours, tied up in the same secret, but that was all.

The Turner household became a place of heavy silences. In life, Archie had united them, they had been a solid conspiracy against him. But the manner of his death divided them. None of them talked about it, but it was always there. They each kept it locked up inside them.

Gradually, without even realizing they were doing it, every one of the brothers and sisters spent more and more time away from home. Harry's job had always taken up most of his time. Now his spare hours were spent almost exclusively with his single friends. Ida and Florrie were courting. Johnny left school and started as an apprentice lighterman, coming home exhausted each night to sleep like the dead. Young Bob was the most faithful member of the Trinidad Street gang, appearing at home only at meal and bedtimes or when he was forced to do chores. From the outside they looked like a normal family. Only Milly, helpless in her pit of depression, seemed any different. But each one of them knew that they were drifting apart, and none of them knew how to stop it. In a way, none of them even wanted to, for to be together was to remember that night when they had acted as one, and they all wanted to forget.

One evening the following April, Jimmy Croft

came to call. He stood in the kitchen doorway, his cap held tightly in front of him, as if uncertain what to do next. Tea was just finished and the girls were clearing away the dishes. Bob had been sent out the back to fetch in some coal, Johnny and Milly were still at the table, Johnny was asleep with his head cradled in his arms, and Milly just sat there, looking down at her hands.

Harry glanced at his sister, expecting her to go and greet her sweetheart, but she just went bright red and whipped out into the scullery. So he nodded to Jimmy.

'Wotcher, mate. You staying till Florrie's ready? Might be a drop left in the pot if you want it.'

'No – er – yeah – that is, I am, but I wanted to have a word with you first.'

'Oh. Right. What was it, then?'

'Er – it's a bit...'

Jimmy was rapidly turning as red as Florrie. Harry suddenly caught on. He grinned, and the weight inside him lifted for the first time in months.

'Got you now, mate. Best come in the parlour.'

They stepped into the chilly little front room. From the other side of the door scrabbling feet and Ida's high-pitched giggle could be heard. Harry guessed there were ears pressed to the door. Jimmy looked acutely uncomfortable. He started several times, but failed to get through a coherent sentence.

'It's our Florrie, ain't it?' Harry said, helping him along.

'Yeah – that's it.' Jimmy snatched eagerly at this lifeline. 'I thought, well, now your dad's gone, it's you I got to see.'

'Want to get married, do you?'

'Yeah, but, it's a bit difficult...'

Harry could see no difficulty. Getting married seemed the best thing Florrie could do, and Jimmy was a good bloke. Briefly he wondered if she was pregnant and a quick wedding was needed. That would account for Jimmy's embarrassment.

'What's the matter, then?' he asked.

'It's her. She don't – it's like she's a different person since your dad went. I can't say how.' He waved his hands about helplessly. 'She's just – different. It's like she's holding out on me, somehow.'

Harry knew what he meant. Florrie was just the same with him. She never had been much of a one for talking, not like Ida, but where once they had been able to discuss things that really mattered, now there was a barrier between them. Of course he knew why, but he could not tell Jimmy that. He tried to decide what he *could* say.

'You still want to marry her, though?' he asked.

'Oh, yeah.' Jimmy was definite on this point.

'And she wants to marry you?'

'I think so.'

'Why don't you just go ahead, then? Florrie, she, well – I think she feels bad because she always wanted him to die, see? And now he has, it's like she wished it on him. What with Mum taking it so bad and all, it's made her go ever so quiet. But I think she might cheer up if you got wed. It's not much of a laugh in this house at the moment, I can tell you. You get her out of here and she'll be her old self again, most like.'

Jimmy relaxed. 'You don't mind, then?'

465

'Mind? I'm pleased for you! Best thing that's happened in our family for ages. Here – shake on it.'

Smiling now, Jimmy grasped Harry's hand in both of his.

'Thanks, mate. Thanks a million. I'll look after her like she's made of glass.'

'I know you will, Jim. She deserves it, does our Florrie.'

They went into the kitchen to break the news to the rest of the family. Amidst the laughter and back-slapping and ribald remarks, nobody noticed that Milly withdrew even further into herself, or that Florrie did not actually say very much.

'My little sister! Ain't it lovely? They'll make a lovely pair, her and Jimmy. Oh, I'm ever so glad. Ain't you glad, Will? Be nice to have a wedding. It'll cheer Mum up and all. We ain't had a wedding since Ellen and Gerry. Been nothing but funerals. I suppose I'll have to wear the same old hat. Still, never mind, eh? Still be nice to think about. Perhaps I can get some flowers for it. What d'you think, Will? D'you think we could afford some new flowers for my hat, seeing as it's my sister and all?'

'What?' As usual, Will was not listening.

'My hat, I can't wear it again, can I? Not for a wedding. Have to get some new flowers.'

'Who bloody cares?' Will shrugged.

'Oh, Will, don't you never care about nothing?' Maisie looked crestfallen. Tears filled her eyes. 'It's my sister getting married. You ought to be pleased.'

'Why? Because that poor sod Jimmy Croft's getting spliced? I only hope he gets more fun out of Florrie than what I done out of you.'

The tears spilled over, trickling down her face. 'You're horrible to me, you are. What have I ever done for you to treat me so horrible? I look after you proper.'

Will groaned in exasperation. 'For God's sake, stop snivelling,' he shouted.

Maisie only cried the more, while Alice, clinging to her skirts, joined in in sympathy. Lily and Albert's faces appeared, pressed against the back window. It was raining outside and they wanted to come in. Their voices were added to the general din.

'Shut your row!'

Will put his hands to his head, but as he did so they caught in the wet washing hanging from the strings across the ceiling. A damp shirt slapped down across his head. It was the last straw.

'It's Saturday night and I worked hard all week. Six days, with overtime every evening. I'm fed up, d'you hear? Fed up! All I want's a bit of peace and quiet in my own home and I get you and your bloody kids howling in my ears. Well, that's it, I'm going out. And don't wait up 'cos I might be late, or I might not come back at all!'

He slammed out of the house, taking pleasure in hearing Maisie's wail of dismay as he did so. He set off down the street, hands in pockets, head down against the rain. He kicked at a stone, venting his anger on it.

'Bloody families!' he growled. 'Bloody women!'

He could see no end to it. Life was just one

long dreary treadmill. The only thing that had happened lately to break the monotony had been his father-in-law's death, and that had done nothing but make Maisie go on and on about how badly her mum had taken it and how worried they all were.

However hard he worked, there never seemed to be enough money. With every baby, Maisie got more scrawny-looking and the house got fuller. He'd been glad when she miscarried the last three. It meant having her weeping about the place for weeks on end, but she got weepy when she did have babies, and it was better than having more mouths to feed.

Without conscious thought, his feet had taken him not to the Rum Puncheon but to the West Ferry Road. He was at the bus stop. He knew then where he was going – off the Island, away from it all, to the place where anything might happen.

The bus was packed with a noisy mass of humanity reeking of wet clothing, sweat and cheap cigarettes. Will had to stand all the way. Then there was a wait in the relentless rain until the tram came. He got a seat this time, but was jammed in by an enormously fat woman who wheezed as if every breath was her last. Will kept his thoughts doggedly on where he was going. Everything would be all right once he got there. He would step into another world. Even the past week of back-breaking overtime was worthwhile now, since he had money in his pocket. Not very much, but enough.

It was pouring when he got off the tram and set off to walk the last part of the journey. His shoulders were soaked to the skin by the time he got there and his trousers were clinging to his legs. One of his boots was leaking. The Saturday-night traffic crawled endlessly past him, cabs, carriages, motor cars, all noisy and smelly in their own way, all driven by men made bad-tempered by the rain. The puddles were slicks of liquid mud composed mostly of oil and horse droppings. Every time he was forced too near the edge of the pavement, he got splashed by passing wheels or hoofs. But through the downpour he could see the bright lights like coloured stars on the front of the theatre, the welcoming yellow warmth of the foyer spilling out on to the pavement. Without realizing he was doing it, he straightened his back and put a spring into his step. He joined on the end of the queue to get in, and was enveloped in the heat, the soft carpets, the glorious red and gold decor.

Then a new worry hit him as he shuffled towards the box office. Supposing there were no seats left?

'Yes?' The attendant did not even look at him.

'One for the gods, please.'

He pushed his money across the counter. A ticket was pushed back. Relief flooded through him. It was all right.

Up the endless flights of stone steps and into the gallery he bounded, as light as a twenty-year-old. A wall of warmth hit him. The excited chatter of hundreds of voices wrapped round him. He found a place on the end of a bench at the very back, so that he had a clear view down the narrow aisle. He was level with the lights up here, but the seats were so steeply raked that it felt as if he was right on top of the stage. One good jump and he would land on it. As the water trickled off the ends of his trousers and his jacket started to steam, the outside world gradually ceased to exist until there was nothing but here and now, and what was to come. He sat taking in the atmosphere as he dried out, anticipation winding pleasurably inside him.

He had been to enough halls to know that this was a good one. There was a proper band, the master of ceremonies handled the audience with skill, and there was a good line-up of acts. He laughed at the comics and joined in the choruses with the singers. All the time the tension was building into a great ball, filling his guts, squeezing his lungs until he could hardly contain it.

The master of ceremonies banged his gavel. His barrel chest inflated, his red nose shone. His voice boomed out to fill every last corner of the auditorium.

'And now, my lords, ladies and gentlemen, for your delectation and delight – with a voice as sweet as the flowers in spring and feet as light as raindrops...'

It had to be her.

'Songs that would melt a heart of stone...' It must be her.

'All the way from the Emerald Isle...'

It *was* her.

'Your sweetheart and mine – Miss Siobhan O'Donaghue!'

'Ye-e-eah!'

Will shouted and whistled and stamped his

feet. He craned forward. The red curtains swept apart. A line of music from the band and there she was, picked out in the beam of the spotlight, as fresh and beautiful and unspoilt as the day he first saw her. In her flouncy green and yellow dress, with her hair tumbling in curls down her back, she did not look a day over sixteen – a fresh, innocent girl with the flowing curves of a woman. Will watched, entranced. The theatre melted away. There was nothing but him and her.

The words and the music swirled around him, a sweet little ditty about the one true love she always remembered. She advanced and retreated, smiling, flirting, seeming to promise everything and snatching it away. She knew he was there, she must do. She was looking right at him. She was singing it for him, his Siobhan. The years rolled away. She was offering him the chance to run away with him again. This time there would be no hesitation.

Her song ended. He applauded until his work-hardened hands hurt. The curtains closed, cutting her off from him. He sat in a daze, seeing and hearing nothing of what was going on around him. He did not even realize the next act was on stage. He had to see her again, face to face. She was waiting for him, he knew it. She had been waiting all this time. He would speak to her after the show. Somehow or other, he had to get to her dressing room. She would let him in, he was sure of it. He sat in a sweat of longing.

Out of nowhere a dreadful thought struck him. She would not be here at the end of the show. All artistes did at least two turns a night, many managed three. She would be at the next theatre. He leapt out of his seat and blundered towards the exit. Down the steps he charged, his boots ringing on the flecked stone, his heart pounding. She could not have left yet. She must not.

'Don't go,' he muttered out loud. 'Wait for me.'

He went out into the cold and wet again. The rain cooled his flushed face as he paused, looking wildly this way and that, trying to get his bearings. Which way was the stage door? He plunged to his right and came to the corner of the building. He peered through the murk for a light or a notice. Nothing. He tried again. There was a cobbled alleyway on the other side of the theatre. A female figure stepped out of the shadows and stood in front of him, blocking his way.

'Hello darling, where're you going so fast? Fancy a nice time?'

A waft of cheap scent in his nostrils, nearly choking him.

'Piss off!' He pushed her out of his way, not even hearing her squall of protest. There was a cab ahead of him, practically filling the alleyway. Level with its roof he could see a dim lamp with lettering on it. He knew what it said: *Stage Door*.

He squeezed between the cab and the wall. There was no one else waiting at all. The rain had seen them off. He poked his head inside the door, to be growled at by the stage doorkeeper.

'Miss O'Donaghue?' he asked. 'She gone yet?'

'Might have. Might not,' was the helpful reply.

Will had not the kind of money to prise a sensible answer from him. He backed out and looked up at the cabby hunched in his seat under a mackintosh cape.

'You waiting for Miss O'Donaghue?'

The man gave no sign that he had even heard.

'Oi! Cloth ears! I said, are you waiting for Miss O'Donaghue?'

'No, I'm waiting for the bleeding Queen o' Sheba.'

Will glowered at him. He stood by the doorway, his hands in his pockets, his ears alert for the first sounds of movement within. The minutes dragged by. Perhaps she had gone. Perhaps she had left the moment her turn was over. She could be halfway across London by now.

Footsteps tapped on wooden stairs. Will sprang to attention and peered into the ill-lit passage. First feet, then skirts appeared. He felt sick with excitement. It was her, he was sure of it.

She was pulling a hood over her head, obscuring her face, but there was no mistaking her.

''Night, Bert!'

''Night, Miss O'Donaghue.'

'Siobhan!'

He moved in front of her, but she sidestepped neatly round him without even looking at his face. She was intent on the cab outside.

'Siobhan, wait.'

'I'm late.'

He caught at her arm but she was past him already and jumping up into the cab.

'Drive on!' she called before she had even shut the doors.

'Siobhan – Siobhan...'

He hurried down the alleyway after her, oblivious of the filthy water sprayed by the cab wheels. As it turned into the narrow backstreet he came alongside. He could just see the shape of her face, a pale circle in the darkness.

'Where are you going, Siobhan?'

The driver whipped the horse into a trot. Will had to run to keep up.

'Siobhan, please! Where are you going?'

'Well, wouldn't you like to know, Will Johnson!'

From the depths of the cab came that familiar laugh, teasing, entrancing.

His heart leapt. He was ready to sing and dance and turn cartwheels in the mud.

'Siobhan, you got to come to the wedding.' He did not know what made him say that. It just came out – anything to catch her attention. 'Florrie and Jimmy. In three weeks' time. Say you'll be there, Siobhan.'

The cab reached the main street. For once, there was a break in the traffic. It crossed into the outside stream. Will plunged after it, heedless of the oncoming wheels. There was a squeal of brakes and the blare of a horn. A large motor car stopped within an inch of him, its polished radiator gleaming in the reflected light from its headlamps. The chauffeur leant out and yelled abuse.

Dazed, Will stepped back on to the safety of the pavement, his eyes still fixed on the back of Siobhan's cab. He felt as if half of him had been wrenched away. He raised his hands and cupped them round his mouth.

'Three weeks!' he bawled above the roar and clatter and rumble of the traffic. 'Three weeks' time, Siobhan!'

He stood in the rain, staring after her. A bus hid

her from his view, but still he stood there. That laugh still rang in his ears, that irresistible, teasing voice. *Wouldn't you like to know, Will Johnson!*

He would like to know, very much. He wanted it with all his being. But all he was left with was the hope that she might just come to Florrie and Jimmy's wedding.

5

The tap on the door made Ellen jump. She wasn't expecting visitors. She got up as Florrie's head came round the front door.

'Oh, Ellen, can I come in?'

''Course you can! What a thing to ask. Come on into the back. Gerry and the others are out.'

Florrie sat hunched up in the chair, with her arms round her raised knees. Her narrow face was pale, her mouth set.

'Nervous?' Ellen asked.

Florrie nodded.

Ellen's heart went out to her. She remembered the night before her own wedding. She too had been nervous, with misgivings about the whole thing, but she had had the support of her mother and the other women of the family. They had all sat chatting and joking while they made last-minute alterations to dresses. Lots of good advice had been given out with the cups of tea and nips of gin. Ellen had felt the arms of the family about her, warm and reassuring. But for Florrie it was not the same. Her mother was still locked in her prison of grief.

'I'm surprised your Aunty Alma ain't come round,' she said.

'She's coming later, she said, and Maisie an' all, if Will don't go out. But – well, you know Aunty Alma when she gets going.'

Ellen knew what she meant. Her mother-in-law had a heart of gold, but could be a bit much, especially on an occasion like this.

'She does get loud, don't she?'

Florrie nodded again.

Ellen wondered how they were going to get on, her and Jimmy, in Alma's house, for, like Maisie before her, Florrie and her new husband were going to lodge with her aunt until such time as they could afford a place of their own. It was a sensible arrangement, since Alma was finding it difficult managing on just her wages and Charlie's intermittent contributions, but Alma was so boisterous and Florrie so quiet and with-drawn that Ellen though she could be swamped.

'You frightened about leaving home?' she asked.

'No, not really. I mean, it's only over the road.'

'Be quite nice to get out of your house. It ain't been the same since – you know.'

'Yeah.'

Florrie did not sound very sure. Ellen had thought she would be only too glad to leave. It never had been a happy place, but since Archie's death it was like a tomb. It was as if Milly's depression was reaching out like a smothering fog, touching each one of them.

'At least Alma's always happy.'

'Yeah.' Florrie sighed. 'It's just – I don't like leaving Mum, that's all. Not in the state she's in at the moment.'

'Oh,' Ellen sought to find a way to put it kindly. 'I would have thought that – things being how they are... I mean, it might be better...'

She left the sentence unfinished, but they both knew what she meant. Florrie was a constant reminder of the manner of Archie's death.

'Perhaps,' Florrie half agreed. 'But Mum does rely on me. Ida's all right, she means well, but she's a bit, you know...'

'Stupid,' Ellen supplied.

'Well, yeah, she is. And I know Maisie comes round, but she's got all them kids and having them miscarriages brung her down, and Aunty Alma does her best, but Mum just goes even quieter when she's there. And I know you do all you can, but you're not her daughter, after all. It's me what's really in charge now.'

'Might do Ida a lot of good. She'll have to think a bit,' Ellen said. 'And you can come over every day and check up on them, can't you?'

'Yeah.' Florrie did not sound convinced.

'Only other thing would've been for Jimmy to move in with your family, but that wouldn't be no good,' Ellen pointed out. 'Not enough room, for a start, and it ain't – well, it ain't exactly cheerful for starting your married life, is it?'

'No, no you're right,' Florrie agreed.

Ellen was worried. Her friend did not seem like a bride looking forward to being with her man. She reached over and took Florrie's hands.

'What is it, eh? What's up?'

'Nothing.' But she did not look Ellen in the eye.

'Come on, there is something. Don't you want to go through with it?'

Florrie pulled her hands away and clawed them into her hair. 'I don't know, I don't know! I do, but...'

'You do love him?' Ellen asked gently.

'Yes! Yes, I do. It's just...'

'What?'

'Nothing.'

'It ain't nothing. Something's bothering you. Is it – about what happened?'

There was a long pause, then Florrie nodded.

Ellen tried to grope her way towards the truth. 'You didn't kill him, you know that, don't you? You hit him, but that's not what killed him.' Then it came to her. 'Ain't you told Jimmy?'

'No,' she whispered, after another long pause.

'Bit of a secret to keep from him,' Ellen said. Harry had always insisted that nobody else should know, not even Maisie. But this was different.

'Yeah.'

'D'you want to tell him?'

Florrie nodded. 'I tried to but I couldn't. I was afraid – you know – afraid what he'd think of me.'

'If he loves you, he'll see it was just a dreadful accident.'

It seemed to Ellen that this had to be cleared up. But Jimmy would be down the Puncheon with the men from the street, and calling him out would cause such a to-do that she dismissed the idea at once. Florrie wouldn't see him again till they met at the church, and then there was the party. They wouldn't get a chance to talk alone until they got to their room at Alma's. It wasn't really the sort of thing to be talking about on your wedding night, but then if Florrie waited till the morning it would be even worse. Wedding nights were bad enough, in her experience, without the prospect of a confession to go through afterwards.

'If you're going to tell him, you want to get it over with as soon as you can,' she said.

'Yeah.'

'Soon as you and him are alone. Once it's out, you'll feel better.'

'Yeah. Yeah, you're right, I know you are. I got to tell him.' Florrie stood up. 'I better get back next door. They'll all be there soon. And thanks, Ellen. Thanks a million.'

Ellen came with her to the door. She put her arms round her friend and hugged her.

'All the best, Florrie. You be very, very happy, you hear me?'

The women clung to each other, both on the verge of tears, then Florrie broke away and hurried home. Ellen was left brushing a sleeve across her eye.

'You be very, very happy,' she repeated in a whisper. 'You're marrying the man you love. Don't let anything spoil it.'

She hoped with all her heart that tomorrow would be a wonderful day for Florrie. God knew, she deserved it.

All the non-Catholic members of the street were at the church the next day, along with the Crofts, most of the Turners and Milly and Alma's side of the family. It was dark inside, after the fine May weather in the streets, and a strong smell of mothballs and camphor from Sunday best and redeemed clothes mixed with the dust, polish and incense of the church. They sat fidgeting in the pews, craning their necks and commenting on each other and their surroundings. The chapel-goers were disdainful of what they considered to be painted idols in the church, while the heathen majority, who only set foot inside the place for weddings and funerals, looked about with awe or exaggerated ease. Babies cried or slept, toddlers ran up and down the aisles. There was a hum of happy anticipation. The women looked smug, as if they as a sex had got one over on the men. They nodded and smiled at each other, the married ones knowing what the bride was up against, the spinsters hoping it would be their turn next. Their menfolk had an air of pained tolerance. Most of them had been drinking with the groom the night before, and were looking forward to further cele-brations once the ceremony was out of the way.

It was drawing near to the time. Jimmy Croft and his brother Joe, uncomfortable in ill-fitting jackets and tight collars, were looking increas-ingly anxious. The vicar had a cold and was sneezing and blowing his nose as he waited.

The outer door opened. Everyone looked round, ready to smile benignly at Florrie leaning on her brother Harry's arm. But the woman who stood framed in the sunlight did not have Florrie's slight figure and made-over dress. In her primrose yellow gown and huge matching hat, she appeared to glow like the sun itself in the doorway. A man appeared beside her – not Harry, but a thin and incredibly tall figure whose height was increased by his shiny top hat. Together they stood, drawing every eye. The entire congregation drew in its breath, then let it out in a buzz of surprise and speculation. Who were they? Why were they here? Nobody in either family dressed like that. It was unknown for toffs to come to weddings on Dog Island.

The man removed his hat. They stepped forward, making a progress into the body of the church. It was then that those with sharp eyes recognized the lady.

'Siobhan! It's Siobhan O'Donaghue – look, just look at her! Siobhan!'

'Who's that with her?'

The buzz grew into a roar as everyone asked everyone else. Heads switched this way and that. Who had she nabbed? Was he one of the nobs? He looked it. They sat down behind the rest of the congregation, so that everyone had to stay screwed round in order to stare at them. Siobhan deliberately avoided looking anyone straight in the face, and a sweet smile of satisfaction curved her lips. The man stared at the windows above the chancel as if there was nobody else there. His thin face with its hooked nose and mysterious dark eyes looked as if it had been carved from alabaster.

When the bride and her brother arrived five minutes later, not a soul noticed.

Florrie and Harry were halfway up the aisle before anyone started to tear their attention away from the exotic uninvited guests. When they did, Florrie looked dowdy and colourless by com-

481

parison. Even Harry, though more handsome and better built than the unknown man, could not compete with his elegant tailcoat and immaculate trousers.

The service started, but the congregation could not settle down. They still kept peering round every now and again to have another look at Siobhan and her escort. Florrie's responses could not be heard at all.

It was Will who finally realized who the stranger was.

'That's no toff,' he muttered to Maisie. 'That's the Great Cornelius, Conjuror Extraordinary.'

'Oh!' Maisie squeaked. 'Just fancy!'

She twisted round to tell her family in the pew behind, and they in turn spread it further. Soon it was all over the church.

'The Great Cornelius – the Great Cornelius–'

The information sighed through the rows like the wind.

The singing of the hymns was ragged and sporadic. There was so much else to concentrate on. Only a few stalwarts ignored Siobhan and the conjuror after the first shock of their entry. Harry steadfastly refused to turn round, and sang loudly in his tuneful baritone. Ellen, raging inwardly at this eclipse of her friend on her special day, also pretended they weren't there. Maisie joined her after a while, and if any of her children did not face front, she clipped them round the ear. The rest of the Turners and Crofts followed suit. But when Florrie and Jimmy emerged from the vestry and processed down the aisle, officially man and wife, it was not them that everyone was staring at.

Outside, precious handfuls of rice were thrown over the happy couple, and people came up and kissed Florrie and shook Jimmy by the hand, but all the while they were eyeing Siobhan and her impressive partner as they stood to one side of the crowd. Gradually they began to move so that Siobhan and the conjuror rather than Jimmy and Florrie were at the centre.

'Time we was moving along,' Harry said loudly.

He shouldered a gap through the bodies and stood back so that his sister and her new husband could lead the way back to Trinidad Street, then took his mother's arm and fell in behind. The rest of the Turners and Crofts followed on, along with Ellen and Gerry, until the others realized what was going on and straggled along as well. Siobhan, seeing that she was being outflanked, used her carrying stage voice to speak to the conjuror.

'Do you want to come and see the next bit? So amusing for you.'

It was a wrong move. Those who still flocked round her were not impressed, but offended. They weren't so dazzled that they had forgotten that she was really one of them.

'Who does she bloody think she is?' they muttered to each other.

Siobhan had to make do with the stares and remarks of passers-by as they made their way along the drab streets to her old home.

Everyone piled in to the Rum Puncheon. The O'Donaghues, hearing that their famous relation had turned up, came along in force. It was only a small pub and everyone was standing shoulder to shoulder, shouting at each other above the din, while glasses were passed from hand to hand over the heads of the crowd to those near the door with no chance of reaching the bar. There was one topic of conversation – Siobhan.

'I could ring her flaming neck,' Ellen said. She felt quite sick with resentment. 'How dare she come along like this and steal Florrie's day? How dare she?'

All the hatred she held for Siobhan on her own behalf came out in defence of her friend.

'What did she have to do it for? What is she trying to prove? She's the most cruel and wicked person I know.'

'Can't bear not to be the star of the show,' Alma agreed. 'Blooming selfish, I call it.'

'Who went and invited her, anyway?' Harry wanted to know. 'The O'Donaghues can't have, not to the church, not with them being Catholic and all.'

'They must've told her about it,' Alma said.

'How? She ain't been near them for months. How come she pops up now?'

'They could've written,' Ellen suggested.

Nobody thought this was likely. Most of them could write, as they had been forced to at school, but only Ellen would have thought of sending a letter. The whole thing was a mystery. Nobody noticed Will's silence on the subject, and only Maisie saw him begin to edge away in Siobhan's direction.

'Sod her,' Alma declared, when their anger had been fully aired. 'What are we talking about her for, anyway? Here's to Florrie and Jimmy. Long life and happiness, and may all their troubles be little ones.'

'Florrie and Jimmy!' they all shouted, raising their glasses.

The toast was taken up round the packed bar.

'Speech, speech!' somebody yelled.

'Yeah, come on, Jim, give us a speech!'

There was much cheering and hushing. Something near to silence was achieved, broken by uncontrolled giggling and shouts of encouragement. Jimmy was red in the face with heat, excitement and embarrassment. With a lot of help from his brother, he managed to stumble through thanks to the Turners and references to his new missus. The whole bar clapped and yelled its approval.

More drinks were called for and everyone toasted the happy couple again. Even Florrie was looking flushed and relaxed now. She hung on Jimmy's arm, smiling at everyone and constantly looking up at her new husband.

It was only then that Harry realized he was no longer supporting his mother. At some point, she had managed to slip away. He almost said 'Where's Mum?' out loud, before stopping himself just in time. Fetching her back would do no good, and pointing out her absence to Florrie would ruin her happiness. He kissed his sister and thumped his new brother-in-law on the back.

'Glad to have you in the family, mate.'

The initiative did not stay long in the hands of the bridal group. Siobhan and the Great Cornelius were slowly threading their way through the guests to join them. A wary hush fell as they approached.

Siobhan stretched out her arms to take Florrie by the shoulders and kiss her on both cheeks.

'Florrie, love! I'm so happy for you. And you too, Jimmy. You're a lucky man, d'you know that?' She kissed the groom as well and made him redder than ever, if that was possible. Even her accent was designed to set her apart. The Irish brogue had almost been wiped away. She did not talk like the rest of them, but neither did she sound like the gentry they had occasionally come into contact with, such as the ladies at the Settlement. She was strangely unplaceable.

She turned to her escort, who was standing at her shoulder, a mysterious area of silence in the midst of the hubbub. He handed her a parcel wrapped in silver paper and tied with white ribbons.

'We brought a little something for you both,' she said, handing it to Florrie.

'Oh.' Florrie was floored. Nothing as exotic as this had ever come her way in all her life. She stood staring at the object.

'Do open it,' Siobhan encouraged her, a patronizing edge to her sweetness.

Florrie tugged at the bows and opened the box. She pulled gingerly at the tissue paper inside. A cut-glass knob appeared. A few more layers of paper and a decanter was revealed, Waterford crystal with a gold rim. The light from the pub lamps danced and sparkled off the facets in tiny rainbows. Florrie and the others stared at it, dumbstruck.

'I thought it might come in handy for your new home,' Siobhan said. Of one accord, they all pictured the one bare room the bridal couple were going to occupy. The contrast with the opulence of the decanter was almost too much to bear.

Ellen was so incensed she thought she was going to burst. She wanted to fly at Siobhan and claw her face for showing up her friends in this way, for lording it over all of them and rubbing their faces in their poverty. She could not let her get away with it.

'You had some of them on the stall, didn't you, Gerry?' she said in her most penetrating voice. 'Didn't sell very well though. People round here don't care for that sort of thing much.'

There was a moment of complete quiet. Scarcely a breath was taken. Everyone looked at Siobhan to see how she would take it. The smile stayed on her face, but her eyes were cold steel.

'You can always take it to the pawnshop if you're a bit short,' she said.

It was such a stark truth that the listeners almost nodded in agreement. With a thing like that to put away, Florrie and Jimmy would be set up.

Florrie found her voice. She thrust the present back at Siobhan.

'Thanks all the same, but I don't think me and Jimmy'll be needing it.'

Siobhan opened her mouth and shut it again. For a moment it looked as if she was going to turn tail and go, defeated. But she did not give up that easily.

'I suppose it was stupid of me to think you'd like anything so fine. It's not what you'd use to put brown ale in, is it? Never mind, it will go with the others I've got on my sideboard. They look nice in the electric light.'

She swept round and made off, people parting to let her through despite the lack of space.

'They look nice in the electric light,' Ellen mimicked savagely.

Everyone gave vent to their feeling in a gust of raucous laughter. The phrase was repeated until all the sting had gone out of it. Or nearly all. Siobhan left without bestowing her attention on anyone else, but she left behind her poison, like a nasty taste in the mouth after an evening's drinking. The celebrations seemed deliberately noisy, the jollity just a shade forced.

Before the evening was half over, Jimmy and Florrie tried to get away. If they thought to slip out unnoticed they were completely foiled. Their move towards the door was spotted and a chorus of hoots, whistles and suggestive remarks went up.

'We know where they're going!'

'Get to it, Jimmy boy!'

'Hold on tight, darling.'

'Give it all you got.'

The younger and rowdier element followed them into the street and waited outside number forty after they went in. They shouted and whistled as a light showed in the front bedroom and again even louder when it went out. They hung around for quite a while, doing their best to put the newlyweds off their stroke, before finally deciding that they needed another drink they ambled back to the Puncheon, where the singing had begun.

Florrie and Jimmy were on their own at last.

It was a long day. Teddy was cutting some back teeth and had been crying on and off during the night and fretful all day. Jessica, jealous of the attention he was getting, was being difficult. By late afternoon, Ellen could cheerfully have murdered both of them. She was beginning to understand why it was that Maisie never seemed to be in control.

'Once the school holidays are here, I'm going to pay some girl to take you off my hands,' she warned them.

Jessica, who could understand, burst into tears. Teddy could not, but picked up the threat in her voice and followed suit. Ellen thrust them both into the back yard.

'If you're going to yell, you can do it out there,' she said, slamming the door and locking it.

She banged around the kitchen, getting tea ready for the lodgers, trying to shut her ears to the wailing coming in through the window.

'And I suppose you'll be late in again,' she said out loud to the absent Gerry. 'Don't know why I bother cooking for you. Never know when you're going to be here.'

Her head ached with fatigue and her whole body felt heavy. She caught hold of a pan handle without using the holder and burnt her hand. Tears welled up in her eyes and threatened to spill over.

'Oh, God,' she said, 'perhaps I'm expecting again.'

She had been tearful like this before both the babies. Another one was the last thing she wanted at the moment. She tried to remember her dates.

No, she couldn't be. But instead of relief she felt only further resentment. She couldn't be, because she and Gerry had not made love since her last period. After the enthusiasm of the first few months of marriage, they had fallen into a habit of a once-weekly session. When she was heavily pregnant and for weeks after the births, Gerry had left her alone, saying that he was sure she would rather not do it at the moment. When the other mothers enquired whether he 'bothered' her too soon, she could reply that he was kindness itself, thinking only of her and how she felt. The women were envious. Despite breast-feeding their babies, nearly all of them had at one time or another fallen pregnant within weeks of giving birth.

But there was no such excuse now. It was just that Gerry did not seem to want her very often. Ellen put down the pan lid with a clatter and went to look at herself in the glass over the mantelpiece in the parlour. The face that looked back at her was haggard with lack of sleep, with bags forming under the eyes. It was flushed from the summer heat and the cooking and framed with lank hair that straggled out of a bun at the back. Still, she decided, that was no reason. Today was a bad day. She didn't always look like this. When she cleaned up and put on a decent dress, she looked just as good as she always had. She smoothed her skirt over her hips. She still had a good figure, not too skinny, not too fat.

It wasn't her, it was Gerry. And into her head slid the thought that Harry would not have gone off her like this. Her eyes were drawn to the front window. He might be back soon. If she sat out on the front step to shell the peas, he might stop and talk before he went in.

The temptation was too much to resist. She acknowledged what it was that was making her so short-tempered and emotional – she needed desperately to be looked on as a woman, a desirable woman, not just a mother and provider of meals. What was more, it wasn't Gerry she wanted to look at her in that way, it was Harry. She hurried out the back to splash cold water over her face and run a comb through her hair, loosening the bun a little for a softer effect and pinning up most of the stray ends. From the back yard came the sounds of pitiful howling. Ellen listened, frozen, pulled between two loves. Then she relented. She unlocked the door and leant out.

'All right, all right, you can come in. Mum ain't really cross with you.'

Both children were dirty, their faces streaked with tears. Teddy hurled himself at her legs, holding on round her knees and effectively stopping her from moving. Jessica just stood glaring at her, sobs racking her small chest.

'Come here, ducks,' Ellen said, holding out her free arm. Slowly Jessica came.

She wiped their faces with a damp rag.

'We'll go and sit out the front. I expect there'll be someone out there for you to play with.'

Jessica immediately perked up, but Teddy stayed clinging to her. With difficulty, Ellen shuffled to the front door, holding a pan and a bag of peas.

'You can play with the pods,' she told them both.

It had been hot all day, and the little houses

were as stuffy as ovens. Outside, it was little better, with the smells from the river and the factories hanging heavily in the still air, but at least Ellen's house faced north, so that the sun was off the front of it. She propped the door open and sat on the step with her back against the frame and the pan on her knees. Teddy leant against her and wiped his nose on her skirt. Up and down the street, other women were peeling potatoes or smearing marge on bread. Ellen waved or nodded to them, calling out to the nearer ones. In the road, children played in a lacklustre fashion, the boys at cricket with a flat piece of wood and a rag ball, the girls at five stones or cat's cradle. Jessica wandered off to watch one pair, and was graciously allowed to hold the string once or twice. Teddy was still snivelling. Ellen looked down at him. She did not want him hanging round making that awful noise when Harry came by.

'Do go and play,' she said, giving him a little push. 'Here, I have some pea pods. Pretty!'

He began to howl again. With his round red face and runny nose, he was a pathetic sight. Ellen's heart contracted in love and guilt.

'Poor little man,' she said, hugging him to her. 'Do those toothies hurt, then?'

The child burrowed into her, comforted a little. She stroked his head. The fine baby hair was damp with sweat.

She did not want to gossip today. After the first greeting, she avoided looking at the other women. She mechanically shelled the peas, her thumb snapping the pods open and running down the insides. They made a pinging noise as they fell into the saucepan. A fresh country smell arose from them. Gradually Teddy loosened his hold on her and began to turn his attention to the empty shells.

Usually this job had a soothing effect on Ellen, but today she found herself getting more and more tense. The heap of pods still to be done grew smaller. Most of the women had gone inside now. Some of the men were coming home, plodding up the street, dusty and weary from the day's work. Ellen worked more and more slowly. Glancing up, she saw the lodgers turning into the street. A wave of anger and disappointment broke over her. She felt cheated. She stood up and stamped back into the house. Harry should have known. He should have got back early today.

She was getting the babies ready for bed by the time Gerry got in. She paused in the middle of scrubbing Teddy's neck, sat back on her heels and looked up at her husband.

'What time d'you call this, then?' she demanded.

Gerry gave a placatory smile. 'Caught a bridger, love.'

Ellen pursed her lips. Anyone could get caught the wrong side of the swing bridge when it opened to let a ship into the dock. It was part of Island life. But she could not help the irrational feeling that Gerry had arranged it just to spite her.

'How's my lovely family, then?' he asked, attempting to give them each a hug.

Ellen shrugged him off. 'Oh, so you remembered you had one, then?'

'Difficult to forget, the row this one made last

493

night.' Gerry squatted down beside Teddy. 'You going to give us a decent night's sleep tonight, old son?'

'Oh, don't worry, I'm slipping him a teaspoon of gin when he goes to bed. That ought to fix him.'

'D'you think that's right? He's only little.' Gerry looked worried.

'Your mum said that's what she used to do with you two, and it ain't done you no harm, has it?'

'No.'

'And anyway, what's it to you? You're never here. If I know anything, you'll be off out the moment you've had your tea. Am I right?'

'Well...' Gerry could not deny it.

'There you are. Same every night. Don't know why you bother coming home. Kids hardly know they got a dad.'

Recognizing trouble coming, the lodgers got up from where they were spinning out an extra cup of tea at the kitchen table.

'Er – think we'll go down the Puncheon for a bit, missus.'

Ellen gave a swift nod of acknowledgement. Gerry tried to pretend all was well, and bade them a cheery good evening.

'You talk to them more than what you do to me,' Ellen complained the moment the door had closed behind them.

'Oh, come on, love.' Gerry put an arm round her shoulders, but she stiffened defensively. 'It ain't as bad as all that. Look, we'll go down the Island Gardens Sunday, how about that? You like that? Jess would, wouldn't you, girl? You like the Gardens. Get you a hokey-pokey, eh?'

Ellen made an effort to be grateful. Any chance of a trip away from the claustrophobic atmosphere of the street was to be snatched at. But the mention of the Island Gardens only brought back aching memories.

'It'll be crowded out there, this weather,' she said.

'Greenwich, then. We'll go through the tunnel, have a cup of tea in the park. That suit you? You like the park, don't you? Plenty of room there – won't be crowded. Do you good to have an outing.'

'Yeah, that'll be nice.' It was hard to inject the right amount of enthusiasm into her voice.

'Good, right, we'll do that. Greenwich on Sunday.' Gerry rubbed his hands together, the problem solved. 'My tea ready, then?'

'All dried up, I expect.'

Ellen fished the plate out of the oven. She was right, it was all dried up, but Gerry made no comment. He sat down and tucked in, telling her in between mouthfuls about an incident at the market. Ellen hardly bothered to listen. She finished washing Teddy and pinned him into his nappy.

''Bout time you was dry an' all,' she told him. 'I'm fed up of washing your stuff.'

Jessica managed to struggle all by herself into the shirt that did duty for a nightie. Ellen planted a kiss on the top of her head.

'There's my clever girl. Sharp as a barrel-load of monkeys. You're going to be top of the class, you are.'

She plaited the child's fair hair and looked at her with satisfaction, the frustrations of the day

495

slipping away for a while. Jessica could be a wilful little madam at times, but when she was washed and ready for bed like this, bright and clean and glowing, she was pure delight.

'She's that bright,' she said to Gerry, interrupting his story. 'She'll go to the Central like her mum, just you wait and see. But she'll stay on. She'll get an office job, will my Jess. Nothing but the best for her.'

The little girl preened while Ellen caught Teddy and expertly dosed him with a teaspoon of gin, followed by one of jam.

'Say goodnight to your dad, then,' Ellen told them.

Upstairs in the front bedroom it was even more stuffy than the kitchen. All the stale air of the day seemed to have gathered there. Ellen squeezed past the big bed to open the window, but it made little difference. She tucked the two babies into their bed with only the sheet over them, but they still looked too hot. It wasn't helped by the fact that the room was so crowded. There was hardly space to get around with all four of them sleeping in there. But then the little ones were lucky to have a bed of their own. Many children slept on the floor or in with their mum and dad.

She gave them each a kiss and smoothed the hair from their hot little foreheads.

'Nightie-night, sleep tight–'

'Make sure the bugs don't bite!' Jessica responded.

Ellen paused at the door, smiling down at them. Her two little cherubs. They were worth any amount of hard work and broken nights.

They gave meaning to her life. She felt ashamed of the way she had treated them today. It was not their fault she was out of sorts. Poor little Teddy couldn't help teething. His eyes were already closing under the influence of the gin. She vowed to be more patient with them in the morning.

'God bless,' she whispered, and trod softly downstairs.

Her gentler mood was broken the moment she arrived back in the kitchen. Gerry was at the sink, washing, ready to go out again.

'So where are you off to, then?' she demanded. As if she didn't know. She mouthed the words as he said them.

'Got to see a bloke about some stuff.'

'You're always seeing a bloke about some stuff,' she complained. 'How much stuff do you need for the stall? You don't sell that much every day.'

It was the usual excuse. He had a business to run.

'You think more about the business than you do about me and the kids,' Ellen accused.

'Now then, love, don't be daft. I said I'd take you all out Sunday, didn't I? What could be fairer than that? Nice trip to Greenwich...'

But Ellen was familiar with his patter.

'I ain't some customer for the stall and you ain't selling me nothing, so come off it. Fact is, you come in, have your tea and go out again. Hardly see hide nor hair of you sometimes. What's up, eh? You got some girl you got your eye on?'

'No!' He sounded so shocked that she knew he was telling the truth. Not that she really suspected him, anyway. She had only said it to stir him up.

'Ellen love, you know what it's like. I got four mouths to feed now. I'm doing it for you and the kids.'

'Good thing there's not much danger of there being any more mouths to feed, then,' Ellen said.

The dangerous note in her voice brought him sharply round to meet her eyes.

'What d'you mean by that?'

Ellen put her hands on her hips, and there was a challenge in the set of her head.

'Just that. Not likely to be any more babies, the way you're going on, is there?'

A slow tide of red seeped into his face. He turned away and picked his jacket up off the chair.

'I got to get out,' he said. 'I ain't got time to talk now. I'll see you later.'

'Oh yeah, much later,' Ellen said to his retreating back. 'And I suppose then you'll be too tired. And then in the morning you'll be up early. It's always the same story, ain't it?'

She followed him to the door, only a sense of self-preservation stopping her from shouting after him into the street. Once she did that, all the neighbours would be avid to know what was up. She did not want to be this evening's topic of gossip. She stood on the step, her arms folded over her stomach, seething, looking after him as he went up the road. His cap was pulled down over his face, his hands stuffed in his pockets and his shoulders defensively hunched. He never had had an impressive figure, product as he was of an impoverished childhood. Now he looked prematurely aged, one more stunted little man in a flat cap. Amidst the rage, Ellen felt sorry for him.

''Evening, Ellen!'

She started. Across the road, Florrie was just coming out with a kitchen chair in one hand and a piece of knitting in the other. The first hint of a swelling could just be seen at her waist.

''Lo Florrie.' Her voice sounded false and uneven to her oversensitive ears. She stayed where she was, not trusting herself to go over and have a chat, even with her best friend. She was about to go inside when a movement in the dark doorway of Florrie's house caught her eye. Jimmy was coming out, laughing and making some remark over his shoulder. Ellen froze. Behind him was Harry. She stood gaping, unable to move.

''Bye, love. Just going to have a quick half.' Jimmy bent over to kiss his new wife. The commonplace words drifted over to Ellen as through a fog.

Harry was looking at her. For an endless moment their eyes locked. Longing flashed between them, an invisible wire joining them across the unbridgeable gulf of the narrow street. She wanted desperately to run across, to fling herself into his arms. She knew with absolute certainty that he wanted it too, and it was only the crushing weight of loyalty, upbringing and fear of public opinion that kept them both rooted to the spot.

'You coming, mate?' Jimmy was already setting off.

'I'm with you.'

The thread was broken. Harry jerked into life. The two men walked together in the direction of the pub.

Ellen stood watching them as she had watched her husband. It was impossible not to make unfair comparisons. Harry walked with a swing to his stride, his broad shoulders unbowed. The slanting rays of the sun glinted on the ends of his blond curls. Ellen was consumed with an unbearable ache. She whisked inside, slammed the door behind her and slumped into the nearest chair in a flood of tears.

'You're a fool, Ellen Billingham,' she told herself, when the weeping finally subsided into sobs. 'You had your chance and you lost it.'

She sat for a long time, aching all over but unable to summon up the energy to move. Nothing had changed. She knew her unhappiness was all of her own making. A saying of her mother's ran round her head, teasing her with its truth, *'If only* never done anyone any good'. If only she had made it up with Harry. If only she had not risen to Siobhan's taunts. If only she had not pig-headedly gone on with marrying Gerry. It was too late now. In a way, she almost wished Harry would find himself a wife. That way, what seemed like a door would finally be closed. She might stop wishing for what she couldn't have.

She stood up at last, cramped and stiff, her eyes tender with crying, and tottered into the kitchen to splash water over her face. Evening was drawing in. She cleared away the remains of the tea and made ready for the night. There was a heap of mending that needed doing, but she could not face it. She got ready for bed and plodded up the narrow stairs.

Jessica and Teddy were sound asleep. Her children. Gerry's children. She crept round their bed and lay down on her own. Her head pounded, and her skin seemed extra sensitive, so that the sheet scraped her nerve endings. She turned this way and that, trying to get comfortable, and the sagging springs creaked beneath her. She was suffocating. There did not seem to be enough air in the room. She lay sleepless as the darkness crept in, listening to the sounds of the street.

The two lodgers let themselves in. She listened as they clumped around. They were a quiet pair, never any trouble, but in the cramped house with its thin walls, they sounded like a couple of giants thundering about. At last they settled in the back bedroom. A snore vibrated through the dividing wall.

She recognized Gerry's footsteps as he came down the street. She could tell he was tired. Maybe the deal had not come off. She lay rigid in bed. She knew what she should do: she should apologize to him for being so horrible. He worked hard to provide for them all. She used to admire him for his ambition, and she had no right to complain now when she found he was wedded to his dreams of advancement.

The front door opened and he came straight up. Ellen lay quite still as he shuffled between the beds and sat down on his side to undo his boots. He undressed slowly, his movements stiff and weary, and lay down beside her in his shirt and underpants. The bed crunched and moaned beneath his extra weight.

'How did it go?' Ellen whispered.

'Oh, I thought you was asleep.' There was wariness in his voice.

'No. It's too hot. Besides – I – I wanted to talk to you.'

'Oh. Well.' For once Gerry was lost for words. He reached across the space between them and clasped her hand. 'I been thinking about –about what you said.'

'I didn't mean it, Gerry. You mustn't take any notice. I was just tired, that's all.'

'No, no, you was right. I'm not – I don't – you mustn't think I don't love you, Ellen. I do. You and the kids, you're everything to me. Everything I do, it's for you. It always has been, ever since – ever since I can remember, since you was still at school. I wanted to marry you then. I was work-ing towards it, trying to make something of myself so I'd be good enough for you. It's all for you, Ellen. I know I'm not like Harry. When you was going out with him, I thought, well, that's it, I ain't got a chance. I couldn't hardly believe it when you said you'd marry me. You're so pretty and quick and good – I couldn't believe my luck. But I know I don't measure up.'

'Don't, don't, you mustn't say that.' Ellen was racked with guilt and remorse. 'I chose you. I never said you wasn't good enough. Of course you are. You're my husband, the father of my children.'

It was all her own fault. She had always thought she was different – too good to go to Dock Street school like the others, too good to work in a factory. Now she was making Gerry unhappy with her mooning over what she couldn't have. She rolled over and put her arms around him.

'I love you,' she whispered, and meant it.

He held her tight. 'The thing is...' he said.

A few feet away, Teddy moaned in his sleep and Jessica turned over. From the next room came steady snores. They were surrounded by people. There was no privacy. Gerry's whisper dropped so low that she could hardly catch what he was saying. He spoke hesitantly, the words coming out through a suffocating barrier of embarrassment.

'The thing is, when I was a kid, when we was all living in one or two rooms in tenement blocks, my mum... We was poor. Really poor, I mean, like we went for weeks on just bread and scrape. No boots in the winter, that sort of thing. I mean, my mum, she just wanted to keep us out of the workhouse. And she brought – there would be men coming in – and sometimes she used to turn us out, Charlie and me. We used to sit on the stairs until they'd gone, like. Once I was older, I stopped it. I got rid of them. But when we was kids, sometimes we'd be asleep when she came in, and then – well, then we'd hear it all. And I couldn't bear it, Ellen. I couldn't bear it. It was horrible. The noises.'

He was curled, rigid, a small boy once more, hiding from what was going on.

Ellen stroked his head and made soothing sounds. 'It's all right. It's all right.'

They lay face to face, foreheads and noses touching. She could feel his lips moving as the words came haltingly.

'You mustn't think I don't love you. I do. I do love you. You're soft and sweet. It's just – I don't want it to be like those men...'

'You're not. You could never be like them.' Ellen could hardly speak for the ache in her throat.

'But I'm letting you down.'

'You're not. Of course you're not. I love you just like you are.' She kissed his lips.

'Oh, Ellen.'

She felt the tension go out of him. They cuddled together until he fell asleep with his arms round her.

Ellen shut the door tight on the part of her that still yearned for something more.

6

The heatwave held the city in its grip. All those who could leave had gone to the country or the seaside in search of shade and clean air and a breath of breeze. But for hundreds upon thousands of souls there was no getting away. They were trapped there, living in small airless houses and tenements, working in factories and shops, forced to carry on through temperatures that soared into the nineties.

'At least there *is* work,' Tom Johnson said when people complained. 'Puts us in a better position.'

Trade, and therefore employment, was on the up. To the men at the calling-on stands it meant that the riff-raff that drifted down to the docks in hard times had disappeared, leaving only the regulars. Just when they would have been glad to have some time off, there was plenty of work.

Tom looked beyond this.

'Don't you see?' he said to his son. 'When there's full employment and ships waiting to be discharged, they need us. That means we can start to bargain with the gov'nors. God knows, we need to. Sixpence an hour is what was fixed in eighty-nine. Look how food's gone up since then.'

Will did not need to be told about the rise in prices. That was Maisie's excuse every time he complained about the paltry teas she provided for him.

'That's all I could get, Will. You should see what they're charging for potatoes now. I don't know what way to turn, that I don't.' She lumbered about the kitchen, pregnant again.

'Got to go,' he would say, getting up as soon as he had finished. 'Working overtime.'

Thank the Lord for overtime. Eightpence an hour and cooler working conditions, and with the extra money he could go and see *her*. She was back in town again after a tour of the provinces.

The moment his back was turned there was a fierce scuffle. Tommy knocked his brother out of the way and grabbed the used plate. In a trice, he had it licked clean. Maisie thought about the food she could buy with the extra earnings.

Down the road at the Johnsons', Martha confided her worries about Tom to her daughter.

'It's all starting up again, this union business. He's not a young man any more. He can't take it, not working all the hours God sends and going to meetings as well. He's never been the same since that time he was set upon.'

'I thought he was looking better,' Ellen said.

'He seemed more, well, more alive. Like what he used to be.'

'That's what I'm afraid of,' her mother argued. 'All this union stuff. Look what trouble it got him into before. I don't like it. I don't like it at all.'

'You won't stop him.'

'No.' Martha sighed. 'No, you're right there. Nothing I say'll make any difference. He's a man of principles, your dad. There's no changing him. But how are you? You're looking peaky yourself these days. The heat, is it, or are you...?' She looked at Ellen's waistline.

'No,' Ellen said shortly.

Her mum gave her a brief hug. 'Best that way really, lovey. Don't do you no good having 'em all close together. Look at Maisie, lost half her teeth already. And she's not as bad as some. You look at the ones what have worn the best and it's the ones what've only had a few kids. Look at Alma – still acting like a blooming twenty-year-old at times, and she's only four years younger than what I am. Only had them two boys, y'see.'

'Yeah,' Ellen said. After Gerry's confession of the other night, she had mixed feelings about her mother-in-law.

At number forty, Florrie felt the same way. She liked Alma, liked her warmth and her cheerfulness, but felt crushed by her at times. She told herself that Alma caused the continual cloud over her marriage, but she knew in her heart of hearts that it was not so. She could have sailed through Alma's loudness and ill-timed jokes, along with Charlie's leering looks and coarse remarks, if it had not been for the secret she still carried. She

506

had never summoned up the courage to tell Jimmy how her father had died. With every day that passed it became more difficult, until it lay there, a dividing wall between them. Time and again it seemed that the moment was right and she actually drew breath to tell him. But when it came to the point, she could not, and the knowledge dragged at her like a great black stone. It even marred her joy in the baby she carried, her child and Jimmy's, a new life. But it would be one more person from whom the terrible secret had to be kept.

Harry had no idea that things were not quite as they should be.

'Nice to see someone happy, sis,' he said.

She smiled and said nothing. She did not want to add to his problems, for their mother was no better.

Alma had lost patience with her sister.

'You got to pull yourself together, girl,' she said, at least twice a week. 'Bloody hell, it ain't as if there was any love lost between you. You're better off without him. You don't have to worry about money. Your Harry's a good provider, better than what Archie ever was. Only thing Archie ever done was knock you around and get you in the family way. You can do without that. And look what you still got – three sons and three daughters, all them grandchildren, and two more on the way. You're bloody lucky, you are, girl. Not everyone's got as much as what you have.'

Though she would not have admitted it to a soul, Alma was finally having to face the unpleasant truth that Charlie was not quite the wonderful son she had always thought he was. She still found it difficult to be civil to Clodagh O'Donaghue, though it was nearly seven years since Theresa had accused Charlie of fathering her baby. She used to be proud of the fact that neither of her boys had conventional jobs. They did not go off to factories or building sites or wait at the dock gates to be called on like all the others. With Gerry making a success of his market stall, she had been able to delude herself that Charlie was some sort of trader as well. His irregular hours and patchy income could be put down to the ups and downs of business life. But even she found it difficult to account for the long idle hours, the mysterious absences from home, the occasional extravagant gift. Still less could she think of a reasonable answer when people remarked that they had seen her Charlie in the company of some character or other with a shady reputation. In comparison with this worry, it seemed to her that Milly's troubles were all her own making.

'I know, I know,' she said, when Alma lectured her, but did nothing to rouse herself.

None of them knew what to do with her.

Harry, working long hours like everyone else and often away overnight on trips upriver, wondered what she did all the time that he was not there. When he asked Ida, she shrugged.

'She just sits there in the kitchen, looking at nothing. If I don't clear the cups away from breakfast, they're still there at tea time.'

Harry sighed. Even getting up was difficult for his mother. If they had not insisted that she got out of bed and dressed, she would probably have lain upstairs all day. A vague memory of a piece from the Bible nagged at him, a remnant of some distant lesson, about a man turning his face to the wall and waiting for death. That was what his mother had done. She had turned her face to the wall.

It was not so bad when everyone was at home. The clatter of himself, Ida, Johnny and Bob all trying to get dressed or washed at the same time, or all swallowing down a meal, masked the underlying silence. But it was there all the same. They all felt it and shied away. Even acting all together, they did not have the strength to face such unremitting despair. Harry was glad to go to work, extra glad to be given longer jobs. Anything for a legitimate reason to escape from home.

Through the distorting glass of her depression, Milly saw them go. It did not surprise her, though it did hurt. She knew she was not worthy of their love. They all turned against her in the end. Archie had. Archie had hated her because she was a bad wife, and now he was gone, gone because she had cried out and brought Florrie crashing in to hit him over the head. It was Milly who had brought death upon him. Now it was too late to make it up to him, to prove that she could be what he wanted. The horror of the last scene in the kitchen haunted her, coming back day and night, forever recurring in her mind. Guilt gnawed into Milly. She wanted to tell, to confess her part. It weighed upon her. Sometimes she felt that if she could just tell someone, anyone, then it would not be so bad.

Because she did not trust herself, she almost stopped speaking altogether. She kept her guilt and fear and grief bottled up inside her, until it seemed that there was nothing else to her. She was empty, worthless. She saw Ida coming in from work to get tea ready, and knew that she was failing in her duty to feed her family. She saw Florrie or Ellen come in to scrub round and tidy up, and knew she was failing to keep her home clean. She heard Alma exhort her to change her blouse or wash her face, and knew she was becoming filthy and repulsive. But she was unable to do anything about it.

Sometimes, when there was drink in the house, she would take refuge in the bottle. When there was not, she did without, for she could not bring herself to go out of the front door and into the street. She had not been outside since the day of the funeral.

The rest of the people in the street had turned against her long ago. When they came in she knew it was only to gloat over her in her despair. Women she had known all her life, like Martha Johnson and Ethel Croft, would push open the door and coo-ee at her. She flinched from their smiles and their offers of help. She knew they despised her. Most of all she flinched from her sister and her lectures. It was all very well for Alma; she was strong. Alma did not know what it was like to be Milly.

The hot summer made it even worse. It closed in on her. Everyone else lived out in the street, playing, gossiping, doing mending or outwork. Milly stayed in the kitchen, staring at the place where Archie had died sprawled across her. She could hear them out there, laughing and calling to each other. She knew they were talking about her, laughing at her.

The day came when she would stand it no longer. She knew what she was going to do. She had known all along, but it had taken until now to come to the front of her mind. She had been afraid when it lurked there like a black dog in the core of her consciousness. But now that it had finally come out into the open, it lost its terror. She welcomed it. It was the only answer.

It was unbearably bright outside. She blinked, blinded like a mole coming out of its tunnel. Through the blur of the brassy glare, she saw the street, saw the women on their doorsteps. She heard their voices and knew that they were calling her.

'It's Milly! Wotcher, Milly, nice to see you again.'

'Come over here, love. How are you?'

But it meant nothing. She was not really there. The sounds came to her as though over a great distance, the movements were heavy and distorted. Even her own body did not belong to her any more. It was simply a means to get her where she was going. She passed along the street, saying nothing, looking neither left nor right, so that as she went by she left a silence behind her, followed by a buzz of speculation.

Heavy footsteps lumbered up behind her. An arm fell round her shoulders, making her start.

'Where're you off to, Milly? You feeling all right?'

She stared, uncomprehending, at the face gazing at hers. Recognition filtered slowly through... Martha Johnson. She had to say something, had to get rid of her.

'Yeah, yeah. I'm all right. I'm going out.'

'That's nice, lovey. Do you good. You want me to come along, keep you company, like?'

It was the last thing that Milly wanted.

'No, no. I'm all right. I just got to go out, that's all. Got to – got to get something. Something for my Harry. Got to get something for my Harry.'

'You sure, lovey? I can come along with you, if you like.'

'No. I'm only going to the shop. That's all. Just up the shop.'

She had not held such a prolonged conversation for weeks. For a moment that felt like half a lifetime, Martha hesitated. Then she gave Milly's arm a squeeze.

'That's all right, then. Can't tell you how pleased I am to see you out again, lovey. We missed you, y'know. It's really nice to have you back.'

Milly hardly heard her. She just knew that she was no longer in danger of being stopped. The exchange had exhausted her powers of speech, so she began to walk on up the street. When she reached the corner, she felt as if she had achieved a great goal. She had escaped from her prison.

Through the dust-laden streets she walked, enclosed in her cocoon. She did not have to think about which corners to turn, for she had walked along these pavements, past these factories, every day of her life. She had been born, gone to school, worked, courted, been married and raised her children within the confines of North Millwall.

She had gone months at a time without leaving the Island at all. So without any conscious effort on her part, her feet took her where she was going. She did not notice the grimy walls or the dirty cobbles; she did not see the sweating faces; she did not smell the reek of leather and chemicals and oil and rotting fruit. The noise of hoofs and iron wheels, steam engines, machinery, hooters and human voices came only faintly through the fog that surrounded her. The fierce sun burnt through the pall of smoke and made the sweat run down her body so that her clothes began to stick to her, but Milly did not notice.

She plodded mechanically, one step after the other. She was nearly there now. Certain signs began to penetrate her consciousness: a stationary queue of buses, trams, carts, delivery vans and innumerable heavy drays; the pavement clogged with pedestrians; a rumble of half-resigned grumbles, dotted with curses and complaints.

The bridge was open. The lock was in use. Milly's heart beat thunderously in her chest. It was a portent. It was meant. Oblivious to protests, she pushed her way through the gathering crowd.

And there were the lock gates, huge, solid walls of oak. On one side, greenish-brown and floating with filth, was the great basin of the West India dock, lined with tall-masted ships and busy with cranes and tugs and lighters and the strain of human muscle power. On the other, fifteen feet down, was the water of the lock, jostling with lighters and barges, for the tide was low and the big ships were trapped. At the river end of the lock, the other pair of gates was closing.

Milly reached the edge of the quay. Just in front of her, a step up, was the hazardous plank walkway attached to the lock gate. A few adventurous souls, unwilling to wait for the bridge, were making their way across it. She fixed her eyes on the halfway point, where the pair of gates met. Beyond that there was nothing. She set her foot upon the walkway. Like a sleepwalker, she made her way along. In the middle, she stopped and turned.

A clanking of iron ratchets sounded as the men opened the sluices. Beneath her feet the water foamed yellow. She watched the churning cataracts, mesmerized by the roar and motion, until her ears and eyes were filled with it. She swayed and her knees buckled, then she pitched forward and gave herself up to the water.

Harry knew there was something wrong even before he got back to the quay. The news passed amongst the watermen's fraternity like wildfire, first that some woman had thrown herself off the West India dock lock gate, then that it was Harry Turner's mother. Harry, coming downriver with the last of the ebb, was hailed by a hoveller sculling his boat home after a spell piloting a barge.

'You better get along home, lad.'

'Why? What's up?' Harry demanded.

The man just shook his head. 'Think you might be needed, like.'

Harry glanced at his brother, who was resting on his oar at the stern of the lighter. The boy looked tired, there were great smudges of circles under his eyes. It had been a difficult trip and they had not got a great deal of sleep last night.

With the weather so sultry, the little cabin had been unbearable stuffy, so they had bedded down on the decks; but passing traffic had kept them awake for much of the time. He had been letting the boy take it easy up till now.

'Bring that sweep up here, Johnny. I think we better get a move on.'

With both of them rowing, the laden lighter moved rapidly down with the tide. As they passed the entrance to the Shadwell dock, a foreman from one of the other companies waved at them, standing up in his skiff as a sweating apprentice rowed him along.

'Harry Turner?'

'That's me.'

'You're wanted back home, mate.'

'What is it? What's wrong?'

But still he did not get a proper answer.

'Been a bit o' trouble.'

Various possibilities raced through his head – somebody ill, young Bob in trouble with the police, the house on fire, his mother... In his heart he knew it was his mother.

'What d'you reckon they're on about?' Johnny asked.

Harry shrugged. 'Dunno,' he lied. 'But we best get along and find out.'

They still had to deliver their load to a wharf down at Woolwich, but as they passed their firm's quay, they were hailed by a colleague and his apprentice, who came alongside in a skiff.

'We'll take over from here,' the lighterman said. 'You two take the boat back and sign off.'

Normally a tyrant, the foreman actually laid a

hand on Harry's shoulder.

'Sorry to hear about this, lad.'

Harry looked him in the eye. 'It's my mum, ain't it?'

Beside him, Johnny drew a sharp breath.

Harry and Johnny hurried home through the sultry streets, fear of what they would find mounting with every footstep.

When they reached Trinidad Street, practically every inhabitant appeared to be out on the doorsteps. It seemed to Harry, as he broke into a run, that a silence fell as they passed. The eyes watched them, sympathetically, but there was no hiding the avid look.

Harry pushed open the front door. Instead of being empty and hollow, the tiny house was full to the seams. He could hardly get in the door for relatives – not just Ida and Bob, but Maisie, with all her brood, Florrie and Jim, Alma, and in the background, Gerry and Ellen. They all looked white and shocked. As one, their eyes turned to him, and a heavy silence fell.

'What's happened?' he asked. 'What's wrong?'

There was an uneasy shuffling of feet. Ida dissolved into tears, to be comforted by Ellen. Alma came forward and put one arm round him and the other round Johnny.

'You better brace y'selves,' she said. 'It's your mum. She – she – well, she's gone and done herself in.'

'What?' His mind refused to take it in at first. It was too terrible to believe.

On the other side of his aunt, he half heard Johnny's shocked voice saying, 'Oh no, oh no.'

'She–' Alma began to repeat.

'I heard, I heard. I just – how did it happen?'

'The lock gates.'

'Oh, my God!'

In his mind's eye he saw the body of his mother turning in the turgid water like a rag doll. A numbness stole over him, slowing thought, dulling feeling, making movement an effort. An all-important question needed to be asked. He knew it was there, knew he wanted to know the answer. With great difficulty, he dredged it from his mind and formed it on his tongue.

'Why? Why did she do it? I knew she was grieving – but to do that...'

'I dunno, lovey.' He had never heard his aunt sound so subdued. 'She'd been down for a long time, y'know.'

'Yeah, but not so – not that she had to...'

Across the room he met with his sister's face. Florrie was ashen; lines of shock were carved into the thin cheeks and her eyes were haggard. And he knew that however much he wanted to ask questions, to lean on someone, here was somebody who needed his strength. He went to her and took her stiff body in his arms.

'You mustn't blame y'self, girl,' he told her.

Florrie was shaking. It was not like when their father had died. Then she had been defiant, even a touch triumphant. Now she trembled with the pain. Harry had the frightening impression that she could shatter at a touch.

'Yes I must,' she said, so low that he could hardly hear her.

Ida's sobs were mounting into a wail. 'I'm never

going to see her again. How can she do this? How can she?'

Some of Maisie's children, not understanding what was going on, but catching the emotion, began to cry in sympathy. Maisie gathered them on to her knee and wept as well. Over Florrie's shoulder, Harry's glance met Ellen's. A silent wave of sympathy and support passed from her. He could feel it wrapping round him and buoying him up. There was nothing they could say to each other with his entire family present, but he knew that she was there, giving what she could to help.

As for the others, he realized that they were looking to him for leadership. He took a steadying breath, trying to think what needed to be done. First his sister. She was always best when given a practical task.

'Florrie, I think a cup of tea might help. It's no use asking Maisie or Ida – they'll just go to pieces. Can you do it?'

Florrie nodded. Harry handed her over to Jimmy and they both squeezed their way through to the kitchen. Bob, who had been standing by himself and refusing any comfort, suddenly pushed past Maisie's family and rushed upstairs. Once again, Harry looked at Ellen, who was still holding Ida.

'Leave him,' she counselled. 'Go and talk to him later when it's quieter.'

Alma filled him in as far as she could.

'It was just after midday, after the kids'd gone back to school. Lot of them saw her going up the street.'

'But didn't no one try to stop her?'

'They thought she was feeling better. Martha Johnson offered to walk along with her, but Milly said she was only going up the shop to get something. Poor Martha, she's in a terrible state. Says she didn't ought to have taken no for an answer.'

Harry was inclined to agree with this, but he let it pass.

'Didn't no one know she was in a bad way today? Had anyone been in to see her?'

'I know Ellen looked in, and Florrie. But you know what she's – she was like. You couldn't hardly get a word out of her. Difficult to know what she was feeling like inside, really.'

That was true enough.

'And at the lock–' He stopped. It was difficult to talk about it. 'Didn't they – didn't anyone try to stop her?'

'Couldn't get to her in time, so they said.'

He knew he was trying to shift the blame. What really gnawed at him was the fact that he and Johnny had been away overnight.

'If I'd been home last night, it might not have happened,' he said. 'She never did like us going. And this time Johnny was with me as well. I should have tried to get the foreman to change us around. I should have seen this was a danger.'

'You couldn't have,' Alma told him. 'None of us knew she was thinking of doing this. I mean, you don't, do you? She never said nothing, never said she wanted to. Maybe she didn't know herself until she done it.'

'I should have done more,' Harry insisted.

Alma gave a great sigh. 'We all should have

done. Maybe we was all at fault. Didn't see what she was going through.'

The guilt and the recriminations carried on for half the evening as the family went over and over the same ground, trying to decide a reason, trying to exorcise the pain, until Harry was almost glad when the police sent for him to formally identify the body. That was the start of a nightmare of official duties, made all the worse because they had been done so recently for his father. Another inquest, another funeral.

They all turned to him whenever something needed deciding or arranging, all with their stained faces and haunted eyes. Bob took to truanting from school, and Harry had to sort it all out and make sure he got there each day. On top of that there was an ever changing makeshift of domestic arrangements, all fitted in between the demands of work. And every day when he came home there was an empty space in the kitchen, the unoccupied chair at the table, reminding him of his failure to help his mother.

At the end of another long hot week, Ida came home from work in tears.

'I hate that place. They been picking on me again. That forewoman, she's got her knife into me. She stands there just waiting for me to do something wrong. Every week I get fined for something, and the others, they just laugh.'

Harry tried to calm her down, but whatever he said she took exception to. He suggested finding a different job, but that would not do either.

'You just don't understand!' she wailed, and took herself off upstairs.

That meant there was no tea on the table.

Harry dug in his pockets. 'Here, Bob, you take this and go down the chip shop,' he said. 'Cod and chips all round.'

'Why me? Why is it always me? Why can't someone else go?' Bob kicked at the table leg, his face thunderous.

Harry reached out and clipped him round the ear. 'Because the rest of us been at work all day and we're starving. Now get a move on.'

Bob glared at him and went, his lower lip thrust out. Harry frowned after him. The boy might be ten years old and tough with it, but he needed someone to mother him. He was probably feeling it worse than any of them, but instead of crying, like Ida, he went about trying to take it out on someone. Behind him there was a sigh. He looked round and saw Johnny slumped over the table, asleep, with his head cradled in his arms. He had grown a lot lately, but it was all upwards and the heavy work he did was too much for him. Through the ceiling came the sound of Ida sobbing on her bed. Harry ran his hands through his hair. They all needed more from him than he was able to give.

He sat on the step after tea, wondering what to do for the best. He could not see his way through the tangle of problems. Gerry emerged from next door.

''Evening, Harry. Coming up the Puncheon for a drink?'

Harry shook his head. It was tempting to go out and forget it in a cheerful evening and a few pints, but that was what his father had always done.

'No thanks, mate. Another time.'

He watched Gerry walk up the street. He didn't look too happy himself these days; unlike the breezy, confident Gerry they all knew, there was an air of worry about him. But Harry had no sympathy to spare for his cousin. Gerry had Ellen.

And then it came to him, like a window opening to the sunshine. He would go and talk to Ellen. Without stopping to consider, he got up and went indoors. Ida was still upstairs. Bob was out with his gang. In less than a minute, Harry was out of his back yard and into hers.

Jessica was grubbing around in the tiny patch of earth where a few cabbages were struggling to survive. She looked up and grinned at him. Little Teddy stopped banging a saucepan with a wooden spoon to babble a welcome. Harry hardly saw them. His eyes were only for Ellen. She was sitting on the back step, darning a sock. Her head was bent over her work, her deft fingers weaving the needle in and out of the spaces in the wool. After the wreck of his own family, she seemed like a haven of peace and calm and order. His shadow fell across her and she looked up, her hazel eyes glowing amber in the low evening light. For a moment she regarded him in silence. Then she stood up.

'Come inside,' she said.

They sat on either side of the kitchen table. Now that he was here, Harry did not quite know what it was he wanted to say. For the moment, just being with her was enough.

'What is it?' Ellen prompted. Her voice was soft and low.

'Oh – everything.'

'Your mother?'

'Yeah.'

'You couldn't have done any more, Harry. We all tried, but it was like she built a wall round her. You couldn't get through it.'

'But I *should've* got through it. She was my mum. I should've done something more. I should've known she was that bad. To do that...'

'I know. It's horrible to even think about it.'

'I can't *stop* thinking about it, Ellen. I lived in the same house as her and saw how she was, and I didn't know just how bad she was. I even – well, I got angry with her, just giving in under it like that. I thought, other women lose their husbands, better husbands than what my dad was, and they don't go like what she did. You couldn't talk to her, you couldn't make her see. Sometimes I wanted to shake her. I had to stop myself. It was awful.'

He had never admitted this to anyone before. It was such a relief to be able to talk, to say just how he felt, to stop having to play the strong one of the family. Once started, he couldn't stop. Ellen sat there and nodded and said yes and no in the right places, and he talked on.

'If only I hadn't gone away for the night. I knew she didn't like it. And taking Johnny too. We was both away when she needed us.'

'But you can't say what job you're going to do, can you? The foreman decides that. It wasn't your fault.'

'I could've asked him to see that we weren't both on the same trip. He might've listened. But I didn't even try. Fact was, I was glad to go, glad to have a night away from home. I thought it'd do

Johnny good and all. I was pleased when we was given that run. It meant I had a night when I didn't have to see her sitting there in the corner, it meant I could forget about her for a while. That's how I felt. I was really glad to put her out of my head for a bit. And just look what came of it.'

His voice broke and he stopped, struggling with himself. And then Ellen was there, standing beside him, an arm round his shoulders.

'Let it out,' she said.

He turned to her and clasped her waist, muffling the harsh sobs in her soft belly while she stroked his head. The pressure of emotion that had been building for so long burst, leaving him hollow and empty and strangely light.

'I'm sorry,' he said automatically, but he did not mean it. Never since he had grown up had he exposed himself like that, and yet he felt perfectly safe. Ellen would not think the worse of him.

'Don't be so silly, there's nothing to be sorry for. You've been carrying it all by yourself. Nobody should do that. Better now?'

He nodded, and gave a crooked smile. 'Much.'

She dropped a kiss on the top of his head, then eased out of his arms.

'Cuppa?'

'Please.'

He was immensely grateful for her matter-of-fact way of taking it. They sat and sipped tea and considered the practical problems facing the Turner family.

'Seems to me you need a bit of a change round. You're just managing from day to day at the moment.'

'I know. Yeah, that's just it.'

'You need someone looking after the home proper. You'd all feel better then. You'd all know where you was.' Ellen chewed her lip, thinking. Harry watched the thought processes in the expressions that passed over her face. 'If Ida hates her job so much, she could stay home. But I can't see her dealing with young Bob... Look, there's only the four of you now. Why don't you ask Florrie and Jimmy to move in? They could have the front bedroom and you and the boys the back one, and Ida the put-you-up. You and Jimmy get on all right, and Florrie's a good housewife. And I think she'd like to get away from your aunt Alma.'

'Of course!' He could not believe it could be so simple. 'Yeah, that's just what we ought to do. You hit it on the head, Ellen. You always was the clever one.'

'Yeah.' She gave a little sigh. 'Sometimes.'

They looked at each other as past mistakes and misunderstandings marched through their minds. Unspoken between them came the acknowledgement that their relationship had progressed to a new level. Harry reached out and took her hand. It was roughened with hard work but still small and dainty. He held it to his lips.

From outside came a wail of distress. Harry started. He had been so immersed that he had forgotten all about the two children playing in the yard. It came as a shock to have to take in all over again the reality of their situation. Ellen broke away from him and opened the back door. She scooped up Teddy and settled him on her hip, jiggling him up and down to soothe his crying. The baby nuzzled against her, his tears turning magically into gurgles of pleasure. Harry was aware of a great ache in his heart. It should have been his son that she held.

'If only,' he began.

She gave a frown. 'Don't say it. You'd best go now. You know what the neighbours are like – if they find out you been in here there's no knowing what they'll say.'

'Yeah.' She was right again. But it was hard to leave. 'I want to thank you, Ellen.'

'You don't have to. I know you'd do the same for me.'

'Yeah, yeah I would. I'll repay you one day.'

'Just go and sort your family out. That's payment enough.'

'I'll do that.'

He walked slowly back next door, so much lighter in heart that his feet hardly touched the ground.

7

'You go and sit with you dad, lovey,' Martha said. 'Me and Daisy'll wash up.'

Ellen did not argue. It was nice to be spoilt for once. Carrying Teddy, she followed her father out to the front, where she set two chairs on the pavement.

The street was emerging from its Sunday-afternoon quiet. Sleeping off hangovers for some, church, chapel or Sunday school for others, and family tea for everyone, were all over and people were coming out of the stuffy houses to find a breath of air. Two little girls immediately swooped on Ellen and begged to be allowed to take Teddy for an airing. She sent them for the pram on the condition that they took Jessica as well. Delighted, the girls agreed and ran off, boasting to their friends that they had a baby to walk.

Mary O'Donaghue as was, trailing babies and heavily pregnant again, passed by on her way to her mother's. She looked Ellen up and down pointedly.

'Still not fallen for another?' she asked. 'Blimey, what's the matter with you? You not giving himself his oats? Or ain't he up to it no more?'

Ellen flushed. It was too near the mark for laughter.

'At least I don't shell 'em out by the dozen like what rabbits do,' she retorted.

Mary sniffed and put her nose in the air. 'I'm raising little souls for Jesus,' she said self-righteously, and lumbered on up the street.

'Riff-raff,' Tom muttered. 'Beats me how a respectable woman like Clodagh O'Donaghue managed to get daughters like Theresa and this one – and the young one's no better, neither. Must break her heart.'

'I ain't got a lot of time for Clodagh O'Donaghue,' Ellen said. 'She ain't spoken to none of the Turners since Milly died. She thinks they're all tainted.'

Tom digested this. 'I'm with you there. What Milly done was a tragedy – no need to take it out on her family. And talking of family, it's a shame your Gerry had to go out today. He should be with his wife and kids on a Sunday.'

'Oh well, you know how it is. If you want to do business over Whitechapel, Sunday's the best day for it.'

Tom lit a cigarette and drew the smoke down into his lungs. Not looking at his daughter, he asked, 'Everything going all right for your Gerry?'

''Course!' Ellen said, too sharply. 'Why shouldn't they be?'

'Come on now, you don't have to take that tone with me. I seen the way young Gerry looks, like he's carrying the world on his shoulders. And your mum says you gone and got rid of all your knick-knacks at home. Needed the money, did you?'

'Just to tide us over,' Ellen said.

She bit her lip. All was not well at home. It was just as her father had said: Gerry did not know which way to turn and they owed money in all directions. What was more, she was sure there was plenty that Gerry had not told her about.

'Well, you know where to come for help, don't you? We ain't got much, you know that, but we'll always do what we can.'

Tears stood in Ellen's eyes. She squeezed her father's knee.

'Thanks, Dad. I'll remember.' And because she could not talk about it, even to him, she changed the subject to the main family topic of the moment. 'Be funny having Daisy married, won't it? I still think of her as my little sister.'

'High time, if you ask me. I told your mum, if

she don't settle down soon, all the decent young men her age'll be spoken for.'

'She'll be all right with Wilf Hodges. He was in my class at school.'

'Yeah, he's fine, is her Wilf. He'll take care of her. Keep her in her place an' all. Needs a firm hand, does your sister.'

'I'll tell you something,' Ellen said. 'If Siobhan turns up and ruins her wedding like what she done to Florrie, I'll get her, that I will. And there's others'll help me an' all.'

'Yeah – that's another blooming O'Donaghue. I been friends with Brian for as long as I can remember, and his lads are as straight as they come, but them girls are the sort what give the Irish a bad name. That Siobhan...' Tom blew smoke out of his nose and frowned at it as it dispersed in the sluggish air.

'What about her?' Ellen prompted.

Tom sighed. 'That brother of yours is still mooning over her, you know. Maisie ain't never going to set the Thames on fire, but she's a good wife to him. He ought to give up hankering over what he can't have.'

'Yes,' Ellen agreed, though her conscience troubled her. Will was not the only one in the family to do that.

'Besides,' Tom went on, 'he ought to be taking an interest in the union. Things are beginning to stir, what with trade being good and everything. If we could get more men interested, we could get somewhere. But we need people to talk, to persuade. We need someone on every quay, getting new members. The stevedores been talking about letting in all cargo handlers to their union, and if they do that, the Dockers Union as such'll just wither away. The stevedores and the lightermen'll have the port stitched up between them.'

Ellen nodded. She had not heard her father talk like this for a long time. She listened as he expounded his hopes for a federation of the three unions, plus the seamen, to really make the owners and the new Port of London Authority sit up.

'If we could only speak with one voice, they'd have to put the hourly rate up,' he said.

'Will never was that taken with the union,' Ellen pointed out.

'He ought to be. It's important to all of us, if he'd only see it,' Tom said. 'And it's only that Siobhan woman getting in the way.'

Ellen wasn't so sure it was that straightforward. 'I suppose I could talk to him, but I don't think he'd listen,' she said.

'No, you'd only set his back up. I tried and it done no good at all. Can't think why a son of mine should turn out so bone-headed. You're the one with the brains of the family, Ellen. Pity you weren't born a boy. You'd've been a big help to me.'

'Can't help that,' she said, but she felt flattered. Then, thinking of things she had read in the newspapers that Gerry sometimes brought home, she added, 'Women do speak at meetings and things. I seen it in the papers. Suffragettes. They're always having meetings about getting the vote for women.'

'Vote!' Tom snorted. 'Can you see the likes of young Mary O'Donaghue and Will's Maisie voting? What do they know about it?'

'They know when they're not being treated right,' Ellen retorted. 'I tell you something, Daisy'd make a good union leader. She'd get 'em all going, she would. She knows what's fair and what ain't. You ought to think about getting women into unions, Dad.'

'Ain't never seen no women dockers,' Tom pointed out.

'True, but look at all the factory workers. They'd show blooming Morton's and Maconochie's a thing or two.'

Tom chuckled to himself. 'I was thinking of a whole bunch of women on the march with young Daisy at the head. That'd be a sight, that would!' He patted his daughter on the knee. 'I'm glad I got you to talk to, girl.'

Mollified, Ellen squeezed his hand. 'I am some use to you, then?'

'You're pure gold, girl.'

Later, going over the conversation in her mind, it struck Ellen just how much Siobhan had influenced their lives for the worse. She couldn't put back the clock and stop the damage Siobhan had done to Harry and herself, but perhaps there was still time to prevent her brother from wasting his life. The trouble was, she could not see how to do it.

She talked it over with Florrie, who was now back next door and bringing a new order and stability to the Turner household. Florrie, who had still not forgiven Siobhan for eclipsing her at her wedding, mentioned it to Harry. Harry mulled it over as he took loaded barges up and down the river. The last thing he wanted was to make contact with Siobhan again, but there was Maisie to consider, together with the urge to do anything he could to help Ellen or her family. So when a friend of his mentioned that he was going to one of the halls that Siobhan was currently appearing in, Harry started working on a plan.

'That the one what your cousin works at?' he asked.

'Not *my* cousin, my old lady's.'

'Same difference. Can you get backstage, see the artistes, like?'

'Depends. He's a funny old sod. Might cost you.'

Harry grinned. 'I got a nice load of tinned pines going upriver.'

His friend smiled in response. 'Think that might do the trick, mate. Saturday night all right?'

He could not be sure that it would work. Harry had met a few music-hall artistes backstage, and the reality had always been a let-down after seeing the glittering performer in the spotlight. The idea was that if Will got near enough to Siobhan to see what she was really like, he would be so disillusioned that he would think no more about her. There was a risk, of course. Will might still be besotted enough to be taken in. But it was worth a try.

It was the work of moments to get Will to agree to a night out. Harry did not even have to let on that Siobhan would be appearing. So far, so good.

That Saturday, all spruced up in their best, with their hair neatly parted and flattened, they arrived at a distinctly second-rate place south of the river.

'Don't think much of this,' Will said, looking at the peeling paint on the columns outside.

'Might not look much but we do get to go backstage,' Harry pointed out.

'If there's anyone worth seeing.'

Will turned his attention to the playbill. Harry watched as his eyes widened and his mouth dropped open.

'Blimey! Sio–'

'Something up, mate?'

Will made a poor attempt at covering up. 'No, no – just surprised, that's all. You never told me Siobhan O'Donaghue was appearing. You remember Siobhan O'Donaghue? Pat and Declan's cousin?'

'Only too blooming well,' Harry assured him. 'Wouldn't never have come if I'd known. Still, too late now – I paid for the tickets.'

'Second from the top!' Will could not be drawn away from the poster. 'Look – she's second from top. She always wanted top billing. She's nearly there.'

All his suspicions confirmed, Harry took him by the arm. 'We're missing it. Come on.'

The first half of the bill was dreadful – old troupers on their way out and young hopefuls who were never going to make it. The comics were painful, with bad timing and worn-out jokes, the singers off-key or unable to fill the auditorium. Harry hoped his plan was going to work, for it was definitely a waste of a Saturday night so far. At half-time, they shoved their way to the bar, where the beer was expensive and on the thin side. Harry was beginning to feel disgruntled. There was so much that was beyond his control. It was not impossible that Siobhan might actually welcome Will, and that would be disastrous. It did not help to see that Will could hardly drink for nerves. Harry scowled into his beer and wondered if the whole idea had been stupid.

The bell rang for the next half.

'We got to wait by the doors into the stalls, left-hand side,' Harry said.

They stood at the appointed place, Will fidgeting with impatience, Harry oppressed by a growling conviction that this was not a good idea at all. Through the closed doors came the sound of yet another mediocre act, a comic duo. Catcalls from the audience punctuated their leaden repartee. Harry was on the point of suggesting that they went somewhere else while there was still time.

'You Harry Turner?'

A small man in shirtsleeves had appeared. Harry introduced himself and Will.

'You got a rum lot in there tonight,' Harry said, indicating the audience with a jerk of the head.

'Always a rum lot in this place,' the little man responded. As he spoke, the cigarette that was stuck to his bottom lip jumped up and down. 'C'mon. The acts get better from now on. They're the ones you want to meet, if you want to meet any of 'em. You want to see the girls, I s'pose. Myself, I wouldn't touch 'em with a barge pole. Lot of little tarts.'

As he shuffled off in front of them, Harry thought that no girl in her senses would want to touch him, either. He let Will get ahead, so that he was close to the small man's shoulder. Sure enough, he heard him ask in a deliberately off-hand way whether Miss O'Donaghue had arrived yet.

'Her? Yeah, she's here. Come a few minutes ago. Can't see her yet. How about a word with the Twistleton Twins? Can't tell 'em apart. They'd be friendly to a pair of young men like you.'

'Fair enough,' Harry said.

'Er, yeah.' Will did not sound at all happy.

They stopped outside a dingy door. The small man stood with his body barring the way.

'They're in here,' he said, with a world of significance in his voice. Harry realized that the tins of pineapples were only to get them backstage. Actually meeting the artistes was going to be extra. It looked as if it was going to be an expensive night out. He produced half-a-crown. It disappeared into the small man's pocket as quick as a conjuring act.

'That's for both of us,' he said.

The man looked disappointed but did not argue. He knocked on the door.

'Visitors for you, Misses T.'

There were squeals from inside. 'No, wait – we're not ready...'

'Want to go in now?' The man gave a gap-toothed grin.

But Will was hanging back. 'Er – which is Miss O'Donaghue's room, then? Ought to see her, y'know. Friend of ours. Used to live in our street. Wouldn't be neighbourly to miss her, would it, Harry? Not right at all.'

'Look, mate.' The small man sidled up to Will.

'I wouldn't go in there if I was you, neighbour or no neighbour,' he said confidentially. 'You go 'n' try your luck with them twins.'

'But which one is it?'

The man indicated the door at the end.

Harry took a chance. 'Come on, Will. You don't want to see Siobhan again. Let's go in here.'

He opened the door and put his head round, and was immediately bombarded in all of his senses. The bright light made him blink, a waft of compounded scent, cigarette smoke and female sweat filled his nose and lungs, and squeals of mock fright and delight vibrated through his ears. The two Misses Twistleton, bright blonde and made up to the nines, bounded up to him and took an arm each, drawing him into the room.

'Oo, you're nice. What's your name? I'm Holly–'

'–And I'm Ivy. Holly and Ivy, get it? We was born at Christmas.'

'Our mum said the Christmas angels brung us!'

Harry's eyes adjusted to the light, and he looked from one to the other. There really was no telling them apart. Two pairs of red lips smiled invitingly at him. Two pairs of blue eyes twinkled roguishly. Two delicious half-dressed bodies exuded animal energy and fun.

'I think Christmas has come early for me this year,' he said.

'You sit down here.' The girls pushed him on to a chair. 'We got to finish getting ready. You can fasten us up.'

'Then afterwards you can unfasten us again, if you're lucky.'

They both shrieked with laughter. Their blonde curls and their high round breasts quivered. Then they spotted Will hesitating at the door.

'Oo, you got a friend! One each – even better. Shame you're not twins. We want to find a pair of twins, don't we?'

'Yeah, we're not getting married till we can find a pair of twins.'

'But they're both very nice, ain't they?'

'Oh yeah, they're both very nice. Come on, darling, come and sit down by your friend. Oo, hasn't he got strong arms? Feel them muscles!'

They pranced about, laughing, joking, getting dressed for their act. Harry and Will were allowed to hook them up at the back and hand them their props.

Their five-minute call came, and they flew around in mock panic, getting in each other's way, tripping over their own and the men's feet, and landing accidentally on purpose on their laps.

'Misses Twistleton, on stage now. On stage now, Misses Twistleton.'

And with a last squeal and flourish, they were gone.

Harry looked at Will. In the overwhelming presence of the twins, he had almost lost sight of the purpose of the evening.

'Reckon we're in with a chance here, eh?' he said.

'Yeah.' Will was not really listening. His attention was elsewhere. Harry chatted on about the two girls, assessing their charms, and all the while Will nodded and grunted.

In no time at all, they were back.

'Ooo, they loved us. Didn't they love us, Holly?'

'They always love us, Ivy. Standing in their seats, they were.'

'Ooo, I love singing.' Ivy gave a shiver of sheer pleasure. 'It makes me feel so – so wonderful. Like I love all the world.'

'All the world! And they all love us!'

They hugged each other and broke into a chorus of their song. Harry laughed out loud, caught up in their sheer exuberance. He threw an arm round each one of them and they all danced together, whirling round in the cramped room in dizzying circles until one of the girls caught her foot on a chair and they all fell in a heap, laughing and shrieking. Harry, swamped in scent and taffeta and young hot bodies, could feel all restraint flying fast out of the window. He kissed one and then the other. They giggled with delight and kissed him back, both at the same time. They tasted salty.

Will sat watching without really seeing them. All his senses were concentrated on listening for Siobhan. He heard the five-minute call for her act, then the on-stage one. Her footsteps went by outside. He knew they were hers. He could bear it no longer. Stepping over Harry and the twins, he slipped out of the door. He just caught sight of Siobhan's skirt as she whisked round the corner.

All the old longing and frustration swept back. He had to see her again, he just had to. He could not stay two rooms away when he could be with her. He knew just what he was going to do; he was going to go into her room and wait for her to come back, and see what she said when she saw him sitting there. Maybe she would be pleased. You never could tell with Siobhan. Standing there in the musty corridor, with the sound of her sweet voice stealing through the walls between him and the stage, he almost managed to convince himself that she would be delighted, that all would be just as it had been on those rare precious occasions when she had allowed him all that he ever wanted. Looking back on it, he always forgot the many times she had stood him up, tried to make him jealous of the Great Cornelius or Sidney Spruce, taken advantage of him, played hard to get or just refused to have anything to do with him. In his memory, she was always sweet and playful and willing.

As he placed his hand on the doorknob, the small man's warning came back to him, but he discounted it. Seeing Siobhan was the only thing that mattered.

The first thing that hit him as he went in was the cigar smoke. At first he thought he had got the wrong room. A man was sitting there, a young man in evening dress with a handsome, insolent face and a broken nose. He was sitting in the one chair, with his feet up on the littered dressing table. It was a woman's dressing table, piled with pots of cream, make-up, scent bottles, flowers, lace handkerchiefs and a bright pink feather boa.

The young man looked Will over slowly, from head to toe, taking in every detail, so that Will was suddenly conscious of his lowly appearance. He became painfully aware that his hair was ill-cut, his collar darned, his hands rough and ingrained with dirt, that his jacket did not match his trousers and his boots were patched. He was every inch the working man on a Saturday night out. In contrast, his rival was impeccably clad in white tie and tailcoat, with a snowy starched shirt covering his broad chest, and patent leather shoes on his feet. He looked very much at home here in Siobhan's dressing room as he blew a puff of expensive smoke into the air.

'Looking for someone?' he asked.

Will was thrown. It was not the accent of a gentleman – that he might almost have been able to handle. Despite appearances, this man was one of his own sort, but successful. Successful and dangerous. A warning instinct set his heart thudding. He was younger than Will, not more than twenty-five, but every inch of him was flint-hard, and behind that smooth smile sat a calculating mind.

'N-no,' he stuttered. 'No – I – I made a mistake. Wrong room.' He was rooted to the spot.

'That so? Who was you looking for?'

'Er – er.' His brain went completely blank. He could not even think to name the Twistletons.

'Nobody? You must've been looking for someone. Friends of Siobhan's, are you?'

'Neighbour.' The word came out before he could stop it. Something in the man's eyes, something cold and snakelike, seemed to drag it from him, like a confession.

'Neighbour? That's funny. Didn't think your type lived round her way.'

Will licked his lips. His mouth was dry. 'W-was,' he enlarged. 'Was her neighbour. Once. On Dog Island.'

'Dog Island,' the man repeated. 'North of the river, eh? Me, I'm from Southwark. This is my home ground, round here.'

It was just a remark, a simple piece of information, said almost pleasantly, and yet there was a distinct menace in it. Will swallowed. He could handle himself in a fight all right, but not with this one. He was the sort that would have a knife in your guts before you knew what had got you.

'Oh, well – I'll be going.'

'Going? But you only just come.'

'Yeah, but I got to–'

'Oh no you ain't. You wait till Siobhan comes back. I wouldn't like her to miss an old friend.'

The power of movement had drained from Will's legs. He stood just where he was, inside the door. He was still there when Siobhan arrived back.

'Got a little surprise for you, petal,' the young man remarked. He did not get up from the seat.

Siobhan stepped round Will and went to his rival. She leant against him and put her arm round his shoulder, so that her breast was pressed against his cheek. He reached up and fondled her.

'Go well?'

'Well enough.'

She was staring at Will as if he was a maggot that had crawled out of an apple she was eating.

'What's he doing here?' she asked.

'Says he knows you, petal. Neighbour of yours from the old days.'

'Never clapped eyes on him in my life.'

Will stared at her, thunderstruck. The costume was the same type she always wore – a fluffy pastel dress with a big flowery hat – and from a distance the rest of her would have seemed the same as well; but close to, it was like seeing a different person. The blue eyes, the pretty round face, the sweet lips, all were hard and calculating and worldly-wise as an alley cat's. Will reeled from the shock, not wanting to believe what his eyes were telling him. In his mind she was the little Irish girl, sweet sixteen and fresh off the boat. This was a woman who had trod the halls for ten years, a bully-boy's mistress.

As if to underline the point, her lover caught at her nipple as it showed through the thin fabric of her dress. He pinched it between his finger and thumb.

'Funny,' he said. 'I knew you was going to say that.'

He looked at Will. 'I think you better be off,' he said.

Sick to the pit of his stomach, Will obeyed.

Ellen stirred and woke up. She listened for a moment, not knowing what it was that had disturbed her. The children were both fast asleep, their breathing light and regular. There was no sound from the lodgers. Perhaps it was just that she was uncomfortable. They had pawned the beds two days ago and the floor was hard.

Then she realized that Gerry had at last returned. He was creeping through the house as soft as a cat burglar. Just as quietly, Ellen got up and tiptoed round the children. She met Gerry at the foot of the stairs.

'Oh.' He was startled. 'I – I was trying not to wake you, love.'

'What, so as you needn't say anything to me?'

'No, no, not that. I was just thinking of you.'

Ellen sighed. 'We got to talk, you and me. You can't go on avoiding me no longer. I got a right to know what's going on.'

Gerry opened his mouth to make an excuse, but Ellen took him by the arm and steered him into the kitchen. She sat down on one of the crates that was serving as a stool and tugged at him to do the same. Too bone tired to protest, Gerry slumped down, his shoulders bowed.

'Now,' she said, 'what's up?'

'Nothing. Nothing much, anyhow. Just a bit of a bad patch. I'll pull through, love. I always have, y'know. Few weeks and it'll all be hunky-dory again.'

'Gerry!' Weeks of worry and frustration surfaced. She felt like hitting him. 'Don't come that one with me. I know. You're in big trouble, ain't you? Why don't you *tell* me, Gerry? I'm not stupid, you know. I was with you last time it happened, remember. You told me about it then and I done what I could to help. Just tell me what's going on.'

Gerry dropped his head into his hands. 'I don't want to worry you. I can deal with it myself.'

'For God's sake, Gerry! I'm worried out of my mind. You're never home, you look like someone's after your blood, we put away the furniture, we owe six weeks' rent, and the only money coming in's from the lodgers – and I can't keep them much longer, not with the place empty like this. Just tell me what it is and maybe I can do something, but don't talk about not worrying me, because not knowing's far worse than whatever it is.'

But Gerry waved his head slowly in denial. 'It wouldn't do no good, Ellen. You can't help this time.'

'Who is it? Who do you owe money to? Is it Praed again?'

'No, no, not him. I steered clear of him this time.'

That was something of a relief. The very mention of Praed's name made her guts crawl with foreboding.

'Except – well, it is, in a way. I mean, that's how it started. I had to borrow off of this other bloke to pay off Praed that time. You know he was leaning on me. Trouble is, now this other bloke's leaning on me just as bad.'

'How much?' Ellen felt sick.

'A lot.'

'How much, Gerry?'

A long pause, then, 'Two hundred quid.'

'*Gerry!*'

'I knew you'd be worried. That's why I didn't want to tell you.'

'*Two hundred quid!*'

'I'll do it, love. I'll get it back to him. I got plenty of stock still and trade's good, people are buying. Like I said, it's just a bad patch.'

More than that, Ellen could not get out of him. She took in outwork to help make ends meet, spending long hours doing repetitive tasks for very little money. Everything they owned that was not absolutely essential to life went along to the pawnshop. But though they just about kept food on the table, it did nothing to pull them out of their debt.

Knowledge of their plight was not long in travelling the street. Some folk who had resented Gerry's status as stall holder gave sly smiles, but most were on their side. Little offerings of food appeared on the doorstep or were slipped into Ellen's hand – a couple of ounces of tea, half a loaf, a saucer of jam.

'For the little 'uns,' people muttered, and slid off before they could be thanked. They all knew what it was like to be on your uppers.

But it was no use. The landlord gave them one more week to pay before sending the bailiffs in.

'They won't find anything worth taking here,' Ellen said. 'Ain't you got nothing we can put 'em off with, Gerry? Just a couple of quid might keep 'em from turning us out.'

Gerry shook his head. For once, he was silenced.

'Then we better go before we're pushed. We'll have to move in with your mum.' She managed to say it in a matter-of-fact way.

Ellen bustled about fixing it with Alma and moving what very little they had left. She told the children what fun it was going to be living with Granny, and put on a brave face. When people sympathized, she just shrugged and smiled, saying that it was only for a while till they got back on their feet again. Nobody, least of all Gerry, guessed how she felt inside.

Pride demanded that the house should be clean before handing the key back to the landlord. Ellen asked her mother to look after the children for the day while she gave the place a good going-over, but put off all offers of help with the scrubbing. She wanted to be alone for once, without having to make the effort to keep cheerful, for she knew that she could not keep it up.

She borrowed bucket, soap, scrubbing brush and even hot water from Florrie, and set to, trying not to think of anything. Doggedly she concentrated on the job in hand, venting her rage and sense of failure on the paintwork. There was plenty to do: the stairs and floors to be scrubbed, the windows to be cleaned, the range to be polished. But when Harry found her she was on her knees by the skirting board in the parlour, crying.

'Oh, love.' He knelt down beside her and put an arm round her shaking shoulders.

Ellen turned to him and buried her face in his chest, giving herself up to her unhappiness. Clinging to him, she let out all the pain that she had been holding to herself for so long. Harry stroked her head and rocked her like a baby until the weeping subsided into hiccuping sobs and she gradually became aware of his strong arms around her, his soothing voice in her ears, her body close to his. She knew she should pull away, but it was good to be held like this, safe in the one haven left in an uncertain world. The crushing weight of debt no longer seemed to matter. She pressed her hot cheek to the damp patch her tears had made on his shirt and closed her eyes, letting the warmth and security of his love flow through her.

Harry bent his head and kissed her gently on the lips.

'My poor darling. He shouldn't've left you all alone like this to clear up.'

'They all offered, but I didn't want anyone.'

'It's a real swine, having to give up your house.'

'Oh, Harry.' She nearly started crying again. 'You don't know. I feel so – so lost. It's horrible, not having a home. I know your aunty Alma'll be good to us, but it ain't the same, it ain't my home. It's like – like I don't belong nowhere.'

'Yeah. Adrift, like.'

'Yeah, that's just it. Adrift.'

'Look.' Harry held her away from him a little so that he could see her face. 'You need taking out of yourself. I can't do nothing about Gerry's problems, but I can see to it that you ain't here all by yourself doing the donkey work. You go and tidy up a bit. We're going out.'

'Out?' She stared at him as if he'd suggested flying to the moon. 'I can't go out. I got this house to clean.'

'Sod the house. It's clean enough already. You go and get yourself ready.'

'But–'

'No buts. Just do it.'

'I can't. I – I got nothing to wear.'

'You got a dress on.'

'I can't go out in this!'

'So you are coming, then?'

She almost smiled, glad to be defeated. 'Yeah. I didn't ought to, but yeah.'

'Right, so come as you are. You look just right to me.'

While she was washing her face and putting her hair in place, Harry slipped out the back way.

They met ten minutes later down at the river's edge. Harry was sitting waiting for her in a small skiff. He stood up and held out a hand to help her onboard. Ellen sat down unsteadily in the stern. It still felt all wrong, running away like this. She worried that the children might need her. What if somebody came running to fetch her and she was not there?

'Whose boat is this? Where are we going?'

'Never mind about the boat. I can have a lend of it any Sunday. And we're going to Battersea.'

'Battersea! I ain't never been there.'

'No, neither's no one else in the street, so it's quite safe. You'll like it. There's a park.'

She sat upright, holding on to the sides of the boat, anxiously chewing her lip. It was another hot late-summer day and people were out. You never knew who might see you.

'Don't worry,' Harry said, reading her thoughts. 'Who's going to be looking out for you here?'

He rowed with a strong, steady stroke through the lines of coasters and small craft moored along the tiers until they were midstream, where the floodtide took hold of them and helped them along.

'Nobody on shore can see who's in a skiff now. The boats on the tiers are hiding us.'

But it was not until they passed under Tower Bridge that Ellen began to feel they were away from prying eyes. She started to unwind a little then, asking Harry about the buildings they were passing.

'There's Fresh Wharf, where we boarded for Southend. Remember?'

'Yeah.' She smiled then at the memory. 'That was a lovely day, weren't it? I'll always remember that. One of the best days of my life.'

'Best days of my life was when we used to go over to Greenwich.'

Ellen was seized with a longing for those uncomplicated times. She had had everything to look forward to then. She changed the subject quickly for fear of giving way to the lump in her throat.

'What's that awful whiff? Is that Billingsgate?'

They were in Harry's own world of boats and wharves and bridges. He had stories to tell of people and places and incidents all along the way. Slowly Ellen relaxed. As they went further and further upriver, the problems of real life faded. She could put Gerry and the house and the debts and even the children to the back of her mind and shut them away in the close little world of Trinidad Street. Out here on the river there was space and light, the sun was dancing on the water and pleasure boats were passing with groups of gaily dressed people on the decks. Best of all, she was with the man she loved. She leant back in the boat, trailing her hand in the water and laughing at Harry's tales.

'There.' Harry nodded over his right shoulder. 'See them trees? That's Battersea Park.'

They tied the skiff up at the jetty. Harry flexed his shoulders, Ellen got her land legs back again.

'Ain't you tired, with all that rowing? We come an awful long way.'

'No – nothing to it, little boat like that. I'm hungry, though. It must be dinner time. Come on, I'll treat you.'

They sat down on flimsy metal chairs at a little round table outside the café and ate pork pies and Chelsea buns, and washed them down with thick sweet tea. Ellen could not recall anything ever tasting so good. Around them families chattered and squabbled, and sparrows hopped right up to their feet to catch the crumbs. The broad leaves of the plane trees above dappled the sunlight into ever changing patterns. Trinidad Street with all its cares was a thousand miles away, almost on a different planet. Ellen looked at Harry, to find that he was looking at her.

'I like it here,' she said.

'I knew you would.'

And they smiled, for they each knew the other's tastes so well.

'Fancy a stroll round?' Harry asked.

She nodded and got up, brushing the crumbs from her skirt. 'Yeah, that'd be lovely.'

All of south London seemed to be in the park that afternoon, from babies in perambulators to old folk in bath chairs, and all ages in between, children bowling hoops, young people in groups eyeing each other, lovers walking hand in hand, noisy families. Harry and Ellen wandered arm in arm round the gravelled paths, engrossed in each other. Sometimes they talked, sometimes they were silent, happy just to be together, away from the prying eyes and clacking tongues of home. They admired the flowers and ate ice cream and listened to the band. Ellen was aware of a great lake of quiet happiness growing and growing inside her, turning the whole world to gold. But at the same time she knew that it was fragile and fleeting, and that every precious moment brought them closer to the time when they would have to go home. The combination produced an almost unbearable ache in her heart.

'Penny for them,' Harry said, as she gazed speechlessly at the display of dahlias.

'Don't you wish you could make time stand still?' she said. 'Just stop it and hold on to it for ever?'

'Yeah.' For the first time that day his cheerfulness slipped and he sighed. 'I wish I could go back an' all, and undo all the stupid mistakes I made.'

'Me too.'

They both stared at the flowers, thinking of all the things they would change if they could only have their time over again.

As they walked on, Ellen became increasingly aware of his physical presence, his arm threaded with hers, his shoulder rubbing against hers, their legs moving in unison. As one, their fingers laced together in a tight knot. She felt her heart thudding in her chest.

In a little copse of trees, Harry stopped and looked into her eyes.

'Look, we can't change anything really, can we? So let's just enjoy what we got.'

Ellen nodded. 'Yes,' she agreed, the word hoarse in her throat.

He set off with a purposeful step, away from the promenading crowds. Ellen, almost trotting to keep up with him, could feel the excitement coursing through him stirring her own body, as if they were one. She knew what it was that she wanted: him, all of him. And she wanted to give all of herself, as a present.

'Where are we going?'

'You'll see.'

They hurried on till they came to a dull part of the park where a large clump of privet bushes grew into a dense hedge. He led the way up a narrow path which opened out into a bare patch by a brick hut.

'What's this?' Ellen was not very impressed.

'It's where the gardeners keep their stuff. But they ain't here today. It's Sunday, remember.'

'Ah.' Ellen was beginning to understand. She let him take her hand and lead her round the back of the hut, and then followed him as he scrambled under the dusty bushes.

When they were completely surrounded by privets, Harry stopped, kneeling with some difficulty under the branches to strip off his jacket. He laid it over the fallen leaves that covered the baked earth.

'There. Not exactly comfortable, but it's well hidden.' He patted the space beside him. 'Make y'self at home.'

Ellen hesitated. She knew that she should not, and yet – and yet she loved him so much, and needed him so much, and they might never get this chance again.

'Come on, love.' He held out a hand to her.

She looked into his blue eyes, and all resistance slid away. She could not refuse, not when she wanted the same thing herself. She sank down, and melted into his arms. It felt so right, it was like coming home. Their lips met in a long, hungry kiss.

'Ellen, Ellen.' He crushed her to his hard body as if he would never let her go. 'You don't know how I needed that.'

'I do.'

As they spoke their lips brushed, their hot breath mingling.

'If I thought you was happy, you and Gerry, I could bear it. I'd never even have thought of bringing you here.'

'Forget Gerry. Just for today. He never made me feel like you do, not one little bit. You're the only one I ever wanted. I see you and it hurts all over that I can't have you.'

They kissed again, lips and tongues searching and demanding. The outside world ceased to exist, leaving just the two of them, and the love they had kept hidden for so long. Ellen felt as if she had opened a door into a new world. She no longer had to pretend. She no longer had to hold back. All the passion and longing that had been damped down could flare up without restraint. She could be her true self. She trembled and moaned with pleasure as Harry's hands caressed her body, awakening breasts and thighs and belly to a burning need. She pressed against him, wanting more, wanting all of him.

'Oh, Harry.'

She tugged at his shirt, eager for the feel of his warm skin and wiry hair beneath her hands, and thrilled at his reaction as she kissed his naked chest. He reached down to gather up her skirt, his hands sending tongues of fire through her as he travelled over calf and knee and found the soft skin of her thigh. She cried out as he lingered, teasing, and again in an agony of pleasure as at last his fingers slipped between her legs. She lay writhing, helpless in the exquisite joy until the need of him became too much to bear and she reached out to touch him. And then they could wait no longer, kissing and biting and tasting as they pulled at their own and each other's clothing in loving desperation. Harry rolled on top of her and she opened to him, rising to meet him as he thrust into her, gripping him as he went deeper, borne on waves of desire that grew higher and higher until they burst in unison into a fountain of ecstasy. They clung to each other, gasping, laughing, sobbing and gradually floating down into a warm golden sea of bliss.

Ellen drew a long, shaking breath. 'I never knew anything like that,' she whispered.

Harry smiled down at her, tracing the line of her cheek with his finger.

'That was good,' he agreed, 'but it was too quick. We was both a bit desperate.'

'Just a bit,' Ellen admitted. It was so wonderful to be able to talk like this without embarrassment. She moved against him so that she could feel the length of him inside her, and found to her delight that she wanted him all over again.

Harry turned over so that she was on top of him.

'Sit up,' he said, 'I want to look at you.'

She complied with difficulty, laughing as her hair tangled with the twiggy bushes. Harry reached up and undid the remaining buttons on her blouse, eased it off and dropped it to the ground. Her corset and chemise followed. Ellen stretched her arms out in a glory of abandonment. She had never felt the air on her body like this before. Sunspots coming through branches played on her naked skin. Harry cupped her breasts in his hands, fondling and caressing.

'You are so beautiful,' he said, wonder in his voice.

Slowly they explored each other's bodies with eyes and lips and fingertips. For Ellen it was a new and wonderful world where part of her that had always been submerged could at last find full expression. She opened like a flower to Harry's loving touch, and revelled in the chance to discover what gave him special pleasure.

'You know what it is?' she said. 'You make me feel like a proper woman.'

'You're the only woman for me.' Harry drew her head down and kissed her.

A renewed excitement began to run through them, mounting by degrees until they were climbing peak after peak of drawn-out pleasure. And just when Ellen felt she could hardly hold so much joy, they flooded with a final molten ecstasy.

For a timeless age they lay locked together, hardly knowing where either began or ended. They slept and woke and sighed, immersed in complete happiness.

'I could die now,' Ellen murmured. 'I have everything.'

'My love.' Harry cradled her head more closely under his chin and pulled her blouse over her shoulders to keep her warm.

But reality came creeping back, nibbling at the

edges of their bliss. Ellen shivered; Harry stirred to avoid the stones digging into his back. With a dragging reluctance, they came back to an awareness of their surroundings. The shadows were beginning to lengthen.

Ellen swallowed, and finally gave voice to the dreadful truth.

'We got to go.'

They clung together a little longer, trying to hold on to the moment, but already the magic was slipping away.

'I suppose,' Ellen ventured, 'I suppose we *could* stay.'

Neither of them dared look at the other as they played with the idea. It was too dangerous. They both knew there was really only one answer. Harry sat up and gathered items of clothing together.

'Come on,' he said gently. 'Arms in.'

Ellen drew in a deep breath, and complied.

They scrambled out from the bushes and brushed each other down. Ellen did the best she could with her dishevelled hair. She smiled feebly.

'Now I know what they mean about going through a hedge backwards.'

Harry held her in his arms as they took one last look at the place where they had discovered heaven.

'We'll always have this to remember,' he said. 'Whatever happens, this day will be ours.'

PART V

1911

1

In the street, the children were playing off-ground touch. There were shrieks of excitement and the scrape of boots as boys and girls leapt for the safety of steps and window ledges. Women who had slaved over scrubbing yelled at them to get off, lending force to their words with well-aimed swipes at legs and ears. The children just laughed and played on. Annoying the grown-ups was part of the fun. When the women started to bring their husbands in with threats of belt-ends, they simply shifted away down the street.

Harry, watching idly through the parlour window, was struck with a fierce nostalgia for the simple rules of childhood. You pushed the adults as far as you could, and if you stepped over the line, you got a clip round the ear. It was the same within the gang. By common consent, the strongest and cleverest boy was leader. You knew exactly what was allowed and what wasn't, and if you broke one of the laws, you were out. It didn't matter how popular you were, how good at fighting rival gangs or playing dares, if you told on a pal or beat up a little kid or stole something off one of the gang, that was it.

His gaze focused on his aunt Alma's place across the road. In some ways, it was still the same now he was an adult. If you broke the rules, you were out. The difference was that you might get away with it if you kept up a good enough pretence. There behind the brown-painted door, Ellen carried on as if nothing had happened between them on that golden day back at the end of last summer. She worked to keep the house clean and bring up the children properly, and supported Gerry as he struggled to get his money problems straight. And all the while, inside her, the fruit of their love was growing.

He was sure it was his baby. She had refused to say, on the one occasion he had managed to get her alone for long enough to ask.

'I dunno. How am I supposed to know? Could be.'

'But you must know. You're the only one who can. You know what – goes on inside of you.'

She glared back at him, eyes hot and defiant. 'Well I don't, so just don't ask, see? Don't ask.'

He knew from the set of her mouth that he would get nothing from her. It was part of the unspoken agreement between them. As long as she did not actually admit it out loud, they could live with it. But he knew, and he was sure that she knew, what the truth was.

The trouble was, it got harder rather than easier to bear. As the months went by and her belly began to swell, he wanted to be there by her side to watch over and protect her. To be forced to stand by like this, pretending no more than a vague neighbourly interest, galled him beyond belief. He could not suppress a growing antagonism towards his cousin. Gerry did not deserve her. Gerry did not look after her properly. Every time he saw Gerry, the resentment and jealousy nearly choked him. He had to stop himself from deliberately picking a quarrel, and keep his fists in his pockets so that he could not smash them into Gerry's anxious, apologetic face.

'Harry?'

He turned away from the window. Florrie was outlined in the doorway.

'What you doing in here? Gave me a turn, you did, standing there in the half-dark, all quiet.'

'Just thinking.'

'Ah.' For a moment it seemed as if she was going to comment, but she changed her mind. 'Well, go and call Bob in for us, would you? Tea's ready.'

Glad to be distracted from the insoluble problem, he went to the door and yelled at his young brother.

There was the usual Saturday wrangle over who was going out and where, who with and for how long. Ida sulked over the necessity to be in by ten o'clock.

'It isn't fair! Johnny's three years younger than what I am and you don't tell him to be in then.'

'You're a girl. I always had to be in by ten, and so do you. Makes 'em respect you if you got family what wants you back at a decent time,' Florrie told her.

Ida pouted. Across the table, Johnny gave an irritating grin.

'I'm going out with my pals,' he said.

'Well, mind you don't get into no trouble,' Harry warned.

'What about you, love?' Florrie asked her husband. 'You going up the Puncheon?'

561

'I will if you come too.'

Florrie shook her head. 'No thanks, I'm too tired.' She smoothed a hand over her vast belly. The baby was due in a couple of weeks.

'Then I'll stay with you, if you like. Bob can go up the Puncheon and get us a jug of mild.'

'Only if I can spend the change.'

'I'll make sure there ain't no blooming change, if you're not careful.'

'I suppose Harry's going somewhere exciting up West,' Ida said, with envy in her voice.

Up to that moment, Harry had not had any definite plans. But the cosy togetherness of his sister and her husband was too stark a contrast with his own bleak situation for him to stick around the neighbourhood for the evening. He certainly could not stand the thought of hanging around in the Puncheon chewing over the doings of the week with the rest of the men from the street. There had been a loose agreement between some friends at work to go out. He decided to take it up.

'Yeah, I'm meeting some mates and going up the Old Vic,' he said.

'Not fair,' Ida complained. 'I bet you wouldn't let me go to a hall with my friends.'

'For God's sake, stop whining,' Harry told her. 'Get that bloke of yours to marry you, and you can both stop out as long as you like.'

That effectively silenced Ida.

An hour or so later, as he walked towards the pub where they were all supposed to be meeting, Harry found himself going slower and slower. He hardly knew why. He needed a good night out; it would make him forget things for a while. He loved the atmosphere of a music hall – the warmth, the jokes, the songs. He liked to have a drink or two, to sing along, to have a laugh with his pals. So why was it no longer the same? He stood still, frowning down at his feet. It was his friends. There was only one of the old crowd left. The rest were all younger than him. The men he used to go about with were married, many of them with two or three children. They took their wives out of a Saturday night, while here he was, twenty-eight years old and still acting like some kid of eighteen.

Around him the cheerful crowds swirled, all intent on a good evening out, all with somewhere to go, someone to go with. He felt lost, disorientated. People bumped into him. He could not decide what to do. He did not want to go home. He did not want to go on to the meeting place. He was tempted just to go into the nearest pub and get drunk, but he had sense enough to realize that that was to start down the same road as his father. While he stood there, he thought he heard a woman's voice call his name.

'Harry? Harry Turner!'

He ignored it. He did not want to talk to anyone, especially a woman.

'Harry, it is you.'

She put a hand on his arm. He was about to shake her off when something in the voice made him look at her.

'Theresa?'

She looked dreadful. Not even the heavy make-up could disguise the ravages of her hard life. She gave a bright, false smile.

'I been looking for you. Months and months I

been looking. Now I found you. You got a minute?'

He groaned inwardly. Another problem. But he had promised to help her, that last time they had met.

'Yeah. Yeah, of course.'

'Can we go and have a drink? I'm gasping.'

'Yeah, right.'

Harry watched her as she downed two double gins, one after the other. In the bright lights of the pub, she looked even worse than she had outside. Her hands were like claws, her face haggard, her hair thin and straggling. There were sores all round her scarlet-painted mouth. It was hard to believe that she was only a year older than himself. She looked closer to forty.

'How you doing, then?' Harry asked. He knew as soon as the words left his lips it was a stupid question.

'Not so bad.' She shrugged.

'So what did you want to see me for?'

'Get us another, Harry. Please – for old times' sake?'

He sighed and stood up.

'Make it two.'

With two more doubles inside her, the harsh lines of her face relaxed a little. She tried to talk to him about himself, but he did not want to say anything. Finding she was getting nowhere, she soon gave up and asked about the street. Harry filled her in with the news of births, marriages and deaths. She nodded, muttering and commenting on each piece of information.

'And Charlie? Charlie Billingham? What's happened to him?'

'I thought you had it in for him?'

She put her hand on his arm, her bony fingers gripping him until it hurt. She leant across the table so that her face was within inches of his. He recoiled from her bad breath.

'I got to see him again, Harry. Can you arrange that, eh? Can you? I got to see him, alone, like.'

'Well, I dunno...'

'Come on, Harry. You said as you wanted to help me, didn't you? Said I only had to ask. Well, now I'm asking. You're not going to go back on what you said, are you?'

'No, of course not.'

He wanted to help, but it was not as easy as all that. He thought it through, anticipating the problems. It was not like getting Will to meet up with Siobhan again. He and Will did sometimes go out together, so Will had not been the least suspicious, and when they got to the hall it had seemed to be just a coincidence that Siobhan happened to be performing there. But with Charlie it was different. He had very little to do with his cousin, beyond the casual meetings in the street or up at the Puncheon. If he suddenly tried to organize something, Charlie would smell a rat. He tried to explain this to Theresa.

'You'll think of something,' she said.

Harry wished he had as much confidence in himself.

'He don't go out with the same people as the rest of us. He might go up the Puncheon during the week sometimes, but Saturday and Sunday he's off with his own mates. I think he goes up Poplar way.'

Theresa latched on to this. 'You find out where,

and tell me.'

'I thought you didn't want to come anywhere near home?'

'Poplar's not home, is it? I would never come near the Island, but I don't mind Poplar – not if I can get that Charlie Billingham.'

'What've you got planned?' Harry asked. He had no respect or liking for his cousin, but family was family.

'Planned? Nothing! I just got things I got to say to him, that's all.' An expression of pained innocence sat incongruously on her ravaged face.

In the end, with many misgivings, he promised to meet her again next Saturday and tell her what he had found out. Satisfied, Theresa stood up.

'Can't sit around here all night gassing to you. I got a living to earn.'

They had not discussed her life at all, so that this barefaced statement caught him unawares.

'Wait, Theresa.'

'What's up? Fancy a bit, do you?'

It turned his stomach. 'Pack it in, Theresa. That ain't funny.'

'Suit y'self.' She shrugged. 'I could get you a nice young girl, if you like. You could have it on the house.'

'Shut it, will you?'

'All right, all right. See you back here next week. Promise?'

'Yeah.'

'You're a real pal, you are, Harry. A brick.'

He watched her as she threaded her way through the noisy bar. Theresa O'Donaghue, nice Irish girl from a strict home. Theresa O'Donaghue, draggled-tailed whore, not even young or attractive any more. He doubted whether she would find many clients round this part of town, except if they were very drunk. It would not be long before she was fit for nothing but the Ratcliff Highway. He was filled with a sick anger. If it really was Charlie Billingham who had been the cause of her downfall, then he deserved anything that Theresa had in mind. Somehow, he would do what she asked.

She knew him the moment he stepped out of the pub. She saw him against the lighted doorway, recognized the figure she had carried in her mind for all these years, first with pain, then with hatred. All this time, she had waited for a chance for revenge, waited without any clear plan beyond the knowledge that somehow, sometime, she would ruin him as he had ruined her. It was only within the last few months that she had realized she had the perfect method at her disposal. And now, at last, the moment was at hand.

She shifted out of the cold alleyway she had been lurking in these past two hours or more and began to walk towards him, keeping to the shadows. He was with friends, which made it difficult, but he was drunk – they were all drunk. She heard them laughing and hooting, saw them staggering about. She was in luck. He tripped and almost fell, then reeled against a wall and leant there while he got his balance. The others, not noticing, went on. Theresa went into action.

'Hullo, darling.'

His first reaction was to push her away, but

Theresa was used to that. She knew how to make a customer out of a man with a skinful. She ducked under his arm and wrapped herself round him, her hand reaching unerringly for his crotch.

'Get out of it!' He grabbed at her arm but she resisted, working expertly at him.

'What's the matter? Don't you like it? 'Fraid you can't get it up?'

They could still get nasty at this stage. It had happened often enough in Theresa's career. She had been punched and kicked and beaten countless times. She had given them what they wanted then been laid out and not paid. But it was not payment she was after this time. Just him. She pushed all her weight against him as he leant on the wall, her breasts rubbing invitingly. She kept her head down so that all he could see was the top of her hat with its gaudy feathers, while her fingers undid his buttons and slid inside, at last getting a sluggish reaction from him.

'That nice? You like that, don't you? You want it, don't you? Come on, it'll cost you a tanner.'

He was far too weak to resist. She managed to get him along to the graveyard she had chosen earlier, holding him up and steering him as he wove unsteadily along. They collapsed on to the rank grass, which was cold and wet from a week's rain. Nearly there. No longer afraid of being recognized now that they were in the dark, her only fear was that he was going to be incapable. She used every trick she knew, a cold excitement growing in her as he responded. Crowing with triumph, she rode him.

It was all over in no time at all. He was too

drunk to keep going. For a moment she panicked, rigid with fury, not knowing if it had been long enough to achieve her purpose. She kept him there for as long as she could, just to make sure, even when he was just lying there making great drunken snores like some wallowing pig. A wild, malicious laugh broke from her. She had done it, she had fixed him. Now he would know what it was to despair.

When she finally could not hang on any more, she got off him, and as an afterthought, went through his pockets. Nothing, absolutely nothing. Suddenly the revenge she had wrought did not seem enough. She had paid him off for what he had done to her, but there were all the others, all the men who had used and humiliated and injured her over the years, all the others who had had what she sold and not paid for it. They had to be seen to as well. She started with his shoes, then, as he was dead to the world, pulled off his trousers and underpants. Even the chill air on his exposed skin failed to wake him. Her mouth stretched in a vindictive grin as she removed his jacket, dragging it carefully from under him. It was only when she tried to take off his shirt that he stirred and grunted in protest. Swiftly feeling around in the darkness, she gathered up his clothes.

'What – whazzermatter? Who...?'

Before he could realize what had happened, Theresa made off, with the bundle clutched to her body.

Charlie Billingham was left nearly naked in a Poplar graveyard at half-past twelve of a March night.

'Charlie in yet?' Alma asked.

'No,' Ellen said. 'Tea?'

'Please, lovey.'

Alma sat down heavily on a kitchen chair. She had not been able to enjoy this evening, not with the worry about Charlie at the back of her mind. It had been the shock of her life last week, when she'd had to go and fetch him back from Poplar police station, taking some clothes with her. They'd brought him up from the cells wearing nothing but his shirt. Thank God it had been his best one, not the old patched thing he wore for every day. He'd not thanked her for it. He'd been right grumpy all week, snapping at her whenever she spoke. But then that was only natural, really. Enough to give anyone the pip, being left like that when you've had one too many.

'I hope he's all right,' she said.

Ellen said nothing. Alma had the feeling that her daughter-in-law didn't much care for Charlie. She didn't say anything against him, but then she didn't say anything for him either. Alma watched her as she moved around making the tea. It was lovely having Gerry and the little ones about the house, and Ellen was no problem, not really. She was quiet and a hard worker, she kept everything nice. She certainly didn't moon around the place like Maisie used to and she looked after the children beautifully. But there was something that Alma could not quite put her finger on. It was as if Ellen was always holding something back, as if she had some secret she wasn't going to let on about and Alma found it frustrating.

'You joining me?' she asked.

Ellen nodded and sat down opposite her. 'Some blokes come to see Charlie this evening,' she said.

'What?' Alma's heart faltered. Charlie's mates never came here: he always met them at some pub or other, well away from the street. 'What did they want?'

'Said they had something for him. I told them he wasn't in and they said they'd leave it anyway.'

'What? What did they leave?'

'Little bag of stuff. I put it down the back of the put-you-up.'

Alma went straight to have a look. She slid her fingers down the gap between the back and the seat, and they closed round the grimy cloth bundle. It was not until then that it occurred to her that it was an odd thing to do, hiding it like this. And even as the thought struck her, she knew that Ellen had been right to put it out of the way. She stood for several moments with the canvas bag in her hand, not wanting to face the fact that anything Charlie's mates might leave for him was likely to be stolen. Charlie's mates, not Charlie. He was in with the wrong crowd, that was all. Unbidden, that dreadful moment at Southend surfaced, and she remembered his hand slipping into a man's back trouser pocket and coming out with a wallet.

Her courage failed. She did not dare look inside the nasty little bag. She was frightened of what it might contain, terrified that it might confirm all the suspicions that she tried so hard to keep at bay. With a shudder, she thrust it back in its hiding place.

'Nothing important,' she said to Ellen.

'Right. I'm going to bed now. Gerry went up ages ago. He's tired.'

'Poor lamb.' With relief, Alma focused on her other son. 'He works so hard. Always has. He'll work himself into an early grave, he will. He does it for you, you know, Ellen – you and the kids.'

'I know,' Ellen said. 'I'd help him on the stall still, if he'd let me. He needs someone with him, but he won't hear of it. Says the children should have their mum looking after them.'

This was a stab at her, Alma realized. It was all very well for Ellen to stand there saying things like that. She had Gerry out there making a living; she didn't have to bring up the children on her own.

'He's a good dad, is Gerry. Thinks the world of Jess and Teddy. And this new one. Real thrilled, he was, when he told me. Had tears in his eyes. Not many men'd be that pleased about their third.'

And there it was again, that secretive look. Alma supposed it was just because she was carrying. Women got a bit odd then. She'd been odd herself, so proud, as if she was making the whole world inside of her.

'Oh yeah, he's good with the little 'uns,' Ellen agreed. ''Night, Mum.'

That was something, anyway – she did call her Mum. Alma liked that. She sat up some while longer, sipping the tea and trying not to worry about her boys. Gerry had married a good 'un there in Ellen, but he was running himself into the ground to provide for her. It was like he was always trying to prove something. As if that was needed.

He was the best, her Gerry. It broke her heart to see him with that hunted look always on his face. In the old days, there was always a smile and a joke from Gerry, always some new plan, some wonderful deal. He never seemed to smile now.

She tried to keep her mind on Gerry, as the lesser worry, but inevitably Charlie crept in on her thoughts. She never knew where he went to or what he was up to. All she did know was that he was in with a very bad crowd. It was no good her saying anything. He'd given up listening to her when he was still at school. She had no power over him at all.

The door banged open and she jumped, then went limp with relief, her hand to her thudding heart.

'That you, lovey?' As if it would be anyone else.

There was a rumble of reply and Charlie appeared, swaying as he held on to the kitchen doorframe. Alma surveyed him anxiously. He was drunk, but he was fully clothed.

'Had a good time?' she asked.

'Yeah.' He lunged past her, blundering into furniture, wrenched open the back door and made for the privy. That was normal enough, and Alma decided she had been worrying about nothing. Last week had been dreadful, but it wasn't going to happen again. Reassured, she went to bed.

She was still half asleep the next morning when there came a banging on the front door. She sat bolt upright in bed, nerves jangling with the shock.

'What the bleeding hell...?'

For a moment she was confused. This couldn't be happening, not first thing of a Sunday morning. She listened. Teddy's high-pitched babble floated up the stairs, then Ellen's voice, wary and measured, and two men's voices, heavily polite. She heard Charlie's name mentioned – 'Charles Albert Billingham' – and then she knew.

'God help us – coppers!'

She shot out of bed and began pulling on clothes, her fingers turning treacherously clumsy. A moaning noise of fear and frustration sounded in her throat. There was nothing she could do to warn him, to protect him. He was right there in the parlour, sleeping on the put-you-up. The put-you-up! She nearly cried out loud. She had not told him about the hidden bag. She put a hand to her side to steady the wild beating of her heart. It was all right; she must keep a hold of herself. He would have noticed it as he went to bed. He would have hidden it somewhere. But a voice inside her head reminded her that he had been pissed as a wheelbarrow last night... Shaking, her hair sticking out, her clothes all anyhow, Alma went downstairs. At the bottom, she took a deep breath. Then she sailed into the parlour.

'Now then, what's all this about? Can't a body have a lie-in of a Sunday morning without you lot coming and marching in here bold as you please–'

She stopped short. The policemen seemed to fill the small room. Charlie was standing in his shirt and underpants, glowering. He seemed small and defenceless beside the large men. One of them had him by the arm and the other was holding the grubby canvas bag. He waved it in front of Alma.

'You know anything about this, missus?'

Alma opened her mouth and shut it again. She

would have said anything, perjured herself, to help Charlie, but she did not know what to say for the best.

'Course she don't. She was out last night and all, weren't she?' Charlie said.

'That's right,' Alma agreed.

The policeman gave her an unbelieving look. 'Got you trained all right, ain't he, missus?'

'I *was* out last night. You saying I'm a liar? I'll have you for that. You ask anyone. I was up the Puncheon.'

He put on a show of patience. 'All right, so who was in last night? This stuff didn't just fly in the window, now did it?'

'I told you, it must've been planted on me,' Charlie said.

'I was in last night.'

They all turned to look at Ellen. In the midst of the drama, she was totally calm. She looked at the policemen with a steady gaze.

'It's all right, Ellen. You don't have to say nothing.' Gerry was at her shoulder, pale and nervous.

'Two men came yesterday evening with that bag. They asked for Charlie and I said he weren't in, so they gave it to me to give to him.'

'There you are!' Charlie crowed. 'It was planted.'

'Friends of Mr Billingham's were they, missus?'

'I never saw them before in my life.'

'So what did they look like?'

'I didn't see them very well. It was dark, and I didn't ask them in.' Ellen hesitated, her brow creased with remembering. 'They was both quite short – no taller than me. They was wearing caps and jackets. One had a spotted necktie. And they was local – I could tell by the voices.'

The policeman holding the bag was unimpressed. 'How old was they?'

'I dunno – twenty, thirty.'

'Short, wearing caps and jackets, twenty or thirty years old, local. That'd fit practically any villain in London, missus.'

Ellen turned her cold stare on him. 'I'm sorry I can't say no more, officer. I don't invite strange men into my house so as I can tell the police about them.'

'Pity.' Wilting ever so slightly before her, he turned on Charlie.

'Charles Albert Billingham, I am arresting you for receiving stolen goods...'

The rest of the caution was lost in Alma's shriek of protest.

'You can't! You can't do this! Not my boy. He's a good boy, my Charlie. You can't take him in – he's done nothing.'

They ignored her and stood over Charlie as he got dressed. Worse was to follow. The house was searched from top to bottom, then they all had to go down to the station to make statements. Gerry was escorted to his lock-up and all his stock was gone through, together with all the receipts he could find. After an endless morning, the rest of them were allowed to go home, but Charlie was marched off to the cells.

Somehow, Alma managed to walk down Trinidad Street with her head high. She could see them all looking at her, some openly from their front doors, some from behind curtains. They must all have had a real morning of it, talking about the whole family being led off by a couple of coppers, but she wasn't going to let them see her defeated. They all sat down round the kitchen table, and Ellen fetched Teddy and Jessica back from her mother, who had been minding them. Alma's control cracked. Great sobs came heaving up from her very soul.

'Oh, my poor boy,' she howled, 'my poor Charlie. What's going to happen to him? I can't bear it.'

She put her head in her arms and gave herself up to weeping, finding a release in the hot tears. She hardly heard Ellen or Gerry, or felt their arms around her. All she knew was the fierce pain and the crushing fear.

Florrie looked up as the bedroom door opened. Not *more* eager visitors. She had had enough of people peering at the baby and finding who he looked like. All Jimmy's family thought he looked like some relation or other of theirs and all her own lot thought he looked like her. Some even went so far as to say he took after her mum, which brought tears to her eyes, or worse still, her dad. She stared long and searchingly at the tiny child after that suggestion, horror in her heart. It couldn't be. Not that. Not her father come back to haunt her in the face of her firstborn son.

Ellen's head appeared round the door, and Florrie relaxed. Ellen was the one person she wanted to see.

'Not asleep?'

'No – come on in, love. I could do with some company.'

'I brought you up some tea.' Ellen handed her a cup.

'Oh, that's nice, but I don't really fancy it.'

'Water, then? Shall I bring you some water? You got to drink a lot to make milk for the baby.'

Whenever anyone else said that, it made her want to throw the drink all over them. But from Ellen she could take it.

'Oh, well, I suppose you're right. Thanks.'

She looked thoughtfully at her friend's face over the rim of the cup. For the first time since the birth of the baby, she considered someone besides herself and the child.

'You look dog tired, Ellen. Things bad over the road?'

'Well, you know Alma – always thought the sun shone out of Charlie's backside. She still doesn't believe he done nothing.'

'But he was picked out, weren't he, at an identity parade?'

'Yeah, but he says as he was framed, and the old boy what picked him was half blind. Alma can't let it rest. She nagged and nagged at him to get all his pals together so as I could have a look at them and find the ones what brought the stuff round, but he won't have any of it. She went on at him so much that he did take Gerry and me to this pub up in Poplar yesterday evening. He wouldn't let us meet his pals. We had to sit in the corner and pretend we didn't know him. And then they all come in, and a right shifty-looking bunch they was an' all. Just like him.'

'And did you see them, the two that knocked?' Florrie asked. It all seemed unreal to her. A pub in

Poplar was as far away as the moon. Ellen looked so worn that she was interested for her sake.

Ellen sighed and ran her hands over her face. 'It was dreadful, Florrie. I stared and I stared, all the while trying to make out that I wasn't. And they all looked the same. Honest. It was like that copper said, all the villains in London are small and about twenty or thirty and wear caps. And I never saw them proper. It was dark when they come, and you know how the streetlamp don't give off much light, not where we are. And Gerry, he really had the wind up. He kept saying, 'What d'you think? Can you see them? Are they there?' And the more I looked, the more I couldn't remember anything about them. Then of course when we got home, Alma was on at me until I just ended up screaming at her.'

'What did she do?' Alma might be all bright and jolly most of the time, but Florrie wouldn't fancy being there when she wasn't.

'She yelled back. And then the children woke up with the noise and they started crying. But I tell you something, Florrie. Gerry surprised me. He really did. He got between us and he said, "You just leave off, Mum. Ellen's done her best. Don't carry on at her or she might lose the baby." I don't think I ever heard him talk to her like that before, not never. And she did calm down a bit. I think she was surprised an' all. But of course it didn't help none, because we still don't know who it was what brought that stuff round for Charlie.'

'At least he's on bail,' Florrie said.

That had been a right to-do, getting the money together. It was Harry who put most of it up.

Jimmy's family had been horrified. They never had any doings with the police, not the Crofts. If it hadn't been for the baby being born right now, they might even have cut her off.

As if catching her thoughts, little George woke up and began to cry.

'Can I?' Ellen asked.

Florrie nodded and her friend bent down and picked the baby out of the drawer he was lying in. She held him on her knee, smiling down at his angry red features.

'He's got a real look of Harry about him, ain't he?' she remarked.

Relief swamped Florrie in a warm wave. She unbuttoned her nightdress and held out her arms for the baby. As he caught hold of her nipple and his face settled into an expression of avid hunger, she regarded him with new eyes.

'Yeah,' she said. 'Yeah, he has, you're right. Just like Harry.'

They were both quiet for a while, watching the sucking baby.

'He's strong,' Ellen said, as he started on the other side. 'Reckon he'll be all right.'

'Hark at you, quite the old hand,' Florrie joked, not looking up.

'Yeah, funny, ain't it, us both being mums now. Don't seem two minutes since we was playing hopscotch.'

'Or wheeling out other people's babies. Remember that time we fought over Maisie's Tommy?'

'Yeah.' They were both silent again, for it had not been Tommy they were fighting over, but Will's behaviour to Maisie. Which brought both their thoughts to Siobhan.

'Are you–'

'I always thought–'

They both spoke at once, wanting to push the Irish troublemaker out of the way. The chat concentrated on babies and motherhood. Ellen fetched a clean square of old sheet for Florrie to change little George.

He definitely did look like Harry, Florrie decided. She still felt quite dizzy with the knowledge. She could not have born having her father in the house all over again, though of course it would be no more than she deserved.

Without thinking first, she said, 'I wonder if Harry'll ever have any of his own?'

The moment the words were out of her mouth, she regretted them. She saw her friend's face pale and her arm curl protectively round the baby she was carrying inside her. Florrie wanted to say she was sorry, but did not know whether that might make it worse.

Ellen was not looking at her. Her eyes were distant and she was stroking the bulge under her skirt.

'I never–' she began. She stopped, bit her lip, then carried on. 'I never thanked you proper for what you done that day – the day we – I had to move out from next door: finishing the house off for me, and covering up. I – we – wouldn't never have got away with it if it hadn't been for you.'

It was the nearest Ellen had ever come to admitting just what had happened. All Florrie knew was that both her friend and her brother had disappeared for the day. She reached out and laid a hand on her knee.

'We all got secrets,' she said.

Ellen turned and for a long time the two women looked at each other, and felt safe.

2

'You been playing around behind my back, ain't you?'

The young man with the broken nose towered above Siobhan as she sat at the dressing table in their gilded bedroom. She cowered from him, shaking her head.

'Me? No, I have not. Playing around? I never have, not in all the time you and me've been together.'

Her lover was unimpressed. He grabbed her arm and pulled her on to her feet.

'Thought you'd get away with it, did you, what with me being away? Even if you can't behave yourself for my sake, you ought to know I got eyes everywhere.' His grip tightened round her arm, making her gasp. 'You been seen.'

'Lies!' Siobhan squealed. 'It's all lies! I been good as gold while you been gone. All I been doing is working and coming back here.'

'And shopping.'

Siobhan went pale. She swallowed, then tried to keep up the defiant tone.

'So I went shopping. What's wrong in that? I got to buy things. I got to keep looking nice. You want me to look nice for you, don't you?'

'For me, yeah. Not for that poncy bastard with the handle to his name.'

'I don't know what you mean!'

She cried out as the back of his hand hit the side of her face.

'Don't know what I mean, my arse. It's not enough for you, is it, having the biggest man in Southwark? You got to go after them bleeding upper-class streaks of nothing. Just 'cos they got fancy names and places in the country. Can't leave it alone, can you?'

'All right, all right,' Siobhan screamed at him. 'So I went down Bond Street with him. That's all there was to it, I swear! I was lonely without you here. None of my friends come here to see me. They're all too scared. All I wanted was a bit of company, someone to talk to.'

'Lying bitch!' He hit her hard this time, cutting her lip.

'It's the truth, I swear it!' she cried, trying to back away from him. 'I was just out walking with him.'

'And after, eh? What happened after, when you went back to his rooms with him? Just having a cup of tea for three hours, were you?'

'No – I never – it was just... I never meant no harm.'

She twisted and struggled, trying to escape from his iron grasp, and when that failed, screamed at him to stop, then tried begging for forgiveness. But this time she had gone too far. There was no mercy in the hard eyes.

When at last he stopped beating her, the ornate

room was a shambles. Siobhan crouched in a corner, her arms curled round her head in an attempt at protection. With a last curse, he flung a vase at her and stormed out of the room.

Behind the bar at the Rum Puncheon, Alma had to keep up a cheerful face. Pulling pints, cleaning glasses, joking with the customers, Alma was the picture of a jolly barmaid. Before she had been there two weeks, Percy Goodhew, the landlord, hardly knew what he used to do without her.

'Life and soul of the place, that's what you are, Alma,' he told her.

'Job after my own heart, this is,' she responded.

What she never told him was how desperately hard it was to drag herself out of bed each day and face the world. It was only the thought that she had to get to work that got her on her feet at all. Now, far too late, she had a glimmer of understanding for how her sister had felt. It was almost as bad as a death, having her Charlie put inside. To the last he protested his innocence, saying he'd been framed. Alma believed him, but no one else did, not even the rest of the family. That really hurt, to have Gerry doubt his own brother.

He had it coming to him, Mum. Those were Gerry's words. Alma could not put them out of her mind. He was wrong, of course. She was sure he was wrong. Somebody had been out to get her Charlie. It was that crowd he went around with. How she wished he was friends with the boys in the street, the boys he went to school with, just like everyone else. She could hardly bear to think of him locked away inside Wormwood Scrubs. It wrung her heart.

So every evening she left the house with something like relief. It was far too quiet at home, even with Ellen and the two little ones about. She stayed in bed for most of the morning, but there was still the afternoon to get through and, try as she might to distract herself with chores or playing with the children, she could not get away from the space that Charlie had left. She wished that Percy would take her on for more hours, but the pub was quiet during the day and he could manage by himself then. It was only in the evenings that he needed Alma there as well.

Once there, she was all right. She had to look bright and lively, and after a while she began believing in her own act. She was happier, too, amongst the men. Women were tolerated in the pub, and even welcomed at weekends, as long as they were with their menfolk, but during the week it was a male retreat, an escape from the rigours of home. The men would come in after a hard day at work, ready to relax.

''Evening, Alma,' they would call out as they came through the door. 'Nice to see a smiling face. Blimey, I wish my old woman'd smile like that when she sees me.'

And Alma would tease them and ask after their work or their chickens or their rabbits or even their children. She had known them all for years and could home in on just the right interest.

All the gossip was chewed over in the bar. They might accuse the women of gossiping, but Alma knew that they were just as bad. They simply thought what they were doing was putting the world to rights. Alma, leaning on the bar with her magnificent bosom straining against her blouse, encouraged confidences.

'And how's the world treating you?' she asked Will, who was staring into his beer with an expression of settled gloom. 'You look like a month o' wet Sundays, you do.'

'So'd you if you had so many blooming kids.'

Alma thought he was lucky. 'Blooming kids? Get away. Lovely little darlings, your lot. Four boys and two girls! Proved y'self there all right, ain't you? Plenty of lead in your pencil.'

Predictably, Will brightened up at this. He gave a silly smile.

'Yeah, well, you could say so.'

'How's your little Billy? Better now, is he?'

The youngest of Will and Maisie's brood had been sickly from birth, but had somehow held on to life.

'No, he's poorly again. Crying and that. Came out to get away from it. And now she tells me she's having another!'

Alma's heart went out to poor Maisie, but it was no use trying to get Will to see it from her point of view. That wasn't what the men came in for. She changed the topic of conversation.

'How's your dad? I ain't seen him in here for days.'

'He's out on union business all the time now, committee meetings, that sort of thing.'

'Well, he always was keen on it, weren't he?'

'Yeah. Wants me to join him. Set his heart on it, he has. Keeps on at me all the time, how I ought to be helping the cause, and if we all pull together we'll win through. I been hearing it for years, ever since I was a nipper, but he don't seem to have won through yet. Still, I might go along with him a bit. Makes a change, like. And it gets me away from *her*.'

The way he spoke, Alma thought, anyone would suppose Maisie was one of those nagging wives and Will a poor little henpecked husband, when nothing could be further from the truth. Will always did exactly what he wanted and left Maisie to get on with it.

'Your dad'd be pleased, anyway,' she said.

A discussion of the Lions' performance last season was breaking up, and one of the Croft men came over to have the glasses refilled.

'They'll have to do a bit better than that if they want me there next winter watching 'em,' he said over his shoulder, and to Alma, 'Same again, love.'

'Them Jennings next door to you are moving, are they?' Alma asked as she pulled the pints.

'Yeah. In a poor way, they are. Going back to his missus' family. Pity. They was all right, them Jennings. Never know who you're going to get in, do you? I asked our Jimmy if him and Florrie'd take it, but he can't afford to, and anyway Florrie's got her family to look after an' all.'

'Young Florrie's doing a good job over there,' Alma said.

'You're right there. She's a nice girl, Florrie. Our Jimmy picked the right one there. But it's all change, ain't it? The Jennings and the O'Malleys both going. Best to keep the street the way it is, I always say. Don't want any bad 'uns getting in here.'

Pat and Declan O'Donaghue came in and bought pints.

'Here's two more looking like the cares of the world are on their shoulders,' Alma said.

'Been having a family meeting,' Pat confided.

'Nothing wrong, I hope?' Alma was all attention.

'No, no.'

'It's Siobhan.'

They both spoke together. Pat dug his brother sharply in the ribs.

'Hold your tongue.'

'It's all very well for you,' Declan retorted. 'My Maureen can't stand her.'

'Your family's still in touch with her, then?' Alma asked.

'Oh yeah. Family's family, when all's said and done,' Pat said.

'We ain't seen her down here since – oh well, it must've been Florrie and Jimmy's wedding.'

'That's right.'

'Bit of a problem then, is there?' Alma asked hopefully.

A full-scale O'Donaghue family meeting sounded interesting. Something must be up. But however she put the questions, Pat and Declan were saying no more. In the end she had to give up.

'We doing anything for this here coronation?' somebody asked.

'We had a rare old knees-up for the old king when he was crowned,' Alma said, smiling in reminiscence. Now *that* had been a party.

'If we was going to do something, we ought to've got it going by now,' one of the Crofts pointed out.

Somehow, there had not been the general will this time around, and nobody had come forward to get things organized. The gathering tension in the port distracted them.

'I can always get a few barrels of coronation special in. We can have a do up here,' Percy suggested.

It seemed like the best idea.

Being a weekday night, the men were on their way by half-past ten. Alma and Percy cleared the tables and swept up. Percy counted the takings. Alma watched him out of the corner of her eyes. He seemed satisfied, giving a little grunt of approval when he got to the final total.

'Not doing bad, are we?' she said. 'Work's good at the moment. Be better still come the summer, when people are on overtime. They'll all be up here spending it. Coronation'll be good for business and all.'

Percy's broad face broke into its ready grin. 'Yeah, nothing like a good celebration to bring on a thirst, eh?'

Alma smiled in response. Perhaps when custom was up, he'd take her on for more hours. It would make all the difference to her life.

He was a cheerful cove, Percy, always willing to look on the bright side. He leant on the bar counter, weighing the small bag of takings in his great beefy hand. An ex-Navy man, he had a chest as big as the barrels he heaved so effortlessly about the cellar, and an amazing art gallery of tattoos up his hairy arms. Alma often wondered if he had them over the rest of his body as well.

'Anyway, you don't have to worry, Alma old girl. I won't be giving you the push, even if things get slow. Best asset I got in this place, you are.'

Alma laughed. 'Get away with you. I bet you say that to all the barmaids.'

Percy shook his head. 'No – useless, some of 'em. What a place like this really needs is a man and his missus running it. That was how it was done before I come here, weren't it?'

There was enough of the old Alma still in her to rise to this and tease him. Percy was a bachelor who claimed to have a girl waiting for him in every port and children of every colour under the sun. Alma spun it out, unwilling to leave the warmth of the pub for the emptiness of home.

But eventually she had to put on her jacket and go out into the dark street. She tried to hold on to the jollity of the evening, going over the conversations, remembering the coronation party. She passed the two houses that were soon to be empty and wondered who would come along to take them. But try as she might, as soon as she opened her own front door the greyness swallowed her up. Even though she knew Gerry and Ellen and the nippers were in their beds in the back bedroom, it was not enough, for there right in front of her was the put-you-up that Charlie used to sleep on. She stood staring down at it. Her poor boy, locked away in a cold cell in the Scrubs. She counted the days till he would be home again.

The street sweltered in the June sunshine. It was late morning, a quiet time of day. The young women and the men had all gone off to work, the children were at school, the early-morning step-and-sill scrubbing was long over. The mothers were mostly indoors, preparing the midday dinners. Only at the Irish end was there any life. A chair-mender was sitting at the kerb, weaving a new seat for a kitchen chair out of split canes. The owner of the chair stood nearby, arms folded over her aproned stomach, seeing that it was done as she wanted it. A couple of her neighbours had come out to keep her company and a collection of toddlers and children too young for school gathered to see what sort of entertainment this might turn out to be. For a while they stood in a semicircle, solemnly staring as the dextrous fingers crossed and recrossed the gaping hole, conjuring a pattern. But it palled after a while. It was slow and tedious compared with the rag-and-bone man or the knife-grinder. A couple of them began to dabble in the bucket of water that was keeping the lengths of cane damp. The mender growled at them and the women slapped their hands. (It did not matter whose children they were. They all had the same standards when it came to bringing them up, and anyone was free to correct a neighbour's offspring as if they were her own.) The little ones were beginning to drift away, or scratch around between the cobbles for pebbles to play with, when their attention was arrested by a large van turning the corner into the street. With a whoop, the oldest ones ran off to get a better look.

The women looked up as well. Anything coming down Trinidad Street was worth checking up on, but this was quite out of the ordinary: a smartly turned-out covered van drawn by two horses, with a driver and his mate up on the box, and on the side, in large brown and gold letters on a green background, JAS. BROWN AND SONS, REMOVALS.

'Will you be looking at that, then!'

'Did you ever see the like?'

'Removals, indeed. Never seen nothing like it in my life. Not round here. Not in Trinidad Street.'

'Pony and cart's always been good enough for us.'

They stared in jealous disapproval.

'Where might that be stopping, might I ask?'

'Has to be the O'Malleys' old place.'

'I never heard it was taken. Did you?'

'Not a word. Been no one look at it, neither.'

All along the road, doors opened and curious heads poked out. By the time the van stopped outside the empty house, half the daytime inhabitants of the street were outside taking a look.

More treats were in store. Dinners were left unattended as the two men opened the rear doors and began unloading the furniture.

Young Jessica Billingham left her little brother standing on the pavement and ran back to tell her mother.

'Mum! Mum, come and look! There's things going into the house!'

Ellen wiped her hands on her apron and followed her excited daughter, rolling slightly as she walked with the bulk of the full-term baby.

'What is it, lovey? My God! Who on earth is this come to live here, Lord and Lady Muck?'

Jessica ran back to see what was going to happen next, while Ellen joined the small group of women at their end of the street. There was plenty to comment on. Out of the van came a procession of furniture; not just the essentials of life like beds and tables, but amazing things such as rolled-up carpet squares, two frilly easy chairs and a table lamp.

'I ain't never seen nothing like it since I had that cleaning job up the minister's house,' one woman said.

Alma appeared, hastily dressed, her hair all anyhow.

'I saw it from the bedroom window. Who is it? Anyone know?'

'That's what we all want to know,' Ellen said.

Tea chests were being lugged into the house now.

'Tea chests? They setting up a shop, d'you think?'

The woman who had worked for the minister aired her knowledge. 'That's what all the crocks and cutlery and stuff is in. All wrapped up in newspaper so's they won't break.'

'What, three chestsful?' Ellen asked. 'Who'd use that much?'

'Some for every day and some for best. Some just for show, like.'

An awed silence fell for fully a minute while they contemplated such riches. Ellen had no utensils of her own at the moment, not a knife or a saucepan. Everything had been pawned or sold, so that she relied on Alma's small resources. True, much of Alma's stuff had come from Gerry in the first place, but it was not the same.

'Blimey!' Alma broke out. 'A cab! A blooming

cab, in Trinidad Street!'

Of one accord, the women began to move nearer the exotic vehicle. They had to see who it was that had taken the O'Malleys' place.

The door opened and a woman stepped out – a woman all by herself, dressed in powder-blue with brown ribbon trimmings, carrying a folded parasol. A large veiled hat hid her face. The women gawped, caught between admiration and envy. Nobody in Trinidad Street looked like that. Nobody on the whole of Dog Island looked like that.

'What the flaming hell is she doing here?' Alma asked, voicing their thoughts.

Ellen knew. The veil did not fool her. The moment she saw that elegant figure, she guessed just who had come back to wreak havoc on their lives.

'It's Siobhan, that's who it is,' she said.

The others looked at her, then back at the woman talking to the removal men, and they saw at once that she was right.

'Bloody hell, we don't want her back here,' Alma said.

Ellen could not have agreed more. Memories of the last time Siobhan tried to move in rose up in her mind. That time had been disastrous. She had got rid of Siobhan at the price of ruining any chance of getting back together with Harry. But whatever it took, she could not let Siobhan back into the street. The need to chase her off boiled inside like a cauldron.

'No,' she muttered. 'I won't let her! I won't!'

Her voice rising with each word, she started forward. She reached the edge of the small crowd gathered on the pavement and began elbowing her way through.

'Get out of it!' she yelled, all the years of hatred spouting out of her. 'Bitch! Slut! We don't want the likes of you round here! Get–'

A sharp pain caught at her back, making her gasp. She faltered, arms coming protectively round her belly. Two of the Irishwomen held her up.

'What is it, dearie? Has the baby started?'

Ellen nodded.

'Best get Mrs O'Donaghue.'

'No!' The last person she wanted was Mrs O'Donaghue. She strained to see between the bobbing heads. Siobhan had gone into the house. Tears of frustration stung her eyes. She looked desperately at the people around her. They were happily craning their necks to see what else might be coming out of the wonderful van. There was a buzz of comment all around her. They had not had such a good free show for months.

'Do you want her back here in the street? *Siobhan O'Donaghue*. Do you?' she asked.

The women shrugged.

Ellen gave a yelp. She was shaking with anger. It might have been a long time ago, but she had not forgotten Florrie's wedding being ruined, or Will being led astray and Maisie being made unhappy. But most of all she had not forgotten that dreadful afternoon when she found Siobhan with Harry. The very thought of it brought on another contraction. She ignored the warning twinge.

'She's nothing but trouble. You all know that!' There was something of a reaction to that.

'What's she want to come back here for, anyway?' Ellen pressed on.

Someone turned round. It was one of the O'Donaghues.

'She's family. Families should be together.' It was said with such finality that heads started nodding all round. It was true. Families should be together. Everyone knew that.

Ellen refused to be beaten and tried to make her way through the crowd. But there were too many people. She was too big and clumsy. They were all firmly planted, watching the men as they closed the van doors, peering unashamedly in at the windows.

'Let me through, let me through!'

An arm went round her shoulders. It was her mother.

'Ellen, Ellen, love. Leave it be.'

'Oh, Mum!'

Something inside her gave. She felt it. And then there was a warm trickle of water down her legs. She just stood there, aghast. It had not happened like this before, not in the street. Martha pulled gently at her.

'Come away, lovey.'

All the fight went out of her. There were more important things to do now. Obediently she turned and stumbled back to Alma's house, while Harry's baby made its first tentative movements towards the world outside.

He never realized it would affect him so deeply, his son, gazing back at him with a fierce un-focused stare. Harry reached out and put a work-hardened finger into the baby's soft palm. The tight grip surprised him. He pulled gently, and the baby hung on. His son, refusing to let him go. He was choked with an overwhelming mix of tenderness, anger and loss.

'Little cracker, ain't he?' Gerry said. He was bubbling with pride. 'Bigger'n our other two by far. Right little bruiser. Poor old Ellen. He come out so fast, I didn't know he was on his way till he arrived. Went out in the morning and he was inside, come back teatime and he was already an hour old. Really caught us on the hop.'

'It was easy,' Ellen said. She did not look at either man. Her eyes were only for her new son.

Harry swallowed. He desperately needed to know what they were calling the baby. If he was named for Gerry he could not bear it. He tried to speak, but the question seemed to stick in his throat.

'She's a brave girl, ain't she?' Gerry chattered on, unheeding. 'Never one to complain, my Ellen. That's how we came to agree on the name, weren't it, love? She wanted him to be Thomas, for her dad. My mum, she said it ought to be Gerald. But I said, if Ellen wants Thomas, then that's it. What my Ellen wants, she gets. And like I said to my mum, we named Teddy for my dad, it's only right Ellen's family should get a look in.'

Some of the tension inside him gave way. Thomas was all right. He could just about live with that. And Tom Johnson was a good bloke.

'Takes after Ellen's side. Don't look like me. My mum said, he ain't no Billingham...'

At last, Ellen looked up. For a brief moment,

their eyes met. A hot tide of blood reddened her cheeks and she looked away again, but in that moment they silently acknowledged the truth. The baby was neither Johnson nor Billingham. He looked just like his father.

Gerry had stopped talking. Harry realized he had to say something. 'He – er – he's a strapping little chap. Credit to his mum.' He stopped, gripped with an urge to hold the little scrap of life in his arms. He had seen new-born babies many a time before but had always shied away from any contact with them. They frightened him; he didn't know what to do with them. But this was different. This was his own flesh and blood. He wanted somehow to make contact with him, let the boy know that he cared. Instead, he thrust his fists into his pockets.

'Florrie said she's coming over later, to see how you are,' he said.

'Thanks,' Ellen responded.

There was so much he wanted to say to her, but there was no chance.

'I'm off, then,' he said, biting back the urge to lecture Gerry on taking good care of Ellen and the baby. He had no right, no right at all beyond that of a friend and neighbour.

He hardly knew where he was going until he reached the Rum Puncheon, and did not hear Alma's cheery greeting. He ordered a pint and drank half of it at one pull. It settled comfortingly in his stomach. The other half rapidly followed. He ordered another, ignoring Alma's comments, and drank that more slowly, hoping for the beginning of a pleasant dulling of the senses. No such luck. By the end of a third pint, his mind was still functioning with full clarity and the hopelessness of his situation was unchanged. Not for the first time, he wondered if it would be better if he went away. There were always jobs going on the deep-sea ships. He could travel to foreign parts, see the world, be away for months at a time. His family could cope without him now that Florrie was married and she and Jimmy could keep an eye on the younger ones, and he would not have to see Gerry bringing up his son.

'...Not with us at all.'

'No, he's in a world of his own.'

He became aware that he was being talked about. A group of men from the street, Crofts and O'Donaghues, were gathered round Tom and Will Johnson. They were looking at him and grinning.

'What's up, Harry boy? Look as if you lost a bob and found a tanner.'

'Nothing.'

'Nothing, eh? Then come and join us and stop looking like a dying duck in a thunderstorm.' This was from Jimmy Croft.

'Yeah, come on, Harry. We need men like you,' Tom Johnson said.

Harry sighed and shifted over to join them.

The subject under discussion, as always when Tom was around, was the situation in the docks. Tom laid a hand on Harry's shoulder.

'Now, you're in the Lightermen's Union, ain't you? So you're one of us now. We're all in the Federation. And that includes the sailors.'

'And the sailors are on strike,' Harry said, trying hard to appear to be on the ball.

'Too true they are, Harry. And in Hull and Manchester and Liverpool the dockers are out in sympathy. The question is, do we come out an' all?'

'What I want to know is, why should we come out for the sailors? When did they ever do anything for us?' Brian O'Donaghue asked.

'That's the whole point of the Federation,' Tom explained patiently. 'We all look after each other. We come out for them. When the gov'nors throw out our claim for eightpence and a shilling, which they surely will, the rest of the unions in the Federation stick by us. Like your lot.' Tom turned to Harry. 'Your lot are putting in a claim for better working conditions, ain't you? We stick by you in that. That way, we got 'em where we want 'em.'

'You'll never get the gov'nors where you want 'em,' one of the Crofts said.

'We will this time,' Tom insisted. 'This time, if we strike, they can't get blacklegs in. You noticed how it is at the call-on stands these days? No fighting for jobs, is there? It's only us regulars there, the proper dockers. You can work as much as you like. They need us. Same as they need Harry's lot. You can't replace a freeman waterman. Ain't a job you can just pick up. Without us, they're stuck. They can't function.' He put his hands in front of him and closed his fists in a grasping motion. 'We got real power in our own hands. We just got to have the courage to use it.'

Harry was listening with growing interest. He had heard Tom speaking on and off for most of his life and he never took a great deal of notice. Tom's dreams of a better life for the working man seemed to him to be just that – dreams. But now it looked as if they really could get somewhere.

'So what can we do about it?' Harry asked.

'Get as many joined to the union as you can,' Tom told him. 'Will and me, we got everyone we know, and we go and talk to men on other quays. The more we got, the better we can act when the time comes. You can do the same amongst the lightermen. They'll listen to you, Harry. They respect you, and you got a tongue in your head; you can persuade people. If enough of us band together, they'll know they got to listen to us when we put in for our rightful claims.'

The more Tom said, the more it appealed to Harry. It was a clear-cut issue with the spice of risk and a good deal to win. What was more, it was a fight with a well-defined enemy – the employers – and he needed a fight, an outlet for all the anger and frustration within him.

'What d'you say, eh, Harry boy?' Tom asked. 'You with us?'

'I'm with you,' Harry agreed.

The women viewed the progress of the dispute apprehensively. They knew what happened when strikes really took hold: hunger far beyond the usual run set in, household goods were sold or pawned until there was nothing left, credit at the corner shop grew so long that it took years to pay it off, and children became ill and the weakest died. They did not want to go through all that again. It was bad enough having to cope with the heatwave, with food going off almost before they carried it home, and all the consequent sickness and diarrhoea.

An ultimatum was sent to the employers, and some of the men at the Surrey docks and some of the grain trimmers walked out. The Port of London Authority promised a conference of employers to consider all the outstanding claims. The men accepted this and carried on working, while the unions ran an increasingly successful recruiting campaign. Men like Tom Johnson found that at last they were speaking to receptive ears, while the rival Stevedores Society decided to abandon its old skilled craft status and let in anyone involved in the handling of port cargo. Throughout July, while the leaders and the employers were locked in negotiations over recognition and a port rate for all men employed in the London docks, the men who did the work began to see the sense in uniting.

Late on the twenty-seventh of July an agreement was at last arrived at. Tom Johnson, who had been waiting together with Will and some others to hear the result, came home to find Martha, Maisie and Ellen all sitting round the kitchen table waiting for him. He and Will clumped into the little house, and the women could tell from the first glance that all was not well.

Martha took the simmering kettle off the hob and made tea. Ellen looked at her father's grim face.

'What happened, Dad? They throw it out?'

Tom sat down with a deep sigh. He rested his elbows on the table and ran both hands over his head.

'Worse,' he said. 'Worse than that, girl. They give in to 'em. Accepted sevenpence and ninepence, with the possibility of eightpence and a shilling for those who are already getting the seven and nine. That and an hour off the working day. We're to start at seven in the morning now, not six. Bloody useless! No port rate, and not a word about union recognition. Just taken the scraps what the gov'nors threw at 'em and touched their caps and said "Thank you kindly, sirs". Makes me sick.'

Martha plumped cups of steaming tea in front of the men. She and Maisie exchanged glances. Sevenpence and ninepence didn't sound too bad to her. Taken over a good week's work, that would make another four or five shillings. It was a whole lot more than nothing. But she knew better than to say so to her husband.

'Going to be a mass meeting tomorrow to ratify it,' Will said.

'I'll tell you something, I'm not voting for it,' Tom said. 'I been a supporter of Ben Tillett these twenty years, but I'm not behind him now. He can tell me to accept these terms till he's blue in the face but I'm having none of it. And I tell you something else, the men ain't going to take it, neither. Will and me've been working away getting new members in, ain't we, Will? We been telling 'em the leaders are going to get eightpence and a shilling for 'em, we been taking their shilling entrance fees off of them and promising 'em it's going to be worth their while. What are they going to say to this?'

'Going to tell 'em where to put it,' Will said succinctly.

'Right. Too true they are. You know what I

603

think, Will? I think we got to get everyone up that meeting tomorrow – everyone we know what's in dock work, all the street, all the blokes what we work with, everyone. And we got to tell Tillett and Gosling what we think of their agreement. They can take it right back to Lord bloody Davenport and start talking fast, or we're all coming out. We waited long enough.'

'But it's Friday tomorrow,' Maisie said, her first contribution to the discussion.

Will groaned dramatically. 'We know it's Friday tomorrow. You don't think we're going to run along to work like good little children, do you? What'd the gov'nors think then? We got to show 'em we mean business. I'm with Dad. I think we ought to get the whole street up there. Them union leaders got to see we ain't going to take it lying down this time. No point in being in a union it they can't get a good deal for us.'

Maisie looked crushed.

'If you do come out on strike, how long is it going to last?' Ellen asked, speaking for all three women.

'As long as it takes,' Tom told her.

Martha's mouth tightened. 'It ain't so bad for us, we ain't got no little 'uns at home no more. But it's hard for them with young families. I remember last time, when the union had to set up food stations – cup of cocoa and a doorstep of bread for the kids before they went to school. Had to see them right through till the next day, that did.'

'But we won in the end, didn't we?' Tom pointed out. 'We got the docker's tanner. This time we're going to get eightpence and a bob.

God knows, it ain't a blooming fortune. You'd think we was asking for life's blood. Eightpence for an hour's hard labour! They're lucky we're only asking that. We deserve more.'

'Of course you do,' Ellen said. She turned to her mother and Maisie. 'One thing, at least it's summer. I always think the worse part of being really on your uppers is being cold. It eats into your bones.'

'It's all right for you to talk. Your Gerry's not in dock work,' Maisie pointed out.

'Let's hope it don't last till winter, then,' Martha said.

'It won't,' Tom told her.

The mood was the same throughout the docks. The men had had enough. They had waited twenty years for a pay rise and they had been persuaded to join one union or another on the promise of twopence an hour more. The mass meeting threw the provisional agreement out and sent the Federation leaders back to try again. The men from Trinidad Street came home in fighting mood, and went up to the Rum Puncheon for a rowdy celebration of their daring in challenging both the employers and their own leaders. The next day the coal porters, who had not been covered by the agreement, started to come out on strike, while the lightermen, who had been trying to negotiate a ten-hour day, threw out the compromise that their leaders had come to.

All through a hot and sultry Sunday, Trinidad Street was buzzing with rumour. The men gathered in little knots, exchanging what they knew of how friends and relations were acting in different sections of the docks and reaffirming their determination to see it through this time. The women stayed on the doorsteps, their arms folded over their stomachs, and muttered amongst themselves. They could feel the tide of battle rising. Even the grandmothers, matriarchs of the clans, did not try to speak out against the coming action. They knew when to bow to the inevitable. The children, picking up the excitement and aggression in the air, marched up and down the street, chanting and waving makeshift flags.

Alma, coming back in the early evening from the long weary journey over to visit Charlie at the Scrubs, could not face them all. She just wanted to hide herself away. But the place was full of Gerry and Ellen and the children, and, anyway, to get there she had to pass all the people out in the street. What she had learnt today was so shaming she felt she could never hold her head up in front of her neighbours again. She hesitated on the corner, looking at the Rum Puncheon. Percy was expecting her in. Teatime was already past and the men were gathering for the evening. He would be needing her behind the bar. Weary and sick at heart, she went round the back way.

As luck would have it, Percy was out there fetching some glasses.

'Ah, there y'are, Alma. Going to be busy tonight, I reckon. Get that hat off and–' Then he noticed the expression on her face and stopped short. He put down the glasses and came over to her. 'Here, what's up, girl? What's happened? Didn't they let you see him?'

Alma shook her head. 'No, it's not that. It's–' A great sob gathered in her throat. She tried to stop it, but it kept coming up. 'Oh, Percy...' And then Percy's big arms were round her and she was crying her heart out on his shoulder. He patted her back and begged her not to cry. When at last she did subside into hiccups, he brought her a whisky and sat her down, ignoring the demands for service coming from the bar.

'Now then, girl, what's the matter, eh? Tell old Perce about it.'

Alma shook her head. 'I can't.'

'Not in solitary, is he? Not been got at?'

'No – no.'

'Been given extra time?'

'No.'

'Sick, then? Is he ill?'

Reluctantly, Alma nodded. Fresh tears welled up. 'Oh, Percy, I'm so ashamed. That a boy of mine...' Words failed her.

'Ashamed? What d'you mean, ashamed? Everyone gets sick sometimes. Even me. Nothing to get into such a state about. Except – oh.' Light dawned. Percy bit his lip. It was a difficult one to ask tactfully. 'He – er – he got something nasty, has he?'

Alma nodded.

'And it's not cancer or TB or nothing like that?'

A shake of the head.

'Ah – so he's got...?'

A nod. Alma pressed her hands to her trembling lips. 'It's horrible. So – so dirty.'

Percy looked disapproving. 'He didn't ought to have told you. You don't go telling your mum that

607

sort of thing. He should've known it'd upset you. Blimey, if I'd had a dose of the clap, I wouldn't've told my mum. Would have broke her heart, it would. That's where a little white lie comes in.' Percy was incensed. He patted Alma's hand. 'But look, it ain't the end of the world, you know. I mean, they got treatment for it, so long as it ain't got too far. When I was at sea, I knew lots of blokes got it. Mind you, one sort's worse than the other. Depends what he's got. But he'll be all right, you'll see.'

'But the treatment. I mean, that's horrible too.'

There was nothing Percy could honestly say to that.

'To think he must of gone with some horrible dirty prostitute. My boy!'

Percy refilled her glass. 'Now, you drink this up, then you go upstairs and have a bit of a lie-down. Then when you're feeling better, you get yourself ready and come on down. But not till you're up to it, mind. I can look after that lot in the bar till then.'

'But it's busy in there this evening. You'll be run off your feet,' Alma tried to protest.

'But nothing. You're all in. I'll manage all right. You just go upstairs and have a rest.'

Gratefully, Alma complied. The last thing she really wanted to do was to go in and be cheerful to the drinkers.

'You're a real pal, Percy,' she said.

Percy gave her shoulder a squeeze. 'It ain't nothing.'

She heaved herself wearily up the narrow stairs. On the dark landing at the top she hesitated. She had never been up here before. It was Percy's private quarters. Feeling as if she was intruding, she opened the doors and peeped into the rooms. There was a neat parlour with a couple of nice easy chairs by the empty grate, then a bare kitchen that looked as if it was hardly used, a tiny spare room piled with boxes and trunks, and the bedroom, Percy's bedroom, with a huge mahogany wardrobe, a marble-topped washstand and an iron bedstead. The curtains were drawn, making an inviting twilight. Alma hovered indecisively in the doorway. He had said to have a lie-down and, God knew, she needed it. Sitting in one of the easy chairs would not be the same. But it did not seem right to go and use his bed. She leant on the doorframe, her head throbbing. From down below a buzz of talk floated up with the smell of beer and Woodbines. Percy would be far too busy to come up and check on her. She tottered across the room and flopped down on top of the green cotton cover.

The room spun round her. The day's events kept popping up in her mind in jagged fragments. The long journey with its changes of bus and tram. The grim exterior of the Scrubs. The clanging doors and distinctive prison smell. And Charlie, always Charlie, small and pathetic in his ugly uniform, sobbing his horror and fury at the loathsome disease he had contracted. She lay on her back, too tired to move a muscle, and stared up at the cracks in the whitewashed ceiling, while Charlie's face danced before her. It was all very well Percy saying there was a cure, but she was gripped with the dreadful uncertainty that she was never going to see him again.

Gradually through the nightmare she became aware of the scent of the room, that comforting male smell of sweat and pipe smoke with a faint whiff of coal-tar soap. It wrapped round her, soothing her. The bed beneath her was soft and comfortable. It was as if Percy's strong arms were holding her. It was so long since she had had a man of her own. There had been nobody since poor Ernie died. The taunting images began to fade, the headache receded, and before she realized it, Alma was drifting into a deep and healing sleep.

3

Will leant forward to catch what his father was trying to say.

'You got to tell 'em, son.' Tom's voice was a painful croak. Just when he needed it most, he had gone down with a bout of laryngitis.

'Me?' Will was alarmed. 'I can't do it.'

'You got to, son. You got to get 'em to act as one. It's vital. Life or death.'

'But what'll I say?'

Tom closed his eyes briefly in exasperation. 'You know. You heard me often enough. You can do it, I know you can. You're my son. Don't let me down.'

Guilt wormed uneasily through his guts. Will had let his father down often enough. He knew he was a disappointment to him. Even now, he would much rather make an excuse and slope off to the easy camaraderie of the pub. It was all right talking to his mates about joining the union and the need to fight, but standing up in front of a whole crowd and making a speech, that was quite different. He was afraid of failing in front of them.

'But,' he began.

'Bloody hell!' His father's face was scarlet with exasperation. 'It ain't as if they don't want to listen. They do. They want to know what to do, they want to be given a lead. That's all they need, boy. Just tell 'em what they can do to make their voices heard. A child could do it. Your sisters could do it. Ellen, she'd tell 'em, or Daisy. They'd know what to say.'

Shamed and angry, Will straightened his back. Pretending a confidence he didn't feel, he gave his father a slap on the shoulder.

'Don't worry, Dad. I'll get 'em going.'

It was the end of a long hot Wednesday, with the stink of summer hanging over the whole West India docks. The men on the quay were caked in sweat and sticky from the raw sugar they had been unloading, and set upon by swarms of flies. All day rumours had been going round the docks. At last Tom had received some firm news.

Will got up on a handy box while his father banged a length of iron against the leg of a crane to gain attention. The men gathered round. The apathy of years had flown. They were all in a state of unrest, ready to stand and fight if they were just given the chance. All the same, as he looked down at the upturned, waiting faces, Will's uncertain resolve quailed. They all expected inspiration and leadership from him, things he felt he couldn't give. He'd seen his father turn rabbles into armies. He had heard the great orators on Tower Hill, Ben Tillett and Tom Mann, putting into words what the men felt, then turn that gut feeling into firm resolve. But he knew in his own heart that he was not the man they were. He was only an ordinary working man, like those gathered round him. He had no right to set himself up like this.

Just behind him, his father was making a painful effort to project the remnants of his voice and get him started.

'Friends, a great fight has started,' he managed to prompt.

Will cleared his throat. 'Friends, a great fight has started,' he repeated.

The buzz of talking died down. All those nearby were listening. Those further off were elbowing each other to be quiet. What next? What did he say now? There was no help from his father. To make it worse, he saw a couple of foremen making their way over, ready to break the meeting up. One of them, he realized, was Alf Grant.

'You know what's been going on these last few days,' he said. A growl of agreement went round. They were an easy audience, but Will knew he had not quite struck the right note. His father wouldn't have put it like that. What was more, if he did not get them all going quickly, Grant and his mate were going to stop him before he started. He tried again.

'We're all in together on this, friends. We been waiting long enough!'

That was it. There were shouts of 'Yeah' and 'Too right, mate'.

Charged with the mood of assent, his mind was starting to function. His father always began by saying what the men already knew and agreed on.

'The gov'nors and the leaders wanted us to accept sevenpence and ninepence. But what did we do? We told 'em to go back and think again!'

More shouts, and even one or two cheers. To his own amazement, Will found he was beginning to enjoy himself. The crowd round him was growing, with men coming in from other quays. He pitched his voice to be heard right to the back of the gathering. Hours of listening to speeches came to his aid. He spoke slowly so that each word could be appreciated, and paused between sentences.

'Now, you probably heard already about the coalies. They weren't in on this agreement in the first place. They started coming out Saturday for more pay. Monday there was over a thousand of 'em on strike. Yesterday the dockers been coming out in the Royals and the Surreys and today there's more of them stopped away. But friends, do you know what our leaders said to 'em, Orbell and Tillett and Gosling? They said, "You men got to go back to work." And do you know what our brothers in the Royals and the Surreys said?'

He paused and looked round. Alf Grant was still there, but he was staying at the edge of the crowd, his arms folded across his chest, silent.

'Stuff going back to work!' came a voice from the crowd.

'Yeah, we want our eightpence a bleeding hour!'

The rumble of agreement swelled. They were all with him, but Will could feel the initiative slipping away. He had to shout louder to get them back again.

'That's right, that's just what they said. And friends, you got a chance to say the same.'

Now they were listening again. He felt a huge exhilaration. He had them. They were hanging on every word. He cast his eyes over them, pulling them in. He spoke with clear emphasis.

'Do you know what else Ben Tillett said, friends? He said it was the dockers' own fault if they couldn't get more than a rotten penny an hour more. Those were his very words. Our own fault! Because he don't believe that we're ready to back him. He don't believe we're ready to come out on strike and demand our rights. Tell me, friends, are *you* ready?'

All around him a great shout of assent went up. It raced through Will's blood like strong liquor. He spread out his arms to quieten them down. Now was the moment.

'Then you got to show him. Show Ben Tillett what you're made of. This very evening, there's a meeting at West Ham, a meeting for every docker in the union. This is your chance, friends. This is when you can say what you think. You got a right to tell 'em, and got to use that right. The gov'nors ain't going to give way on this, friends. We got to show 'em we mean business. We got to show 'em this evening. I'm going to West Ham. My dad here's going. What about you, brothers? Are you going to have your say?'

There was a roar. They were with him, every

one. Will was borne up by it, the concerted power of all these men. He felt ten feet tall. He was a giant. He could fly. He waved his clenched fists in the air.

'*Eight* pence! *Eight* pence!' he yelled above the shouting.

Out of the corner of his eye, he spotted Alf Grant and the other foreman disappearing into the safety of a transit shed.

The men took up his chant. Will jumped down off the box and the men parted to let him through. With his father at his shoulder, he strode towards the gates. The men fell in after him, still chanting, and they all marched out of the docks, the leader and his army. Will had at last found something to fill the hole Siobhan had left in his life.

'You should've seen it. It was wonderful, flaming wonderful. You ever been to Trafalgar Square, girl?'

'Once,' Ellen said.

It had been with Harry, on a cold winter's evening almost unimaginable in today's stunning heat. She remembered the lights reflecting in the waters of the fountains, and the great lions, and the way she and Harry had laughed at the pigeons landing on the head of a woman foolish enough to encourage them with seed.

'...As far as you can see,' her father was saying. Ellen dragged her attention back to the present. This was important, what her father was telling them. He and the other men had just come back from a mass rally in the square.

'Hundreds and hundreds of men – dockers,

615

lightermen, stevedores, carmen, tugmen, sailing bargemen, ship repairers, coalies, deal porters – every trade you can think of what works in the port. They was all there. And the banners – you'd've liked the banners, all bright colours and silk embroidery. Beautiful. And the bands. I tell you, it brought a lump to my throat, it did, seeing us all there. We are the people, you know. We're what England's all about, not the King, nor the bloody government, nor the Army. It's us, the working people. We are something. And do you know, I think a lot of us knew that today. We knew we counted.'

Ellen nodded. She understood what her father meant.

Martha said nothing. Ellen guessed that she just wanted to hear the outcome of the meeting. But her father was too full of the day's events to give it away. Flushed with heat and triumph, he was spinning the tale out, savouring every moment as he relived it.

'We got 'em on the run now. Sir Albert Rollit, him what was arbitrating for the men working on the overseas ships, he decided for us. Said we should be paid eightpence and a shilling. You should've heard the cheering! Rang round the square, it did. I reckon they could've heard it at Buckingham Palace.'

'So you got it, then? Got what you was asking for?' Martha said. The men would be going back to work in that case, and the worry about rent and food would be over.

'Ah no, not all of us. Just the men on the overseas trade. Clever, see? Keeping us divided, hoping we'll fall out and squabble amongst ourselves.'

'No port rate, then?' Ellen said.

'That's it, girl, no port rate, and not a word about union recognition, neither. And nothing for the coalies or the lightermen. So do you know what happened?'

Both women shook their heads. There was no stopping Tom now. They were required to be a sympathetic audience.

'Harry Gosling, he tells us as how this is a test case for the Federation, how the gov'nors'll be expecting us to take what's offered and go back to work. He says we got to stick together and support each other until the job is finished.'

'Just what you been saying,' Ellen commented.

'That's right. And all them men, from all them trades, including the ones what have been granted the eightpence and a shilling, they all agreed with him. When it was put to the show of hands, they all voted to stay out until everyone's got what they are rightfully due. It was a wonderful moment. I don't think I'll ever forget it. I was so proud of 'em. All them hands so straight and determined, all them men willing to stay out till we won the day. I could've cried, honest to God I could. This is a turning point, just you wait and see; a turning point in the history of the docks. The men have found the way to make themselves heard at last.'

When Ellen left a little later to see if Gerry had arrived home, she found that the whole street was buzzing with the news. Nearly all the men who were employed in dock work had been to the meeting, and the women had been awaiting word of the outcome. Now they were gathered in small groups, chewing it over.

It was another sweltering day, and what with that and the uncertainty over the strike, tempers were getting short. It gave Ellen an uneasy feeling, walking the short stretch of pavement to Alma's house. At her parents' place, she was at one with the strikers; it was her family right in the heart of it. But once she went back to Alma's it was not the same. Gerry was unaffected by the stoppage, as plenty of his customers worked in the myriad manufacturing trades of the East End, and Alma's job at the Rum Puncheon was still going, despite the fact that the men no longer had drinking money. For the time being, it was going on the slate, and the temperature and the idle hours made for good custom. Ellen had the impression that people fell silent as she passed and that the eyes following her were not altogether friendly. She pretended she had not noticed. She nodded and spoke to people as she went by, refusing to believe that those she had been brought up with would turn against her just because she was not directly affected by the strike. All the same, she was quite relieved to reach the safety of the house and put the front door between herself and the street.

Later on in the day, an amazing piece of news reached them. All over the docklands, the women were coming out on strike and marching round the streets encouraging others to join them. In Millwall, the workers were leaving the great food-processing factories and demanding a better

618

hourly rate. Most exciting of all, at Maconochie's the ringleader was said to be Daisy.

The whole street turned out to welcome the girls home. Tired and sweaty but euphoric, they arrived back, still headed by the triumphant Daisy. Ellen fell on her sister and hugged her.

'I always said you'd make a union leader.'

Tom patted her on the back. 'You done wonderful, girl. Wonderful! I'm that proud of you.'

Basking in the glory, they all went to Ellen's for tea, since she was the only one who still had food on the table.

Gerry returned home to find a full house.

'Mum gone?' he asked, seeing nothing but various Johnsons.

'Yeah, she went in early. Percy's busy up the Puncheon today, what with the girls coming out and all. Chalk on that slate's going to be a mile long at this rate,' Ellen said.

'He won't have no beer to sell soon. They're saying up the market the breweries have only got three more days' hops and four days' coal.'

This really did silence them for a moment.

'Blimey,' Wilf Hodges said at last. 'We thought we'd run short of food, but we never thought we'd run out of beer.'

'Food's getting blooming ridiculous,' Ellen said. 'There's hardly anything up the West Ferry Road, not fresh stuff, and what there is is a dreadful price.'

'You shouldn't buy nothing what's more expensive than usual, girl,' her father told her. 'That's profiteering, that is. Making money out of the working man just because there's shortages.

Shopkeepers ought to be shot for lining their own pockets at a time like this.'

He turned to Gerry. 'What's it like up in Poplar now the carmen are out, eh? Made a difference, I'll be bound.'

'Made life blooming impossible, that's what,' Gerry said gloomily. Though he did not dare say so in front of his father-in-law, he thoroughly disapproved of the strikes. They interrupted trade something dreadful.

'Good, good. I knew it would. Do you know how many men are out now? Sixty thousand! Sixty thousand men all refusing to work.'

'River's at a standstill,' Jack said. 'I went down and had a look this morning. Not a ship nor a barge nor hardly a skiff moving. I never seen nothing like it.'

'Don't forget the women an' all,' Daisy put in.

'I ain't forgetting, girl. That was real brave of you, that was. We're all proud of you.'

'They say there's troops standing by,' Gerry said.

'What? Who says?'

'Up the market, they're saying it. Soldiers, supplies and forty army motor lorries, all ready and waiting to drive into the East End and go down the docks.'

'I tell you something, they won't get past us. We'll stand up to 'em.'

'Oh, Tom.' Martha was moved to protest at last. 'Oh, Tom, you won't go facing soldiers, will you? Not that. Leave that to–' She stopped herself just in time, but they all knew what she meant to say – *leave it to the younger men.*

620

'If a job's got to be done, it's got to be done.'

'What do they need to send the Army in for, anyway?' Ellen asked. 'London's starving, girl. You said it y'self. Ain't nothing fresh in the shops. And the stuff in the docks is stinking to high heaven. Ain't you smelt it, all the stuff left in the sheds and on the ships? Rotting away in this weather, it is.' Tom spoke with relish. 'We might not have no money left, but London's got no food and no coal and the carmen are fighting on every corner.'

'You're telling me,' Gerry said. 'You should see 'em. Anyone comes along in any sort of cart, a dray or a flatcart or a van, the strikers jump up and drag the driver off and cut the traces.'

'Hooray!' cried Daisy. 'That's the stuff!'

Teddy and Jess joined in, cheering and clapping, and the rest of the family laughed. They were all in it now, and they were going to win. Only Gerry remained silent.

It was not until all the Johnsons went off home that he ventured to say anything.

'I don't think your dad and his mates know just what they're doing,' he told Ellen.

'Of course they do,' Ellen said, loyal to the last.

'You ain't seen them carmen at work,' Gerry went on. 'Blooming madmen, they are. Won't let a thing through. If this goes on much longer, I'm not going to have anything left in the lock-up to sell.'

'Dad says it'll be over soon,' Ellen told him.

'Yeah, but what does he mean by soon? There's this bloke told me of this load of stuff going begging over Stepney. Nice stuff, he said – chinaware, tea sets, just what I need. But it's no

621

use if I can't get it back to the lock-up. Someone else'll get it and that'll be a good bargain lost. God knows, I can't afford to miss a good bargain. In fact, I got a mind to go over there with a pony and cart and fetch it myself.'

'Oh, Gerry!' Ellen thought of the tense atmosphere in the street, the looks she had been getting, how she brought in through the back way what little food she could buy. 'Don't you go saying nothing like that out there. They're all of them right behind this strike. They'll have your guts for garters.'

'Them out there? It weren't them I was thinking about. It's them flaming carmen.'

'Is it worth the risk, Gerry, just to get a bit of stock?'

Gerry looked at her as if she had spoken heresy. 'But it's a bargain, love!'

She sighed. It was no use even trying to deflect him when he was in pursuit of a fast penny.

'You just be careful,' she said. 'And keep your mouth shut about it round here an' all.'

'Don't worry, love. They'll get the troops in soon and things'll soon go back to normal. We'll be all right, you and me and the kiddies.'

But that was what worried Ellen. Heaven knows, she and Gerry had had their hard times, but at last their debts were paid off and they would be all right. But the rest of the street would suffer. And that caused jealousy and resentment. Of course, she did what she could to help, slipping half-loaves and saucers of marge and twists of tea to worried mothers with young families to feed, but it was difficult when nearly the whole street was going short. She could not perform miracles. She took a look outside before she went to bed. People were still out there, even in the dark. It was still hot and nobody had to go to work the next day. To her overwrought imagination, it seemed that they were talking about her family.

The next day Maisie arrived at Ellen's, trailing children, with little Billy wailing feebly in her arms. Ellen sent the older ones out to play in the street and made a cup of tea, generously sugared. Maisie drank thankfully.

'Oo, that's lovely, that is. We run out of tea two days ago.'

An appalling smell rose from the baby.

'He got the runs?' Ellen asked.

Maisie sighed. 'Yeah. I'm out of things to put him in. Can't get the washing proper clean with no hot water. Poor little soul.'

Ellen rummaged around in the laundry pile and produced some baby clothes.

'Here, they ain't ironed yet, but they are clean. I'll get you some water to wash him in.'

Between them, they cleaned up the baby.

Only his mother, Ellen decided, could think that Billy was lovable. He was a scrawny-looking little thing at the best of times, always poorly. Just at the moment, stinking to high heaven, he was really quite revolting. She dropped the soiled clothes into a bucket and put them outside the door.

'I'll boil those up for you later, if you like,' she offered.

'Oh, would you, Ellen? I'd be ever so grateful.'

They were interrupted by Jessica coming into the house in tears. Teddy was trailing behind her.

623

'What's the matter, pet?' Ellen took her daughter in her arms.

'They w-won't p-play with me.'

'They won't? Why not?' But she knew the answer before it came.

''Cos my dad's not on strike.'

Anger filled Ellen's heart. They could cut her if they liked – she didn't care. But she was not having her children upset. She stood up.

'We'll see about that,' she said.

She marched to the front door and wrenched it open, ignoring Maisie's entreaty to leave off. The glare outside made her blink and the heat coming off the brickwork was like an oven. She could practically feel the doorstep burning up through her boots. Everyone was over the other side of the road, using what shade there was.

'Who said it to you?' she asked Jessica.

The child pointed.

Assorted young children were sitting on the kerb, staring at her. Behind them was ranged a group of mothers, including the woman who had moved into her old home. She had managed to give something to all of them in the last few days – not much, but enough to tide them over one more meal. But they stood, arms folded across their stomachs, shoulders leant against the wall, ignoring her. Ellen could not believe this was happening. These people had always been her friends and neighbours. They had all been through so much together. She walked across the street.

'What's all this about my Jessica not being allowed to play because her dad's not on strike?' she asked loudly.

Each of the five women shifted a little and stood more upright or moved her arms or tightened her expression.

'Ain't no lie in that.'

''S all right for some, with money still coming in.'

'Rest of us are in it together.'

Uneasy on her mind was the fact that Gerry had been blacklegging, fetching goods on a cart while the carmen were on strike. It made her all the fiercer.

'Bloody hell! If my Gerry was a docker or a lighterman, he'd be out. What do you expect him to do, shut up the stall?'

'Some might do that, if they was really neighbourly.'

'Yeah, but she always did set herself up, didn't she? Went to the Central when all the rest of us was out to work.'

'Yeah, didn't marry a decent working man. Waited till she could get Gerry Billingham. Him with his stalls and his shop and all his fancy ideas.'

'Jealous, that's what you are,' Ellen accused.

She became aware of someone standing beside her.

'You just lay off!' Florrie cried. 'Ellen's got her troubles. No call to go picking on her just 'cos her old man's not in dock work.'

Eager for entertainment, people were gathering round. There was nothing like a good row to spice up the day. If it developed into a fight, so much the better.

'That's right, girl, you tell 'em,' a male voice encouraged.

'Give it what for!'

Daisy came marching up, belligerence in every line of her body. 'Who's getting at my sister?' she demanded. 'No one gets at my sister. You lot of old witches better pipe down.'

Some backed down a little before the heroine of the Maconochie's walk-out. But not all of them.

''S all right for them without kids and all. Don't have to worry then, do you?'

Daisy went white. Her marriage to Wilf Hodges had not yet produced any children. This time it was Ellen who flew to her defence.

'That's a wicked cruel thing to say! You just take that back.'

'Yeah, take it back,' Florrie echoed.

The menfolk began to line up with their women. Jimmy appeared at Florrie's side, Wilf draped an arm round Daisy.

'You take no notice of 'em, girl.'

Ellen felt raw and undefended. Gerry, of course, was at work. And even if he had been there, he would not have been much use. He never had been any use in fights.

'What's all this flaming fuss about, then?'

Harry was shouldering his way through the knot of onlookers. When they saw who it was, they parted to let him pass. Ellen felt a great wave of love and gratitude and relief. It was all right; Harry was here.

'Ain't we got enough on our hands with the gov'nors to fight?' he demanded.

'Her and her old man ain't got no fight with them,' one woman stated, waving an arm in Ellen's direction.

'No more has Percy Goodhew up at the Puncheon. But there'd be trouble if he shut down in sympathy,' Harry said.

'That's different.'

'No, it ain't. And what's more, Gerry Billingham's my cousin. He's one of our own. So are the Johnsons. So if anyone wants to pick a fight with one of them, they got to get through me first.' Harry looked slowly round. He was balanced lightly on the balls of his feet, and his hands beckoned, inviting anyone who chose to take a swing at him.

'Come on, then. Who says the Billinghams ain't one of our own, eh? Anyone want to have it out?'

All round the circle, men and women subsided, some with reluctance, many muttering, but backing down all the same. When it came to the point, they weren't serious enough to want to tangle with Harry Turner. The crowd began to melt away. Some of the men went off to the Puncheon. The women retreated to their doorsteps. The children resumed their games. Ellen and her supporters were left in a group at the kerbside. She wanted to hurl herself at Harry and hug him, to feel his arms round her and the strength of his body against hers. She wanted to have him stroke her hair and say, 'Nobody threatens my Ellen and gets away with it!' Instead she just gave him a tight smile.

'Thanks, Harry. That was a nasty moment.'

'No trouble.' He shrugged, avoiding her eyes. 'They ought to know better than to fight amongst themselves at a time like this. But I don't think they'll have a go at you again now.'

'They wouldn't dare,' Ellen agreed.

But it was an uneasy peace. Ellen retreated to Alma's, where Maisie was nervously waiting and Billy again needed changing. At midday she hardly liked to call the children in for their dinner, since she knew that for many there was next to nothing on the table.

When she went out to collect them, hoping to do it without attracting too much attention, there was a distinctive smell hanging in the still, hot air. She stood outside the door, sniffing, and as she did so, she could see that others were doing the same.

'Someone's having a nice fry-up,' Ellen's neighbour remarked. 'All right for some.'

'Well, it ain't me,' Ellen snapped.

'Never said it was, girl. Where's it coming from, though? That's what I'd like to know. Who's found eggs and bacon for their dinner?'

'And kippers, I'm sure I can smell kippers,' someone else said.

'Smells more like sausage to me. Blimey, what I wouldn't give for a plate of nice juicy bangers and a good heap of mash.'

'Shrimps are what I fancy. Nice dish of shrimps and one of winkles, with plenty of vinegar to dip 'em in.'

'Or whelks, while you're about it, or jellied eels.'

The fantasies came thick and fast, fuelled by hunger and the knowledge that at the very most there was a thin slice of bread and scrape for dinner.

'Where *is* that smell coming from?'

Ellen could guess, but something made her keep

quiet. She let her neighbour voice her suspicions.

'You know what I think? I think it's that Siobhan O'Donaghue. She's the only one round here what can have a fry-up for her dinner.'

'Breakfast, more like. Never gets up of a morning, she don't. Gets up at dinnertime.'

'Had a good supper last night an' all, most like.' Ellen could not longer resist joining in. 'At one of them fancy chop-houses or something. Supper and a couple of bottles of beer, or even wine. With some gentleman friend.'

'Yeah, that's all she cares about,' Maisie chipped in.

There were dangerous rumblings all round.

'I saw her the other day, talking to Micky Docherty.'

'Best not tell Maureen Docherty. You know what a one she is.'

'Why ever not? I'd like to see Maureen Docherty give her what for. Sight for sore eyes, that'd be.'

'It's not just the Catholics, neither. I saw her talking to Bobby Croft. Slobbering over her, he was.'

'Shame! And him ten years younger than what she is!'

Ellen sensed she was back in the fold. They all knew there was no love lost between her and Siobhan O'Donaghue.

'I got a big pot of tea brewing,' she said. 'Anyone want a cup?'

Only a while ago she would have been afraid to ask in case it was interpreted as showing off. Now the offer was gratefully accepted. Cups were produced, tea was poured. There was no milk, since the strike had stopped deliveries, but Ellen still had some sugar. They all took steaming cups back to their meagre meals. And the smell of fried eggs and bacon still hung over the street, adding to the simmering unrest.

Far away upriver, a solitary figure walked slowly along the Strand. Respectable people avoided looking at her, since her clothes gave her away. The low-cut purple dress and scarlet feathered hat could only be worn by a woman of one profession. Women drew their skirts to one side to avoid contamination as they passed her. Men assumed expressions of moral righteousness. They might stray from the straight and narrow more than once in a while, but never did they sink as low as something like that. The woman appeared not to notice them. Slowly she plodded, one foot then the other, on and on, keeping close to the kerb as if she knew that her real place was the gutter.

All that morning she had walked, doggedly going west. At first if she stopped to rest, nobody cared. She was just one more unfortunate like themselves, too poor to trouble to rob. Once she reached the better class of street, things were different. If she stopped, a policemen would materialize as if out of nowhere and move her on with threats of arrest. Slower and slower her footsteps dragged as the sun rose higher in the brazen sky. Several times she just avoided death beneath spinning wheels as she stepped unheeding into traffic. She seemed not to hear the curses of drivers.

It was exactly midday when she arrived at

Westminster. She swayed and clutched at a lamp post as Big Ben's chimes rang out majestically across the richest city on earth. She leant precariously, staring across at the tower. She could go no further. It would have to be here. She began to walk across Westminster Bridge.

She had nothing on her that might identify her. She had thought of all that beforehand. She had walked all this way so that she would not end up anywhere near home, for she still thought of Millwall as home. Nobody must ever know her shame, not even after she was gone – *especially* then, since to take your own life was a mortal sin. The lessons of childhood could never really be eradicated, even by the life she had led.

By the time she reached the centre of the bridge, her strength was nearly spent. But for once, fate was with her. There was nobody near enough to stop her. She hesitated only long enough to pull out a heavy gold cross on a piece of string and hold it tightly in her hand. Then she jumped.

The planning worked. Her body was pulled out long before it was washed down to Millwall. The inquest stated her to be an unknown prostitute, about thirty years old, suffering from advanced syphilis. Theresa O'Donaghue had taken her secret to the grave.

4

Practically the whole street turned out after dinner that day. The strikers were to march through the streets of Millwall to the East India Dock Road for a mass meeting. The men assembled in the road, some with serious faces, others looking self-conscious, many of the younger ones larking about and showing off. Despite the blazing heat, all were respectably dressed. No shirtsleeves or bare heads were to be seen. If the world and possibly the press was going to see them, they were going to look decent. The women, children and old folk gathered on the pavements to see the show.

Harry, speaking for Tom Johnson, gave last-minute instructions. Will Johnson appeared with the contingent from his street. The children were wild with excitement, shrieking and jumping around, while the young girls giggled together and called out to the lads they fancied. And above the racket, from away along the West Ferry Road, the faint sound of a brass band could be heard.

'Listen!' somebody shouted.

After a great deal of hushing, some of the voices piped down. The band could definitely be heard, playing 'The Girl I Left Behind Me'. A cheer broke out. Nearer and nearer the music came, till Tom judged it was about time they started off. A forward wave of his arm, together with a shout from Harry, and the procession set forth, an army in grey and brown and black, with patched boots and flat caps, off to stand up and be counted for what they believed in.

The children skipped and marched and ran alongside. Some of the women followed at a modest distance, the mothers with babies on their hips and toddlers hanging on their skirts. They stopped at the West Ferry Road and watched as their menfolk joined the main procession, waving and cheering as they all filed by.

It was a stirring sight. Poorly dressed and badly shod and undernourished they might be, but all together they made up something to be reckoned with. Against the drab buildings and dull clothing, the banners of the union branches made bold splashes of colour, scarlet and royal blue and green, with lettering and fringes of gold. Up the thoroughfare they tramped, accompanied by a posse of special policemen, past shops half empty or closed because of the strike action, and halted what traffic was left on the road. A second band brought up the rear, and a froth of children and stray dogs frolicked behind. And then they were gone, off to make their statement to the world.

The spectators hung about for a while, watching as the band retreated up the road, and discussing the latest news with friends from other streets. But after a while it seemed that nothing much else was going to happen, so they began to trail back home. There was a sense of anticlimax in the stale air. The houses were too stuffy to sit indoors. The heat reflecting back off the brickwork and cobbles was stifling. The men might have looked fine, but now they had gone the women were left with squabbling children and a sense of powerlessness. And to top it all, hardly anyone had any tea leaves that had not been used twice before. A restless feeling of dissatisfaction seethed just beneath the surface.

'I wish I was out there marching with them,' Daisy said to her sister. 'When we all walked out yesterday, I really thought I was doing something.'

Ellen sighed. She knew just what Daisy meant. The last time she had made a bold gesture like that was when she ran away with Harry for the afternoon.

'I know. We spend most of our lives just – just plodding, don't we? Getting from day to day. But if you do go and do something different, you feel – well, you feel like you're really living, don't you? Like you're making your mark in the world. Trouble is, you feel all sort of let down afterwards.'

'You said it right there,' Daisy agreed.

They could see that other women up and down the road felt the same. Nobody could settle to anything. The least misdemeanour on the part of a child brought a sharp clip round the ear. Many of the older girls were sent off with babies and toddlers to take them for walks, while the older boys, the members of the street gang, decided to go down to the river for a swim.

And then Siobhan appeared.

She was wearing a white muslin dress and a large shady hat trimmed with white silk flowers. She put up a pretty frilly nonsense of a parasol and tripped daintily across the street to speak to her aunt Clodagh. She looked totally out of place in the mean little street, a butterfly on a dunghill.

Staring at her, each and every woman became conscious of her own dowdy appearance. She was fresh and cool and pale in the impractical white. They were hot and sweating with sleeves rolled up and hair straggling down. Their feet had swollen inside ill-fitting boots. They had on old cotton skirts or dresses which had been washed so many times that the original colours could only be guessed at. Most of them wore aprons over the top, also washed almost out of existence, so that the general effect was of various shades of grey – blueish grey, greenish grey, brownish grey. One flower from Siobhan's hat could have bought any one of the whole outfits that the others were wearing, and still left some change.

Resentment churned in every heart.

'Look at that. Dolled up to the nines. Makes me sick,' Alma remarked to Ellen and Daisy.

'All that finery and she ain't done an honest day's work since she left Morton's,' Daisy agreed.

They were joined by Florrie and Ida.

'You looking at what we're looking at?'

'Yeah, Lady Muck there. What makes her think she can set herself up like she's better than what we are?'

'Flaunting her white dress and her posh hat like that when folks are on their uppers. Ain't right.'

'It ain't neighbourly, that's for sure.'

Up and down the road, the same feelings were being expressed in a chorus of envious mutterings.

'She ain't never given nothing back, that one. Other folk, when they're in the money, they help those what're down.'

'Yeah well, that's what we all do, don't we? We all help where we can.'

'Not her. She don't. Just goes flashing it around.'

'Yeah, I didn't see none of her relations asked in for a share of that fry-up what she had for dinner, let alone anyone else in the street.'

'Now what's she up to? I hope she ain't coming up to speak to me.'

'I hope she is. Give her the rough side of my tongue, I will.'

Siobhan appeared to have finished her conversation with Clodagh, but instead of going back to her house or off out, she was coming back down the street, sublimely indifferent to the looks she was being given. She stopped by the little group in which Ellen was standing.

''Afternoon, Ellen. All friends again now, are we?'

Ellen glared at her. She did not want to be reminded of this morning's argument. It was only a few hours behind her and she was still feeling very raw.

'Yeah,' she said.

'Lucky for you that Harry spoke up for you. Might have been a bit nasty otherwise.'

'I don't see why.'

Siobhan gave a little smile. 'What with your husband not here and all. It must be nice to have another man there ready to take your side.'

Ellen flushed. She held her temper in check with difficulty. 'What d'you mean by that?'

The smile became a shade more provocative. 'Of course, you always did try to keep Harry to yourself, didn't you? Doesn't seem to have changed now that you're married to Gerry.'

Guilt hit Ellen, winding her like a kick in the stomach, and along with it an awful irrational fear. She gaped wordlessly while questions chased round her head. What did Siobhan know? Had she seen her, that day they went to Battersea? Was that why she came back to Trinidad Street?

Daisy and Florrie had nothing to silence them. As one, they stepped forward.

'Just what are you trying to say?'

'You keep your filthy trap shut.'

The nearer neighbours began to sidle up. Those further away asked each other what was going on.

'Come on, what d'you mean, eh?' Daisy was insisting on an answer. 'What are you trying to say about my sister and Harry Turner? You trying to pin something on them, 'cos if you are you better come out with it proper.'

'I know what I heard this morning.' Siobhan was not cowed.

'Yeah? And?'

'I'm only saying what other people think.' She shrugged insolently. 'Everyone knows Ellen Johnson only married Gerry Billingham because she couldn't get Harry.'

'You're just jealous because you didn't get him,' Florrie said. 'But I'll tell you this for nothing, my brother wouldn't touch you if you came to him on a plate.'

'Thank you, but that's hardly likely to happen, is it? I'm not going to stoop to lightermen when I have titled gentlemen lining up for me night after night.'

'Funny none of them ain't never married you.'

'Funny she comes back here to live, and by herself an' all, when she's got all these men,' Daisy put in.

'What's happening? What's she saying?' someone at the back wanted to know.

'She's saying there's something going on with my sister and Harry Turner,' Daisy said loudly.

Women who only that morning had been baiting Ellen were immediately on her side.

'Blooming cheek! She's one to talk.'

'Yeah, we all know what went on with her and Harry Turner.'

'Who does she think she is, spreading lies like that?'

'Yeah, who *does* she think she is?'

That was what really needled all of them.

'Parading about in her expensive dress and her posh hat.'

'Coming back at all hours of the night in cabs.'

'Eating eggs and bacon when our kids are going hungry.'

'Thinks she's better than us, that's what.'

Daisy snatched at the hated hat. Siobhan screamed and clutched at it, but Daisy was too strong for her. She wrenched it from Siobhan's grasp and set it on her own head, an incongruous piece of frippery above her broad face and sturdy body. She held it firmly with one hand and placed the other on her hip. Then she minced a few steps up and down the street.

'I'm a famous music-hall artiste, I am. I'm a cut above all you lot in Trinidad Street,' she trilled, in a recognizable imitation of Siobhan's new accent.

The women shrieked with laughter. Someone wrested the parasol from Siobhan's hands while the others held on to her to stop her from snatching it back. In the fray some of the trimming got pulled off.

'Stop it, you're breaking it!' Siobhan cried.

'Stop it, you're breaking it!' they chorused.

The tension of the last few weeks, long held back, was bursting out. Siobhan tried to pull away from the hands that gripped her, and the fragile sleeve of her dress ripped at the seams. That did it.

'Look, look, a pretty hanky,' yelled its new owner, and loudly blew her nose on it.

The women screamed with delight. Hands reached out to grab at Siobhan's clothing. This way and that she was pulled as the fabric ripped and split.

'Bitches! Ugly cows!' Howling with rage and humiliation, she tried to hit and scratch and kick.

The women just laughed at her. They were enjoying themselves. Every just cause for jealousy was being avenged: Will's desertion, Florrie's spoilt wedding, the rift between Harry and Ellen, all the girls jilted because of her – it all came out in handfuls of dainty muslin.

From the other end of the street, the O'Donaghues and the Irish contingent waded in.

'What are you doing to our Siobhan?'

'Lay off, will you, or–'

'*Your* Siobhan?' the others flung back. 'You related to this whore, then?'

Battle was joined. The street was a blur of yelling, punching, scratching women. Caught up with all the rest, Ellen found herself face to face with Siobhan. Skirt, bodice and petticoats had all come away and Siobhan was left standing in her corset and drawers, tears of hatred running down her face.

'You – you done this!' she screamed, and flew at Ellen, grabbing a handful of hair.

The unbearable strain of living with Gerry while rearing Harry's child pounded in Ellen's head and broke out in a fury of revenge. With a spurt of fierce pleasure, she slapped Siobhan hard round the face, glorying in the sting on her palm and the squeal from Siobhan. Her own head was being forced back by Siobhan's grip on her hair. Twisting against the pressure, she sank her teeth into the enemy's arm, and Siobhan let go with a cry of pain.

All restraint gone now, Ellen attacked, enjoying the rake of her nails on flesh, the tearing of hair coming out by the roots. Siobhan was wailing now, begging her to stop.

'Stop? You should've stopped. You should've left us all alone. You're the cause of all the trouble round here!'

She flew at her with renewed force, slapping her head from side to side. Siobhan tried to back away, tripped and fell sprawling on the cobbles. Ellen stood over her, hands on hips, breath rasping in her lungs.

'Now,' she gasped. 'Now you know what it feels like.'

Siobhan's lovely curls were a tangled mess, her remaining clothes were torn and she was bleeding from a dozen scratch-marks. Not taking her terrified eyes from Ellen's face, she scrambled to her feet, then made a run for the safety of her own home.

'She's going, she's going!' someone shouted.

Howling and calling, the women pursued her. The front door was slammed in their faces and the bolts shot. Ragged cheers of victory arose. Cheated of their prey, they milled about, while the Irish retreated to their end of the street to mutter among themselves.

Exhausted but elated, the others straggled back to their own front steps, agreeing amongst themselves that they had shown *her* what for. Ellen brewed up the last of her tea and they sat about, bruised and scratched and glowing with victory, and obscurely satisfied that they too had stood up for the values they believed in, whilst the toddlers gathered up the tattered remains of Siobhan's clothing and sat in the road to play with them. If the shade of Theresa O'Donaghue was watching, she had cause to be well pleased.

Ellen lay awake long after Gerry had fallen asleep. Everyone had been up late, what with there being no work in the morning and then the parade and the fracas over Siobhan to chew over. Gerry had sat uncharacteristically silent as the others went over the day's events. Ellen became very aware that it was true what they had said about him earlier: he *was* out of it. The strike affected his supplies and reduced his trade, but it did not change his life the way it had everyone else's in the street. In fact, he had been strike-breaking, fetching that wonderful bargain from Stepney. To cover this, she kept trying to draw him in, and included him in her remarks and opinions.

'Ain't that so, Gerry? That's what you always said, ain't it, Gerry?'

It was only when they got to bed that he said what he really felt.

'I'm surprised at you, Ellen. Scrapping with that Siobhan O'Donaghue. I never thought you was the sort.'

'Huh! I can fight with the best of 'em when I have to. And I always hated that woman. Anyway, it weren't me what started it, it was her. She come and picked on me. I was only defending myself.'

'That's as maybe. But it just goes to show what this strike is doing to people when women like you start getting into fights.'

Ellen stopped listening to him at this point as little Tom was sick. All her concern now for him, she mopped him up.

'That's not like you, my pet. You ain't a sicky baby. What's the matter, eh? I hope you ain't got the runs.'

Worried, she checked his nappy, though she could smell that he was all right. She was reassured to find that he was clean. Diarrhoea carried off more babies each year than any other disease. He was hot and fretful, though, hardly taking any feed, and it took her a long time to soothe him to sleep. When she finally succeeded, she was still wide awake herself, and she lay listening to the breathing of her family around her.

In the quiet of the sultry night, Gerry's words came back to her, and she had to admit, reluctantly, that he was right. She was not one to fight, unlike some of the women in the street who would fall out and come to blows over the slightest little incident. The last time she let fly at anyone was when she had found Siobhan and Harry together. As time trickled by, a niggling feeling of remorse crept in.

Hoofs and wheels could be heard out on the deserted street. Ellen slipped from the bed and crept downstairs. Peeping out through the parlour window, she saw a cab pull up outside Siobhan's house and Siobhan herself step down and pay off the cabby. On impulse, she snatched a shawl from the peg and stepped outside. She flew down the street and reached the door just as Siobhan was shutting it. She placed her foot in the gap.

'Siobhan? Can I come in?'

A suspicious face appeared. 'Ellen? What the devil do you want? I've nothing to say to you.'

'But I want to talk to you.'

She didn't know quite why, just that it was important. She leant her shoulder against the door and pushed. With a sigh, Siobhan relented and let her in. There was a scratch of a match and then the lamp flared. Ellen caught her breath. She had heard rumours of the magnificence of Siobhan's home, she had even seen the stuff going in, but it had not prepared her for the full effect. There was a blue and fawn patterned carpet square on the floor, where other people just had oilcloth. There were two upholstered armchairs covered in a flowery chintz. There were lamps with frilly shades. There was a sideboard with glassware that glistened and sparkled in the light. And all over the walls there were photographs of Siobhan in her many stage costumes, smiling, preening, asking to be admired. Speechless, Ellen could only gape.

'Like it?' Siobhan was watching her, that superior smile on her face again.

'Very pretty,' Ellen said.

Something was wrong, but she could not put her finger on it. She was too dazzled by the opulence. Instead she said, off the top of her head, 'What happened to the conjuror?'

'I beg your pardon?'

'The conjuror. What's-his-name. The Great Cornelius.'

'Oh, him. I gave him the push. He wasn't good enough for me.' She gave a shrug, as if the man had been nothing more than a troublesome fly, Ellen decided. Yet at the time she had been glad enough to drag him down here for Florrie's wedding. Siobhan stood there in her fashionable gown, with the smell of greasepaint and powder still on her, not asking Ellen in as a neighbour might, just standing, barring the way further into the house.

'Ain't no one good enough for you, then?' Ellen asked.

'No, they are not that.'

'Must be lonely for you, on your own.'

'I'm not on my own. My cousin Shelagh's here.'

Shelagh was the widowed relation who kept house for her. But that was not what Ellen meant, and they both knew it.

'Anyway, what's it to you?'

'Just wondered.'

And then it came to her what was wrong with the room. It was all brand spanking new, as if Siobhan had gone out and bought it all at one go especially to come here. She followed the train of thought. If that was so, then Siobhan had brought nothing with her from wherever she had been.

'Why did you come back here?' she asked abruptly.

'Why are you here asking me all these questions?' Siobhan countered. 'I didn't ask you to call. I don't have to say nothing to you. This is my house. All mine.' She walked slowly round the room, touching pieces of furniture and ornaments, glancing at Ellen from time to time, watching for signs of envy.

Ellen did not give her the pleasure. She kept doggedly to what she now knew was the reason for her visit. 'I can't see why you come back. If you're so rich and no man's good enough for you, what are you doing back on Dog Island? I'd've thought this street wasn't good enough for you.'

Siobhan paused by the sideboard. Above it was a row of photographs. Four faces smiled sweetly down from the wall, a completely different person from the live one who stared back at Ellen with eyes as hard as slate and lines of cruelty round the mouth.

'You're just like all the rest. In fact, you're worse than all the rest, because you're even more jealous than they are. You can't bear it that I took Harry away from you.'

'I'm not jealous,' Ellen said, and it was true. The fight had released her, had drained away all the hatred that had built up over the years. She could

645

see Siobhan clearly now, beyond the front she put up to the world. 'I'm not jealous of you, I'm sorry for you. I'm sorry that you got nobody what cares for you. That's why you come back, weren't it? You come back because nobody wanted you. You had to run away from something, didn't you? Or someone. That's why all this stuff is new. You ran back to your family to be safe. Blood's thicker than water and all that, so they got to back you up, and they do, because they're good people. But they don't like you, Siobhan, they don't like you any more than what all the rest of us do. They're just putting up with you because you're related. I think it's sad. I'm glad I'm not you.'

There was a tense stillness about Siobhan. 'Have you finished?' she asked, her voice dangerously level.

Ellen briefly considered mentioning the baby, saying she was sorry about that as well, but she abandoned the thought. It was not necessary.

'Yes, thank you. I found out what I wanted to know. I'll go now. Good night.'

Siobhan moved so swiftly that for a precious few seconds Ellen could only gape at her. Then, just in time, she dodged. A vase came flying across the room to hit the wall just inches away from her head. It broke with a crash and shattered, glass splinters scattering over half the room. One grazed Ellen's cheek, others lodged in her hair, pieces opened cuts on her bare arms. Too shocked for speech, she stared at Siobhan, choking down the scream that rose in her throat.

'I hate you, Ellen Johnson. I'll hate you till I die!' Siobhan was shaking, her face contorted

646

with fury. She reached behind her for another missile. This time a sense of self-preservation came to Ellen's rescue. She whisked out of the door and pulled it shut behind her just as something else crashed against it. Then she ran.

She reached the safety of Alma's house and went straight through to the kitchen and shook her head over the sink. Only when she was sure she had got all the glass out of her hair and her clothes did she sit down, and then she did so with a rush, for her legs had gone to string. And for a long time she just sat there, while the scene played over and over in her head. The more she thought about it, the more she knew she had spoken the truth. She was sorry for Siobhan. Her life was empty. She was not a great success as a music-hall artiste, she was just a third-rate act. She had nobody to call her own, no children to love, and her relations only put up with her because she was family. And she was left nursing a murderous hatred. Ellen knew all about that. She had felt the same and it was a terrible thing. She was glad to be purged of it.

By comparison, she knew herself to be rich. She might not have the man she loved, she might not have a place of her own at the moment, but when she looked at what Siobhan had, she was blessed. Slowly, she stood up and went upstairs to join her family.

It was late Friday morning and the air of tension over the street was so thick it could almost be tasted. Rumour was rife about the outcome of the various strike negotiations. First it was said that the Government had made all the employers agree to the men's terms, then that the Army was moving in and martial law had been proclaimed, then that the unions had given in and everything was back to how it was before the strike. With each rumour, hopes soared or slumped, till nobody knew what to believe. Of one thing they were sure, though: today was the day. Now that the Government had stepped in, there would soon be a settlement one way or the other.

The women were better off than the men. There were still steps to scrub, beds to make, children to care for. Despite the lack of money, food had to be got from somewhere, even if it was just bread and scrape. They still had a purpose in life. The men just hung about, waiting for news.

Martha stopped by to see Ellen.

'I don't think we'll be seeing too much of Siobhan today,' she remarked, glancing towards the closed door and drawn curtains.

'No,' Ellen agreed.

'How's my latest grandson, then?'

'I dunno, Mum. He's still poorly. He don't seem to keep anything down. You come and look.'

The two women went into the stuffy kitchen and looked down at the baby lying in his pram. His face was scarlet and he was whimpering. Martha reached out to feel his forehead.

'Poor little soul, he's ever so hot.'

'And look at his arms and legs, Mum. I'll swear they're thinner. He's hardly taking anything from me, and what he does have he throws right back.'

'You been giving him anything to drink?'

'I tried giving water from a teaspoon, but most

of it just dribbles out.'

'Well, I should keep trying, lovey. He needs to have something inside of him. He's going to starve otherwise. Seems to me he's got the same as what little Billy's got. I'm just off round to see Maisie now. You know what she's like. With Will gone off with your dad to find out about these blooming strikes, she'll be all at sixes and sevens, and Billy's always been poorly. She needs someone to help.'

'Yeah.' Ellen could not spare a great deal of concern for Maisie at the moment. She was too worried about Tom.

Her mother gave a brief hug. 'He'll be all right, lovey. Jess and Teddy both been ill like this and they was all right after. And it's not as if he's a weakly baby. He's a strong little scrap, like his grandad. He'll pull through, you'll see.'

Ellen was not reassured. She knew, as her mother did, that these stomach upsets carried off more babies than anything else.

'I hope so, Mum. I couldn't bear to lose him.'

'Yeah, well, he's a bit special to you, ain't he?' Martha's tone was carefully neutral.

Ellen looked at her. Her mother's face was unreadable. 'They're all special, all three of 'em.'

'That's right, lovey. So they are. I got to go now. I'll stop by later and see how he is.'

Ellen was left wondering just how much her mother knew. She sat by herself in the kitchen, spooning water into the baby's unwilling mouth and cleaning him up each time he vomited or soiled himself. She could not think where it was all still coming from. He had not had a proper feed since yesterday evening.

Outside, the street was divided into two camps. Of Siobhan they saw nothing, just as Martha had predicted, but led by Clodagh O'Donaghue, the Irish community kept to their end of the road and refused to talk to anyone else. Clodagh had never really forgiven the Billinghams and everyone connected with them for Theresa's downfall, and however much she might disapprove of Siobhan, this new attack on her family was not to be passed off with a shrug and a laugh. She stood with folded arms and glared at the enemy, forbidding Brian to go off with the Johnsons to find out what was happening about the pay negotiations.

'Ye'll find out soon enough without having to associate with the likes of them,' she declared.

Brian, who knew her moods of old, contented himself with the thought of a pint at the Puncheon directly Percy opened up for the day.

Many of the men were already in the pub when the Johnsons and Harry arrived back. The two younger men sprinted ahead, eager to tell the news. Tom followed them at a fast walk, breaking into a jog at times, borne along by the euphoria of victory. He could still hardly believe it had happened. He scarcely felt the ground beneath his feet or the protesting rasp of his lungs as he hurried along. When he reached Trinidad Street, a crowd was already gathering round Harry and Will. Out of the Rum Puncheon they came, off the doorsteps and through from the kitchens, men, women and children, all keen to hear what had happened.

'What's up?'

'Have we won?'

'Is it over?'

Everyone was asking everyone else and calling out to Harry and Will. English and Irish alike were pushing to get to the front and hear the latest.

'Come on, Will, let's have it.'

'We got to wait for Dad. Where's Dad got to?'

The outer edge of the crowd surged forward to meet Tom, surrounding him and bearing him towards his son and Harry at the centre. They could tell it was good tidings by the glow on his face. Friendly hands slapped him on the back as he passed by. He reached Will's side at last.

'Come on, Dad. It's your day. You tell 'em.'

Tom shook his head. He was breathless. His heart was thudding painfully in his chest.

'I can't, son. You do it.'

Will had learnt a lot since that first time his father made him stand up and address a meeting. He spread his arms and waited till nearly everyone was quiet.

'Friends, this morning great things have been happening.'

Cheers broke out.

'The carmen have come to an agreement. They have been given nearly everything they asked for.'

Slightly less enthusiastic cheers, since nobody in the street was actually a carman.

'What about us?' Jimmy Croft shouted.

'I'm coming to that, friends.' Will paused, and something approaching a hush fell over the expectant crowd.

'The employers have finally agreed that all

651

dockers and stevedores, whether casual or permanent, on deep-sea or coastal trades, in the enclosed docks or on the wharves, shall now work from seven in the morning till six in the evening.'

An hour less was good, but that was not what they were waiting for.

'What about the money?'

'And–' Again there was a pause for quiet. 'And every man shall be paid eightpence an hour, with a shilling overtime!'

The gathering erupted into whistles and yells. Caps were thrown in the air, men shook each other by the hand, some of the women wept with relief and children capered around.

'We done it, we done it!'

'But what about the lightermen?'

Will turned to Harry. 'Come on, you tell 'em.'

Harry had some difficulty in making himself heard. The dockers and stevedores and their families were still laughing and shouting and congratulating each other. The lightermen who lived in the street had to push their way to the front.

'We got our ten-hour day and a shilling overtime. They're still arguing over the weekly wage, but I reckon they ain't got no choice now. They'll have to give us our two quid.'

The whole crowd was now cheering. Tom stood in the thick of it, the voices ringing in his ears. This was what he had been working for, all these years: a brotherhood of working men, supporting each other for the common good. At first he hardly heard Harry speaking urgently to him.

'...the message?'

'What?' he asked.

'The message from Gosling and Tillett. You're the one what ought to give it.'

'Yeah,' he agreed. 'Yeah, I'll do that, if they'll listen.'

'They'll listen,' Harry said, and bellowed for silence.

A patchy hush was enforced with a great deal of effort.

'Friends and neighbours...'

Tom had dreamed of this day, and had made this speech or one very much like it in his head a hundred times. Now the words could be said.

'Your courage and your steadfastness have opened a new age for the men of the waterfront. Never again will we be put upon and exploited. We have stood up and made our voices heard in high places. We are a power in the land. And we have been an example to other working people in different trades and different parts of the country. Even now, the railwaymen, the miners, the printers and the cotton workers are demanding better wages and conditions. You have been an inspiration to them.' He stopped, choked with emotion. Hastily he tried to dear his aching throat. He still had something he wanted to say.

'I have a message for you from our leaders, from Harry Gosling and Ben Tillett. They congratulate you on your success, and they say this: "We now declare the strike at an end, and thank every man, woman and child for your loyal support of our efforts."'

Happy faces swam before his eyes. People were wringing his hands. Someone's arm was across his shoulders.

'Three cheers for Tom Johnson! Hip, hip–'
Harry's voice belted out over the joyful row.

The heartfelt hurrahs reverberated up and down the street, raising the sparrows from the rooftops. Tom stood, dazed, with tears running unashamedly down his face.

'Chair, chair!' somebody shouted.

The idea caught on at once. Before he could protest, Tom found himself lifted up on a precarious platform of shoulders. Laughing and shouting and singing, his human chariot bore him the length of the street and finally deposited him at his own front door. He stood with shaking knees, saying he knew not what to everyone who spoke to him, until Martha managed to work her way through to his side. He threw an arm round her ample body and held her close to him, as if they were a newlywed couple, while their neighbours whistled and cheered anew.

For a while everyone milled about, then a bright spark realized that the very best excuse for a drink was to hand, and a large majority made off for the Puncheon, where Percy broached his very last barrel in the fervent hope that deliveries would soon be back to normal and money available to pay off the amounts run up on the slate.

Tom resisted all invitations to buy him a pint. He stood and watched them disperse, his arm still round his wife.

'So you done it, then?' It was Martha who spoke first.

'We all done it, girl. All of us, the women as well as the men.'

'It's a proud day for you.'

'Yeah.' He shook his head slowly. 'I still can't take it in. After all this time, years and years of trying to make people see what they could do if they would only stand together, and in the end it all blew up so quick. Even when it did start, I thought it'd be a long fight, like what we had back in eighty-nine. It looked like it even up to a couple of days ago, yesterday even. All that talk about the Army standing by. And it was, too. People seen 'em, making ready to come and break the strike.'

'Thank God they didn't,' Martha said.

'Yeah, it would've been nasty, that.'

'You coming in?' Martha said. 'Our Ellen give us a twist of tea. Her Gerry got hold of some up the market yesterday.'

Tom looked at the families still busily discussing the news – his friends, his neighbours, the people he had been working for. But right now he did not need the hurly-burly and the acclaim. He had had his moment. Now he just wanted the peace and quiet of his own kitchen. He followed Martha inside.

'So it's been worth it, then, in the end?' Martha said, pouring hot water into the teapot.

'The end? It's not the end, it's the beginning. The start of a new age.'

'Ah.'

He went and put his arms round her waist as she stood at the sink. 'I couldn't never have done it without you, love. You been a real brick, you have. Best wife a man could have.'

'Oh, get away with you.' Martha's voice was rough with tears.

'I mean it, love. The way you put up with it all. Never a cross word. And me not taking notice of you and the family like what I ought.'

Martha leaned back against him, resting her head on his shoulder. 'I know how much it means to you, this union business. And I'm happy for you. This is your big day, ain't it?'

'Yeah – yeah, it is. What we all been working for.'

'Then I'm glad you got what you wanted. You enjoy it, love. We don't often get what we want, do we?'

Tom kissed her cheek.

'You're the best, you are. Best wife a man could hope to have.'

5

Harry sat in the Puncheon, nursing a mean half-pint. The strikes might be over but life had not got back to normal straight away.

'Half a blooming pint,' Jimmy Croft grumbled. 'Can't hardly wet your whistle with this. 'Specially with it still so hot and all.'

'Some pubs have run out altogether,' Percy told him. 'It's not just a case of the deliveries from the breweries starting up again. The breweries themselves ain't got no hops or malt left. They're waiting for you lot to unload 'em from the wharves. Then we might get some beer back on tap again.'

'Blimey, that's going to take days. You seen the

boats waiting to be unloaded?' Jimmy said.

'They say there's three weeks' work just clearing the ships in the West India dock, let alone starting on them moored up in the river,' Harry said.

After the celebrations of the day before, everyone was restless and irritable. Somehow, they had expected Tom Johnson's new age to dawn at once. Instead, they were still in debt, with no food on the table and Percy down to the dregs of the last barrel.

The groups in the bar were divided sharply into English and Irish. Though the men had not been involved in the fight over Siobhan, there was a lot of bad feeling in the air.

At that moment a skinny boy of about twelve came hurtling into the pub.

'Quick, quick! It's Gerry Billingham, he needs help!' he shrieked, his shrill voice cutting through the noise. 'They got Gerry Billingham! They're giving him a right pasting!'

Harry caught the boy by the arm. 'Who? Who's got him?'

'It's the carmen on the West Ferry Road. Quick! You got to help!'

Harry looked round at the men hunched over their drinks. 'You heard that? Them mad bleeders have got our Gerry! Are we going to stand for that?'

'No!' howled those around him.

The Catholics said nothing, but Harry knew how to get them behind him. Not for nothing had he led the street gang for two whole years.

'Nobody touches someone from Trinidad

Street and lives! Death or Glory!'

'Death or Glory!' came the battle cry.

Harry turned to the boy.

'Where are they? Show us.'

The lad sped off down the street, with Harry at his heels. Behind him, Harry could hear the pounding boots of his lifetime friends, and glancing back over his shoulder he was heartened to see that the Catholics were with him. With an army like this, he could face anyone.

They raced into the West Ferry Road. There on the other side of the cobbled highway a knot of assorted vans and drays was held up while a mêlée of men staggered this way and that, fists flying. Harry plunged straight through the nearside traffic, ignoring the curses of a tram driver. Fuelled with anger and anxiety, he waded in, trying to get to the centre of the trouble.

'Gerry!' he yelled. 'Hold on, Gerry! We're here!'

Around and behind him he could hear and see the Trinidad Street men laying in. Shouts and curses greeted their arrival.

'Blimey, it's his mates!' someone shouted. 'Scarper!'

But Harry's army was not going to let them get away just like that. They were spoiling for a fight, and this was just the outlet they were looking for. Passers-by gathered round and shouted encouragement while the Trinidad Street men wreaked revenge on the carmen.

Through the tangle of flailing arms and falling bodies, Harry could see his cousin. He looked for all the world like an abandoned heap of old clothing, pitifully small and vulnerable. Even as he tried to fight his way through to him, he saw men tripping over him, iron-shod boots ramming into soft flesh.

'Gerry! Move – get out of it!' he bellowed.

But there was no response.

Harry put his head down and barged a way through. Gerry was lying curled up, foetus-like, with his hands protectively over his head. He was quite still. Harry straddled him, bracing his body against the ebb and flow of the battle. He had to get Gerry to safety, he was in danger of being kicked to death here. He bent down and gripped his cousin under the arms, then backed towards the pavement, dragging the inert body with him. Gerry's boots bumped and grated against the cobbles. A retreating carman fell backwards over his legs and was pounced on by an O'Ryan. Harry yelled at them to get off, but they were oblivious of him. It was only when the Irishmen hauled up the carman to punch him more easily that Harry could continue his journey. To his horror, he realized that Gerry was leaving a trail of blood on the road. He redoubled his efforts, heaved him up into his arms like a baby, and carried him out of the brawl and through the ring of spectators till he finally made the safe haven of a shop doorway.

'Oi!' The shopkeeper was incensed. 'You can't put him there, he'll make a mess.'

Harry drew himself up to his full height and glared at the man. 'Not half as much of a mess as I could make of you, mate. Now go and fetch us some water and a cloth.'

For a moment the man held his eyes. Then he backed down and disappeared into the back of the shop.

Harry knelt down beside his cousin. What he saw sickened him. Gerry's face was a pulp of cuts and bruises and his hair was matted with blood. Harry laid a hand on his chest. Beneath the protruding ribs, his heart was still beating. His worst fear was allayed. But what really alarmed him was Gerry's right arm. The left sleeves of his jacket and shirt were hanging loose, cut almost through, revealing a huge jagged wound that was oozing bright red blood. Harry was tight with anger. That had not come from a fair fight. That had been made by a piece of glass or sharp metal.

He tried to stop the bleeding by wrapping the flap of cut sleeve round the arm. But when he pressed down, he found blood welling up through his fingers.

'I think this is a job for the hospital,' he said to the shopkeeper's wife. 'You got anything I can borrow to wheel him in? A flat cart, a barrow, even?'

She shook her head. 'Them mad carmen are the ones to ask.'

'They're not going to help, are they?'

'Him next door but one's got a barrow. He's all right, is Jim. He'll lend it you,' a passer-by chipped in.

Harry thanked him, and while the man went to ask he and the shopkeeper's wife set to work, cleaning the worst of Gerry's cuts and bandaging up the open wounds. Within a minute the water in the bowl was scarlet.

The battle with the carmen was coming to an end. A couple of policemen appeared on the scene and all those who could make a break for it had gone. Everyone was explaining to everyone else what had happened. A large navy-blue-clad figure loomed over Harry.

'Right then. What's been going on? Is he hurt bad?'

'What's it bloody well look like?'

'Them carmen said as he was blacklegging during the strike. They was out to get him for it,' explained the man who had asked for the barrow.

'We got to get him to hospital,' Harry insisted. 'He could be bleeding to death lying here.'

The constable rose to the occasion magnificently, calling a police ambulance and assisting with the first aid. The next fifteen minutes felt like the longest Harry had spent in his life. He answered the constable's questions without thinking, believing that Gerry was slipping away before his very eyes. He was so deeply unconscious, it was only by feeling his chest that Harry could tell that he was still alive.

'Married, is he?' the constable asked, flipping a page in his notebook.

With a jolt it hit Harry that if Gerry were to die... He tried to brush the thought away, ashamed that he should even have entertained it. But it lingered, tantalizing, refusing to be banished.

The policeman repeated the question.

'Oh – yeah. He is.'

'Name of the wife? Living at the same address?'

If Ellen were free...

The ambulance arrived. Full of concern and guilt, Harry tried to go along with his cousin.

'No need for that, sir. Doesn't exactly want you

to hold his hand, now does he?'

Along with all the others, he was rounded up and taken down to the station for further questioning.

Ellen and Alma waited for what seemed like hours in the echoing brown-tiled hall. Around them, accident victims and emergency cases were brought in, porters and nurses and doctors passed to and fro, other relatives sat anxiously waiting for news. The place had a hostile feel to it. In the harsh light, everyone's faces looked tired and drawn. They were all stiff from sitting on the uncomfortable benches, their nostrils offended by the overpowering smell of disinfectant. At first they talked, putting their gnawing worry into words, repeating their fears over and over to each other, as if they might work like an incantation and stop the worst from happening. But as time went on and it became more and more likely that Gerry was seriously injured, Ellen subsided into silence, no longer able to keep the horrors at bay.

Here in the hospital Gerry was fighting for his life. Back at home little Tom was getting weaker by the hour and she felt as if she was being torn in half. Hardly able to contain herself, she paced up and down in front of the hard wooden bench, chewing at her knuckles.

'Sit down, lovey. You'll wear yourself out,' Alma begged.

'I can't. I can't sit still,' Ellen said.

At last the pressure of guilt was too much to bear.

'It's all my fault. I should've told him not to get

that stuff. I should have stopped him.'

'What stuff? What d'you mean?' Alma was mystified.

'When the strike was on. He said he was going to fetch some stuff from over Stepney and he wasn't going to let no blooming carmen stop him. I told him, I said, "You be careful, Gerry", but I should've done more than that. I should've stopped him. If I'd've stopped him, he wouldn't be here now.'

If she was hoping for some reassurance from Alma, she was disappointed.

'Well, bloody hell, girl, why didn't you?'

'I didn't think he'd listen! You know what he's like when it comes to getting a bargain. There's no stopping him. And he never believed in the strike. He never said it, but I knew what he thought. He thought it was a nuisance, getting in the way of trade.'

'You still could've tried! For God's sake, girl...'

'I told him to be careful–'

A nurse appeared, stiffly disapproving, and told them to keep their voices down or they would be asked to leave.

Alma was not cowed. 'How much longer are we going to be kept waiting here? That's my son in there. I got a right to see him. I'm his mother.'

'You'll not be allowed to see him if Doctor thinks you'll disturb him,' the nurse said chillingly. 'Patients' welfare always comes first.'

After another excruciating wait in which neither Alma nor Ellen said anything to each other, an exhausted-looking junior nurse came and informed them that Mr Billingham had been taken to one of the wards upstairs.

'Can we see him?' both women chorused.

'I don't know.' The young girl was confused.

'You take us there,' Alma told her.

'I can't, I'm on duty here.'

'Tell us where it is,' Ellen urged.

They were both of them far too upset to listen properly. They got lost round the endless stairways and corridors and argued over which way to go next. At last they found a porter who was willing to help them and discovered they were in quite the wrong part of the building. With his directions, they finally got to the right ward.

The sister barred their way.

'All patients are settled for the night now.'

'But he's my son.'

'My husband...'

'I can't have my patients disturbed.'

Ellen laid a hand on her immaculate arm. 'Please, just tell us how he is.'

The sister regarded her for several seconds, her lips pressed closely together.

'I want to see him,' Alma insisted.

But the sister was adamant: no visitors outside visiting hours. That was the rule. If they tried to disobey, a porter would be fetched to evict them.

'I'm staying till he wakes up,' Alma decided.

'Then you will have to wait downstairs. We have no facilities for relatives here.'

Defeated, Ellen and Alma made their way back to the hall.

'Old cow,' Alma muttered. 'Keeping a mother from her sick son. Ain't right.'

On and on she went, making dire threats. Ellen

could hardly bear it. She was doing no good here, and Tom must be wanting her at home. Her breasts ached with unused milk. But if she went now, Alma would suspect the truth, the secret she had kept so carefully all this time, that she was not the devoted wife she made herself out to be, that there were others that came way before Gerry in her heart. But Tom might be awake, he might be crying for her, he might have taken a turn for the worse…

First Gerry pulled at her guilt, then the baby at her heart, turn and turn about, until she did not know what to do. Time ticked slowly by, measured by the large clock on the tiled wall.

Something made her turn and look towards the big double doorway. Her brother Jack stood there, searching the room with his eyes. Terror clutched at her, taking her breath away, striking her speechless. In that moment, she knew. Jack spotted her and came striding across, his boots ringing on the stone floor.

'Ellen.' His voice was unusually gentle, his eyes large with compassion. 'Mum says she thinks you ought to come home.'

Ellen ran as she had never run before. On and on through the dark streets she ran, till she felt as if her legs were about to splinter and her lungs to burst. She had no breath even to whimper. Only the terrible fear pressing round her heart drove her on.

How she got the last half-mile down the West Ferry Road she did not know. She was dimly aware of Jack clutching her waist and holding her up. Round the last corner and into Trinidad Street they went, and then they were there at her parents' house.

Martha was sitting in the kitchen with little Tom in her arms. A stub end of candle lit her worn features.

'Ellen, love.'

Ellen licked her dry lips. 'Is – is he...?' she croaked.

Martha held out the baby to her. Ellen took him, searching his tiny face by the feeble light of the candle flame. He seemed to have shrunk even in the short time since last she saw him. His little nose and chin were not softly rounded but pointed, so that he took on the look of a wizened elf. But he was still breathing.

Silent tears of relief slid down her face. She dropped on to a chair and held Tom to her. It was all right. He was alive. Her whole body throbbed from the nightmare journey home, but it did not matter. She hardly noticed Jack going off to bed or her mother wearily making a cup of tea and asking after Gerry. Her entire being was focused on the little bundle in her arms. Gradually she realized that she could feel his bones through the threadbare shawl.

'He's so thin, Mum. He's – he's fading away. Has he been sick much?'

'No, love. Not at all.'

'Perhaps he's getting better.' She refused to acknowledge the worry in her mother's voice.

Martha sat down beside her and put an arm round her shoulders. 'Ellen, he's very poorly. You know that?'

Ellen nodded. 'But he's getting better, Mum. He's sleeping quiet and you said he's stopped being sick.'

'He's got a very bad dose, love. Very bad.'

'But Billy, he had the same and he's pulled through, ain't he?'

'Yeah – I think he's on the mend.'

'And Billy was always sickly. Tom's a strong baby.'

'Don't always follow, lovey. You know we none of us raise all our kids.'

Ellen closed her mind. 'He's going to be all right,' she stated.

She repeated it as his shallow breathing quickened a little and his eyelids flickered open to show dull, sunken eyes too big for his pinched face.

'See – he's awake.'

The small mouth opened as if to cry but no sound came out.

'What is it, darling?' Ellen whispered. 'What do you want, eh? A feed?'

She pulled at the buttons of her blouse, her fingers useless with fatigue. But before she could get them undone, Tom's eyes had closed again. Frustration filled her. The only thing she could do for him was feed him, and he was too weak to stay awake.

'You must wake up, darling,' she begged him. 'You must feed. I got to make you strong and well again.'

She stared at the pointed features, and somewhere in her heart a cold terror started. Even as she spoke to him, he had slipped away.

Alma stood in the waiting hall. The morning activity washed round her: crying children, shuffling old folk, people limping and moaning from road or work accidents. She saw none of it. She was cold and numb, unable to think or even feel very much.

They had let her see him. They led her behind the screens and drew back the sheet from his poor bruised face. Internal bleeding, they said. He had never regained consciousness, so he had felt no pain.

He hardly looked like her son, lying there so still and white. He belonged to them, to the starched and stiffly efficient nurses. She reached out to touch him, feeling for the hands crossed over his chest. He was cold. A great shudder of revulsion went through her, followed swiftly by anger. She would not let him go. They would not have him.

'Gerry, Gerry!' She gathered him up in her arms, trying to rouse him, to give him her life, to banish the suffocating smell of hospital and death. She cradled his head to her breast, great sobs tearing from her.

'Come back to me, Gerry. Speak to me. Oh, please don't go, Gerry, don't go.'

They tried to pull her away, but she fought them, with tears streaming down her face, and threw herself forward on to the bed, her large living body covering and protecting his fragile dead one. Frantic in her grief and loss, she knew only that she must not let him go.

It took three strong porters to pull her away. The nurses clucked with disapproval at the disturbance to their orderly ward. She did not know what happened next. There were rooms and faces and voices and papers to sign. And then she was here, in the hall, with a small bag of Gerry's belongings at her side. She was quite empty, a great hollow shell, and totally devoid of any idea what to do next.

'Alma?'

The name meant nothing. She ignored it.

'Alma, it's me, Perce. What's the matter, girl? He's not...?'

Slowly her eyes focused, her brain took note. Percy, large and familiar, his battered face creased with concern – Percy had come to find her. The numbness dissolved. The pain came back, but with it was life. She fell into his arms and buried her face in his barrel chest, weeping anew.

He held her tight, patting her shoulder and rocking her. He was warm and alive, he smelt of sweat and pipe smoke and beer. She clung to him, crying until she could cry no more. Only then did he release his hold. With one arm still round her, he bent to pick up the pathetic little bag.

'Come on,' he said gruffly. 'I'm taking you home.'

She let him take charge, raising no protest against the criminal expense when he hailed a cab and bundled her into it. They sat squashed together in the stuffy interior. Percy was still holding her hand.

'He – er – he...' Percy began, and faltered to an embarrassed halt.

'Yes,' she whispered. She had no tears left now.

Her voice was hoarse and her throat aching, but it was nothing to the terrible pain inside. One son dying, the other dead. Everything had been taken away from her.

He gave her hand a squeeze. 'He was a good boy, your Gerry. And you was always a good mum. No one could've had a better mum than you. He was lucky there.'

She nodded. It did nothing to ease the hurt, but she recognized that he was trying to comfort her. She gave voice to the very worst part of all.

'Oh, Perce, I never said goodbye to him. I was in bed when he left for work and I never got up to say goodbye. And then he never woke up in the hospital. Oh, Perce, if only I'd got up.'

'You wasn't to know, girl. It was just another day. You wasn't to know that he wasn't, well...'

'I know, but it don't make it any better. He's gone without me saying goodbye.'

She would never be able to make it right now. The awful finality of it washed over her again. He had gone. A low moan escaped from her very soul.

Percy took her hand between his two great meaty paws. 'We'll give him a good send-off, girl. The whole works. And drinks for everyone to remember him by in the Puncheon after.'

'Oh, God.' She had not thought of the funeral. She hadn't a penny to pay for it. All her life she had spent everything as soon as it came into her hand.

'Now don't you go worrying about anything. I'll see to it. I got savings. I'll see he's sent off proper.'

'Oh no, Percy.' She came out of her miasma of loss enough to realize that this was not right. 'No, you can't do that. He's–' She stopped, and for the first of many times, corrected herself. 'He was my boy.'

For a while they were both silent, while the cab creaked round them. Alma had no idea where they were. Percy could be taking her anywhere, and she did not care. Nothing mattered any more.

'Look, er–' Percy began, an unusual hesitancy in his voice. 'I know this ain't the best time for it. In fact, I s'pose it's the worst time for it, but I got to say it. I been wanting to say it for a long time now. Weeks. I want you to marry me, Alma. I want you to be my old lady. Will you, Alma? Let me take care of you, eh? What d'you say? Will you?'

'What? Oh I don't know, Percy, I can't say. I just can't say.' She could not fully take in what he was saying.

'I'll take care of you, Alma. A woman like you, you need someone to take care of you. Since you come to work at the Puncheon, I been looking forward to you arriving each day. It don't feel right when you're not there. I need you there, Alma. I – well – got very fond of you.'

The words buzzed and jangled round her head, making no sense. She could think of nothing but the still figure on the bed, the great aching void in her heart. But this solid male presence was a vague comfort. She would certainly rather he was there than not. She gave his hand a feeble squeeze.

'Later, Percy,' she said. 'Later.'

'Yeah, right.' He was contrite. 'I knew it was the wrong time. I just couldn't help it. But let me take care of the funeral, Alma. Let me do that.'

'Yeah.' She hadn't the strength to resist him. 'Yeah, if you want to. Thanks.'

He patted her knee. 'I'll do it right. You wait and see. You won't regret it.'

People were in and out all day, saying what a fine man Gerry had been, what a dear little boy Tom had been, saying how sorry they were, what a loss it was, how they felt for her. And all the while Ellen mechanically thanked them and said no, there wasn't anything they could do for her right now. After all, nothing was going to bring them back. Jessica and Teddy clung to her like two little wraiths, bewildered by what was going on around them, not understanding why their mother was crying and their granny was crying, or why their father did not come home. Ellen hugged them to her, taking what scant comfort she could from the small round bodies.

Then there was the agony of the funerals. First Tom was buried, in his pathetically tiny coffin, then, after a post-mortem, Gerry. Ellen did not know how she got through the days. Having to look after the little ones helped. She could not be totally absorbed in her grief when they needed her so much. And her family was around her. Martha came every day; so did Daisy, and so did Maisie, though Ellen usually ended up support-ing her. But it was Florrie who helped the most. With Florrie she could be totally open.

'Aunty Alma's off up the Puncheon again, then,' Florrie remarked one day.

'Yeah, she spends all her time up there now.'

'D'you reckon she'll marry Percy?'

'Wouldn't be surprised. When she's got over it a bit. She was that close to Gerry.'

Florrie looked at her for a moment, then she said, 'Just as you was to little Tom.'

Ellen held her eyes. There was something waiting to be said, and she was not quite sure what it was, only that Florrie knew she still had a lot locked up inside her.

'I had to come home,' she said defensively. 'I had to choose between them, and I had to come to Tom. Gerry had Alma there. But Tom was so little, he was my baby, I couldn't let him go all alone.'

'Of course not. You done the right thing, Ellen. You was with him when he went. So why are you still blaming yourself for leaving Gerry?'

'Because...' The pressure of guilt had always been there. It had built up almost unbearably on the night he was injured. Now she could hold it back no longer. 'Because I didn't love him. Not proper, like I ought to. I was – I was fond of him, like I'm fond of your Jimmy or Daisy's Wilf. I didn't even love him like what I do our Jack or Will. Like, they drive me silly sometimes, 'specially Will, but I love them just the same, 'cos they're my brothers. But Gerry – it, well, it just wasn't the same...' She trailed off. It all sounded so lame. For a dreadful moment, she was seized with a doubt as to whether even Florrie would understand. But Florrie was nodding in sympathy.

'You made him happy, you know. That's what counts. He never knew.'

'But I knew!' Ellen burst out. 'I knew. I was

wicked, Florrie. It was all my fault. I was wicked and now I been punished. Gerry and Tom have both been taken away from me and I'll never be able to make it up to him.'

Florrie was silent, waiting. Ellen took a breath. She could not quite meet her friend's gaze.

'Tom wasn't Gerry's baby, you know.'

Florrie reached out and took her restless hands. 'I guessed that. He was Harry's, wasn't he?'

'Yes.' Her whisper was so low it was hardly audible.

'Harry's been ever so upset too, you know. Ever so. But he can't show it.'

'Oh.' In her preoccupation with her own loss, she had not thought of Harry's. It brought a new source of pain and guilt. 'I never thought – but that's someone else I hurt. I didn't ought to live. I just hurt people.'

'Ellen!' Florrie jumped up. Ellen looked at her in amazement. Her friend was glaring down at her, arms akimbo, stiff with anger. 'For God's sake, stop it! You're being bloody stupid. You're just heaping blame on yourself, like you're enjoying it. I could – I could shake you, I really could. You just stop it, d'you hear? You was a good wife to Gerry, you're a lovely mum to them kids, you're a good daughter to your mum and dad and you're the best friend I'll ever have. So what if you and Harry went off that day? Where's the harm? You suffered enough for it since, so stop piling it on. You got to get up and go on. We all got secrets we got to live with, God knows.'

For several moments Ellen just gaped at her, stunned. Nobody had given her a talking-to like

674

that for years, not even her mum. And as the words sank slowly into her head, she realized they were true. She *was* almost enjoying making the pain worse. She opened and closed her mouth, but nothing came out.

'There! That told you, didn't it?' Florrie declared triumphantly. 'You just think on that, Ellen Billingham.'

'I – I–' Ellen stuttered.

Then, to her amazement, Florrie's face began to twitch. First her lips, then her eyes. She made a great effort to control herself, but there was no stopping it. Laughter bubbled through.

'Oh, Ellen,' she gasped. 'Oh, Ellen, if you could see your face! It's a picture, it really is – an – an army could walk inside of your mouth and you'd not notice.'

A strange feeling began inside her as she watched her friend. Florrie was hysterical, doubled up, with tears streaming down her face. Slowly, she stood up. A smile was beginning to pull at her own mouth. She held out her arms, and Florrie fell into them. The two women hugged each other, laughing and crying until they did not know which was which.

When they finally subsided into sobs and hiccups, they were both weak and aching. Ellen made tea and they both looked out to check up on the children. Jessica was proudly minding Florrie's little George, wheeling him up and down the street. Ellen watched her as she bent over the ancient pram, tenderly tucking in a sheet where the baby had kicked it off. Into the hollow left by so much spent emotion, Florrie's words came echoing back.

'Florrie,' she said. 'What did you mean by "We all got secrets"?'

'Well, you know...'

'Your dad, you mean?'

'Yeah.'

'But I thought that was...'

After being so tied up in herself, she found the sudden release made her see more clearly.

'I thought that was all over and done with,' she said slowly, watching Florrie's face.

Florrie said nothing.

'Do you mean to tell me...? Florrie, you ain't still carrying that around with you, are you? You mean you ain't never told your Jimmy?'

Florrie shook her head.

'But you was going to tell him on your wedding night. You said you was. We talked about it the night before. I remember it like it was yesterday.'

'I know, I know.' Florrie's features creased into helpless frustration.

'But when it come to it, I couldn't. Not then. I mean, not on our wedding night. And after that, it was on the tip of my tongue dozens of times. I really meant to tell him, Ellen. I wanted to, but – I never got it out. It was never quite the right moment.'

'So you gone on keeping it from him?'

'Yeah,' Florrie admitted. 'And now it's too late. I can't tell him now.'

Ellen took the first decision she had made since Gerry and Tom died. She caught Florrie by the arm and looked at her in the eyes.

'Oh yes you can. You done me a favour telling

me what for. Now I'm going to do the same to you. You can't keep it to yourself no longer, Florrie. It ain't fair to you and it ain't fair to Jimmy neither. It's like you don't trust him. You got to promise me you'll tell him.'

'But – but I can't. It's much too late.'

'Promise! Promise or – or I'll never speak to you again. Cross my heart and hope to die.'

Florrie looked at her. They both giggled feebly at the old childish threat.

'All right,' Florrie agreed. 'All right, I'll do it.'

Two days later, Florrie came flying over the road while Ellen was still scrubbing the step.

'Ellen, Ellen, I got to tell you...'

Ellen took a quick glance up and down the street to where other women were busy with their brushes and pails. You could almost see the interest quickening.

'Come inside,' she said.

They sat down at the kitchen table. Florrie was glowing. She could hardly keep still.

'I did it, Ellen. I told him. I really did.'

'You never!'

'I did an' all. I can't hardly believe it. I was so nervous, I couldn't hardly speak. My throat all closed up. But I thought of you, and how you said I got to, and somehow I done it. I told him. And Ellen, he was wonderful. He said, "I'd've done just the same in your place, girl. Don't you think no more about it." Oh, Ellen, it's such a weight off my mind, I can't tell you. It's like a big cloud's been lifted. There's always been this thing between me and Jimmy, keeping us apart, and now it's gone.'

'I'm so pleased for you. I really am.' Ellen smiled at her shining face.

'And it's all down to you, Ellen. I wouldn't never have done it if it wasn't for you making me. I'd've gone on keeping it all inside of me, and it would've made things all wrong with me and Jimmy, and that would've been dreadful, 'cos I really do love him. He's the best, he is. Just look at how he took it! On my side without even thinking about it. Knew I was right, whatever. That's how he is.'

'You're good for each other, you two,' Ellen said. 'I'm so pleased. It makes me all warm inside to see people like you and Jimmy, and my mum and dad, and now Alma and Percy. Like, it is possible to be happy.'

Florrie leant forward. 'It's because of you, Ellen,' she said earnestly. 'With me and Jimmy, that is. You are good for people. You do believe that, don't you? You do believe it wasn't because of what you done that Gerry and Tom died?'

Ellen smiled back at her, taking pleasure from the knowledge that for Florrie and Jimmy there was going to be a marriage that would hold true whatever life might throw at them.

'Yes,' she said. 'I do see that now. I think I was off my head a bit.'

'And it will get better, you know. Maybe you won't never really get over little Tom, but you will be happy again some day. I know you will.'

Ellen could not quite believe that, not at that moment. But, for Florrie, she was willing to try.

'We'll see,' was all she could say.

6

The river slid smooth and calm, steel-grey beneath a pale blue sky. It was a still March afternoon with a promise of spring in the air. Ellen sat on the top step of the Torrington Stairs. She liked to come here on a Sunday. It got her away from Trinidad Street and the continual claustrophobic discussion of everyone's doings. There was space to collect her thoughts.

Below her, Jess and Teddy played on the edge of the dirty strip of pebbles, poking about in the mess of flotsam and jetsam, lobbing stones to land with a satisfying splat in the ooze. Beyond them, the evil-smelling low-water mud banks gleamed grey-brown, fringed with filthy scum. The river was settled into its Sunday quiet, with only the odd few vessels moving. Ellen watched a stately old three-master being towed downstream by a steam tug, and a couple of lighters coming down on the ebb, while a boy in a skiff sculled between ships in the tiers and the shore, running errands. It being Sunday, the factories and foundries and repair yards were shut for the day and the air was free of their clamour. Behind her, the drinkers in the Torrington Arms could be heard, but she could easily ignore them. They were not her friends or neighbours, they would make no demands on her. Ellen let the peace wrap round her. It was nice here; just herself, and

679

the children playing contentedly together at the foot of the steps. It was soothing to sit and watch the water slipping away to the distant sea.

She tried to think of nothing at all, to let her mind drift with the boats going by. The recent past was too painful to dwell upon, and she was only now beginning to come to terms with it; the future was unsure. Better to chase it all away, to become still and empty. But try as she might, thoughts and images kept crowding in. So much of her life was tied up with the river. The highlights kept coming back to taunt her – the day they all went to Southend, the day she and Harry went to Battersea.

The skiff passed close by. It was just like the one she and Harry had gone in. She heard the creak of the oars in the rowlocks, the dip of the blades in the water. She could almost feel the lift of the waves beneath her. She was out there again, the sun dancing on the river, Harry's feet braced on either side of her as he rowed, a whole daring adventure in front of them.

To Harry, coming across from the Torrington Arms, she seemed still and distant and alone. It wrung his heart to see her there all by herself, staring at the river. He had to try to break through, to find her again.

'Ellen?'

She started, then turned slowly round, a hand pressed tightly to her chest. Her eyes widened a bit on recognizing him, but he couldn't tell whether she was pleased to see him or not. He stepped forward so that he was standing beside her.

'Can I join you?'

For a long and nerve-stretching moment he thought she was going to refuse. Then she gave a brief nod.

'Y–yeah. 'Course.'

He found that he had been holding his breath. He let it out in a great sigh of relief and sat down on the top step, carefully leaving a good yard separating them.

'Nice day,' he remarked, starting on neutral ground.

'Yeah. Quiet. I like it quiet.'

The children caught sight of him and came scampering up the slippery steps to hurl themselves at him.

'Uncle Harry! Shell. Look!'

'I made a dock. Come and see my dock.'

He obligingly looked and admired, then pushed them away. 'Go and play now, your mum wants a bit of peace.'

They both watched as Jess and Teddy settled back into their games.

He ventured a compliment. 'They're fine kids. A credit to you.'

It was as if the old Ellen had come back again. Her drawn face lit from within and real enthusiasm lifted her voice.

'They're that bright an' all. Little Teddy, he's sharp as a barrow-load of monkeys. Never misses a trick, he don't. And Jess, she picks words out of books I read, she does. She's going to go to the Central if it's the last thing I do. She's going to get her chance. I don't care if I have to work for the rest of my life, but she's going to get a proper education.'

He could believe that. 'I'm sure she will, if you say so. You always were strong-willed, Ellen.'

It was a wrong move. The closed looked came back into her face again. He tried to think of something less personal to talk about.

'What's your job like? Are you managing all right?'

'Yeah, it's all right. Took a bit of getting used to.'

She had considered carrying on with the stall herself, but the more she delved into Gerry's finances, the more she realized that he was still badly in debt. When he had told her that he was beginning to see daylight, it had merely meant that he was no longer actually being threatened for money. In her shocked state, she had taken an offer from a fellow stall holder and used the money to pay off the largest of the creditors. Which left her and the children with nothing in the world to live on, so back to work she went, at a shop on the West Ferry Road.

'Maybe I didn't ought to have sold the stall and the stock. I wonder if I'd kept it on perhaps I could've made a go of it. And the kids could have come up the market with me instead of having to leave them with my mum. I mean, they love their gran, but I miss 'em something dreadful, and when I come home, I'm too tired to enjoy being with 'em.'

'At least it's not Maconochie's,' Harry said.

'Yeah. That's something, I suppose. I couldn't have stood Maconochie's again.'

He thought about her running the stall herself. 'You would have been good at the selling side, up the market. But it was the buying, weren't it? That was Gerry's line really. He had the contacts, and a nasty lot they were, some of 'em. Wouldn't have been right for you to go getting mixed up with that sort.'

'Maybe not. But that was Gerry's life, that stall. He had worked and dreamed and planned for that stall since – oh, since he was a kid. It was like – well, it was like I didn't care, selling it off like that.'

'He'd've understood,' Harry said.

'I dunno. I hope so.'

She stared bleakly down at the two children, chin in hand. He longed to take her in his arms, to tell her that he would protect her against everything. But she was still so far away from him.

'You know what the latest is in the street?' he asked.

'No. What?'

'Siobhan's moving out.'

'She never!' That jolted her out of herself. She looked fully at him. 'When did you hear that? Who said?'

'Got it off of Declan O'Donaghue, so it must be true. Said she was going off on a tour of Scotland and how she was giving up the house. All that fancy furniture is going into store.'

'Well, who'd've thought it? Mind you, we thought she'd gone for good last time, and she come back.'

'A real bad penny.'

A glimmer of a smile touched her eyes. 'I reckon she thinks she's more of a sov than a penny.'

Harry smiled back, not so much at the joke as at the old Ellen showing through again. He waited, sensing that she was about to spill a secret.

'I went round and spoke to her,' she admitted.

'You never!' That did surprise him. 'When?'

'After – after that fight in the street. I had to, I dunno why. And do you know, I ended up almost feeling sorry for her. She's so – so cold. She don't give anything, there's no loving feeling in her for anyone but herself. She may be beautiful and she may have this wonderful singing career, but I wouldn't be her, not for all the tea in China I wouldn't.'

'You could never be like her, Ellen. I can't think of anyone more different.'

She did not answer. Her eyes still focused on the ebbing water.

'I'm glad she's going,' she said. 'I couldn't be easy with her there in the street. You never knew what she might do next to hurt someone. I always had this feeling she'd get to know about what happened, you know, the night your dad died. There's no knowing what she might've done if she'd've found that out.'

The very thought of it gave Harry the shivers. 'She'd've had a field day with us,' he agreed.

'Mm. We all got secrets.'

He drew breath, studying her profile. 'There's one secret that don't have to be kept no more.'

The statement hung in the air between them.

Ellen could scarcely breathe. All the defensive layers she had gathered so carefully about her seemed to be floating away, leaving her naked and exposed. She needed them to blur her feelings, to stop any more love and pain from getting in. She could just about cope with life, if she did not think about Harry. It was frightening, being made to face him again.

But he was waiting for an answer.

'I – suppose not,' she admitted. Her throat was dry, so that her voice came out in an odd croak.

'We made a good team, you and me.'

'Yes.'

It might be frightening, but it was also hugely exhilarating. She was coming alive again, so that she could almost feel the blood pumping through her body. Something she barely recognized was gathering inside her like a fragile bubble.

'We mustn't let the past hang on to us. You was a good wife to old Gerry. You ain't got nothing to blame yourself for.'

She dared to look at him at last. 'I know,' she said, and found that she really meant it. She had done her best. There was no need for guilt. 'You neither,' she told him. 'You went and tried to rescue him.'

The shadow of deceit that had lain between them ever since she married Gerry rolled away. She was free.

'Oh, Harry,' she cried. 'I do love you–'

And then she was in his arms, laughing and crying, the whole world reduced to just the two of them and the love they had denied for so long.

'Never, never leave me again,' Harry said, holding her head in his hands, looking into her eyes. 'Promise me.'

'I promise,' she said, and kissed him with passionate intensity.

'You never gave up, did you?' she said, her lips on his. 'Sometimes I almost wished you would. I thought it would be easier if you found someone else.'

'There was only ever you. Anyone else would've been second best.'

The pressure of happiness was almost too much to bear. She found herself sobbing, the tears running down her face. Harry held her, kissing the top of her head.

'What is it, darling? Tell me.'

'The worst – the very worst – part of Tom – dying – was not being able to grieve with you. I had to shut you out.'

'I know, I know. I felt shut out all along. I hated it, Ellen, hated it. But there will be others, I promise you. I know it will never bring Tom back, but we will have others, children we can share.'

'Yes.' She was filled with a sense of wonder. 'Do you know, I never used to look forward, except for Jess. She was the only one I made plans for. I just went on, one day after another. But now it's like a door opening. I can see ahead.'

He smiled, her delight mirrored in his eyes.

'And does it look good, what you can see?'

'Yes.' She put a hand to his face. Her fingers explored the contours she had longed to touch so many times. 'Yes, it looks very good.'

The publishers hope that this book has given you enjoyable reading. Large Print Books are especially designed to be as easy to see and hold as possible. If you wish a complete list of our books please ask at your local library or write directly to:

Magna Large Print Books
Magna House, Long Preston,
Skipton, North Yorkshire.
BD23 4ND

This Large Print Book for the partially sighted, who cannot read normal print, is published under the auspices of

THE ULVERSCROFT FOUNDATION